The Inheritance Game

by
Joe Platt

Bloomington, IN Milton Keynes, UK

AuthorHouse™
1663 Liberty Drive, Suite 200
Bloomington, IN 47403
www.authorhouse.com
Phone: 1-800-839-8640

AuthorHouse™ UK Ltd.
500 Avebury Boulevard
Central Milton Keynes, MK9 2BE
www.authorhouse.co.uk
Phone: 08001974150

First published by AuthorHouse 7/3/2006

ISBN: 1-4259-0882-9 (sc)

Printed in the United States of America
Bloomington, Indiana

This book is printed on acid-free paper.

For Catherine and Alexia.

Prologue

"If you had to choose what would you say is the single most important thing in the world to you?" Dougie asked as he put down his tumbler and lit his cigar.

"Mates" Dean replied as he poured himself another generous measure of whiskey.

"Not family?" Dougie asked.

"Not my family" Dean replied as he took a long drink from his glass. "I don't really get what my parents are about and as I haven't got any brothers or sisters I suppose I regard my mates as closer than my real family."

"What about money?" Dougie asked as he blew a large smoke ring.

"Money comes and goes. As long as you've got enough cash to pay the bills and go out at the weekend you don't really need much more but mates are always there for you" Dean replied.

"But don't you dream of having loads of money, going on flash holidays and owning loads of cars and houses?" Dougie asked.

"I'm not saying I don't want all of that but you asked me what I consider to be the most important thing in the world and I think mates rank ahead of money."

"What if we were talking about millions of pounds? Would mates still rank ahead of money then?" Dougie asked.

"Oh course they would. You can't put a value on your mates so it doesn't matter how much money you're talking about. Where's all this leading to anyway Dougie?"

"Nowhere really, I was just making conversation" said Dougie asked as he drained his tumbler and reached for the whiskey bottle.

Chapter 1
Week 0 - Friday

"Where the fuck am I?"

Dean woke to find himself lying on the floor with his head propped up against a wall at a forty five degree angle to the rest of his body. As his blinding headache stabilised he made out a couple of blokes lying on the floor on the other side of the room who also looked like they had fallen unconscious at body-breaking angles that would haunt them for the rest of the day. Despite having no idea where he was Dean decided it was definitely time to get up and fuck off home. As he lifted himself up from the floor he was hit by an overpowering smell. It was at that point he noticed the perfectly formed turd sitting proudly on his bare chest with the words 'FUCK YOU' written underneath in what looked like red marker pen. He grabbed a towel that was lying on the floor next to him and used it to scoop the majority of the shite off his chest. However, as soon as he'd done that he realised the towel was actually the white D&G T-shirt he'd been wearing the previous night.

"Bollocks, shit, twat, fuck!"

He sat up and wiped the remainder of the excrement off his chest with his expensive new T-shirt. He briefly considered rinsing it under the tap and taking it home but decided that even if he could get it clean (which was unlikely as it had been a rather large and worryingly dark turd) he would always associate it with handfuls of soft stinky human shit. Despite having a vicious crick in his neck, a raging hangover and feeling physically sick Dean still had an appetite for mischief and stuffed the rancid garment down behind the back of the radiator he was lying next to. It was a modern slim fitting design that sat underneath a large window and the only way of spotting there was anything behind it was to try to squeeze your head underneath the wooden window ledge. As a result Dean was confident the T-shirt would stay down there undetected until the next time the central heating kicked in, when it would act like one of those plug in air fresheners although it would clearly give a completely new meaning to the phrase 'eau-de-toilette'.

Having successfully planted his version of an incendiary device Dean decided it was now definitely time to go. He stood up and looked around the room. He didn't recognise the room or either of the two blokes who were still asleep on the other side of the room. He tried to piece together the events of the previous evening. It had started, like most Thursday nights, with a few beers with the guys from work. He'd then met up with a few of the lads in Covent Garden and from there it had developed into a full-on drinking session. After that he was very sketchy on the detail but a few black and white snapshots started to form in his mind. He vaguely remembered dancing (like a twat) in some club and snogging some girl at the bar. From there he remembered being in a taxi with the girl and a couple of other people and then being at some sort of party in the house where he was now. He remembered more drinking and more dancing (like a twat). The very last thing that he could remember was getting it on with the girl and...

"Oh fuck no....!"

The last few minutes before he passed out came flooding back to him in glorious technicolour. He'd been dancing erotically with the girl and suggested that they adjourn to her bedroom. Unfortunately it turned out that she didn't live in the flat and that the bedrooms were all occupied. Somehow Dean had persuaded her to go with him for a 'cuddle' behind the sofa which, at the time, he considered acceptable on the basis that it was out of sight of the other people in the room. When they got behind the sofa they'd started some serious bump and grind. After a few minutes it was clear that the girl wasn't going to take the initiative so to get the ball rolling he'd decided to go down on her. He'd slithered his way into position and hitched up her short skirt without any fuss. She was wearing big un-sexy pants but he decided that there were more appropriate times to raise the issue and let it pass. He distinctly remembered pulling her pants down and being hit by the overpowering smell. At exactly that point the eleven pints of Guinness, six vodka red bulls and various flavoured vodka shots caught up with him and he'd started to feel sick. However, being a trooper, he decided not to let the young lady down and to crack on with the job at hand. The final thing that Dean remembered was the uncontrollable Exorcist-like projectile vomit that occurred about thirty seconds later, which completely drenched the girl's lower torso and thighs in Guinness-black beer sick. After that it was all a blank but Dean thought it was fairly safe to bet that he'd passed out and that the girl (or possibly one of her mates) had decided that shitting on his chest was suitable retribution.

"Fair enough to be honest" Dean thought. *"I wish I'd just shagged her as it would've been a lot less messy and much more fun for both of us."*

Dean picked up a discarded jacket (not his) from the sofa, put it on over his bare chest and made his way out of the flat. He stopped the first passer by he came across.

"Excuse me mate is there a tube station near here?"

"Yeah, Tooting Bec tube is straight down the end of this road" the guy replied.

Dean looked at his watch. It was just after 7am.

"Ah well at least I'm only a couple of stops from Clapham. I've got time for a shower and a bit of brekkie before I need to head off to work. Then again it is Friday, my neck is quite sore and I haven't had a sickie for ages….."

Chapter 2
Week 0 - Saturday

"Are we going to the pub tonight or what?"

Dean stood at the foot of the stairs shouting up at the bedroom for the third time in twenty minutes. It was a familiar scene on a Saturday night. Dean would get ready in around five minutes (sometimes extended to ten minutes if he needed a dump) and then spend what seemed like an eternity hanging around.

"Right, if you're not ready in the next ten seconds I'm going down the boozer on my todd" he shouted in his mild Scouse accent.

"I'm almost ready, I just need another two minutes" came the response from upstairs.

Dean opened the front door and waited impatiently for another five minutes. "Right that's it. If you aren't down here by the time I've counted to five I'm fucking going out on my own. One, two, three, four….."

"No need to get all upset just because I've taken a couple of minutes longer than you to get ready."

"A couple of minutes? I could've watched every episode of the Simpsons while you were up there."

"Oh stop talking bollocks. Anyway do you think this looks OK?"

Dean had been here a million times before; maybe more. He knew that this was a double-edged sword of the highest order. If you don't like the outfit and you tell the truth then you're fucked, consigned back to purgatory waiting for the next outfit to be selected. Merely stating that it looked 'OK' was also not an option as this inevitably led to the "You're just saying that" response which then led to "You don't really like it do you?" and ultimately to "No I'm going to change it anyway now." Having already spent the best part of half an hour waiting there was no way he was taking any chances.

"Yeah, it looks shit hot" Dean said unconvincingly.

"Honestly? Do you think I'll pull?"

Dean looked Glynn up and down. He was wearing a bright red silk shirt with 'MOCHINO' written down one arm in huge white letters, black drainpipe trousers and a pair of brogues. He looked a complete twat. It was the kind of look that could just-about be carried off by a model at an outrageous designer fashion show. Dean had known Glynn since his first day at university, where they had both studied law and had initially dismissed him as a geek as he was tall, thin, gangly and spoke with a strong Welsh accent. However Glynn had later impressed him with his sharp wit, his ability to drink copious amounts of alcohol without ever puking but most of all by the fact that he was a total genius and was always willing to help Dean out with coursework. Six years on this latter trait was still handy as they'd both landed a job with the same law firm. They shared a flat near Islington together and Dean considered Glynn to be his best friend, despite the fact that he had absolutely no dress sense. Glynn struggled to pull at the best of times but in this outfit he was an absolute dead cert to be heading home at two thirty with only a kebab for company.

"Yeah mate, the birds are gonna love it. I'd be surprised if you're not fighting them off with a shitty stick before the night's out. I've got to ask though, where *did* you get that shirt from?"

"I thought you'd like it, it's the dogs bollocks isn't it? I got it from Camden market. The bloke I bought it from said that it's an exact copy of the latest Mochino design. The Mochino version costs £200 but mine was only £17.50, a fucking bargain, particularly if it gets me a shag. He had loads of other colours mate, so we can go up and get you one tomorrow if you fancy."

"Nah, I don't think that I can carry it off in the same way you can" Dean said although what he really meant was that it was the worst shirt he'd ever set eyes on and that he wouldn't even wear it for a bet. As he continued to stare in amazement Dean noticed that the stitching holding one of the arms on at the shoulder was starting to come loose and that the buttons didn't seem to be stitched on in a straight line. "Anyway mate although I'd love to discuss the ins and outs of your wardrobe for the next couple of days we've already spent far too long hanging around, so let's get down the boozer."

****

Dean and Glynn arrived at Covent Garden just after eight forty five and headed straight for the basement bar of the Punch & Judy. Dean went to scout around for the lads whilst Glynn got the drinks in. He soon spotted Rod standing outside in the courtyard.

"Oi, Oi Saveloy!" Rod shouted as he saw Dean approaching. Despite being from Leeds Rod insisted on using as many Cockney phrases and rhyming slang that he possibly could. He claimed it made him 'blend in' although his strong Yorkshire accent made the rest of the lads slightly dubious. Rod was twenty four and was a mate of Dean's from university, where they'd played football together. In those days Rod had been the midfield dynamo of the team but in the three years since they'd graduated he'd moved into computers and piled on the pounds. He had shoulder length hair, was into heavy metal and now resembled a stereotypical overweight, long haired IT guy that constantly wore black T-shirts emblazoned with the name of rock bands. Tonight he was wearing an AC/DC T-shirt, black leather trousers and a denim jacket. Standing with Rod were two other blokes: Urban and a huge black guy built like an American football player.

Urban was the same age as Rod, Dean and Glynn and had also played for the university football team. He was originally from Birmingham and although he didn't have a strong accent, the occasional word was pronounced with a distinctive Brummie twang. Like Glynn he always tried to keep up with the latest dress trends but unlike Glynn he managed to carry it off most of the time. His real name was John Lawson but Dean never felt the name John suited his cheeky livewire character. He'd christened him Urban during the first week at Uni due partly to the fact that he continually dressed like an urban warrior (combat trousers, black T-shirt, big boots) but mainly because of the continual stream of bollocks stories that he came out with. Despite swearing they were all true Dean was convinced that most of the stories were simply urban myths and so his new name was born. Urban now worked as an accountant and had a very attractive girlfriend called Charlotte who he was engaged to. However he liked to lead a double life, playing the dutiful doting boyfriend when he was with Charlotte and leading the charge on the pulling front whenever he was out with the lads.

"Evening Rod, Urban and….I don't believe we've met" Dean said nodding to each in turn and holding out his hand to the black guy.

"I work with Urban. Call me Daisy, mate" he said in a broad Cockney accent.

"Daisy? That's a funny name for a big lad like you isn't it?" asked Dean staring at the six foot five, fifteen stone bloke standing in front of him.

"My real name is Colin Day but at school everyone called me Daisy, you know Day-sie. I decided that I prefer it to Colin so it just sort of stuck."

"Fair enough, Daisy it is then" said Dean.

Over the next few hours the five of them downed numerous pints, shots of tequila, sambuca, black sambuca, whiskey, gin, pernod and enough vodka red bull to make a doped elephant hyperactive. As eleven o'clock approached Dean suggested that they move to a club to avoid the queues. They headed across the square to the Roadhouse and after the obligatory laddish banter with the bouncers they found themselves inside. As usual the place was full of blokes who'd also had the idea of 'beating the queues.' The evening continued much as it had in the pub with each member of the group feeling it their obligation to buy a 'cheeky shot' with their round.

"I don't know about you mate but I was feeling a bit pissed earlier on. I feel fine now though" Dean slurred to Rod, whilst swaying slightly.

"Me too mate. It was that fucking Pernod that Glynn bought. If he does anything like that again I'm gonna chin him. I can still taste that aniseed bollocks every time I burp."

"You'll have to wake him up first if you want to chin him" said Dean pointing to Glynn, who was slumped unconscious in a booth with his head on the table.

"You should really take him home mate. If the bouncers see him they'll chuck him out" said Rod.

"I've just fucking got here, I'm not going home yet. All he needs are a couple of vodka red bulls and he'll be sorted. I'll tell you what though come and have a laugh at this" Dean said as he sat down next to Glynn. He gave Glynn a prod to see how cabbaged he was. Glynn didn't move so Dean slapped him full on in the face which also failed to bring a reaction. "Great, I've been waiting to do this all fucking night," said Dean as he proceeded to pull down on the sleeve with 'MOCHINO' written on it. The stitching came away sweetly from the shoulder leaving a perfect cap sleeve. Dean lifted Glynn up from the table and Rod effortlessly removed the other sleeve so that Glynn was now wearing a red silk cap-sleeved shirt, a look that Dean thought would not have been out of place in a German porn flick (and he should know as he'd seen enough of them).

"You know when we left the house I thought that Glynn had surpassed himself and had achieved the definitive cock look. I didn't think it was possible for him to look any more stupid than he did but I reckon we've helped him reach a higher plain now. That deserves a celebratory drink I reckon. Let's get to the bar."

"What about Glynn?"

"We'll pick him up on the way out, unless some bird decides that an unconscious, pissed-up twat in a red silk capped sleeve shirt is the man of her dreams and whisks him off to a better life."

"Yeah I see your point; he's going nowhere" said Rod.

Whilst Dean and Rod had been amusing themselves with Glynn, Urban and Daisy had been attempting to pull. Their technique involved an entirely random process of wandering around the club attempting to find two girls who didn't walk off as soon as they saw them coming or tell them to "Fuck off" before they'd got to the end of their first sentence. Urban finally spotted two likely candidates.

"What d'ya reckon on those two?" Urban asked Daisy.

"The blonde one's fit but the other one is fuckin' horrible. I wouldn't touch her with yours."

"Yeah but she looks quite pissed and I think she's giving me the eye."

"Giving you the eye? How can you tell with those stupid fucking glasses on?"

"Fuck off, she's alright. Anyway can I count on you to be my wing man?"

"What about your bird? I thought you were engaged?" Daisy asked.

"Look, I keep telling you that when I'm out with the lads I'm effectively single. I'm not looking for a new girlfriend, just a bit of fun so where's the harm in that? Charlotte's not here so let's just keep that to ourselves. Are you up for it or not?" asked Urban.

"Alright then, but only as long as I get the fit one" Daisy replied.

"Agreed. Right let's get over to them before two other fuckers get in there."

****

Heather and Mel were both twenty five years old, worked for the same law firm and shared a two-bedroomed flat together. Mel was tall, blonde and attractive. She'd spilt up with her long term boyfriend six months earlier and was constantly on the lookout for a new man. Heather was short, dumpy, wore glasses and was the not-very-attractive mate that good looking girls always seem to hang around with. She hadn't had a boyfriend since she left university, almost four years ago. After drinking large glasses of Chardonnay in a pub in Covent Garden all evening neither of them had pulled and they found themselves in the queue to Roadhouse at eleven o'clock.

Once inside they positioned themselves on two high stools from which they had a good view of half of the club. After a few minutes of looking around trying to catch someone's eye Heather noticed a couple of blokes who were clearly interested and looked like they were plucking up the courage to come over.

"What do you think of those two Mel?"

Mel looked over at the two blokes at the bar. One of them was a well built tall black bloke with a shaved head, wearing jeans, a trendy white shirt and who looked cool. The other was wearing a round floppy hat, a fitted T-shirt and combat trousers.

"The black lad is alright but his mate looks like a bit of a prick."

"I think he looks alright. Not too sure about the hat but other than that he's quite fit."

"Right well that's that decided then, you can have the dick with the hat and I'll have the hunky guy. Look out, here they come."

****

"Evening ladies. My friend and I were just discussing the last ten years of Eastenders and were trying to compile a list of all of the landlords and landladies of the Queen Vic in chronological order. We've got up to Pat & Frank Butcher but have got a bit stuck. Is there any chance you could give us a hand?" Urban said with a cheeky smile.

This was a tried and tested chat up line that Urban had used in the past, despite the fact that he'd never seen a full episode of Eastenders in his life. After a number of years failing to make an impact with cheeky one liners ('I'll save you the embarrassment of asking love, here's my number,' 'Before you ask I am single and I love kids' etc) he'd finally been persuaded by one of his best mates that the key to getting a conversation started was to discuss something that girls might be interested in. After a few unsuccessful attempts (football, women's football, computer games etc) Urban had finally hit upon the idea of soaps. The only drawback was that he hated soaps and didn't have a clue who was in any of them or what any of the current story lines were. He could have forced himself to start watching them but that would've been too time consuming and his knowledge base would've been too thin. Instead he picked a central theme to each of the major soaps, the pub, and then asked his mum (who religiously watched every single soap) to write down in chronological order the landlords and landladies since each soap began.

"Sorry mate we don't watch Eastenders" said Mel. This was actually a lie but Mel could see it was clearly a chat up line as she didn't believe that this bloke in his stupid hat and combat trousers settled down to watch the Eastenders omnibus every Sunday afternoon.

"Oh right then" said Urban. He was just about to ask if they watched Coronation Street when Heather cut in.

"I used to watch it" she said. Mel smiled as she knew from this reaction that Heather was obviously interested in Urban. Within a split second Urban positioned himself next to Heather's stool.

"So what's your name anyway Mr Eastenders?" Heather said after they had spent a full fifteen minutes running through the names of every publican from the show's history.

"Everyone calls me Urban."

"Why?"

"Well I do like to tell a good story and at uni I was always coming out with those 'strange but true' stories. You know like Aliens found at Roswell, snakes emerging from toilets after being flushed down by their former owners that sort of thing. Anyway one of my mates, Dean, decided that none of them were true. We had this huge argument about it and after that he christened me Urban Myth Man. It was then shortened to Urban and it just sort of stuck."

"So do you think that they're all Urban Myths?"

"Some of the things you hear are obviously bollocks but I reckon a lot of them are true. For instance I heard this top story yesterday about a party at a house that four girls shared. The party is pretty fucking boring so one of the lads decides to have a bit of fun. He finds a jumbo tub of margarine in the fridge, one of those two litre jobs the size of a shoe box. He scoops out all of the margarine, does a king size turd in the bottom of the box, puts the margarine back in the tub and smoothes the whole lot down so that it looks good as new. After the party the girls are totally unaware of what's happened and continue to use the margarine for the following couple of weeks until one day someone digs in to butter their toast and discovers what's been lurking underneath all along. Of course by the time they discovered it there was no chance of finding out who did it so it was the perfect crime" said Urban laughing. Heather shook her head to show that she didn't think it was very funny.

"Oh fuck, don't tell me that it was your house?"

"Don't be stupid" Heather replied.

"Anyway are you going to give me a kiss or not?" Urban asked as he grabbed Heather around the waist and they started snogging.

Mel was impressed that Daisy was even better looking up close. He was a big man but his strong features, dress sense and general manner made him appear more like a fashion model than a thug.

"So do you like Eastenders as well then?" she said to Daisy.

"No I hate all soaps, too depressing for my liking" Daisy replied. He suddenly felt really pissed and was concentrating on staying with it.

"So what do you like then? Football I suppose?" Mel asked.

"Football's OK but my real passion is hard core porn" he replied with a cheeky smile. Mel burst out laughing and Daisy knew that he'd broken the ice.

"Well you never know we might have more in common than I first thought" said Mel cheekily. "If you get me a drink I'll tell you what else I like."

Chapter 3
Week 0 - Sunday

The first thought Daisy had when he awoke from his alcohol-induced coma was "*Jesus Christ, my head!*" This was rapidly followed by "*Where the Fuck am I?*"

He opened his eyes and immediately felt a wave of nausea sweep over him. His tongue felt like a piece of wood and he was mildly amused to note that it was actually dry to the touch, although he was just about coherent enough to realise that this probably wasn't healthy. He was sweating profusely and could have murdered for a drink of water. Without moving his head he looked around the room. It was clearly a girl's bedroom but not one that he'd been in before. He gingerly turned to see who was in bed alongside him and was relieved to see that the other side of the bed was empty.

He trawled his mind for some hint of what had happened; a clue from the night before that would lead him to crack the mystery of how he had got to this bed in god-knows-where. For the moment his memory was not prepared to throw up anything so he decided to get dressed and face the walk into the living room to meet whoever had taken him home. After a couple of minutes searching for his boxers he eventually found them rolled up in a ball at the bottom of the sheets (which were still tucked into the mattress). Their whereabouts confirmed that it was extremely unlikely that he'd been taken home by a kindly soul wishing to offer him a place to rest for the evening and far more likely that some form of bedroom gymnastics had taken place before he'd passed out.

He got dressed quickly and tiptoed out of the room. He was obviously in a flat and the bedroom door led into a hallway with four other doors leading from it. One of the doors was slightly ajar and led to the bathroom, the other three were closed. Daisy tried the door nearest to him and was relieved to see it led into the lounge. Urban was lying fully clothed on the sofa.

"Morning mate. How are you feeling? I'm feeling like shit" said Urban as he sat up.

"Can you remember how we got here and what happened?" Daisy asked.

"Yeah, we pulled those two birds in the club and they invited us back here. Well when I say they invited us, we sort of invited ourselves but they were game on for it. Once we got back here we had a glass of wine and then headed off to the bedrooms with our birds."

"God, I really don't remember that. What was mine like?" Daisy asked.

"Can't you remember mate? She was an absolute minger. I mean you've had some rotten birds in the past but she was different gravy."

"Honestly? I can't remember a thing. I think I might have shagged her though. What happened with yours?"

"We went back to her room and did the business but as soon as I'd shagged her she started to look really ugly and I decided that it was time to leave. She was really pissed off that I wanted to go and got all arsey about it. I then realised that I didn't have any money for a cab home and she got even more upset when I asked her to lend me £20 for a taxi. She refused to give me the money and then demanded that I leave. As I didn't fancy walking halfway across London in the middle of the night I finally persuaded her to let me sleep on the sofa instead" Urban replied.

"You're a nightmare mate. Anyway I don't know about you but I quite fancy getting out of here."

"I couldn't agree with you more mate; let's go."

Just as they were about to make a move Heather appeared in the doorway of the room. Daisy still had a complete blank as to which girl he had spent the night with and so deliberately said nothing to avoid making an arse of himself. However his worst fears were confirmed when she smiled at him.

"How are you this morning BIG boy?" she said.

"I feel a bit hung over to be honest" he replied feeling sick that this was the girl he'd spent the night with. Daisy took a good look at her. She was around five foot tall, about three stone overweight (which she didn't wear well), had brown hair (although it looked a shade red and he bet her pubes were ginger), was wearing glasses and had what looked like a bum-fluff moustache. Daisy started to feel nauseous at the thought of the ginger pubes and wondered if he had any entwined in his own. That thought started to make him feel really itchy and it was all he could do not to thrust his hand down his boxers and give himself a really good scratch. He decided it was definitely time to go.

"Anyway we've got to be going erm…" Daisy realised that he had no idea what the girl's name was.

"…Heather" she interjected.

"Yeah, Heather. As I say we've got to get on as we've got to wash the football kit" said Daisy saying the first thing that came into his mind.

"But it's eight o'clock on a Sunday morning. Why do you have to wash it now?"

"Because we're playing at ten thirty and dipshit here hasn't got round to doing it all week as he's a lazy fucker" replied Urban helping Daisy out of a hole.

"Yeah so it's been great and everything but we've got to go now" said Daisy desperate to get out of the front door.

"But aren't you going to wait for Mel to come back from the shops? She's gone down to get the papers and some bacon and eggs."

"We'd love to but we've really got to go" said Urban just as they heard the front door open.

"Oh here's Mel now" said Heather.

Daisy reluctantly stayed where he was as Mel entered the room. She could not have been more of a contrast to her friend Heather. She was tall (almost six foot), slim, with shoulder length straight blonde hair, a very pretty face and most importantly no hint of a moustache. Daisy looked at Mel and then at Heather and couldn't believe that he had gone for the pig-dog. In fact he was genuinely baffled as he normally had very high standards and would usually rather have gone home for a wank than end up with a bird like Heather. *"Must've been very, very pissed"* he mused to himself.

His bemusement was broken when Mel bounded over to him and gave him a big kiss on the lips.

"Morning Colin, you must be ready for a hearty breakfast after the night you've had" she said.

"Absolutely" replied Daisy making sure that Mel didn't catch the look of daggers that he flicked in Urban's direction. Urban responded with a quick shrug of the shoulders and a cheeky smile that neither of the girls saw.

As Mel and Heather set about making the fry up Daisy nodded over to Urban. "Have you just farted?"

"No, I was just about to ask you the same thing. Honestly!" Urban replied in protest to Daisy's accusing look.

"Hey ladies, I don't mean to be rude about your place or anything but has anyone ever told you that it stinks in here?" Urban said in his usual blunt fashion.

"It's funny you should say that as there has been a funny smell that has been coming and going for the last week or so. We had a party on Friday night and since then there has been a really funny smell in here" Heather replied as she laid out four plates on the dining table whilst Heather prepared the food.

"Yeah it's funny isn't it, must be the sewers. You need to call the council about it tomorrow, Heather" replied Mel as she sat down to have breakfast with what she hoped was her new boyfriend and his slightly dodgy mate.

"Well it fucking stinks and I'd get it sorted ASAP if I was you" said Urban as he opened the News of the World.

"Thanks for the advice" Heather replied sarcastically. She desperately wanted Urban to leave but Mel had pleaded with her to make sure they both stayed until she got back with the papers and the breakfast.

"Fuck off!" thought Urban, who was now regretting that he'd shagged Heather and was feeling guilty about his girlfriend, Charlotte.

After breakfast was over, Urban and Daisy made their excuses and headed to the front door. Mel grabbed Daisy, threw her arms around him and gave him a long passionate kiss goodbye. This left Urban standing awkwardly directly in front of Heather who he was sure wanted to do the same to him. As he stood frozen to the spot thinking *"Please God no"* Heather was feeling very cheap due to the way that Urban had treated her. She had been looking for a boyfriend for a long time and didn't usually sleep with blokes on the first night. She'd made an exception with Urban and he'd made her feel like a prostitute by getting dressed and wanting to leave immediately afterwards. She now couldn't believe how stupid she had been and never wanted to see him ever again.

In order to prevent events escalating Urban suddenly thrust out his hand and said "Well it's been great meeting you Heather, we'll have to do this again sometime soon." As soon as the words left his mouth he thought "*what the fuck am I saying?*" and immediately followed up with "well not exactly this but you know what I mean." Heather gave him a withering glare and said "bye *Urban*" emphasising how stupid she thought his nick-name was.

Mel eventually let Daisy out of her clinch.

"Can I have your number then?" Daisy asked.

"You've already got it. Don't you remember I sent you a text last night?"

"Oh yeah, stupid of me" said Daisy having no recollection of the text. He wasn't even sure if he still had his phone or if it was missing in action. "Right then, I'll give you a bell" he said making his way to the front door where Urban was standing looking impatient.

"Look forward to it" said Mel shutting the door.

"What a pair of twats" said Heather as soon as the door was shut.

"Ooooh get you, just because yours was minging" said Mel.

"Well if you think that I'm going on a double date with you two and that tit you can fuck off!" Heather said as she headed back to bed.

****

Dean was woken by the sound of his mobile ringing. He picked it up and saw that it was his mum calling. He wasn't really in the mood for the usual 'How are you? How's work? Have you found yourself a nice girlfriend yet?' chat so he let it divert to voicemail, switched the phone off and went back to sleep.

Three hours later, when he finally got up, he was surprised to see that he had four voicemails when he switched his phone on. They were all from his mother saying that something terrible had happened and that he needed to call her immediately. His mother was prone to bouts of histrionics and so Dean imagined that the terrible news might be to do with her cat or his dad's new car. Reluctantly he selected her number and pushed the call button.

"Hi mum, it's me."

"Oh thank god. I've been trying to get hold of you all day."

"I know, you've left four voicemails – although as they are all identical I'm not really sure why you bothered to leave the last three. Anyway what's so terrible that it merits four voicemails?"

"It's your friend Dougie."

"Oh yeah? He hasn't gone and got himself arrested again has he?"

"No. I don't really know how to tell you this but he's dead."

"Dead? He can't be. I only saw him last week. What happened?"

"Well I don't know the full details but a friend of his called Danny rang this morning. He didn't have your mobile number and got our number from the phone book. He said that Dougie was found floating in the Thames at around five o'clock this morning. Nobody really knows what happened yet but they think that he was drunk and fell in on his way home."

"Fucking hell…."

"Dean, what have I told you about swearing?"

"Oh yeah, sorry mum. Thanks for the call" said Dean as he hung up the phone and started to get dressed.

****

Dean had met Dougie MacKenzie around five years previously when he'd seen him playing guitar in a pub in Islington. After Dougie's set they had got chatting at the bar, which turned out to be a real touch for Dean as the women were falling over themselves to talk to Dougie. They hit it off straight away and Dougie told a couple of birds that came over that Dean was actually the usual singer but hadn't been able to sing that night due to doctor's orders to rest. Dean played along with the 'I'm pretty much Liam Gallagher to his Noel' routine and the four of them ended up back at Dean's flat. Glynn had been visiting his parents that weekend and Dean was more than happy for Dougie to take Glynn's room (and bed) for the night ("That'll be the first bit of non-solo action that it's seen for some time" Dean had said making Dougie laugh out loud).

In the morning, after the girls were sent packing, the two of them had gone out for brunch and ended up on an impromptu all day drinking session, which cemented their new-found friendship. From that day onwards Dougie was added to Dean's circle of friends. One of the things that Dean loved about London was that you could make good friends very quickly, if you met somebody of the same mind set. Back in Liverpool things were much less dynamic as most people had an established group of mates that they'd known for years. On top of that most people were surrounded by family and operated in set routines; going out with the lads on a Friday night, the girlfriend on a Saturday, playing football on a Sunday and maybe snooker on a Tuesday. The same people went to the same places every week so it became like a recurring school disco nightmare.

London was very different. Every night was like a Saturday night if you knew the right place to go. There were always loads of women around that you had never seen before and that you would never see again (unless you wanted to). The place was so big that you were anonymous and you could be whoever or whatever you wanted to be on a night out. The fact that few of the people living there had grown up there meant you made friends quicker and there was always somebody up for going out on the piss.

Dougie fell very much into the category of 'always up for the cup.' In the five years that Dean knew him he couldn't recall one occasion when Dougie had declined a night out boozing unless he had a prior engagement (like a gig) and even then he would usually turn up later. He was at least ten years older than Dean (Dean wasn't sure of his exact age but guessed that he was in his early thirties) but that didn't matter as they both had the same interests; drinking, music, football and women. The only issue that they disagreed on was football. As Dougie was Scottish he was a staunch Celtic man and hated English football. He would occasionally bore the arse off everyone with his tales of the Lisbon Lions but it happened infrequently enough to let him off. The other passion that Dean and Dougie shared was music. Dean was not musical himself but had a very wide taste in music from heavy metal through to hard core dance. Dougie was a talented guitarist who could also play a number of other instruments. Dean had asked him on a number of occasions why he had never pursued a career in music properly rather than just gigging in pubs. Dougie always replied that he couldn't be arsed and that he was happy enough doing the pub scene as it made him a few quid and provided a steady supply of women.

Dean had actually dated Dougie's sister, who moved to London for a year, but broke it off when she became very possessive and clingy. Dougie had been pissed off about their relationship and Dean hadn't seen much of him whilst they were dating but after they split their drinking friendship was soon rekindled. Despite the fact that they were great drinking buddies and that they had shared lots of wild drunken nights out Dean still felt that he didn't know much about Dougie. He had never been to his flat (Dougie said that he lived in a shithole in Fulham and that he didn't want anyone to see it) and he had never met any of his friends from Scotland. Still that didn't matter as he was a good laugh and had always up for a bit of fun.

Chapter 4
Week 0 - Tuesday

The morning of the funeral was suitably depressing; freezing cold, windy and pissing down. The ceremony was set for two o'clock at a crematorium in Fulham. Luckily it was directly opposite a half decent boozer so Dean arranged to meet the other lads at twelve thirty so that they could have a few jars beforehand. By the time Dean and Glynn arrived at the Red Lion all of the other lads were already tucking into their first pints but there was none of the usual buzz and banter. Everyone looked shell shocked and there was a distinct awkwardness in the air.

"I've never been to a funeral before" Dean said to Urban.

"I don't think that many of us have mate. You don't really expect to know people that have died when you're in your early twenties. Well, maybe a few old relatives but not your mates. Do you know what the format is for today?"

"When I spoke to Dougie's mate Danny he said that it's going to be a really quick service and then it's over to some place in town for the reception, or whatever it is they call the party after a funeral."

"This is all fucking mad isn't it? I mean I only met Dougie for a pint last week and less than seven days later I'm attending his fucking funeral. How come it was organised so quickly?" said Urban.

"Danny said that Dougie had made a will which had clear instructions in it and as the police are happy that it was an accident the funeral can take place straight away. Apparently the funeral directors had a spare slot and so it all got sorted out on Sunday night. I think the only thing we can do to mark the occasion is to have a few drinks in Dougie's honour mate. Mine's a Guinness and Glynn'll have a pint of Stella."

Four pints later Dean, Glynn, Urban and Rod all felt a lot more comfortable about the funeral and made their way over the road to the crematorium. Once inside Dean spotted some of the other lads he knew and went to sit with them. After a couple of minutes of beer fuelled chit chat the hushed tones were split apart by the sound of some seriously large bells clanging. Everybody took this as the start of the ceremony and the signal to stand up. However there was a ripple of laughter a few seconds later as the bells were followed up by a guitar and it was clear (to those who knew the tune) that the bells had been from the intro to "Hell's Bells" by AC/DC, which Dougie had obviously chosen to mark the opening of the ceremony.

"Hell's Bells eh? Good old Dougie. Still managing to give us all a laugh even when he's dead" Dean said to Glynn.

"*Hells* bells? Just as well were not in a church" Glynn responded.

"Well I'm no expert but I don't think that you get rock music played at your funeral if it's in a church, you gimp."

"I was only saying…" Glynn started to say but abandoned the sentence before he dug himself in any deeper.

The ceremony passed by very quickly and once it ended (Dougie had chosen "No Regrets" by Robbie Williams as his closing song) a coach arrived and took everybody to the reception.

The reception turned out to be at a small club in Greek Street in Soho which didn't look much from the outside, just a small doorway leading down a set of stairs. It was around three o'clock when they arrived but once inside the dark basement bar it could have been a Friday night. Dougie had arranged for a DJ and a high tempo dance tune was banging out as they arrived.

"Fucking Hell, what sort of funeral is this?" Dean said to Glynn.

"Well, funeral is an anagram of real fun you know" Glynn responded.

"Fuck off Glynn. Get me a Guinness."

Once they had their drinks Dean took a look around the room at the other attendees of the party. There were at least fifty people, mostly blokes, some of whom he knew well and others that he had never seen in his life before. There didn't seem to be any old family members present. There was a distinct split in the ages with around a third of the room in their early twenties and the rest of them around forty. Dean looked around at the lads in their twenties. He obviously knew Glynn, Rod and Urban but there were also three other lads there that he classified as mates:

Mick Brady - a scruffy Irish lad who was a short, stocky prop forward rugby player and a monster drinker. Dean had met him when Dougie got into a fight with Mick at a party around four years earlier. Bizarrely they started drinking together straight after the fight and ended up becoming the best of mates. Since then Dean had seen Mick get into numerous other sticky situations but he was a great laugh and always good to have along on a night out. Mick was in his mid twenties and worked for a foreign bank.

Tim Patterson - a product of the English public school system who spoke with a plum in his mouth and was a mate of Mick's from university. Like Mick, Tim was also a rugby player but he played in the backs so he was much taller than Mick. He was also quite well built and could handle himself if there was any bother. He had very straight, neatly kept blonde hair and his looks, combined with his accent, made him generally popular with the ladies. Despite the fact that he came from a very wealthy family he hated everything to do with the public school system. Tim and Mick were inseparable and a night out with the pair of them usually ended in some form of fiasco. Tim was also in his mid twenties and worked in banking.

Ray Peach - six foot tall, white lad with a shaved bald head and was the archetypal cockney geezer. Known to everyone as Razor, it suited his personality as he had a sharp wit and would skin anyone for cash if he got the chance. Always had various dodgy deals on the go and his gift of the gab and muscular swimmer's physique made him popular with the ladies. Razor was one of Dougie's drinking buddies and Dean had known him ever since he started knocking around with Dougie. He was in his late twenties and found his perfect vocation working as a recruitment consultant.

Dean recognised five or six other young lads from nights out with Dougie but didn't know any of the older blokes. Dougie had obviously decided to keep his two sets of friends entirely separate and Dean decided to head over and introduce himself to a small group of older guys that were chatting on the other side of the room.

"Afternoon chaps, I'm Dean, one of Dougie's mates from London."

"Alright big man, I'm Don" replied a small fat Scottish guy standing in the group. "I've heard Dougie mention you a few times in the past."

"How do you fellas know Dougie?"

"Most of us went to school with him. He moved to London when he was eighteen when he went off to the Royal Academy but he used to come back fairly regularly for the piss ups."

"The Royal Academy? For Music?" said Dean shocked. "I didn't realise he'd had any formal training."

"Oh yeah. He could play any instrument but his main passion was the piano in those days" said Don.

"I didn't even know he could play the piano" said Dean. "What happened when he left? Did he get a job in music or did he just start gigging in pubs?"

"No, he became a freelance musician and used to write various bits and pieces, you know theme tunes for TV programmes and that sort of stuff."

"Really? Did he make any money from it?"

"I dunno. All I know is that after about five years he packed it all in to be a pub singer. He said that he'd had enough of the corporate side of music and just wanted to get back to performing. As far as I know he was much happier doing that."

"Well you learn something everyday, thanks mate" said Dean heading back over to Glynn and the rest of the lads.

"What about ya Deano. Fancy a shot?" shouted Mick. "We're all having one in memory of Dougie."

"Very appropriate. What are we having?"

"Aftershock mate. We're doing the red one first then the blue one" replied Mick as he simultaneously downed both the red and blue shooter glasses that he had lined up in front of him. He handed two glasses to Dean who drank the red one, winced and then swallowed the blue one.

"Why is it that shooters always make you shiver and feel sick after you've had them?" Dean asked.

"Because that's what it's all about isn't it? Getting pissed" replied Mick. "Right, who fancies a black sambuca?"

"How much money have you got Mick? This place doesn't look cheap" Dean asked.

"It's a free bar, you tit. That's why we're all on the shooters; quickest way to get pissed for free" said Tim putting on his best Mockney accent but still sounding like one of the royal family.

"Well if you put it like that make mine a double" replied Dean.

Just before Dean got completely cabbaged an old, serious looking man came over and asked if he could have a word with him in private. As they stepped out into the stairwell that doubled up as the entrance area of the club, Dean was shocked to see that it was still light outside despite the fact that he felt half cut. He looked at his watch and saw that it was still only four thirty. The elderly man introduced himself:

"My name is Peter Jacob. I have acted as Mr MacKenzie's legal advisor for the past fifteen years and I have been appointed as the Executor of his estate. There will be a private reading of Mr Mackenzie's will at my offices on Thursday afternoon at three pm. The details are in this letter" he said handing an envelope over to Dean. "Please try not to be late as I have additional appointments later in the afternoon." Without saying anything more he picked up his briefcase and coat and headed off up the stairs.

Dean opened the envelope and read the enclosed letter:

Dear Mr Williams,

It is the final wish of Douglas Forsythe Mackenzie that a private reading of his will be held at the offices of Jacobs & Co at three pm on Thursday 14th May. You alone are cordially invited. Please do not bring any other party with you to the hearing as they will not be permitted to enter.

> *Yours Sincerely,*
> *Peter Jacob*
> *Partner*
> *Jacobs & Co*

Dean put the letter back in the envelope and tucked it into the inside pocket of his suit jacket. He returned to the bar and shouted:

"Right, let's stop pissing about and get the fucking tequila out!"

****

Dean, Glynn, Mick, Tim and Razor were the last to leave the bar, after the manager told them that they had run out of tequila, aftershock and sambuca (although Dean secretly suspected that it was because Mick had been caught having a piss in the plant pots and that Tim was so pissed that he had just knocked over a table of full drinks). They stumbled out into Greek Street and were blinded by the sunshine. Dean looked at his watch and was shocked to see that it was still only eight pm. He surveyed the rest of the squad to see how they were doing.

Glynn looked in the best shape of all of them. Despite being the butt of all of the jokes and not particularly good with the ladies one of Glynn's key strengths was that he always appeared to be sober right up until the point when he would fall asleep, usually at the bar or in a club. Razor could booze with the best of them and his instinctive blagger nature kicked in when he was hammered making it difficult to know if he was pissed or not. Mick and Tim however were a different story. Mick always looked a mess but once he'd had three or four drinks he seemed to enter a new dimension of scruffiness and would have made a good scarecrow at a fancy dress party. It also didn't help that once he was pissed he only had one volume; loud. Tim who was more cultured than Mick but could be just as wild when pissed, still looked relatively sober. Overall Dean summed up that all in they were in reasonable shape to get into another bar, especially as it was only a Tuesday.

They managed to find a pub without any doormen and made their way inside. Glynn headed to the bar whilst the rest of them stumbled over to a table. A few minutes later Glynn returned with five bottles of Barcardi Breezer.

"What the fuck's this shit?" Mick shouted.

"I couldn't be bothered asking everyone what they wanted and it's easier to carry five bottles than five pints" Glynn responded.

"Fair enough. Anyway have you fuckers seen my new jacket? It's the bollocks isn't it? Cost me the best part of £500 this did" Mick shouted to make himself heard over the music.

"I was just about to ask why you were wearing your mum's jacket" said Razor, winking at the rest of the lads. "£500 they must have seen you coming Mickey son".

"Well you can fuck right off you flash Cockney twat. I got it from Selfridges after I had a couple of big wins on the horses. The personal shopper said that it would be a bit hit with the ladies."

"Personal Shopper?!!" Dean and Razor both shouted.

"I never knew you were gay" Razor followed up "Well bugger me, hang on, that's not an invitation Mickey."

"Fuck you. You all know it's quality. You're are all just jealous."

"Absolutely correct Michael" Tim cut in with his plummy tones. "Right who's for another one of these" he said waiving the empty bottle. Everybody nodded in agreement and Tim headed off to the bar.

"Now who fancies being my wing man for a crack at those two birds at the bar" slurred Mick.

"Count me in fella" said Dean putting his arm around Mick's shoulder and they both headed off to the bar.

****

"Right lads it's one thirty and this club shuts in half an hour. It's last chance saloon if we're gonna pull any birds" slurred Razor as he stood swaying next to the bar. Glynn was asleep standing up and Tim was in an alcohol-fuelled trance staring across the dance floor.

"Right then, I'm off to trawl through the wreckage and see if there are any survivors" said Razor. "Are you coming Tim?"

"What about Glynn? He's cabbaged." Tim responded.

"He's not going anywhere is he? If we can't find any birds then we'll come back and take him home. If we do then I'm sure the bouncers will wake him up before they chuck him out."

"Or the cleaners will in the morning" Tim replied satisfied that that Glynn was in good hands.

"OK then lets start with these two, they look hammered" said Razor gesturing to two girls dancing together who looked a bit worse for wear.

"Yeah alright" replied Tim. "What's it going to be tonight then?"

"Police frogmen mate, best of both world's exotic and safe. There's no way they'll be able to resist."

"Right you are. I'll follow your lead" replied Tim as they wandered over to the girls that they had targeted.

"Hi ladies, my name's Ray and this is Tim. We're in London on a new case and as we don't know the lay of the land at all we were wondering whether you know anywhere where we can get a late drink when this place closes."

"Case? What sort of case?" asked the shorter fatter girl falling head first into the trap laid by Razor. Unfortunately he'd already allocated the ugly one to Tim and so he ignored her and directed his response to the more attractive of the two girls.

"We're police frogmen down here on a new murder case. We've spent the whole day trawling through the Thames looking for a murder weapon that was thrown in a few days ago."

"Hang on Ray. I think you've said a bit too much. You know the rules about confidentiality. It's probably best if we were going now ladies" Tim interjected.

"Point taken Tim. Can I ask if you would keep that information to yourselves as we wouldn't want to jeopardise the case."

"Of course" both girls responded together.

"So what's it like being a police frogman then?" the prettier of the two girls asked Razor as she stared directly into his eyes and moved a little closer to him.

"Well it all sounds very exciting, diving in rivers and canals looking for clues or bodies but it has its ups and downs like any job. Although it is very satisfying when you find that vital piece of evidence and crack the case."

"But it can be hard as well especially if you find a body that's been in the water for a long time" Tim followed up.

"Yeah, do you remember that time we had to fly over to New York to help Interpol and we found that headless corpse that had been there for a couple of weeks" said Razor upping the ante.

"Remember it? I still wake up twice a week thinking about it." Tim replied, enjoying the game of verbal tennis that they had started up.

"But most of the time it's quite mundane and boring" said Razor aware of the fact that it was important not to give the game away by over-egging the pudding.

"God, I don't know how you do it. I know I couldn't" said Razor's bird.

Razor winked knowingly at Tim. The police frogman cover was one of the best in his armoury and he'd never failed to pull when he used it (well at some point in the evening anyway, even if it was at the seventh or eighth attempt).

Just as Razor was about to give himself a well deserved pat on the back he noticed a disturbance at the bar and saw that Glynn had somehow managed to get himself into an argument with two blokes which looked like it was about to boil over. Razor tapped Tim on the shoulder and gestured towards Glynn with a nod of his head. By that time one of the blokes had his hand around Glynn's throat and looked like he was about to punch him. Tim put down his bottle and was over in the blink of an eye. He punched the guy holding Glynn square on the jaw so hard that he was out before he hit the floor. In one continual sweeping motion he then punched the second guy who didn't go down but the blow caused him to stagger back and he held his hands up in front of his to indicate that he didn't want any trouble. From previous experience Tim had learnt not to waste time asking questions and wait for the bouncers to arrive so he grabbed Glynn.

"Let's get the fuck out of here" he said.

Glynn had never had a fight in his life but decided to take the opportunity to give the guy on the floor a quick kick in the bollocks as he stepped over him. Tim managed to get Glynn about twenty feet away from the scene of the incident before the bouncers arrived.

"What the fuck happened?" said the first bouncer who was a gorilla of a man and looked like he had been waiting all night for something to happen.

"That geezer there just decked him" said Razor pointing at the second guy that Tim had punched.

"You what? That cunt over there just decked my mate and then chinned me" he shouted indignantly pointing to where Tim and Glynn had been standing but both had now disappeared.

"Which cunt? Anyway it doesn't matter as you're out anyway mate" said the bouncer hoisting the bloke's arm behind his back and pushing him towards the door as the other bouncer picked his mate up off the floor.

"Tell your mate that he's fuckin dead if I see him again" the guy screamed as he was frogmarched past Razor.

"Don't know what you're talking about geez" replied Razor with a smile. After a quick scoot around he couldn't see Tim or Glynn and decided that they must have left. As he came outside he saw them waiting for him on the other side of the road and headed over.

"What was all that about Glynn? Didn't have you down as the sort of lad to start fights in clubs" said Razor

"That bloke tried to nick my wallet. I must have dropped off for a second and woke up to find him trying to take my wallet out of my kecks. When I asked him what the fuck he was doing he grabbed me round the throat and said that he was 'nicking my wallet and if I didn't like it he'd give me a kicking as well.' Just after that Tim turned up and lamped him. Cheers Tim, you saved my bacon"

"Glad to be of assistance Glynn. I'm sure you'd do the same for me."

"Probably not actually" Glynn replied. "But I'll sort your PC out for you if it goes wrong."

"Cheers" said Tim. "Do you fellas fancy coming back to my place as I've got a bit of booze in"

"Yeah, why not. We can have a game of cards" said Razor. They made their way over to the rank of dodgy geezers with beat up old cars offering illegal mini cab rides home and arrived at Tim's flat about fifteen minutes later.

"Fucking hell Tim have you had a party? This place is a right tip" said Glynn as they walked into the lounge.

"No, it's Mick he's an untidy fucker. Never does any clearing up. I do a bit but most of the time I can't be arsed either."

"What booze have you got in?" asked Razor

"We've got six cans of Stella and a half bottle of vodka" said Tim looking in the fridge.

"Right let's neck the Stella before we got onto the hard stuff" said Razor. "Have you got any tucker?"

"A can of beans and a half a loaf of bread" said Tim.

"Great, you get the toast on and I'll sort out some tunes" Razor responded, looking through the CD's stacked next to the stereo.

In his usual style Glynn passed out on the sofa before they had finished the first can of lager.

"Hey Tim have you got a marker pen?"

"Yeah, why are you going to draw a beard and glasses on Glynn?"

"Nah that's a bit childish, give me the pen and I'll show you."

"He's plays squash with his boss on a Wednesday or Thursday lunchtime doesn't he?

"Yeah?" said Tim not entirely sure where this was leading as he handed over the large black marker.

"Right, lift him up and pull his T-shirt up his back."

Tim pulled Glynn up into a sitting position and yanked his T-shirt up. Glynn was completely out of it and showed no signs of stirring. Razor pushed his trousers down to the point where you could see the crack of his arse and then wrote in large letters on Glynn's back:

INSERT

COCK

HERE

↓

"There we are, job done. The next time anyone sees that will be when Glynn gets to the changing rooms at his boss's stuck-up private health club. That should cause a bit of commotion amongst the members" said Razor unable to contain his laughter. By this stage Tim was rolling on his back on the floor and quite literally crying with laughter.

Once they'd finished the cans of lager Tim and Razor moved onto the vodka.

"What have you got as a mixer? Razor asked.

"We've got a two litre bottle of coke somewhere, but no clean glasses."

"Don't worry about the glasses mate, all we need to do is pour out some of the coke and tip the vodka into the bottle, hey presto instant vodka and coke."

"Good idea" replied Tim who got the coke bottle from the fridge and poured the half bottle of vodka into it.

Chapter 5
Week 0 - Wednesday

"Where the fuck am I?" thought Glynn as he woke up and realised he was sleeping fully clothed on a sofa. He then saw Razor lying starfished on the floor and remembered taking a taxi back to Tim's place after the club. He looked at his watch and saw it was ten past four. He was desperate for a piss and decided to find the bathroom. He stood up and had to grab the sofa to stop himself falling over. He stepped over Razor, opened the door. Tim was lying unconscious on the bathroom floor with his head propped up between the side of the toilet and the bath. Glynn bent down and gave him a shake.

"Tim, get up mate and go to your bed."

Tim showed no sign of stirring and Glynn was relieved to see that he was still breathing. Glynn was desperate for a piss and decided to move Tim's head away from the toilet bowl to avoid splashing him. As he dragged him by his feet Tim's head slipped from between the toilet bowl and the side of the bath and gave off a loud crack as it dropped about eighteen inches onto the wooden floorboards. Tim uttered a groan but still didn't wake up. Glynn didn't want to risk inflicting any more injuries and decided to straddle Tim's prostrate body in order to have a piss. He had just started urinating when Tim opened his eyes and saw Glynn standing directly above him with his nob in his hand. Alarmed, Tim sat bolt upright, causing him to headbutt Glynn in the bollocks which sent him flying backwards and threw a jet of piss up into the air and over the pair of them.

"What the fuck are you doing with your nob out in my bedroom Glynn? Tim said, still groggy from the blow to the head and the booze.

"This isn't your bedroom it's the fucking bathroom and I was trying to have a piss" said Glynn quickly tucking his nob back into his trousers.

"The bathroom?" said Tim, confused. "What the fuck would I be doing sleeping in the bathroom?"

"Good fucking question" said Glynn pulling himself up off the floor and heading back to the lounge.

When Glynn got back to the lounge Razor, who still appeared to be unconscious, had somehow managed to pick himself up off the floor and had taken Glynn's place on the sofa.

"Fucking great. I haven't got any cash to get home, that fucker has just nicked the sofa, I've got a mouth that's as dry as a granny's fanny and I can't even have a piss in peace" thought Glynn as he pushed the two armchairs together to make an impromptu, uncomfortable bed. As he moved the second armchair into position he noticed the two litre bottle of coke that was around two-thirds full.

"You fucking beauty!" he thought as he unscrewed the cap and gulped down half of the liquid in a oner. *"Tastes a bit dodgy but at least it's wet"* Glynn thought as he curled up onto the sleeping space he had created across the two chairs.

Glynn woke up again about two hours later at around six am. It was just starting to get light outside and he felt a sharp pain as the sunlight hit his retina. *"Jesus, I feel worse than I did before I went to sleep and my throat feels like sandpaper"* he thought as he reached for the coke bottle again. He downed the rest of the liquid and a little shiver went down his spine. *"That stuff tastes like shit"* he thought as he drifted back to sleep.

The next time Glynn woke up it was seven thirty and Razor was shaking him. Rather confusingly he felt worse than he had on the previous two occasions that he had woken. Razor was speaking to him but he couldn't seem to focus on the words. He could see that Razor was laughing and holding up the coke bottle and an empty vodka bottle but couldn't really understand why. Razor then started shouting and Tim appeared. Eventually Glynn managed to get himself together enough to speak.

"Fucking hell lads I still feel really pissed!"

At which point both Razor and Tim both starting rolling around the floor laughing and even Glynn had to admit that it was one of the funniest things that he'd ever heard (although he couldn't quite work out why). They finally stopped killing themselves laughing a good ten minutes later.

"I'll tell you something really funny though Glynn" Tim said, "it's fucking Wednesday morning and we're all got to be in work in an hour" which caused another outbreak of uncontrollable laughter.

****

Mick woke up with a start. He had no idea where he was but knew that he was lying in a bed with no clothes on, which was a step up from being in a field, or a bush, or a prison cell so all in things could've been worse. He could see that it was a girl's bedroom as it had pink curtains and he could vaguely make out a few cuddly toys on a chair in the corner of the room. That was another plus point then, as waking up in a bloke's bedroom was always a bit of worry.

Mick lay perfectly still as he thought about his predicament and the various potential scenarios. He had absolutely no idea who he was in bed with him. It could be a hot, fit attractive bird that had taken a fancy to his Irish charms and that he could spend the rest of the day frolicking with rather than going into work. Alternatively it might be some fat old moose that he'd picked up when he was too pissed to care and who might try to get him to stay all day against his will. Then again it could be some underage bird whose whole family were now downstairs waiting to lynch him. Mick's mind quickly raced through a hundred different scenarios as he lay perfectly still. He decided that given how bad he felt and the fact that he couldn't remember much after leaving the reception for the funeral it was quite likely that the lady in bed alongside him probably wouldn't be troubling the judges at Miss United Kingdom that year and was probably nearer to her bus pass than her teens. As a result he decided that discretion was the better part of valour and that the best course of action was to allow her the luxury of a lie in by quietly creeping out of bed, grabbing his clothes and fucking off as quickly as he possibly could before she could get his name or phone number (assuming that she didn't already have them).

As he inched his way towards the edge of the bed he got the feeling that there wasn't anybody in the bed with him and plucked up the courage to cast a quick glance over his shoulder. To his relief he saw that the other side of the double bed was empty. There was evidence that someone had previously been in alongside him (indentations in the pillows and the bedcovers were pulled back) and as Mick never slept naked he was fairly confident that there had been some frantic activity the previous evening. He now faced a new dilemma. The bird had clearly got up before him without wanting to wake him; but why? On the upside there was the possibility that a gorgeous twenty-something nymphette was currently cooking him the fried breakfast of a lifetime in order to re-fuel his body for a full day of rampant sex. At the opposite end of the spectrum there was the chance that a fifty-something grandmother of six was downstairs with all of her family waiting for granny's new 'special friend' to appear. Worst still it could be that a fourteen year old schoolgirl was frantically trying to explain why she had gotten home so late and was trying to persuade her parents to go to work before her soon-to-be-on-the-sex-offender-register-boyfriend appeared.

Mick very quietly got out of bed and crept over to the window. "*Fuck!*" he thought as he saw that the bedroom was at least two stories up and that it would be a certain broken leg if he tried to jump it. Despite this he still considered it an option and decided to make it plan B in the event that he encountered either of the family gathering scenarios he had just thought up. At the foot of the bed he found his trousers, shoes, socks and pants in one pile and guessed that he had taken them all off in one sweeping movement at the height of sexual anticipation for both of them (or at least for him). His T-shirt was on the floor over by the door some ten feet away and from this additional clue he guessed, in a sleuth like manner, that they had been in a passionate embrace from the moment they had entered the room and his lady friend had been clearly gagging for it. He looked around for his jacket but there was no sign.

"Where's my fucking £500 jacket?" he said to himself. Mick was not good at keeping his cool at the best of times but when he was pissed or hungover he had a very short fuse. He suddenly forgot about all of the potentially nightmare scenarios, got dressed and yanked open the bedroom door. The property turned out to be a small flat, thus ruling out the possibility of a large family gathering. The bedroom door opened onto a small landing which had two other doors running off it and a steep staircase down to the front door of the flat. Mick stood and listened but couldn't hear any movement from the other two rooms. He looked at his watch, saw it was almost seven thirty and decided that the best course of action was to grab his jacket, hotfoot it home and get to work as soon as he could. He walked across the landing and popped his head through the first door he came to. It was obviously a girls bathroom as there were candles dotted about all over the place and at least ten different bottles of shampoo lined up neatly along the bath. He carried on down the landing and came to the other door, which was closed. He slowly opened the door and quietly said "Morning" in a sheepish manner, just in case anybody was in the room. The room was a decent sized living room but felt cramped due to the dining table and chairs which had been squeezed in behind the sofa. He walked over to a freestanding shelf unit and grabbed the framed photograph that was on display. It was a snapshot of what looked like a mother and her daughter. The daughter was about twenty five, plump and not particularly attractive. The mother was in her fifties, had clearly been decent looking in her day but was now on a downward path. Mick couldn't decide which possibility was worse; that he had shagged the fat young pig or the wrinkly old mum. Either way he decided that he wasn't going to hang around to see whose flat this actually was.

Mick looked all over the living room for his jacket but couldn't find it anywhere. He could feel himself getting more and more irate. *"It is a fucking great jacket"* he thought in his drunken haze. "S*he must have nicked it hoping that I'd have to get off to work in a hurry. Well fuck you bird! No one pulls a fast one on Mick Brady and gets away with it."*

With that thought in his mind Mick went back to the bedroom, pulled back the duvet, dropped his trousers and had a huge shit right in the middle of the double bed. Just as he finished he heard a key in the door.

"OH FUCK!!!" he thought as he quickly pulled up his trousers and threw the duvet over the offending mound.

"Hi, are you up yet Mick?" shouted a female voice that was ascending the stairs.

"Yeah" he replied, shocked that she knew his name, "I've just got up and am coming out."

"Why don't you stay there and I'll join you" she responded. As she reached the top of the stairs the bedroom door flew open and Mick appeared looking flustered.

Mick started to feel both sick and puzzled as he stared at the very attractive black haired girl standing opposite him. She was wearing his jacket and holding a packet of bacon in one hand and a loaf of bread in the other.

"I borrowed your jacket to nip to the shop, hope you don't mind."

"No, not at all" Mick lied, feeling even worse about what he had just done in the girl's bed.

"Right. I've phoned in sick today so my diary's totally free. How about I make us some bacon sarnies, you call your work to say that you won't be in and we go for a little lie down as we didn't really get much sleep last night did we?" said the girl who was becoming more and more attractive by the second.

"I'll tell you what why don't we have those sarnies before we decide what else we're going to do today?" Mick said, deliberately closing the bedroom door behind him and ushering the girl into the living room. "Who are these two in the photo" he asked picking up the photo he'd inspected with disgust earlier.

"Oh that's my mum and my sister."

"You take after your mum don't you?" said Mick trying to be casual about the situation but feeling a wave of panic every time the girl made any sort of movement towards the door.

"Yeah everybody says that, which is very flattering as she was a model when she was younger."

"That's fascinating" said Mick who, despite his faux pas, now had the raging horn. "I'll tell you what why don't you leave the bacon for a minute and come here" he said patting the sofa next to him as he sat down.

"Why?" the girl replied coyly.

"There's something I want you to have a look at" said Mick unzipping his trousers.

"Oh let's go to the bedroom, it'll be a lot more comfortable."

"It fucking won't" thought Mick but managed to say "No, let's stay here, it's more spontaneous."

"Alright then" she responded as she dived on top of him "but let's go back to bed after breakfast.

"Of course" said Mick pulling off her top.

As soon as they finished having sex Mick's hangover suddenly felt a lot worse and he knew that it was time to make a decision on the way forward. This girl was very attractive, rampant in bed and for some god-unknown reason had taken a real shine to him. Ideally he would have liked to see her again. However the main sticking point was the enormous turd that he had just laid in her bed. As he saw it he had three real options available to him:

1. Pretend that he had had some sort of accident whilst she was at the shops, claim to be highly embarrassed and hope that she was sympathetic towards his plight so that they could put it behind them.

2. Admit what he had done, offer to clean up all of the mess and claim that one day (possibly their wedding day) they would look back and laugh about it.

3. Get his coat and fuck off.

Mick quickly made his decision. "I'll tell you what I really fancy, apart from you of course, is a full fry up. I'll pop back to the shop and get some sausages and eggs and then phone in sick. How's that sound?"

"Great, I'll come with you."

"No, you're alright, you've already been once. I'll go" said Mick rapidly fastening his trousers and grabbing his jacket as he made his way to the front door.

"OK then. The shop is straight down the road just past the tube station but don't be long."

"Don't worry I won't be" said Mick as he closed the door behind him and broke into a full sprint. After about twenty seconds he thought he could hear a faint scream coming from the direction of the flat but decided not to look back. He sprinted past the commuters making their way to the tube station and jumped straight into a black cab that was parked outside.

"I'm running really late for a meeting mate, just drive in that direction" he panted as he slumped onto the back seat. The cab driver looked at Mick disbelievingly in his mirror as he pulled off. Mick turned round and looked out the back window to see the bird running down the middle of the road screaming. He waived at her, held his hand to his mouth in a phone gesture and mouthed the words "Call me." He started laughing to himself as he watched the girl shouting obscenities and waiving her hands in the air as the cab turned the bend and she disappeared out of sight. He settled back down into the seat and as he put his hand inside the pocket of his jacket found the girl's purse. *"Oh shit"* he thought.

****

Dean was woken by the noise of post being forced through the letterbox. He wouldn't normally have heard it but the fact that he was lying fully clothed in the hallway meant that he was a lot nearer to the sound that he would normally have been at that time of the morning. He sat up on and rubbed his eyes. He had absolutely no recollection of how he got home, what time it had been or why he had decided to kip on the floor in the hallway rather than making an extra thirty seconds of effort and going to bed. Sheepishly he decided to assess the damage of the night before, in the usual order of importance:

1. Face – he felt his face and was relieved to discover that it was blood / bruise / cut free. *"Well at least nobody chinned me last night so I can go to work today"* he thought.

2. Hands – no signs of any blood, cuts or dirt. *"Great, looks like I didn't chin anybody either so the police won't be looking for me."*

3. Wallet – check. *"Thank God!"*

4. Cash – none. *"No surprise there then. As usual, I have once again managed to spend every single penny that I took out with me last night. I am truly a master of budgeting."*

5. Mobile – check. *"Miracle. It's a bit early to check who I called or texted last night though,*

I'll do that later on when I'm feeling a bit more up to it. In fact probably best to switch it off in case anybody I did contact last night tries to call me back."

6. Keys – check. *"Obvious really seeing as I am lying on the floor of my flat, although there is always the possibility that Glynn let me in."*

"All in as good a result as I could have hoped for. What a great night out" thought Dean to himself as he stood up and made his way into the living room. He flopped down onto the sofa and switched the telly on with the remote. The clock on the breakfast news showed it was seven forty five and that he had half an hour before he had to leave for work. He looked at the suit he had worn to the funeral the previous day (that he had used as an impromptu set of pyjamas) and wished he'd done what he'd been promising to do for weeks and bought a second suit. *"No problem, I'll just have to go in smart-casual today"* he thought but just as he was about to settle back and watch the sports news he remembered he had a client meeting later that day. Given his lack of options he decided to take the suit off and give it a quick steam clean, which involved hanging it up in the bathroom for half an hour whilst running the shower on full heat. As Dean took off his suit jacket he spotted the letter in his inside pocket, which he opened.

Dear Mr Williams,

It is the final wish of Douglas Forsythe Mackenzie that a private reading of his will be held at the offices of Jacobs & Co at three pm on Thursday 14th May. You alone are cordially invited. Please do not bring any other party with you to the hearing as they will not be permitted to enter.

*   Yours Sincerely,*
*   Peter Jacob*
*   Partner*
*   Jacobs & Co*

Dean sat up and carefully re-read the letter. He hadn't seen the old guy hand out letters to any of the other guys and he certainly couldn't remember any of them telling him that they had received one. *"The reading of a will? How exciting!"* he thought, allowing himself for a second to dream of the untold riches that he might be about to inherit. He then remembered that this was Dougie's will, his mate that gigged in pubs a couple of times a week. *"He's probably stitched me up with his fucking debts"* though Dean as he screwed up the letter, He then returned to the more pressing matter of his crumpled, stinking suit and headed off to the bathroom to try to convert it into a sauna.

Chapter 6
Week 0 - Thursday

The offices of Jacobs & Co were not quite what Dean had been expecting. He had imagined a gothic old building steeped in history, with a huge wooden front door, stone gargoyles in the shape of judges and a large brass plate announcing the year that the firm was founded. What he actually found was that Jacobs & Co occupied the fourteenth floor of a newly constructed glass and steel office block in Canary Wharf that had an enormous banner declaring "Office Space to Let" covering the front of it. The building was huge, with at least a fifty floors and twelve huge lifts serving different blocks of floors. After a couple of minutes of searching Dean managed to locate the correct lift and took it to the 14th floor. On his way up he imagined the receptionist to be a friendly grey haired old lady who'd been with the firm for twenty years however as the lift doors opened he was actually greeted by an Australian bloke in his twenties.

"Hi, my name's Dean Williams and I'm here for the three o'clock reading of the will of Dougie Mackenzie" said Dean.

"That meeting started fifteen minutes ago, sir" the receptionist responded looking at the clock above him which showed it was three fifteen.

"There was a problem on the tube" Dean lied. The receptionist gave him an insincere smile as he picked up the phone and advised the person on the other end that Dean had arrived.

A couple of minutes later the old guy that had given Dean the letter at the funeral appeared. Dean followed him into his office, where three other people were seated. Mr Jacob took his seat behind the large wooden desk and motioned for Dean to take the one remaining empty seat. Dean looked at his fellow attendees. In the furthest seat from him was an elderly woman who Dean guessed was in her late sixties. She had grey hair, gold rimmed spectacles, was dressed like a primary school teacher (skirt over the knee, knitted pullover and pearls) and looked exactly how he expected Dougie's mother to look. Seated in the next-but-one chair was the small fat Scottish guy that Dean had spoken to at the funeral the previous day and in the seat next to his was Ray 'Razor' Peach. Dean nodded to all three of them as he sat down. The elderly woman gave a polite smile, the Scottish guy nodded and Razor whispered "Alright geezer?"

"Now that Mr Williams has finally joined us we can start" Mr Jacob said flashing an insincere smile at Dean that made him shuffle in his seat.

"As you know you have each been invited here today to hear the final will and testament of Douglas Forsythe

58

Mackenzie. Before we start I must advise you that as Mr Mackenzie passed away only recently his estate has yet to be finalised. Before we will know the final amount of his estate there are a number of costs that must be paid out, such as this firm's fees and the funeral costs. As a result any cash inheritance will not be distributed until the estate is finalised. However tangible assets will be released immediately as the responsibility to pay any taxes due on the value of these assets falls upon the person who inherits them.

As, as you may or may not be aware Mr Mackenzie was a very wealthy man" Mr Jacob continued.

Dean shot a puzzled look over to Razor who responded with an equally puzzled look.

"He was a highly accomplished musician who composed a number of original pieces that have generated, and continue to generate, large royalties."

"Erm, excuse me. Is it OK to ask questions?" Dean asked, cutting in.

"Providing that the question is relevant to the information that I have given you so far" Mr Jacob replied.

"When you say that Dougie wrote a number of original pieces, what sort of pieces do you mean exactly?"

"I have a list somewhere" Mr Jacob replied as he started rummaging through a large stack of papers on his desk. "Ah yes, here it is. Mr Mackenzie's speciality was composing jingles for advertisements. I have a long list of the jingles but by far the most successful one was for a major UK insurance company."

"An insurance company? That doesn't sound very exciting" said Dean looking disappointed.

"Maybe not very exciting Mr Williams but the jingle that Mr Mackenzie composed is played at the end of every single advertisement that the company puts out on both TV and radio. Each time the jingle is played a fee is payable to Mr Mackenzie. When you consider the number of satellite TV channels and commercial radio stations in the UK that adds up to lot of royalty payments. Shall I continue with the will or do you have any further questions Mr Williams?"

"No, please carry on" said Dean starting to get excited.

"Good. In view of the size of Mr Mackenzie's estate he drew up a comprehensive will and updated it annually. The will I have here in front of me was prepared on 6th January this year and therefore represents Mr Mackenzie's most recent wishes" Mr Jacob said as he opened the folder on the desk in front of him and put his glasses on. "To my oldest friend Donald Scott I leave my Triumph Spitfire and the sum of £100,000 in cash. In addition I leave a further sum of £10,000 that is to be used to fund an invitation-only party in my home town of Ayr. The details for the arrangements and the guests to be invited for this are listed on a schedule that Mr Jacob will provide separately."

"Get in! You fuckin beauty Dougie!" Don shouted as Mr Jacob handed over the guest list.

"Quite" said Mr Jacob smiling politely. "If I may now ask you to leave the reading please Mr Scott."

"What? But I wannie hear what everyone else is getting" Don responded.

"Well I'm afraid that Mr Mackenzie has left specific instructions on the order that the will is to be read out and he has specifically stated that you should leave now" Mr Jacob replied.

"OK then. When do I get the money?" Don asked.

"As the car is a tangible asset it will be delivered to you by a representative of this firm within the next few days. However as I stated earlier you will have to wait until the estate is finally settled before the cash will be made available."

"So when will that be?" Don asked.

"I can't give you a definitive date but it may take up to six months to agree all of the tax issues with the Inland Revenue."

"For fuck's sake. Six months? But I am definitely going to get it aren't I?"

"Yes, providing that the Inland Revenue are satisfied that the money is available for distribution."

"Great, then I think it's time for a wee dram to celebrate" said Don as he walked out of the office.

Once Don had closed the door Mr Jacobs continued. "To my mother, Annette McCloud Mackenzie, I leave all of my ongoing royalties together with the balance of all of my bank accounts once the sums due to all other parties have been settled."

"Oh that's nice" the old lady responded. "Do you have any idea how much we are talking about as I am considering buying a new car."

"I am not able to give you precise details as to the exact amount however I can tell you that in the past twelve months the ongoing royalties amounted to over one million pounds and Mr Mackenzie's bank account currently holds considerably more than that figure."

"Goodness me!" said the old lady.

"I think she means 'Fuck me!'" Razor whispered to Dean.

As the words 'one million pounds' registered in Dean's mind he started to feel that he was having an out of body experience. Fifteen minutes ago he thought he was coming to his mate Dougie's will reading to hear who'd be getting his clothes and maybe the odd DVD. However over the past quarter of an hour he'd discovered that Dougie was a multi millionaire jingle writer who owned a Triumph Spitfire. After hearing the first two readings Dean started to get very excited about what Dougie might have left him.

Mr Jacob then asked Dougie's mother to leave the office. Once she had gone he turned to Razor and Dean.

"Now gentlemen the final part of the will is a little unusual but was a specific instruction of Mr Mackenzie."

Dean glanced at Razor who looked just as confused as he was.

"'To my best friend in London and my valued drinking partner, Dean Williams, I leave my eight bedroom house in Battersea."

Dean had been leaning back on the rear two legs of his chair and quite literally fell off his seat as it toppled backwards. As he lay on the floor time seemed to stand still as he thought *"Eight bedroomed house in Battersea? I'm fucking rich!"*

He clambered back onto his chair and before he could ask any questions Mr Jacob continued.

"Mr Williams will initially be allowed to occupy the house on a rent-free basis for a maximum period of ten weeks. Ownership will then pass to Mr Williams providing that he meets the following conditions:

1. He must arrange for six of the rooms to be occupied by six single men of his choice for the entire ten weeks. The other two rooms will be filled by Mr Williams himself and my Personal Representative. The ten week period will commence on the day that Mr Williams moves into the property which must be within one week of the reading of this will.

2. Each week Mr Jacob will provide my Personal Representative with an envelope containing a challenge that Mr Williams will have a maximum of seven days to complete. This challenge must be completed to the satisfaction of my Personal Representative. There will be a total of ten challenges and photographic evidence that each task has been completed will be required.

3. Each person in the house must participate in at least one challenge each over the course of the ten weeks. Failure to comply with this ruling will make it impossible to complete all ten tasks and will therefore result in forfeiture of ownership.

4. None of the other members of the house must be aware that Mr Williams will take ownership of the property upon successful completion of the

challenges. If any of the other members of the house become aware of any of this information then it will result in failure to comply with the conditions of my will and Mr Williams will not take ownership at the end of the ten week period.

5. My Personal Representative is exempt from participating in the challenges unless it is his personal choice to do so.
6. If all ten tasks are completed to the satisfaction of my Personal Representative, debt free ownership of the property will be transferred to Mr Dean Williams at the end of the ten week period.
7. If all ten tasks are not been completed to the satisfaction of my Personal Representative then the property will revert to my overall estate and will be distributed accordingly."

"So what are these so challenges then?" Dean asked.

"I'm sorry Mr Williams but I do not have access to that information. Mr Mackenzie left me ten sealed envelopes together with instructions to release one per week to his appointed representative. I do not have any further information that I can give you at this stage. My only future involvement will be to provide the envelopes to the appointed representative and to receive weekly confirmation that the terms of the will continue to be complied with.

"You mean that the challenge for that week has been completed?" Dean asked.

"Yes. Thereafter my only remaining involvement from your perspective will be to complete the transfer of ownership of the property."

"Is there anything else I need to be aware of?" asked Dean.

"Not for you Mr Williams, but under the terms of the will you are permitted to stay here and hear the reading for Mr Peach."

"Finally to my other closest friend in London, Ray Peach, I leave the sum of £500,000. Payment of this sum is conditional on the following:

1. Mr Peach acts as my Personal Representative with regards to the Battersea property.

2. Mr Peach provides a sealed envelope to Mr Williams each week containing that week's challenge and also a sealed envelope containing photographic evidence that each challenge has been met to Mr Jacob each week. Mr Jacob will retain these photographs in safe keeping and is not required to check their contents.

3. This photographic evidence must subsequently be verified by a further representative of my estate at the end of the ten week period.

4. To avoid any collusion the identity of my additional representative will not be released to any party but will only be released by Mr Jacob at the end of the ten week period.

5. If all ten tasks are not completed then Mr Peach will forfeit his inheritance and it will revert to my overall estate.

"That, gentlemen, concludes the reading of Mr Mackenzie's final will and testament" said Mr Jacob packing away his papers. He handed over a large brown envelope to Dean. Dean took the envelope and opened it. Inside was a piece of paper with the address of the property together with a set of keys.

"Looks like we're moving house then Deano" Razor said.

"Fancy a pint?" Dean replied "I think we need one."

****

Razor brought the two pints over to the table where Dean was sitting in the corner of All Bar One at Canary Wharf. Dean was staring vacantly at the keys for the house and the piece of paper containing the address.

"Here we go then geezer, this'll sort you out" said Razor placing the pint of Guinness in front of Dean.

"I just don't get it" said Dean still staring suspiciously at the two objects in front of him. "How can you know somebody for that long and still not know anything about them? I mean fair enough if you don't know the name of the school they went to or their pet dog when they were a kid but to not know somebody is a millionaire musician with an eight bedroom house is taking the piss."

"I know, it's mad isn't it" Razor said settling into his seat and lighting a cigarette. "Well let's think about it all for a minute; where did you meet Dougie?"

"In a boozer in town. He played a few songs on his guitar, I ended up talking to him at the bar and we just hit it off."

"So did you befriend him because of his successful music career or his enormous wealth?" Razor asked, playing devil's advocate.

"I see your point" Dean responded. "Maybe Dougie wanted people to like him for who he was rather than for his money but I'm still saying that he could have told me the truth once I got to know him."

"And I'm saying that it doesn't matter when he told you, it would still have changed things" Razor replied. "I can't remember how many pissed up nights that me and Dougie ended up with no cash walking home from town to my place. Obviously we now know that he could've bankrolled the lot of us every night if he'd wanted to, but part of the fun of those nights was the scrapes that we ended up getting into on the way home. If we'd have known that Dougie was loaded we'd have been plaguing him on every one of those nights to pay for a cab or to lend us £20. It definitely would have changed things if we'd have known he was wedged-up even if we say now that it wouldn't. Although, having said that, the tight arsed twat could've kept an emergency few quid aside to have saved me walking home all those fucking nights!" he followed up with a chuckle.

"I still can't get my head around it" said Dean finishing off his drink and indicating to Razor that he wanted another one by shaking his empty glass at him.

"I think you'll find it's your round, you cheeky fucker" Razor responded.

"Technically it is, but you have just inherited half a million quid" said Dean smiling.

"And you're wondering why Dougie never told you that he had any cash? Mine's a Stella when you're ready" replied Razor.

"Worth a try" said Dean as he headed to the bar. He returned a few minutes later with the two pints. "OK then Razor how's all this Personal Representative business going to work then?"

"You know as much as I do Deano. You heard what the old geezer said, all I have to do is give you an envelope every week containing some sort of challenge and then get photographic evidence from you that it's been completed. When we deliver all ten photos, I collect my cash and you get your house."

"So what sort of thing do you reckon these challenges will be?" said Dean.

"I dunno, but Dougie did have quite a fucked up sense of humour so they could be anything" said Razor.

"Great" Dean replied sarcastically.

"Anyway, are we going to see this house or not?" Razor asked as he downed his pint.

****

The house was located off Northcote Road, about a ten minute walk from Clapham Junction station, and was a grand double fronted Victorian terraced property with a huge white front door. Dean opened the door and stepped inside, avoiding the mound of post on the floor, and walked into the hallway which had a high ceiling and two large modern art paintings opposite each other. Two doors faced each other and Dean turned right into the first. The room was enormous and was obviously the main living room in the house. Mounted on the wall above the marble fireplace was the largest plasma screen TV that he had ever seen, the type that they have in the lobby of large office buildings or in car showrooms. The room had been decorated in a minimalist, ultra modern fashion, with two large black leather sofas and a large coffee table sitting on a wooden oak floor. The room opened out into a huge bay window that was covered with oversized wooden blinds. On the wall opposite the plasma screen was another large painting that was similar in style to the two in the hallway.

"Fucking hell" said Dean "this place is amazing."

"Unbelievable" said Razor shaking his head.

They crossed over the hallway to the other doorway and entered an equally large room that was set up as dining room. The furniture was ultra modern, with a huge glass table in the middle surrounded by sleek, curved perspex chairs.

They made their way back into the hall, past the grand wooden staircase, opened the other door on the ground floor and entered the kitchen. Dean had only ever seen kitchens like this on TV. The room was designed on an open plan basis, had a conservatory at the far end, a grey stone floor and a fully fitted kitchen with opaque glass-doored units and black granite worktops. In the middle of the kitchen was a huge square island and suspended above it were a variety of pots, pans and other cooking implements. To the left hand side was an enormous American-style fridge and a large counter which served as a breakfast bar. Beyond the kitchen was a large conservatory made up of one brick and three glass walls. On the brick wall was another plasma screen and opposite it were two sofas. At the far end were concertina doors leading out to the garden, which consisted of a hundred foot lawn, edged with a variety of exotic looking trees.

Next to the fridge was a locked door. Dean checked the key ring and found the appropriate key. He opened the door revealing a set of stone stairs leading into the basement. The footprint for the basement was roughly the size of the living room and dining room combined and the floor had obviously been excavated, making the place cavernous. This huge space was set up as a music studio. Mounted along the whole of one wall were at least twenty guitars as well as a host of other string instruments and on the opposite wall was artwork from various album covers. At the far end of the room was what looked like a mixing desk (although neither Dean nor Razor knew what one actually looked like) and strewn around the floor were various keyboards, drumkits, wind instruments and sheets of handwritten music.

"Looks like Dougie was still working hard right up until the end" said Razor.

"Freaky isn't it? It's like an Aladdin's cave in here" Dean responded.

Upstairs Dean and Razor found four double bedrooms (two ensuite) and a family bathroom on the first floor and two double ensuite bedrooms, two single bedrooms and a further bathroom on the second floor.

After they finished their tour of the house they headed back to the kitchen and grabbed a couple of beers from the fridge, which freaked them out as it was still stocked with Dougie's groceries.

"So how much do you reckon this place is worth then Razor?"

"Well I'm no expert but it's got to be a couple of mill at least" he responded.

"I'd better make damn sure that all of those challenges are completed then hadn't I?" Dean said staring at his new garden.

"Seeing as my cash is also on the line I reckon you fucking should" said Razor laughing as he clinked his bottle against Dean's.

****

Dean was sitting in the front room of the flat watching TV when Glynn came storming in from work.

"Fucking hell mate, what's wrong with you?"

"Those fucking bastards have gone too far this time. I mean I don't mind a joke but this is too much" Glynn shouted as he marched into his room and slammed the door. Dean got up from the sofa and knocked on Glynn's bedroom door.

"Fuck off Dean, I mean it."

Dean and Glynn had lived with each other for the past four years and now knew each other's moods pretty well. Dean hadn't seen Glynn this upset since the time that he'd accidentally shagged his girlfriend.

The problem on that occasion was that neither Dean nor the girl herself knew that she was actually Glynn's girlfriend. The situation had started when Dean had left Glynn asleep (as usual) in a nightclub at Uni. Miraculously Glynn somehow recovered sufficiently to pull and end up back at a girl's flat. They never actually had sex but Glynn, who never really had much luck with

71

women, instantly fell madly in love with the girl. She was freaked out by Glynn getting all heavy and decided to treat the whole thing as a drunken mistake. Glynn refused to believe that a girl who would let him sleep in her bed didn't want to see him again and he refused to go out on the following Saturday night just in case she called. Glynn was then mortified to bump into her again in his own kitchen the following morning when she came waltzing out of Dean's room wearing one of Dean's T-shirts. Dean had tried to explain that he hadn't actually done anything wrong as he didn't know it was Glynn's 'girlfriend' (an argument supported by the girl herself who pointed out that she *wasn't* actually Glynn's girlfriend). However Glynn had taken it very badly, especially as Dean had actually shagged her. It had taken almost a month before Dean and Glynn were back on normal speaking terms and the topic was still a sore subject that both of them avoided mentioning.

"Come on mate it can't be that bad" said Dean through the door.

"Oh yeah, well look at this" said Glynn yanking the door open. He was standing in his boxer shorts and turned around to reveal the slogan on his back:

INSERT

COCK

HERE

↓

"How long have you had a tattoo?" said Dean unable to contain his laughter.

"It's not a fucking tattoo; it's indelible marker pen which won't fucking come off" Glynn responded curtly. "Those fuckers did it to me on Tuesday night."

"Which fuckers?"

"Tim and Razor. I never noticed it yesterday and I might be able to see the funny side any other time but I play squash at my boss's club on a Thursday. The changing rooms were packed and a couple of the older members lodged a complaint about him bringing a rent boy in at lunchtime" said Glynn almost in tears.

Dean was also fighting back the tears; of laughter. "So what happened?" asked Dean, only just able to speak.

"We were both asked to leave and he's had his membership suspended pending a Committee hearing" said Glynn. "I think I might get sacked."

"They can't sack you for that, it'd be homophobic. You'd be able to take them to tribunal and claim that they were discriminating against your sexual preference" said Dean.

"But I'm not fucking gay" said Glynn "and even if I was I wouldn't have 'INSERT COCK HERE' written on my back would I?"

"I dunno, it might be helpful for those occasions when you fall asleep in night clubs" Dean responded.

"Oh fuck off" said Glynn slamming the door in Dean's face.

"Oh I forgot to mention" said Dean, shouting through the door, "we're moving out on Saturday."

"What?" said Glynn suddenly yanking open the bedroom door. "What do you mean we're moving out? We've still got another two weeks to go on the rent that we've paid for this month and we've also got to give a month's notice."

"Well" said Dean sitting down on the sofa "I was invited to a reading of Dougie's will today and it turns out that he was really rich."

"Dougie was really rich? Oh pull the other one Dean" Glynn replied shaking his head.

"No, seriously. Apparently he wrote a few jingles that were used on adverts and he made millions from it. Anyway he owns this fuck off big house in Battersea which he's left to one of his relatives in the will but as a way of saying thanks to his mates he's made it available for eight of us to live there rent-free for six months" Dean said, stretching the truth a little. Technically Dean only had access to the house for ten weeks but he didn't think that he would be able to persuade anyone to move in for ten weeks so he decided to tell the lads that it was a full six months. He didn't see this as a problem as he was confident that he would meet the terms of Dougie's will and take possession after the ten weeks and then he would simply let everyone stay on until the end of the six months period. "So, seeing as we are paying £1,000 a month for this shithole we may as well move in there and save a bit of cash for the next six months. Also the place is absolutely pukker so it's going to be a blast."

"Sounds great" replied Glynn "what's the catch?"

"There isn't one" Dean lied.

"We'd better start packing then" said Glynn suddenly forgetting his problems and closing his bedroom door.

"You do that mate, I'm going out for a bit. See you later" said Dean picking up his jacket and heading out the front door.

****

Dean arrived at Mick and Tim's flat about half an hour later. Mick claimed that he was 'keeping it real' by living in Hackney as it had a diverse ethnic population and wasn't full of stuck up public school types. Tim (who technically was a stuck up public school type himself) said that he lived there because it was cheap and he couldn't be arsed to look for anywhere to live on his own. Dean couldn't stand the area and tried to avoid going there unless he really had to. He rang the bell and had to wait for a couple of minutes before anyone came to the door. Tim eventually opened the door about a quarter of an inch, just enough to see who it was whilst still being able to slam it closed if it was someone that he didn't want it to be. When he saw it was Dean he opened the door fully.

"Hi Dean, how's it going?" Tim said in his clipped accent. He stood aside to let Dean in.

"Yeah, alright thanks Tim. What's with all the cloak and dagger door opening routine?" Dean asked, as he walked down the hall to the living room.

"Well I had a bit of a run in with a couple of likely lads on Tuesday whilst Michael here got himself into all sorts of bother with one of those lovely ladies that you two were talking to in the boozer" said Tim.

"What lovely ladies?" said Dean trying to recall the events of Tuesday evening.

"Apparently we decided to chat up two birds in a boozer after we got kicked out of the funeral reception" said Mick who was sprawled on the sofa watching TV. "I probably wouldn't remember either except I woke up with one of them yesterday morning."

"Result" said Dean.

"Not when you hear what the fuckwit did" said Tim.

"You didn't go bareback did you?" asked Dean.

"No, nothing like that. I wish it was something that simple as she was really fit. No, it's a long story but I ended up having a dump in her bed" said Mick

"What? Did she have one of those shit fetishes? I've seen porn where people eat each other's shit, it's disgusting" said Dean pulling a horrified face.

"No, it was nothing like that. I thought that she'd nicked my new jacket" Mick replied.

"But I thought you said you were at her flat? How could she nick it when you were at her flat?" Dean asked.

"Yeah it all sounds a bit stupid now but it seemed feasible when my brain was still full of Stella in the morning. Still at least I still got to nob her again before I left."

"What? After you'd shat in her bed? So she did she have some sort of fetish then?" asked Dean looking puzzled.

"No. Anyway what the fuck do you want?" said Mick rapidly changing the subject.

"How would you two like the opportunity to live rent free in a state of the art mansion in Battersea for the next six months?" said Dean.

"That would be great Dean. I'd also like the opportunity to have a threesome with a couple of page three birds and to drive a Ferrari round the streets of Monaco but I don't think it'll happen this week" Mick replied sarcastically.

"I'm serious" said Dean. "Wait til you hear this. It turns out that Dougie made a mint out of writing jingles for TV adverts, was worth millions and owned a fuck-off big mansion in Battersea" said Dean.

"Dougie? Bollocks!" Mick replied.

"No, honestly he was worth at least five million" said Dean.

"What and his dying wish was for us lot to wreck his house by letting us live there rent free for six months?" Mick asked unconvinced.

"Not wreck it, no. Dougie has left the place to one of his relatives but as a thank you for being his mates he inserted a clause into the will saying that we can live there rent free for six months if we fancy it. So what d'ya reckon?"

"Where is it? Battersea?" asked Mick.

"Yeah, I went there today and it's a fucking top-banana house. Eight bedrooms, plasma screens everywhere, near the station, big garden" said Dean sensing that Mick was taking the bait.

"Nah, it's full of stuck up public school nonces round there. I'm quite happy here thanks" Mick responded.

"Don't be a prick Mick. This place is a shithole and we could do with a change of scene as we've done a bit too much shitting on our own doorstep around here" said Tim.

"Are you having another pop?" said Mick standing up.

"I don't mean actual shitting, oh you know what I meant" said Tim laughing.

"Eight bedrooms, rent free?" said Mick. "Alright Deano you're on. When do we get to move in?" asked Mick.

"Saturday" replied Dean.

"Fucking hell you don't hang around do you? Right then give us the address and we'll see you there on Saturday. But this had better not be a wind up or I'll be coming over to shit in your bed" said Mick laughing.

"It's not a wind up lads, just a way of Dougie saying thanks for helping him have a laugh over the last few years" Dean replied as he made his way to the front door.

"Right, including Razor that's five of the rooms filled, just need to get another three of the lads on board and we're off and running" Dean thought as he left the flat. He pulled out his mobile phone, called up his list of contacts and pressed the call button.

"Hey Urban, it's Dean. What you up to?"

"Still nursing my hangover from last night mate" Urban responded.

"Fancy meeting for a pint? I'm over at Mick and Tim's place and could be at yours in about twenty minutes" said Dean.

"I'm actually in the Maple Leaf waiting for Daisy and a couple of other lads to turn up but feel free to come along."

Dean flagged a passing black cab and jumped in. *"Right if I can get Urban to sign up I'll just need two more to complete the set"* Dean thought whilst searching his contacts list. He called up another number "Rodney my old mucker, fancy meeting me and Urban down the Maple Leaf for a couple of jars?"

"I can't mate I'm up in town with a few of my mates" Rod replied in his thick Yorkshire accent.

"Oh right. Are you going to be out for long?"

"Yeah, we're going to a gig at a club later."

"Any chance I could join you?" asked Dean.

"I don't really think it's your scene mate" said Rod.

"But I really need to have a chat with you tonight, it's about Dougie" Dean responded.

"Alright then mate, I'll be in the Hellfire club on Tottenham Court Road from eleven o'clock onwards. It'll be the place surrounded by hairy arsed bikers. You can't miss it" replied Rod.

"Right, I'll see you in there" said Dean hanging up and desperately trying to think of somebody else that he could call. The taxi arrived outside the Maple Leaf. Dean paid the driver and headed into the pub. In the corner he saw Urban, Daisy and a couple of other big black lads.

"Alright fellas, anybody in need of a refill?" asked Dean as he arrived at the table.

"Yeah, great timing Deano, I'll have a Stella" replied Urban and the other three all nodded and waived their almost empty pints of Stella to indicate that they wanted the same.

When Dean came back from the bar he shook hands with all of the lads and asked Urban if he could have a word in private. They moved to another table and Dean repeated the same story that he had told Glynn, Mick and Tim earlier.

"So what do you reckon then Urban, are you up for it?"

"I'm not sure. My bird is constantly nagging at me that as we're engaged we should get a place together. As you know that's the last thing that I want to do but if I move in with you she'll get all upset that I'm moving in with even more lads" Urban replied.

"Yeah, but it'll be rent free for six months so you can tell her that you're doing it in order to save up for a place of your own. That way she'll see it as a step closer to getting a place with you" Dean replied.

"Good point" said Urban nodding "so who else is going to be moving in then?

"So far it's me, you, Glynn, Mick, Tim and Razor" Dean responded.

"Razor? Ray Peach?" Urban responded "He's a right dodgy fucker that bloke. There something about him that I don't trust. I can't out my finger on it but I'm not sure that I want to live in the same house as him."

"He's alright once you get to know him. I wouldn't normally have asked him but Dougie specifically requested that he be invited so I didn't really have a choice."

"I'm not really sure about Mick and Tim either. I mean don't get me wrong they are both a good laugh to go out on the piss with but I think they could be a nightmare to live with" said Urban.

"Oh I'm sure they'll be much calmer when you're living with them. Anyway did I mention that it's rent free and you'll definitely have a much better room than you've got in that flea pit of a bed sit that you live in at the moment."

"Yeah, but it's cheap and the landlady treats me like a son" said Urban.

"Does she shag her sons then?" Dean asked smiling

"Fuck off. That was just once and I was really pissed" replied Urban not joining in the joke.

"But she's a fat old moose who's at least sixty" Dean followed up. "I'd have thought the fact that you've shagged her and that she's constantly up for seconds would mean that you'd be out of there like a shot."

"I'm not sure that I've got the heart to move out, I feel a bit sorry for her really" said Urban.

"You've shagged her again haven't you?" Dean asked accusingly, moving in like a shark sensing blood.

"Look, when do you need to know about this?" said Urban changing the subject.

"Tomorrow at the latest. Everyone is moving in on Saturday."

"Fucking hell, you don't hang around do you? OK I'll let you know tomorrow then" said Urban standing up.

"Great. Can you see if Daisy fancies it as well as we've got room" asked Dean.

"Why don't you ask him yourself" said Urban walking back to the group.

"I've got to get off, I'm meeting Rod" Dean replied.

"Why didn't you get him to come here?"

"I did but he wouldn't come as he's going to see some shite band so I'm meeting him there" said Dean.

"Rock On Dude!" Urban responded, holding up two clenched fists with the index and little fingers pointing up in the air.

"Fuck off" muttered Dean as he made his way out of the pub and looked for a black cab to run him up to Tottenham Court Road. The cabbie had never heard of the Hellfire club so he dropped him on the corner of Charing Cross Road and Tottenham Court Road. The road was full of large groups of pissed up people queuing for clubs, waiting for buses or crowding around dodgy burger stalls. During the day this part of Oxford Street contained all of the downmarket shops and the tourist tat shops but at night it took on a new perspective, becoming a myriad of neon, fast food outlets and trendy clubs.

Unfortunately Dean wasn't heading to one of the trendy clubs but rather was looking for some scanky rock club that he was certain would be 90% full of long haired greasy blokes. When Dean was younger (around thirteen) he had briefly flirted with rock music and had often fantasised about the cool rock-chick scene in LA where gorgeous glamour models with huge breasts would be clambering to get into the rock clubs and shag good looking British guys like him. He'd imagined rock clubs being the coolest place to be seen and that he'd be fighting off the women. As he continued down the street he suddenly saw where he was heading to. The club was obviously set up in the basement under a shop and didn't even have its own signage. What it did have was an old bed sheet hanging above it on which somebody had scrawled "Hellfire Club" in red paint however they had clearly hung it up before the paint had dried as each letter had large drips running off them. *"Oh Jesus"* thought Dean as he approached the doorway. All thoughts of meeting Pamela Anderson evaporated from his mind and he started thinking more along the lines of Urban's landlady in leather trousers.

Dean arrived at the entrance and was greeted by a queue of about fifty people, all of whom had long hair, leather jackets and a multitude of piercings. Dean looked at his jeans and white FCUK T-shirt and wished that he'd worn something vaguely more appropriate. He reluctantly joined the back of the queue. Directly in front of him in the queue were a couple in their early twenties who were all over each other. The girl broke off from the necking and stared at Dean, making him feel even more uncomfortable. He shrugged his shoulders and gave a weak smile to which she responded by poking her tongue out to reveal two piercings. *"Rod had better fucking be in here"* thought Dean.

Chapter 7
Week 1 - Friday

After calling in sick for the second day in a row Dean headed over to the house. It looked even more impressive than he remembered as he wandered around and he allowed himself to dream of owning it. Dean was still trying to work out what Dougie meant by the 'challenges' he wanted him to complete. Would they be real tasks, like world record attempts, or would they be something more like the sort of thing they used to get up to on nights out? The main thing concerning Dean was that he needed to get photographic evidence. There was an unwritten rule on nights out that nobody was allowed to take pictures which could incriminate anyone at a later date. Therefore it would be difficult for Dean to take photos if the challenges turned out to be anything remotely dodgy. He had the camera on his phone for emergencies but decided he would need something more discrete to record anything the lads wouldn't want him to photograph. He pulled his phone out of his pocket and made a call.

"Razor, it's Dean. I'm at the house. Do you know anyone who's good with computers?"

"Yeah, Glynn."

"I know Glynn is but do you know anybody else, preferably someone who doesn't know me" said Dean.

"Why? What do you need?"

"It's this photographic evidence thing. I want to set up a hidden camera in the living room so that I can record everything that goes on there and then use the recordings to print off any photos that I need to" said Dean.

"Nice idea Deano. Leave it with me, I'll make a few calls and get back to you" said Razor.

Twenty minutes later Dean received a text saying that Razor was on his way over to the house with someone who could help. An hour later Razor arrived in a white van with a small stocky bloke aged about forty.

"Right Dean, this is Dave. He knows everything there is to know about spying on people. Isn't that right Dave?"

"You're not fackin wrong Razor son" Dave replied in a strong cockney accent. "It all started when I thought me missus was having an affair so I wired up every room in the house with digital cameras in order to catch her at it. It turned out she fackin was as well, the slag. She tried to deny it and almost shat herself when I stuck the video on showing her and that cunt at it. Still he got what was coming to him just after that, didn't he?" Dave said winking at Razor. "Anyway it turned out that a lot of people are interested in this sort of thing and so she sort of done me a favour as I've now started doing this for a living. What's your problem, your missus playing away is she?" Dave asked Dean.

"Erm, yeah she might be" Dean responded pleased that Razor had not told Dave the real reason why he wanted the cameras.

"Well you're doing the best thing" said Dave "best to be sure I reckon and once you've got the evidence she's fucked, so to speak. Which rooms do you want me to set everything up, in all the bedrooms?"

"Well I was just going to do the living room but now that you mention it I think it will be safer if we do all of the bedrooms as well" Dean replied.

"Except for your granny's room mate" said Razor, winking at Dean to indicate that he didn't want a camera in his room.

"Yeah, that's a good point" said Dean. "If you've got your kit with you I'll show you which rooms to put the cameras in Dave."

"I've got everything in the van. Hang on a minute" said Dave heading back outside. He returned a few minutes later with a large cardboard box and a ladder. "You'll love these little beauties, I made 'em all myself" he said pulling a camera the size of a marble out of the box. "The cameras are so small they can be hidden inside burglar alarm casings so that anyone in the bedroom will simply think it's a burglar alarm system rather than someone spying on them. Let's have a look at the alarm system" said Dave as he climbed up his ladder and started fiddling around with the casing for the alarm sensor. "Great, there's enough space in the existing housings to bury the camera without it being visible and I can connect the camera to the same power supply so that nobody will know the difference. The cameras will then transmit their signal directly to the receiver which plugs into the back of your PC."

"Excellent, I'll show you which rooms to set up then" said Dean.

Three hours later all of the cameras were in place. Dave set up a laptop in Dean's bedroom which had a built-in recordable-DVD drive. "Right Dean, all of the cameras are in place and the DVD drive is set up to record everything that happens. All you need to do is select which room you want the signal to be recorded from and Bob's your uncle. I've left you a box of twenty blank DVD's and all you need to do is change the disk every six hours. If you have any problems or need anything else here's my mobile number" Dave said handing Dean a business card. "The only other thing left to say is good luck catching the bitch out."

"Erm yeah" said Dean remembering the story he'd told Dave about his 'missus.' "How much do I owe you?"

"I still owe Razor for a favour he did for me recently, so don't worry about it" Dave replied grabbing his equipment and heading out to the van.

"Right then we're all set. All we need to do now is see what Dougie's got in store for us from beyond the grave" said Dean as he closed the front door behind Dave.

As Dean made his way to the living room his mobile rang. He saw that it was Urban. "Alright fella? Made a decision on the offer of a lifetime yet?"

"Yeah, I'm in" Urban replied. "I've done my sums and even if having all those maniacs in the house does turn out to be a living hell I'll be at least six grand better off at the end of it and that's gotta be worth it."

"My point exactly mate. Did you get a chance to ask Daisy?"

"Yeah he's bang up for it. I told him that a few of the lads can be a bit lively but he's from Camberwell so I think he'll be able to hold his own."

"Brilliant mate, are you all set to move in tomorrow then? We're gonna have a bit of a party tomorrow night to mark the occasion" said Dean.

"Yeah we've hired a van and should be round late afternoon."

"OK, see you then" said Dean hanging up.

"Who was that?" said Razor as he entered the room and handed Dean a bottle of beer. They sat down on opposite sofas.

"Urban. He's up for it and so's his mate Daisy" Dean replied.

"Daisy? What sort of a name's that? Don't tell me that he's another twatish mate of Urban's trying to make himself sound a bit more interesting than he is?"

"No he seems a decent lad, I think you'll like him" said Dean.

"So is that all the rooms filled then?" Razor asked.

"Almost. We've got seven confirmed - me, you, Glynn, Mick, Tim, Urban and Daisy and I'm just waiting for Rod to call me back. I asked him last night at some thrash metal gig in town"

"I didn't know that sort of stuff was your scene?"

"It isn't" said Dean chugging back on his bottle. "Basically the set up was lots of long haired fat sweaty bikers headbanging to shit music, whilst me and Rod had a chat at the bar."

"Sounds dreadful."

"It was. Anyway Rod has been crashing with his latest bird for the past month or so and wanted to talk to her about it and give me an answer today. I've arranged to go over to his place about three o'clock."

"Rod's got a bird? Fucking hell, what's she like?" asked Razor.

"She's one of the long haired fat sweaty bikers that was there last night" Dean replied, laughing.

"Nice" said Razor. "By the way mate you'd better get your skates on, it's ten past three."

"Shit" said Dean jumping up and spilling his beer over his jeans. "Right, now that everything is set up the only other thing you need to do is get the first week's envelope from Mr Jacob. I'm going to have to shoot off now but if you can get round there this afternoon it'll mean that we will have a full week to do whatever it is Dougie has cooked up for us. Let yourself out and I'll see you here tomorrow."

"OK" said Razor as he flicked the huge plasma screen onto one of the music channels and settled back on the sofa.

****

Dean arrived at the Docklands Light Railway station at a quarter to four. Despite being an overweight heavy metal fan who rode a scooter (he couldn't afford a bike) Rod had somehow managed to find himself a half decent looking girlfriend called Helen. He'd been kicked out of his last flat for not paying his rent and had wangled his way into moving into her flat even though they had been going out for only a month. Helen owned a new-build flat in Docklands, which was a complete no-go East End ghetto until the developers moved in and converted all of the disused warehouses into luxury apartments.

"Fucking apartments" thought Dean as he made his way from the station. *"When I was growing up you either had a house or a flat and apartments only existed on the telly in New York. Now all these big developers have got involved it's all studios, penthouses, duplexes and designer living but at the end of the day it's still a fucking flat, apart from the fact that it costs a fuck of a lot more money."*

All of the luxury apartments were plonked down alongside the poor quality housing stock on the former council estates which meant the area had a surreal feel. Ostentatious glass fronted apartment blocks sat uncomfortably next to run down gritty estates and it was common to see groups of school kids terrorising young idiots in suits who thought that this would be a cosmopolitan place to live. The whole area was soulless and as Dean walked along the road he was amused to see a couple of blokes in suits scurrying along the street, desperate to get to the safety of their apartment block with its video camera surveillance systems and twenty four hour security guards. He arrived at Rod's block and entered the lobby. The guard was watching TV on the large plasma screen behind him and Dean had to clear his throat before he noticed him. The guard quickly swivelled in his chair and grabbed a bunch of papers to make it look like he was in the middle of something.

However once he saw that Dean was obviously nobody important he gave up the pretence.

"Can I help you *sir*?" he said with more than a little sarcasm cast onto the final word of the sentence.

"I'm here to see Rod Duncan, flat 609" said Dean.

"*Apartment* 609" the security guard replied correcting Dean on his mistake. "Can I take your name *sir*" he asked continuing to make it clear that he would not normally refer to Dean as 'sir' but that it was something he was required to do for this job.

"Dean Williams."

"I'll just call Mr Duncan to see if he would like me to send you up" he said punching the number into his phone. "Mr Duncan? It's Henry on the front desk. I have a Mr Williams here to see you. Shall I send him up?" He hung up and gestured to the lift behind him. "It's the sixth floor, just follow the signs."

"Thanks" said Dean heading to the lifts. When he arrived at flat 609 the door was already open for him. He knocked and shouted "Hello" as he entered.

"In here mate" shouted Rod from the room at the end of the hallway. Dean closed the front door and walked into the room. Rod was lying on the sofa in a pair of jogging bottoms and an old 'Simpsons' T-shirt and looked rough. Dean sat on the armchair opposite Rod.

"You look fucking terrible mate. Anything the matter?"

"Erm, well, yeah, sort of" Rod responded without sitting up.

"Well there either is or isn't something up with you. You seemed OK when I left you at the Hellhole club last night" Dean said.

"Hell*fire* club" Rod replied. "Yeah I was OK when you left. In fact things initially ended up more than OK."

"How d'ya mean" asked Dean.

"Well after you left Helen said she had to go home as she had a meeting this morning. I didn't want to miss the band's second set and so she suggested that I stay on without her and crash over with one of the other lads. So she left at about one and I stayed behind with a few mates."

"Sounds brilliant" said Dean sarcastically. "Any chance of a brew?"

"You'll have to make it yourself mate, I'm still feeling a bit delicate after last night. The kitchen's the first door on the left and the tea bags are in the jar marked 'Tea Bags'."

"Really? I'd never have worked that out" Dean replied "and don't tell me the water is in the tap and the cups are on the tree mug."

"Fuck off, you cheeky twat!" Rod replied. "Anyway do you want to hear what happened or not?"

"Yeah, carry on" Dean shouted from the kitchen.

"Anyway I had a few more beers and a couple of cheeky spliffs. The last spliff that I had was a bigun and before the band came on I started feeling a bit dodgy. I decided to nip out for a bit of fresh air to clear my head. When I got to the doorway there was this bird there who was doing the same and we ended up having a bit of a laugh about being a pair of lightweights. Anyway one thing led to another and we ended up getting a cab back to her place in Stoke Newington."

Dean started to feel a bit jealous that he'd missed out on some shagging action until he remembered that the Hellfire had been full of horrific fat birds. He consoled himself by imagining that Rod had gone home with an eighteen stone monster. He interrupted Rod's flow "So hang on, you bumped into this bird who was puking outside the club and she then invited you back to Stoke Newington, which is a right shit hole. She must have been really classy."

"Do you want to hear what happened or not?" Rod responded.

"I'm all ears" said Dean as he brought his tea into the living room.

"For your information she was fit, although you are right about the puking part as she still had a few lumpy bits in her mouth when I kissed her" said Rod laughing.

"Feel free to leave out the stomach-churning parts of this sordid tale, although having seen the quality of birds at that gig I think the whole thing is probably stomach-churning" said Dean indicating his distaste with a shiver.

"Anyway" said Rod continuing "we got back to her place and headed straight to her bedroom. She opened a bottle of JD and put on some AC/DC."

"It all sounds so romantic, I think I'm going to cry" said Dean.

"You might do when you hear what happened" said Rod, grabbing Dean's attention again. "Right, so after a bit of necking and fumbling about on her bed she decides to go down on me. She gets the old fella out and puts it in her mouth but rather than sucking it she decides to use her teeth. At first it felt quite nice, a sort of S&M pleasure and pain thing, so I didn't say anything. Then she started biting a bit harder and she had a few jagged bits on her teeth which were quite sharp. I shouted out in pain and she took that as an indication that I was enjoying it and started going at it even harder. I tried to pull her off, no pun intended, but by that stage she was like a wild banshee and started wanking me off really hard with her hand as well. I was literally screaming when all of a sudden I felt this hot sensation and she stopped."

"Had you come?" asked Dean.

"No, she'd pulled so hard that she'd split my banjo and the hot sensation was the blood that had started pissing out of the end of my nob. She was so pissed that she thought I'd come and didn't notice it wasn't spunk. She then stood up and tried to kiss me with her face all covered in my blood."

"I told you that fucking club was full of freaks and vampires" said Dean laughing.

"So there I was in agony with blood squirting out of the end of my nob and this bird, whose face is covered in blood, says "I think you enjoyed that didn't you, we can do it again when you're ready!" It was at that point that I puked and things went really pear shaped."

"What?" said Dean "How could it possibly go any more pear shaped?"

"Well after I threw up she started screaming and going mental. Then one of her flatmates came in, saw the blood on her face and thought that I'd been knocking her about. He was all for kicking the shit out of me but luckily I had my bleeding nob to use as exhibit A in my defence and I managed to persuade him that I had actually come off a lot worse out of the incident and avoided getting a kicking."

"Jesus, what a nightmare" said Dean.

"Yeah but it didn't end there. By the time I'd washed most of the blood off and got dressed it was still only three o'clock. The bird was having none of me staying over and chucked me out. I obviously couldn't come back here as Helen would have killed me so the only place that I could think of going was the all night café near Kings Cross."

"What, the place all the cabbies hang out? It's a bit of a shit hole isn't it?"

"Totally, but the state I was in they almost didn't let me in" said Rod.

"So what did you do then?" Dean asked.

"Well I had to wait until Helen had gone to work and then I came back here. I daren't go to bed as my nob has only just stopped bleeding and I don't want to accidentally knock the scab off it. So I've just been lying here in agony for the past few hours."

"Are you going to go to see the doctor about it?" Dean asked.

"Well I wasn't intending to, I was hoping that it'll just heal naturally" Rod replied.

"Let's have a look at it then" said Dean sitting forward in his chair.

"Fuck off you bender."

"No seriously let's have a look and I can give you my opinion as to whether you need to go to the hospital or not" said Dean adopting a more serious tone.

"Alright then" said Rod as he swivelled on the sofa and sat up. He stood up and gingerly pulled the front of his jogging bottoms down revealing his blood encrusted penis.

"Fucking hell mate, I thought you said you'd cleaned the blood off it?" said Dean recoiling back into his chair.

"Well I tried to but it's bloody sore" said Rod. "So what do you reckon?"

"It doesn't look good mate. You might need a stitch or two to sort it out. I'll tell you this though, you won't be shagging Helen with that for some time and if she sees it you'll have a lot of explaining to do!"

"I know. Is the offer of that room in Dougie's house still available? I need to avoid seeing Helen for the next few weeks."

"It certainly is mate" Dean replied smiling to himself "although only if you promise not to get up to anything like this again."

"I don't think I'll be getting up to anything for a while" Rod replied as he lay back down on the sofa and winced with pain.

Chapter 8
Week 1 - Saturday

Despite downing the best part of a case of Budweiser the previous night Dean hadn't managed to get much sleep. As he watched his digital clock flick over to seven o'clock he decided to get up. He'd already packed most of his clothes and looked around his room at what was left to pack. Despite the fact that he was now twenty four and had been working for three years since leaving university he didn't have many possessions to show for it. He had his Technics stereo system (which had cost him the best part of his first month's salary but was still the dog's bollocks three years on), his extensive CD collection, a Tag Heuer watch (which he'd bought with his second month's salary), some clothes and that was about it. *"That's all about to change though"* he thought, *"once I get this house business sorted out it'll be champagne, caviar and tailor made suits all the way!"*

He stood up and starting gathering the remainder of his clothes from the floor. He stuffed them into the open suitcase, stripped his bed and packed the bedding. *"OK then, ready to go"* he thought to himself.

"Oi Glynn, are you up yet?" he shouted.

There was no response from Glynn's room so Dean headed out of his room and opened Glynn's bedroom door. "Oi, lazy bones, are you up yet?"

"Of course I'm not fucking up yet, it's ridiculous o'clock on a Saturday morning" Glynn responded from under his duvet.

"Come on mate, we're moving out today so it's time to get up" said Dean pulling off the duvet to reveal Glynn lying in the foetal position in a pair of grubby boxer shorts.

"It's just as well that I hadn't smuggled a bird into bed with me last night isn't it? Glynn said sitting up and rubbing his eyes.

"It's not very likely given your track record though is it? The only bird that you're likely to smuggle back is from KFC and it's closed for refurbishment at the moment" Dean replied, laughing at his own joke.

"Ha ha" said Glynn sarcastically as he got out of bed.

Two hours later, Dean and Glynn pulled up in the van outside the house in Battersea. The street was deserted and although it was nine o'clock it felt earlier.

"It's like the whole street has got a hangover and has decided to have a bit of a lie-in" Glynn said to Dean as they got out of the van. "You can almost hear the drunken snores coming from the windows."

"Well I'm sure by this time tomorrow you will *actually* be able to hear those drunken snores" said Dean referring to the eight new residents that were about to move into the area.

"Do you think that we should ask a few of the neighbours round tonight for a few housewarming drinks? You never know there might be a house full of fit totty next door that's gagging for it" said Glynn getting excited.

"Are you fucking mad? We're looking to stay here for six months" said Dean (who had now resigned himself to the fact that he would have to honour his offer to let everyone stay on a rent free basis for six months). "We don't want to get everyone's backs up on the first night do we?"

"Good point" said Glynn remembering who else was moving in with them.

"Anyway, stop waffling and give me a hand with my stereo" said Dean as he opened the back of the van.

By eleven o'clock Dean and Glynn had moved all of their stuff into their chosen rooms and were settled in front of the giant plasma screen watching Soccer AM on Sky Sports.

Dean had taken the room he assumed had been Dougie's. It was situated on the first floor at the front of the house and had a huge bay window overlooking the street. Dougie had mounted another plasma screen (not as large as the one on the living room but still massive) on the wall opposite the bed and had installed a combination stereo-home cinema system with speakers all over the room. The bed was a king sized water bed that had various controls allowing you to set the temperature to match the time of year. You could also get the whole bed to vibrate or give a massage which Dean thought would be useful the next time he pulled. The room also had an air conditioning system, an ensuite shower room and mirror fronted wardrobes which made it appear even bigger.

Glynn's room was also on the first floor but was at the back of the house, overlooking the garden. It had obviously been used as a guest bedroom but was considerably large than any bedroom Glynn had ever had before. It had a small en-suite shower room and a wide screen TV.

It was three o'clock before any of the other lads turned up. Razor was the first to arrive, bowling up in a huge black Hummer with blacked out windows. Dean and Glynn heard the music that the vehicle was spewing out as soon as it turned the corner around two hundred yards from the house and were both standing on the doorstep as the pimp-mobile pulled up.

"The eagle has landed!" shouted Razor with what looked like a huge reefer hanging out of his mouth.

"Nothing like being discrete" Dean said to Glynn raising his eyebrows.

"You're probably right about not asking the neighbours round" Glynn replied.

"If he carries on at this rate I think the neighbours will be coming round tonight anyway" said Dean "but they're more likely to bring the bizzies with them rather than a moving in present."

Razor walked up the path carrying a large bag. Behind him were two stocky black blokes each carrying a suitcase.

"Afternoon chaps, am I the first? Razor asked.

"Yep and you'll be the last if you don't tone it down a bit" said Dean nodding towards the spliff that Razor had in his mouth.

"Oh this stuff is practically legal these days, everyone's doing it" Razor responded.

"Maybe they are down the East End but not in this street they're not" Dean responded taking the roll-up out of Razor's mouth and stubbing it out on the floor with his foot.

"Fair enough" Razor responded. "Right fellas if you follow me I'll show you to my room" he said nodding for the two guys to follow him as he walked into the hallway.

"This is going to be an interesting six months" said Glynn closing the front door.

"You're not wrong" Dean nodded still wondering to himself what Dougie actually had in store for him.

Urban and Daisy arrived about an hour after Razor. They were followed by Mick and Tim and Rod was the last to arrive at six thirty. Dean opened the front door to let Rod in and saw that he'd arrived in a pick up truck which had his moped tied to the back of it.

"You've left it late mate. How come you never came over on the bike this morning? Dean asked.

"I tried to mate but with my little problem it was agony sitting on the bike so I had to run out and hire this thing."

"What did you tell Helen?" Dean asked.

"Err, well I never actually told her I was moving out" Rod replied, looking guilty.

"You haven't told her? She's going to kill you when she gets hold of you mate."

"I did leave her a note" Rod replied, putting forward a weak defence for his actions.

"A note? What did it say? 'I've fed the fish, we need some milk and by the way I've moved out?" Dean said, clearly loving it.

"No. It said that I need a bit of time and space to contemplate where our relationship is going and that I've decided to move out for a few days to clear my head" Rod said with a smirk.

"A few days? You are staying for the whole six months aren't you?" Dean asked, worried that Rod would ruin his plans to meet Dougie's requirement to keep the house full.

"Yeah, of course I am. I just said a few days to take the sting out of it for her. I'm working on the basis that it'll give my nob a bit of time to sort itself out so that when we do get back together everything will be in full working order and we can do what comes naturally."

"So when is she likely to read it?

"She's away at her parents place this weekend so she won't get it until she gets back on Sunday night" Rod replied.

"Best have your phone switched off tomorrow then mate" Dean said.

"Too fucking right, especially with the hangover that I intend to have tomorrow" Rod said laughing. "Right then give me a hand bringing in my stuff."

****

Whilst everyone was busy unpacking boxes and working out where they wanted to position their beds, Dean went to see Razor.

"Did you go and see the old boy yesterday then?" Dean asked desperate to know if Razor had the envelope containing the first challenge.

"Erm, yeah. I went to his office but he wasn't there" Razor replied.

"Bollocks!" Dean responded "I was hoping that we could have a crack at the first one tonight as everyone will be together for the first time."

"As I was saying before you interrupted me, *he* wasn't there but the receptionist had this little fella for me" said Razor pulling a crumpled envelope out of the back pocket of his jeans.

"Fucking hell" said Dean "have you opened it yet?"

"No. Dougie's rules state that I give each sealed envelope to you" said Razor handing it over to Dean.

"Oh god, I wonder what it says?" Dean said as he sat down on the bed. He was holding the envelope out in front of him on his open palms as if it was an original parchment from the bible.

"Only one way to find out" said Razor as he snatched it out of Dean's hands. He opened the envelope and took out the single piece of paper inside. He held it out in front of him and Dean sat next to him so they could both read it simultaneously.

"Dear Dean,

If you are reading this letter it means firstly that I am dead (which is a real bummer I can tell you) and secondly that you have agreed to take on my challenges. As you know by now I have a few bob tucked away (who'd have thought that those annoying jingles at the end of an advert could be worth so much dosh?). Anyway I found out very quickly that having money doesn't bring happiness and that there are a lot of people out there (both birds and blokes) who just want to know you for what they can from you. After a few bitter experiences I decided that I'd been happier before I was rich and that's why I never told you or any of the other lads about the money. It wasn't because I thought you were a money grabber but it would have changed things and I liked things the way they were, with us all going out, getting pissed, pulling birds and having a laugh.

I thought long and hard about what to do with the money - whether to leave it to charity, my family or just dish it out amongst my friends. I rapidly decided that I didn't give a fuck about any particular charities and discounted that as an option. Out of my family the only one that stuck with me through thick and thin was my mum and she'll have more than enough with what I have left her. So the real decision was who to leave the rest to and how to do it. You and Razor have been my best mates for the past five years and we've had some right laughs. I therefore decided that you should get the chance to get some of the cash but I didn't just want to give it to you as that'd be too boring. I've therefore decided to use my untimely demise as an opportunity to create a final period of mayhem and to get you lot to have a few more laughs before you forget about me, sort of like my legacy if you like. It has taken me a while to think up a good way of doing this but I think the ten challenges you will be set will be exciting, fun and will definitely make the next ten weeks very interesting. Just to re-iterate the rules are as follows:

1. *You must get six other lads to move in the house with you & Razor.*

2. *There will be one challenge set every week for ten weeks.*

3. *Every member of the house (except Razor) must participate in at least one of the ten challenges.*

4. *None of the other members of the house must be aware that you are working towards an end game (i.e. that you will inherit the house). The only exception to this is where a cash incentive is provided for a challenge. You may then advise them that they can earn some cash from my will in return for doing certain things although this should be expressed as a one-off dare rather than as part of a bigger scheme..*

5. *Photographic evidence is required that each challenge has been completed. This evidence will be held by Mr Jacob and will be checked by an independent representative of my choosing at the end of the ten week period (just to make sure that you and Razor don't try to cheat!).*

6. *Ownership of the house will pass to you if you pass all ten challenges. If you fail any of the challenges the game is over and you will all have to move out immediately.*

I'm sure by now that you are dying (excuse the pun) to know what the first of these challenges is. I thought I'd break you in gently with an easy one:

'PARTY TRICKS'

All you need to do is to get at least three members of the house to perform an 'impressive' party trick, which should be a piece of piss given some of the lads you know.

Anyway, good luck mate and hopefully we'll be in touch again in a week's time.

Your friend,
Dougie"

"Party tricks? That really is going to be a piece of piss" said Razor lying back on the bed and relighting his reefer.

"What a fucking relief" said Dean. "I've been shitting myself for the past two days worrying what Dougie was going to come up with but this will be a doddle. I'll tell you Razor if the rest of these so called challenges are like this then we'll both be rich before we know it."

"Knowing Dougie, I wouldn't fucking bank on it. That part about cash incentives indicates to me that you might have to bribe people to do some of the stuff" Razor responded, closing his eyes and taking another long drag.

"Well I haven't got time to worry about that just now. I need to make sure that these fucking digital cameras are working" said Dean as he stood up and headed back to his room. Once inside he closed the door and locked it. He switched on his PC and called up the programme that Razor's mate Dave had set up for him. After a few seconds a video image of the living room came onto the screen, showing the room to be empty. Dean then clicked onto each of the bedrooms to show

Glynn sitting writing at the desk in his room, Mick bending over a box pulling out items of clothing, Tim making his bed, Daisy hanging his clothes neatly in the wardrobe, Urban sitting on the floor surrounded by hundreds of CD's and finally Rod standing in front of a mirror with his trousers round his ankles inspecting his swollen nob. Dean winced at the sight of Rod's battered penis and quickly switched back to the shot of the living room.

Although he felt guilty that he was technically spying on his friends the voyeuristic element made him feel excited. He checked the DVD drive was set up and ready to record the evening's events, switched off the screen and headed downstairs to grab a beer.

****

By eight thirty all of the housemates had either finished their packing or given up for the day. Dean, Urban, Daisy and Rod were gathered in the kitchen, drinking bottles of beer and discussing who should make it into the top five foxiest female singers of all time and in which order they would like to shag them.

"Well you've got to have Madonna in there for starters" said Dean.

"What? She's a right old trout who's got two or three kids" Rod responded, almost spilling his beer in outrage.

"I don't mean now you nobhead! I mean when she was doing all that 'Sex' book stuff and was mega famous in the 90's. The whole point of this is not who you would like to shag now but anyone from any period in the past" Dean replied.

"Oh, so we could have the blonde bird from Abba or one of the Spice Girls then?" Rod asked.

"Absolutely, except for the fact that all of the Spice Girls were complete hounds" Dean replied.

At that point Glynn walked into the room. "What are we doing tonight then lads? Fancy a night out in Battersea?"

"The conservatory is full of cases of beer and wine. Why don't we take advantage of that first and then head out to a club later? The Clapham Grand is meant to be full of women and it's only down the road" Dean said before anybody else could suggest anything else.

"Sounds like a good idea Deano" Urban said nodding. "Anybody else for another beer?" he said opening the oversized-fridge door and grabbing himself another bottle.

"Yeah" came the collective response and Urban tossed them each a bottle.

A few hours and a good percentage of the beer supply later, all eight of the housemates were in the living room. Razor had brought his extensive collection of porn on DVD with him and one of the films was showing on the huge plasma screen. Razor, Rod, Mick and Tim were watching intently and commenting on the movie like a group of film critics.

"You see the director should have zoomed in a bit more here as I think it's always good to have a close up of a blow job early on, just to set the tone" said Mick.

"Having said that Mick I'd stay on the wider angle as they can then change position without you needing to pan out or change the shot" Rod responded.

"That's a very good point and as they've only just got started there isn't going to be a cum shot yet, so I think you might have zoomed in a bit prematurely there Mick" said Tim, laughing.

"That's always been your problem though hasn't it Mickey son?" said Razor picking up on Tim's premature statement.

"Fuck off and watch the film" Mick responded.

On the other side of the room the rest of the lads were continuing the discussion started earlier in the kitchen but had now widened the scope to include actresses.

"So we're all agreed on Angelina Jolie, Cameron Diaz and Pamela Anderson then? Glynn asked.

"Well I'm not totally convinced by Cameron Diaz" Daisy responded, "although she definitely ranks ahead of Madonna" he continued shaking his head towards Dean.

"I'm talking about Madonna from 1993, not now" Dean said, although as it was the fifth or sixth time he'd repeated this statement he knew Daisy was just taking the piss. Whilst Glynn continued reeling off the short list of ladies for the last two places in the top five Dean looked over at the other lads who were all intently watching the plasma screen. He looked at his watch and saw that it was eleven thirty. *"Right this is it"* he thought *"If I don't start the ball rolling now one of these fuckers will suggest going clubbing and I'll have missed the chance."*

"Does anyone want to see my party trick?" Dean said in an attempt to catch everyone's attention.

"Not really" said Glynn who had seen it numerous times in the past and was still trying to finalise the top five women of all time.

"What is it?" asked Daisy.

"Well that'd spoil the surprise if I told you what it is wouldn't it?" Dean responded. "Right, switch the porn off and I'll show you something impressive."

After a couple of minutes of moaning the plasma screen was duly turned off and Dean stood up in the middle of the room. "OK, has anyone got a condom on them?" Dean asked. Everyone immediately reached for their wallets. "Forget it Glynn, I don't want one that's five years past its sell by date" Dean quipped. Glynn responded by flipping Dean the bird with his middle finger.

"Here's one" said Daisy throwing a red sachet at Dean.

"Oi, I don't want one of your extra large ones" Dean replied drawing a ripple of laughter from everyone.

"It's not that crap thing where you stretch it over your head and blow it up like a balloon is it?" Daisy asked.

"You'll see" said Dean as he opened the sachet and pulled out the contents to reveal a red condom. "Is this strawberry flavoured?" Dean asked.

"Yeah, I always think that there's more chance of a blow job if you've got the flavoured ones" Daisy responded.

Dean unrolled the condom and stretched out the open end as far as it would reach, in the same way that somebody about to blow up a long thin balloon would do. He then leaned his head back, pushed the enclosed end of the condom into his left nostril and stuffed the remainder up his nostril whilst making sure he held onto the open end with the thumb and forefinger of his left hand. Dean then leaned his head forward, pressed the forefinger of his right hand against his right nostril and started sniffing as hard as he could. He let out a gagging sound as the enclosed end of the condom shot up his nostril and popped out at the back of his throat. Whilst continuing to hold the open end with his left hand he reached into the back of his throat and pulled the enclosed end out of his mouth with his right hand. He then stood in front of them all with one end of the condom hanging out of his left nostril and the other end out of his mouth and started pulling the condom backwards and forwards rapidly like a pulley.

Daisy, Urban, Razor, Mick and Tim all started to clap and cheer whilst Rod and Glynn both shook their heads and looked disgusted.

"That's fucking horrible" Rod said as Dean pulled the entire condom out of his mouth.

"That's fucking quality, you mean" Daisy corrected him. "Where did you learn to do that?"

"I saw some bloke do it at a party once and decided to give it a go" Dean replied, simultaneously spitting and trying to clear the snot from his left nostril. "The only problem is it rips the fuck out of you nose and throat lining so they'll be killing all week now. Added to that all can taste now is that artificial strawberry crap that it had on it."

"I fancy having a crack at that" Tim said standing up.

"Well feel free, later" Dean responded. "Does anyone have any other tricks?"

"How about this old favourite" said Rod as he rolled onto his back on the sofa, and struck his Zippo lighter just as he let loose a rip roaring fart which duly flared briefly into a ball of flames around his crotch.

"Ow! Ow! Ow! Fuck!" Rod screamed, as he jumped off the sofa and frantically started patting his arse, causing an outbreak of hysterical laughter from the rest of the room. "Fucking blow-backs" he said whilst still jumping up and down.

"Well if you don't clean your pipes properly you can't complain when the engine backfires" said Urban through his tears of laughter.

"Yeah, it's just the same as sticking a potato up someone's exhaust Rod, it's going to end in tears when you switch on the gas" Razor followed up.

"Very good Rod, although you might want to practice that one a bit more at home before your next public appearance" said Dean attempting to steer the group away from Rod's unintentionally comical performance. "Now has anyone got any real party tricks?"

Razor stood up. "Yeah, I have. Rod have you got a light?" he asked causing the room to break out into another session of laughter. "Oh don't bother your arse, I've got one here" he followed up, taking his lighter out of his pocket as Rod pulled a sarcastic 'ha ha' face and flicked him the bird. Razor proceeded to light the cigarette, took a couple of drags, so that it was glowing red, took it from his lips and stubbed it out completely on his tongue.

"Oooh! Doesn't that hurt?" Glynn asked.

"No, but it tastes like shit" Razor replied as he spat out the ash from his tongue. "All you've got to do is make sure that your tongue's really wet before you do it and you don't feel a thing."

"I'm definitely having a go at that one" said Tim "give us a fag Razor." Razor threw him a cigarette. Tim lit it, took a couple of puffs and then pressed it onto his tongue. "Jesus Christ!" he screamed "that's fucking burnt my bastard tongue."

"Oh yeah, the other thing is that you need to do it really fast and in the middle of your tongue otherwise it will burn like fuck!" Razor said pissing himself laughing.

"It's a bit fucking late now, you twat!" Tim replied, dipping his tongue in his beer.

"Hey, it's not quite a party trick, more of a challenge really. I've heard that it's impossible to put a whole raw egg in your mouth and close your lips around it" said Daisy.

"Bollocks!" Urban responded.

"Have you ever done it?" Daisy replied.

"No but that doesn't mean that I can't" said Urban.

"Right, has anyone ever done it or seen it done?" Daisy said looking around at the other six blokes. Everyone shook their heads. "Well there you go then, nobody has ever seen it done because it's impossible."

"No it fucking isn't" Urban replied. "Right there's only one way to sort this out" he said getting up from his seat and heading off towards the kitchen. He returned a minute or so later with a carton containing half a dozen eggs. He selected the smallest one and showed it to everyone. "Right then you losers, you're about to see somebody perform an 'impossible feat,' putting this egg in my mouth and then closing it" Urban said as if he was a master magician about to perform a death defying stunt. He stood up in the middle of the room, cleared his throat, placed the egg carefully in his mouth and slowly closed his lips around it. Before he could do anything else Daisy leapt up from the sofa and in the blink of an eye slapped both of Urban's cheeks simultaneously, causing the egg to explode inside his mouth. The whole room erupted into laughter.

"You fucking bastard!" Urban shouted as he spat the broken egg into the nearest plant pot.

"I can't believe you fell for that one" Daisy laughed.

"I wasn't sure whether that was a wind up or for real until you smashed it" said Razor nodding at Daisy. "Top work fella!"

"Yeah, very good" Urban said "but you know that I'm going to have to get you back for that, maybe not today, but I'll get you."

"Give it your best shot Urban, but better men than you have tried and failed" said Daisy as he pulled a new bottle of beer from the box in the middle of the floor.

"I'll tell you what though and this isn't a challenge but is definitely true. If you put a light bulb in your mouth it instantly gives you lockjaw" Urban said.

"Really?" Daisy replied sarcastically "and you expect me to go and try it now that you've said that do you?"

"No, of course you're not going to try it now after what's just happened to me. I'm just telling you that it gives you lockjaw."

"Now I can see why they all call you Urban, although I think Bullshit would be a more appropriate name" said Daisy laughing.

"Right, enough of all these namby-pamby tricks, I'll show you a real fucking show stopper" said Mick as he stood up and headed off to the kitchen. After a lot of banging about he returned with a bucket and a length of rubber tubing around 2 foot long. He placed the bucket on the table in the middle of the room and cocked his head back as far as it could go, so that he was staring directly up at the ceiling. He then took the rubber tube and fed it very slowly into his mouth and down his throat. He started to gag as the tube entered his oesophagus but after pausing briefly he continued until he had swallowed almost half of it. He continued to gag and his chest started to convulse as he motioned to Tim to help him. Tim, who had clearly done this before, took hold of the other end of the tube, put it into his mouth and gave a brief but strong suck on the end. He then quickly moved the open end of the tube over the bucket as the contents of Mick's stomach came flooding out. The liquid was mainly lager but had enough bile and other substances in it to make it an opaque brown-green colour. As Mick hadn't really eaten anything since lunchtime there were very few lumps except for a few obligatory pieces of carrot.

The room was filled with a mixture of genuine groans, cheers and laughter. Mick let around half a pint of the liquid empty out before whipping the tube out of his throat and breaking into a coughing and gagging fit. Glynn suddenly leapt forward and vomited into the bucket which had a domino effect on Rod and Urban (who was still complaining about feeling sick from the raw egg incident before Mick had started). Unfortunately Rod hadn't finished puking by the time the urge came to Urban and, as Rod still had his head over the bucket, Urban was sick all over the back of Rod's head. When Rod sat up his shoulder length hair was matted and full of lumps which caused him to bring up another mouthful of vomit.

"So, what d'ya reckon?" asked Mick, smiling like a mad-man.

"Well these three loved it" said Razor pissing himself laughing as he gestured towards Glynn, Urban and Rod. "Especially Rod!" he said breaking into a further fit of laughter.

"Yeah, any chance you could do it again?" said Rod seeing the funny side of things as he spat out the remaining bits from his mouth.

"Better still why don't you teach Rod how to do it" said Dean "he's obviously got the stomach for it."

"Seriously though, how come you don't just puke when you put the tube into your throat as it must feel the same as sticking your fingers down there?" asked Daisy.

"I've never puked in my whole life, apart from when I was a baby" said Mick. I've got a cast iron stomach and I saw some bloke do this once on telly and thought that it'd be a laugh to give it a go. That's the fourth or fifth time I've done it now and it fucking kills your throat for days after though" he said grabbing a new bottle of beer as he flopped back onto the sofa. "Of course it wouldn't be possible without my glamorous assistant though" he said nodding to Tim.

"It's a team effort" said Tim being sarcastically modest.

"Great trick though Mick, and impossible to top" said Dean.

"Oh I don't know about that" said Daisy as he stood up and headed out of the lounge. Everyone looked at each other and wondered what Daisy could possibly come up with to top Mick's stomach wrenching feat. As Daisy was new to the group everyone looked at Urban who had known him the longest.

"I honestly have no idea what he's going to do" Urban said shaking his head.

Daisy returned a few minutes later with a hand sized lump hammer, about a foot long with a rubber head the size of a packet of biscuits. Daisy stood in the middle of the room with the hammer in his right hand and stared at each of the lads one by one. An eerie silence descended on the group and a few of the guys started feeling a bit worried that they'd only just met Daisy and didn't really know him. Daisy put the hammer down on the table and started to unbuckle his belt. Everyone looked at each other and the level of concern in the room increased. He then dropped his trousers and his boxers, knelt down on the floor and placed his nob and balls onto the table.

"Hang on a minute, I think you're a bit too pissed mate. Probably best to stop there" said Dean standing up.

Before he could do anything Daisy picked up the lump hammer and smashed it down onto his left ball.

"Aaaaarrgggggghhhh!" he cried. All of the other 7 lads instinctively grabbed their groin, bent forward and winced in knowing pain.

"Oh fuck!" said Dean "where's the nearest hospital?"

Urban and Glynn both jumped up however just as they were about to start helping Daisy to his feet he stood up and started laughing hysterically. The rest of the group fired puzzled looks at each other as Daisy pulled his pants back up and fastened his belt.

"I don't get it" said Urban "how did you manage to do that without your ball exploding?"

"Because I've got a false one" Daisy responded grabbing his beer as he sat back onto the sofa alongside Urban.

"How come?" Urban continued

"I had testicular cancer when I was eighteen and had to have one of my balls removed. Rather than leaving me lopsided they replaced it with a prosthetic one."

"So you can't feel that at all then?" Glynn asked

"Not apart from a bit of a pitch on the skin. The ball itself is made of silicon so there's no feeling in it at all" Daisy responded.

"Well that trick is very impressive and just about tops Mick's effort I reckon" said Dean, desperately hoping that the PC upstairs had recorded everything. "Right then who fancies heading out to a club?"

The group gave a variety of positive responses "Yeah, sure, ok, only if we have to, as long as there's loads of birds there..." as they all went back to their rooms to spruce themselves up.

"Hey did you know that Hitler had one of his balls removed? Urban said as they all headed upstairs.

"Fuck off! That's just another one of your bollocks stories. Hey do you get it? Bollocks story?" said Mick pleased with his unintended pun.

"No, but that one's definitely true" said Urban as he went into his bedroom.

Chapter 9
Week 1 - Sunday

Dean was woken by the streaming sunlight coming through the window. As he opened his eyes he could see he still had all his clothes on and was lying on top of a bed in a strange room. *"Where the fuck am I"* he thought as he sat up. Thankfully he suddenly remembered he'd moved house the previous day and was actually in his new room in Dougie's house. He looked around and was relieved to see that he was alone, he still had all of his essential belongings and he didn't appear to have been in any sort of altercation. He couldn't remember getting home but assumed that at least one of his fellow housemates had made it back with him as he could hear music coming from somewhere in the house.

He sat up and spotted the computer in the corner. His thoughts turned to Dougie's challenge and he turned on the PC. A shot of the living room flicked on. There were beer bottles scattered everywhere and the bucket of sick from different house members still sat on the table in the centre of the room. *"Probably best to avoid heading down there until someone else decides to clean up"* he thought.

Dean reached for the mouse, clicked onto the DVD drive and waited for the disk to fire up. The playback programme opened up and he watched as he saw the events of the previous evening unfold on the screen. He fast forwarded the action and stopped at his condom-up-the-nose trick. He had no idea what Dougie had in store for him over the course of the next couple of months so he wanted to make sure that he'd been involved in the first challenge, just in case the rest of them involved things he didn't want to do. He paused the DVD and zoomed in to show a close up of his face with half the condom coming out of his mouth and the other half hanging out of his nose. The still shot showed a huge blob of snot hanging from his nose. *"Not the most attractive of poses"* he thought as he sent it to print. He then flicked through the rest of the footage and printed off appropriate photos of Mick and Daisy. He decided Rod's 'trick' was not worthy of printing as despite being unintentionally amusing it wasn't what Dean classified as impressive. He placed the three photos in a 'do not bend' style A4 envelope, wrote 'Week 1, Confidential' on it in large letters and sealed it. He then placed it in his bedside drawer, locked it and headed off for a shower.

Chapter 10
Week 1 - Tuesday

"Look Tim, I'm asking you to do this as a mate. If you asked me to do something like this I'd do it like a shot, no question. It seems to me that I'm a better mate to you that you are to me" Mick said shaking his head and looking serious.

"Don't give me all that shit" said Tim shaking his head to indicate that Mick was talking bollocks. "The situation is quite simple; you pulled a bird, shagged her twice, then decided to shit in her bed and nick her purse and now you're asking me as a 'mate' to go round to her house and give it her back. No fucking way. You can go round and clear your own shit up this time Mick."

"I'm sure she's cleaned it up by now" said Mick laughing.

"I was talking metaphorically" Tim responded but couldn't help smiling. "Anyway she might try to get the police involved or something. I think your best bet is to ditch the purse and forget the whole thing ever happened."

"But she's really fit" Mick pleaded.

"What? Do you think that by returning her purse she'll suddenly forget everything that happened and want to go out with you? Are you fucking mental? You shat in her bed Mick. In fact, worse than that you shagged her in her front room *after* you shat in her bed. Do you think that's the sort of boyfriend she's looking for?"

"Dunno" mumbled Mick realising he may have been a little optimistic. "Anyway whatever happens I never meant to take her purse, that was a genuine accident. She left it in my jacket pocket after she went to the shops..."

"...to buy your breakfast" Tim finished Mick's sentence for him causing Mick to put his head in his hands.

"Look, I could just chuck the purse away but there are a few things in there that look like they've got sentimental value. There's an old locket containing a couple of black and white photos, a couple of newspaper clippings and an old ring. If it was just cash and cards then I probably would just bin it but I've lost my wallet a couple of times and once it's gone all you want are the things that can't be replaced by insurance. I've really fucked this up Tim but I am asking you as a mate. Please, please take the purse round to her house for me. I'll owe you big time if you do."

"Alright then" Tim replied, finally giving in. "You're fucking right about owing me big time and if she does want to get the police involved then I'm giving her all your details straight away."

"Fine" Mick replied. "And if, on the off chance, she wants my phone number you can give her that as well."

"You really are fucking mad aren't you?" Tim replied as he walked out of the room.

****

Tim arrived in Islington just after eight o'clock and headed to the address written on the inside of the purse. It was close to the tube station and turned out to be a flat above a hairdresser's shop. He loitered for a few minutes wondering how he was going to introduce himself.

"Hello, my name's Tim. Do you, by chance, remember a one night stand that you had last week. One where the bloke shat in your bed? Oh, you do? Good, well I'm that bloke's best friend and he's asked me to give you this." "No, too direct" he thought.

"Hi I think you know my friend Mick. He's had to leave the country on important business for the next six months but before he left he gave me this to pass onto you. Goodbye." "No, still too much association with Mick."

Tim was still weighing up the options when the front door of the flat suddenly opened and a very attractive black haired girl literally ran into him, causing him to stumble backwards and drop the purse onto the floor.

"What are you doing standing in my doorway?" She said as she watched Tim reaching for her purse. "Is that my purse? How did you get that? Did that fucking bastard Mick send you?" she asked, clearly enraged. Tim decided to take the only possible course of action left available to him under the circumstances and lie.

"Mick? I'm sorry I don't know what you're talking about" he said in his clipped accent, sounding like a cross between Prince Charles and Hugh Grant. "I came across this purse earlier today and as I was unable to find a phone number I thought I would do the gentlemanly thing and return it to you by hand. Clearly my actions are not welcomed and I will bid you goodnight" he said acting like he was delivering a speech from a 1940's black and white film.

"Oh! Oh! I'm really sorry" she said, calming down. "Somebody stole my purse last week and when I saw it I just assumed that you knew the guy who'd done it."

"You called him Mick?" said Tim continuing to pretend that he had come across the purse by chance. "If you know him how come you didn't just get it back from him?"

"I know his name but I don't really know him" she responded. "I haven't got a phone number or an address for him otherwise I would've got my brother and a couple of his mates to go and get it for me."

"So is he a thief, this Mick?" Tim asked starting to enjoy the situation.

"He is a complete and utter scumbag and should be strung up from the nearest lamppost by his goolies" she replied with a smile.

"Anyway I won't hold you up any longer you're obviously in a rush" said Tim continuing to play the role of a perfect gent.

"Err to be honest it can wait" she replied impressed by Tim's charm and good looks. "I really should buy you a drink to thank you for returning this" she said opening the purse. "Oh thank god, my grandmother's ring and locket are still in there. That's all I was really bothered about as I cancelled all the cards. Have you got time for a quick drink?"

Tim took a good look at the girl. She was around five foot eight, had jet black long curly hair and a pretty face. She was wearing a three quarter length T-shirt, which showed off her ultra flat stomach, and a long flowing skirt. All in she was absolutely gorgeous. "Yeah, I think I've got time for a quick one" he replied whilst looking at his watch to make it look like he had other plans.

"Good, we can go to my local over there" she said pointing to a trendy looking wine bar over the road.

They headed over to the bar, ordered two white wines and took a couple of seats near the window.

"I'm sorry I haven't introduced myself, I'm Tim."

"Pleased to meet you Tim" she responded jokily as if it was the first time they had met, "I'm Sam, although you probably already know that" she said holding up the purse and smiling.

"Well I knew it was Samantha but wasn't sure whether you were a Sam or not" Tim said making conversation.

"So what do you do for a living Tim?" she asked.

"I'm a police frogman" he replied nodding as if it was obvious.

"Really? That must be very exciting" she said.

"Yes it is" Tim replied "it's quite dangerous as well but I try to play that aspect of the job down to be honest. I'll tell you what" he said "why don't we make a night of it and have dinner. I can tell you all about it and you can tell me all about whatever it is that you do."

"OK then, you're on! Just let me make a couple of calls" she said picking up her bag and heading towards the door.

"What do you do, by the way?" Tim asked as Sam headed towards the door of the bar.

"I'm a policewoman" she replied smiling.

"Oh fuck" Tim thought as he sat back down and drank half of his glass of wine in one gulp.

She returned a few minutes later. "So which division of the force do you work for? Maybe we know some of the same people. Who's your sergeant?"

"Err, well actually I'm not really a police frogman" Tim said with an embarrassed smile.

"Really?" Sam said sarcastically "Let me guess, you're an accountant?"

"Close, I'm a banker."

"So why didn't you say that?"

"Because it sounds completely dull and is usually a conversation killer. Nobody wants to talk about banking, not even me, and if they do then it's always about some problem that they've had with their personal account or to ask how to steal a million pounds."

"So you thought that a police frogman sounded more exciting and would have women swooning at your feet did you?"

"Well it's the first time that I've ever used it really. A friend of mine uses it quite a lot and it seems to work for him."

"Well if I was you I'd stick to the truth as starting a relationship on a lie is like building a house with no foundations, it'll come crashing down on you in the end" Sam said taking a sip from her wine glass.

Tim briefly considered coming clean on his story about the purse but decided that telling the truth would actually have far worse consequences in this case. "Are you really a policewoman?" he asked.

"Oh course I'm not, I work in marketing but I could tell that you were talking absolute nonsense."

"Fair enough" Tim replied. "So is there anywhere decent to eat around here, I'm starving."

"There's a really good Italian that I know around the corner. We should be able to get a table if we're there in the next ten mins or so."

"After you" said Tim and they both made their way towards the door.

Chapter 11
Week 1 - Wednesday

Tim woke up with a splitting headache and a severely parched mouth. He opened his eyes, blinked twice to clear his vision and realised that he wasn't in his own room. He glanced to the side and saw Sam lying in bed with him and the memories of the previous evening instantly came rushing back to him. They had gone for a pizza (washed down with a couple of bottles of red wine), returned to the wine bar they had started in, where they had attempted to drink every cocktail on the list, before coming back to her flat and opening another bottle of wine. The rest was extremely hazy but he had a few snapshots in his mind of having sex in various positions and he could sense that he was naked under the duvet.

He suddenly thought of Mick and the fact that less than a week ago this bed had been home to what he had described to Tim as 'one of the largest turds I have ever managed; a genuine masterpiece!' Tim started to feel uncomfortable and a bit itchy as he thought about it.

By all accounts it was at least half an hour before Sam could have found it and that would have given it time to soak into the mattress. Tim felt his hangover getting worse at the thought of lying in Mick's excrement. He turned to Sam and gave her a shake to wake her up. She opened her eyes and gave a groan to indicate that she also had a severe hangover.

"Morning" said Tim hoarsely "How are you today?"

"Rough" she replied "What time is it?"

Tim looked at his watch. "It's just gone seven thirty. Look I need to go as I need to get home and get changed before work."

"I think I've got a spare wetsuit you can borrow" she said referring to the running joke they'd shared the previous evening about his bogus frogman career.

"Pink's not really my colour" Tim replied getting out of bed. "Where are my clothes?"

"I think they're in the front room" Sam replied sitting up and rubbing her eyes. Tim headed out of the room and returned wearing his trousers a minute or so later. He started putting his shirt back on.

"Look I really do have to go but can I see you again?"

"That would be great "she replied. "You've got my number, I texted it to you last night. Thanks again for bringing my purse back. In a funny way I'm quite glad that all that business with that bastard Mick happened last week as if it hadn't I would never have met you."

Tim smiled and started to feel really guilty about lying. He briefly considered confessing but decided that he really liked Sam and would like to see her again.

"Great, well I'll give you a call soon then" he said as he gave her a quick kiss goodbye and headed down the stairs to the front door. As he made his way to the tube station he decided that it was now too late to tell her the truth about their 'chance' meeting and that the best way forward was to simply ensure that she never found out that he knew Mick.

Chapter 12
Week 2 - Friday

Dean waited nervously for Razor in the vast lobby of the building that housed the offices of Jacobs & Co. The huge clock on the opposite wall showed it was just after five thirty. Razor had gone to provide the solicitor with verification that Dean had successfully completed the first of Dougie's challenges and had taken the envelope with the three photos that Dean had printed from the PC with him.

It had been an absolute doddle getting the lads to partake in the party games and Dean allowed himself to dream about his future life as an international playboy. His dreams were cut short when Razor appeared from one of the many lifts. He spotted Dean and headed over waiving the A4 envelope as if it was a ticket he had just managed to get hold of for a big football match.

"Here's the next one fella" said Razor handing over the envelope.

"How did it go? Was he happy with the photos?" Dean asked.

"The old boy wasn't there so I left the photos with the bird on reception" Razor replied, lighting a fag as they made their way out of the building.

"What do you mean you left the photos with the receptionist? What if she loses them?"

"How's she going to lose the photos? You're just being paranoid" said Razor as they left the building.

"Yeah, you're right but there's a lot at stake here so I don't want any fuck ups."

"Are you going to open that envelope or not?" Razor asked as they made their way into the tube station.

"Give us a chance" Dean responded.

They made their way down the escalators at Canary Wharf tube station and the electronic boards showed it was four minutes until the next train was due. They took a seat at the far end of the platform Dean opened the envelope. The letter was much shorter that the first one. It read:

"Dear Dean,

The fact that you are reading this letter must mean that you've successfully completed my first challenge, so well done. Don't get too cocky just yet though as I thought I'd start you off on something easy and then build things up gradually. You know the rules by now so I won't repeat them. The second challenge is

'DRUGS'

You need to get photographic evidence of at least three members of the house taking 'class A' drugs (i.e not pot). I'll leave the choice of which 'class A' drugs up to you.

Good luck mate and hopefully we'll be in touch again in a week's time.

Your friend,
Dougie"

"Here's the train" Razor said, standing up and walking towards the glass doors.

Dean stood up and put the letter back into the envelope. "This one's going to be more difficult than the last one. No-one in the house takes proper drugs. You and Rod smoke a bit of weed but as far as I know no-one takes anything harder than that" he said as they boarded the tube.

"I think your first issue should be which drugs you're going to take and where are you going to get them from" said Razor as they sat down.

"Do you know anyone Razor?"

"Well I know a few geezers that could probably help you out but I only ever buy weed from them. I can see if they're around tonight if you want."

"Yeah, that'd be great. I mean I'd rather not but if we're going to do this it'll have to be tomorrow night as no-one's going to take anything when they've got work the next day."

"OK, I'll make a few calls once we get out of the underground" said Razor.

****

"I managed to get hold of a bloke who can sort us out with some coke but we've got to go over to his place to get it" Razor said to Dean as they stood outside Waterloo station.

"We? What do you mean *we*? I'm a lawyer. I don't want to go on some dodgy fucking drug deal. Can't you go on your own?"

"Look, you're the one that wants the fucking drugs, not me so if you want to buy them you'll have to come with me" Razor responded. "I don't want to run the risk of getting lifted with class A drugs on me."

"Well neither do I. If I get caught I'll get sacked and never be able to practice law again. Where does this bloke live anyway?" Dean asked.

"Mile End. I've never been there before but he said he'd pick us up at the station and take us back to his place."

"Can't he just give them to us at the station?"

"Don't be fucking stupid Dean. They've got CCTV all over the place at tube stations."

"It just all sounds a bit dodgy to me."

"Of course it's a *bit* fucking dodgy" said Razor. "We're buying class A drugs not popping down to Marks & Spencer to pick up some fruit and veg. But I know this bloke a bit so it should be sound."

"OK, when did you say we'd go over?" Dean asked.

"Now" Razor replied. "We need to find a cash machine and then work out how we get to Mile End from here. There's a machine over there" said Razor as he marched off towards a cash machine.

"How much cash do I need?" asked Dean.

"Well it depends on how much you want to buy, but a couple of hundred should see you right."

"A couple of hundred? Really? How the fuck do normal people afford to buy drugs?" Dean replied.

"Well for a start not too many 'normal' people as you put it are regularly using class A drugs. But the ones that are tend to be well-paid suited and booted types.

The rest just go round nicking cars and beating up old ladies, that sort of stuff" said Razor sarcastically.

"Right, let's get this over with as quickly as possibly" said Dean as he put £200 in his pocket and headed back into the underground station. They arrived at Mile End tube station around thirty minutes later. Razor called his contact on his mobile and were told to wait by the traffic lights at the corner of the road.

"Fucking hell, it's a bit rough round here isn't it?" Dean said.

"Keep your voice down, dickhead" Razor whispered back to him.

"When you imagine the 'East End' of London you have all these romantic ideas of what it'll look like but when you get here it's actually a shit-hole."

"Well spotted Sherlock" Razor replied whilst lighting a fag.

Before either of them could say anything else the air was filled with the sound of loud rap music. Dean watched as a 'pimped up' Vauxhall Nova pulled up at the lights. The car looked like a ten year old kid's dream. It had blacked out windows, skirting that was almost touching the road, bright red bodywork with flames down each side and blue neon lighting underneath that flashed in unison with the music.

Dean was just about to pass comment on the ridiculousness of the vehicle when the passenger side window wound down, releasing the music that had previously been trapped inside. The driver was a scrawny white guy wearing a black Nike tracksuit and a Burberry baseball cap. He gestured to Razor to get in. Razor opened the passenger door and motioned to

Dean to get into the back. Dean momentarily questioned whether the risk was worth it but the adventure of the situation and the thought of the playboy lifestyle spurred him on and he got in. Razor jumped into the passenger seat and shut the door. Despite the fact that he now had two passengers the driver opted to turn the music up even louder. Sitting in the back, between the oversized speakers, Dean had the same feeling he'd had when he'd stood directly in front of a speaker at a Motorhead gig at the age of thirteen. He could see Razor and the driver having a conversation of sorts but couldn't hear a thing they were saying.

"This must be what it'd be like to be deaf, but obviously without the really loud music blasting in your ears" he thought to himself. Just then the driver pulled on the hand break as they rounded a corner and the back end of the car flipped out. Dean was thrown hard against the side window and the driver raised his hand to apologise and Dean waved back to show that he was 'cool' with the situation, although the reality was that he was far from cool. Dean was actually thinking about his career and how it would all be over if he was caught in a drugs bust by the vice squad and, worst still, how his mum and dad would be very disappointed to discover that he had become a drug addict. Before he could think of any more negatives that could arise from the situation the car screeched to a halt outside of a large block of flats.

The driver got out and slammed his door without any thought for Dean in the back. Razor opened his door and flipped the passenger seat forward to let Dean out. As he stepped out two rough looking kids about five years old came peddling over on their bikes.

"Oi geezer, give us fifty pence for some sweets" the first shouted.

"Nah, make it a pound" the second followed up.

"You two fuck off or I'll tell yer mum" the driver shouted back in a broad Cockney accent as he made his way towards the doorway to the flats. Dean and Razor followed him. The entrance lobby was a stark contrast to the lobby of the office building that they'd been in an hour or so earlier. Rather than the floor to ceiling glass and ornate water-feature wall that the Canary Wharf building had, this building had bare concrete walls, broken panes of glass and the water dripping down the walls was far from ornate. As a finishing touch the place was blessed with a strong aroma of stale urine. The driver walked straight past the lifts and into the stairwell.

"Come on, it's on the third floor" he said without looking back. Razor and Dean followed him up the stairs and they all arrived at a huge steel door which looked like it had been on a bank vault. The driver gave the door a distinctive rat-a-tat-tat knock and after a few seconds a huge black guy opened the door. He introduced himself as 'Yida' and gave Razor and Dean a long unfriendly stare as they entered.

Inside was a sharp contrast to the exterior of the building. The flat was spacious and had family photos hanging on the walls, revealing that the guy who opened the door lived here rather than the driver. They went through to the lounge which was dominated by a huge plasma screen and had two large leather sofas facing each other across a square wooden coffee table. A Bang and Olufsen stereo was mounted on the adjacent wall. A set of professional-looking record decks sat next to the stereo and two huge speakers, sitting like a pair of giant bookends, were blasting out hard core rap music.

"Right then what can I get for you two geezers?" Yida asked.

Dean was about to suggest that a cup of tea would be nice when Razor cut across him. "Have you got any Charlie?"

"Yeah man. Got some new stuff in this week. It's wicked, real pure you know? How much do you want?"

"A couple of grams. How much is it?" Razor said before Dean could say anything that might have embarrassed them.

"Well as I said, bro, this stuff is the real deal so it's a bit more pricey than usual. A couple of grams is going to cost you £120 but I'll tell you what I'll let you have three grams for £150, providing that we can join you in having a little toot now."

"I'd love to but we've got to be somewhere like an hour ago" Razor replied.

"I'm not asking you, bro, I'm telling you. That's the deal. Take it or leave it."

"Well if you put it like that we'd love to" said Razor looking to avoid the situation escalating.

"OK, it's cash up front so that'll be £150" Yida said holding out his huge hand.

"This is where it could start to go pear shaped" thought Razor as Dean reached into his pocket and handed over the cash.

"OK, me and my boy here will go and get it and will be back in a minute" Yida said nodding to the driver to follow him.

"Hang on, where are you going?" asked Razor, starting to get nervous that they were being set up.

"Calm down, bro, it's cool" Yida replied. "I don't keep the stuff here, too risky, but it's close. As I said I'll just be a minute or two."

Just after Yida and 'his boy' left the room Dean and Razor heard the giant front door slam behind them.

"Is this normal procedure?" Dean asked.

"I'm not sure that there is a 'normal procedure' but if there is then this isn't it" Razor replied.

"Should I start to get worried yet?" Dean asked.

"Not yet. If they both come back wearing ice hockey masks and carrying chainsaws then that's probably the time to get a bit worried" Razor said with a smile that showed he was getting a bit anxious.

"Chainsaws? What do you mean chainsaws? Do you think they're going to try and kill us?" Dean asked starting to get really concerned.

"Probably not, but you never know" said Razor with a shrug.

A minute or so later Yida and the driver returned (without any chainsaws). They sat down next to each other on one of the leather sofas and Yida motioned to Dean and Razor to sit on the opposite one. He then took three small paper parcels out of his pocket, placed them onto the table and carefully opened out the first one. Inside was a mound of white powder that looked to Dean like talcum powder. Yida reached under the sofa and brought out a mirror and a large hatchet knife. *"Oh fuck, they are going to kill us"* thought Dean, but Yida proceeded to use the knife to lift off a small amount of the powder and tap it onto the mirror. He shaped it into a line, took out one of the £20's that Dean had just given him and snorted the lot up his left nostril. He sat back and sniffed a few more times before handing the knife to the driver. Dean watched Yida closely to see what effect the coke had on him but was surprised to note that he didn't seem to be any different. He was nodding to the music now but that seemed to be the only real change.

Suddenly the driver slid the mirror, knife and cocaine over to Dean and Razor. Dean was relieved when Razor reached out and picked up the knife. He followed the same routine as Yida, pulled a £5 note out of his pocket and snorted the white powder.

"Hey man, don't you know it's disrespectful to use less than a £20?" Yida said smiling. "In fact I'm usually only seen in public with a £50 but I'm a bit short today. I went to Scotland once and they've got £100's up there and in Amsterdam that you can get a €500. Now that's the way to do it!"

Yida, the driver and Razor all burst out into hysterical laughter. Dean didn't really think it was that funny and was hoping that he might get away without taking any of the coke until Yida caught his eye and nodded towards the white mound with a frown. Resigned to his fate, Dean followed the same procedure that the others had been through, borrowed Razor's rolled up £5 and snorted the cocaine. He suddenly felt his heart rate quicken and started to feel hot. He waited for the effects to kick in but felt nothing, no hallucinations, no headspin, absolutely nothing. Dean was just starting to think that it hadn't had any effect on him when he suddenly noticed the music.

"I love this fucking tune" Dean said nodding along with the beat.

"It truly is a top fucking track" said Razor in complete agreement.

"Hey Yida, this is a great place you've got yourself here" Dean said suddenly feeling very talkative and comfortable with his new 'friends'.

"Do you want one man? We can do you one for £500. It's an upfront payment but that's it, no rent, no nothing" Yida responded.

"How d'ya mean?" Dean asked.

"This block used to be owned by the council but they gave up on it a long time ago and the place has been taken over by squatters and drug addicts. If somebody wants a flat we go in, evict anyone who's living there and put one of these steel doors on the place. You get the key and that's it. It's a public service really."

"You're like a modern day Robin Hood" said Razor as he lit a fag.

"Absolutely" Yida agreed, nodding at Razor to throw him a cigarette.

"Anyway chaps it's been great but we've got to shoot" Razor said standing up.

"Really?" Dean asked, starting to feel very much at home.

"Really!" Razor confirmed as he folded up the open packet of coke and placed all three in his pocket. "Any chance of a lift back to the station?"

"'Fraid not mate. I've got to be somewhere like an hour ago" the driver replied with a cheeky smile.

As Razor and Dean made there way down the stairs to the ground floor Razor asked "So what d'ya reckon then?"

"About what?" Dean replied

"The fucking charlie?"

"Oh yeah. I feel great. To be honest I'd forgotten I'd taken it" said Dean.

"Yeah, I think you'll find that that's the problem with it" said Razor as they made their way out of the estate.

Chapter 13
Week 2 - Saturday

Dean was in the kitchen doing the washing up for what seemed like the 100th time since they moved in. *"Why the fuck doesn't everyone just wash their own stuff once they've used it rather than stockpiling every plate, bowl and dish in the house until some stupid twat like me decides to do it?"* he thought to himself as he changed the horribly dirty water and looked at the teetering mass of crockery still waiting to be cleaned. "You fuckers need to start washing your fucking plates after you" he shouted into the hallway to no-one in particular.

A minute later Glynn appeared at the kitchen door.

"Were you shouting me?" Glynn asked.

"No. Yeah. Sort of. Why doesn't any bastard in this house do any washing up apart from me?" Dean asked holding out his soap-sud covered palms.

"What d'ya mean? I did a tonne of washing up yesterday" Glynn replied.

"Well some fuckers in here aren't pulling their weight. I think we should set up a rota so that someone has to do it every day."

"But there's eight of us in the house so you can't have a rota where one person does a particular day."

"Fuck off, smart arse. Look the point is that we need to set something up before I end up killing somebody" Dean said starting to rant as he finally finished washing the last spoon.

"Calm down mate, it's only a bit of washing up. Are you OK? Glynn asked.

Dean had been feeling very edgy all morning and although he wasn't sure he thought it might be related to the coke that he'd had with Razor the previous night.

"Anyway, fuck the washing up, what are you up to tonight?" Dean asked thinking about Dougie's challenge and the coke he had upstairs.

"I'm meeting an old school mate of mine who I haven't seen for ages. He's in London for the weekend. You're welcome to join us if you're at a loose end" said Glynn.

"What and listen to you two going on about the Welsh rugby team all night. No thanks. I'm intending to have a few beers in the house and then head out locally" Dean responded, not wanting to admit that he was planning not only to snort cocaine but that he was also hoping to persuade a couple of the other housemates to join him. "Do you know what anyone else is up to?"

"Mick and Tim are playing in a rugby sevens tournament in Richmond so they probably won't be back until tomorrow and I think Daisy said that he's out with a few of his mates from Camberwell. I don't know about the rest of the lads though" Glynn replied.

"It sounds like I need to speak to Urban and Rod then, otherwise I might end up staying in on my own, which is practically a criminal offence on a Saturday night at my age" Dean said laughing. He now started to feel even more anxious as he desperately needed Urban and Rod to not only have no plans but to also agree to take coke with him. "Are they around?" he asked Glynn.

"I think Urban's in his room but I haven't seen Rod at all today."

Dean dried his hands and headed to Urban's room. As he approached he could hear Coldplay blasting out from hi stereo and after knocking on the door was greeted with a muffled "come in." Urban was lying on his bed reading FHM.

"Alright mate" he said without getting up.

"I was just checking whether you've got any plans for tonight?" Dean asked. "I thought we could have a few beers in the house and then check out a few of the local bars later."

"Err, yeah, that sounds good. My bird's off on a hen weekend in Brighton which is great as it leaves me free to go out on the pull. No doubt she'll come back with her head all full of marriage ideas but that's alright as it means she won't ask me too many questions about what I've been up to" said Urban.

"Why is it that you constantly feel the need to go out on the pull when you've already got a really fit girlfriend? I wouldn't mind but the birds you end up pulling are usually total mingers" Dean said as he sat down on the end of Urban's bed.

"It's the thrill of the chase mate. Charlotte is lovely and definitely the sort of girl that you'd want as a wife but I'm only twenty four and I just haven't shagged enough women yet to be thinking of settling down" Urban replied.

"So why don't you just finish with her then and play the field?"

"Because it doesn't work like that does it? For some reason when I've got a girlfriend I find it really easy to pull but if I haven't then it's much harder. I must give off a smell of desperation when I'm single. I don't know what it is but all I know is that since I've been seeing Charlotte I seem to be able to pull everytime I go out, which is great."

"I'm not sure she'd agree with that. Anyway are you up for it tonight?" Dean asked looking to firm up the evening's arrangements.

"Definitely. Shall we say meet in the living room about seven o'clock? I'll be wearing a red rose and carrying a copy of the Evening Standard, you won't be able to miss me" Urban responded. "Who else is up for it?"

"Well I'm hoping that Rod will be, but apart from that I think it's just you and me as Razor's on an all day bender, Mick and Tim are egg-chasing and Daisy and Glynn are going out with some other mates."

Dean closed Urban's bedroom door and headed down to Rod's bedroom. There was usually some shite heavy metal blasting out from inside and as the room appeared to be silent he wasn't too hopeful that Rod was in. He knocked and after a few seconds opened the door. There was no sign of Rod. In fact it didn't look like he had been home at all the previous night. *"Shit"* thought Dean to himself as he closed the door. He looked at his watch and saw that it was almost one thirty. He'd agreed to play football for his firm that afternoon and was now running late so he made his was back to his room, quickly gathered his kit together and headed off.

****

Dean got back to the house around six thirty. Urban and Rod were in the living room watching football on the plasma screen. They had clearly been drinking for a couple of hours and as Dean popped his head in the door they gave a loud cheer.

"Alright chaps, what's going on?" Dean asked.

As Rod turned round Dean saw that his eye was puffed and swollen and that he also had a cut on his lip. "Fucking hell Rod, what happened to you?"

"I'm back on the bare knuckle boxing circuit Deano. I know I promised you I wouldn't go back to it but it's in my blood and I just can't give it up" Rod replied holding out his hands.

"Yeah and back in the real world what actually happened?" Dean asked as he sat on the sofa opposite Rod.

"Well, like all good nights out it all started with one quick beer after work. One led to another which led to another dozen. Before I knew what was going on I'd somehow managed to call Helen, tell her I'd had time to think everything over, that I love her and I want to spend the rest of my life with her" Rod replied.

"Heavy stuff" said Dean.

"Yeah, well I never really meant any of it I was just pissed and looking for a shag. Anyway she was all happy and crying and everything and asked me to go over to her place. When I got there she'd put on one of her fancy dresses, got all made up and looked fucking gorgeous. We fell into each other's arms and headed off to the bedroom. She went down on me and as I'm lying back in my drunken stupor I suddenly remembered why I've been avoiding her. I scream in pain as she grabs the old fella and discovers that it looks like it's been in a food processor. Next thing I know she's hitting me in the face with her shoe and screaming the place down."

"So why didn't you come back here?" Dean asked.

"Well we sat up most of the night with me trying to explain that I caught it in my zip and her refusing to believe a word of it."

"Which is understandable, as it's total bollocks" Urban cut in.

"Yeah but she doesn't know that does she?" Rod replied. "Anyway she ended up deciding that she needs some space to think things through and asked me to move out again. I wouldn't mind but I hadn't even moved back in before she kicked me out. I did feel like pointing out that I'd technically chucked her before she chucked me but decided against it in the end."

"Probably for the best, no need to pour petrol on the flames" said Dean. "So where have you been since then?"

"Well I remembered this biker and rocker's bar in town that's open all hours so I went up there and started drinking."

"What time was that?" Dean asked

"About eight o'clock this morning" Rod replied.

"Fucking hell mate, you must be cabbaged."

"I don't feel too bad actually. I felt a bit pissed about midday but I've managed to drink myself sober again."

"I feel a bit pissed though" said Urban.

"Right let me get changed and I'll join you" said Dean heading upstairs. *"Perfect"* he though as he checked the PC was set up to record the events in the living room before heading downstairs. He grabbed three bottles of beer from the fridge and joined Rod and Urban. The football was finished and they were now watching some garbage Saturday evening family entertainment show.

"Get this crap off and stick some music on" Dean said grabbing the remote control. He flicked through the music channels, stopped at VH2 and sat down.

"Have you two had anything to eat yet?" Dean asked. Urban and Rod both shook their heads. "Right I'll order up three pizza's. What d'ya want?"

"Large American Hot" said Rod instinctively.

"Mighty Meaty" Urban added.

Dean pulled out his mobile and ordered the pizzas. He was desperately wondering how to drop the subject of the coke into the conversation and decided that the best option was to just go for it. "Hey, what drugs have you two ever done?"

"Drugs?" Rod replied "Well I've obviously have done a bit of pot, I've tried speed a couple of times and did acid once at Uni, although I'd never do that shit ever again."

"What about you Urban?" Dean asked.

"Just a bit of pot really. I'm more into my beer to be honest. You know where you are with lager, you still get wasted and make an arse of yourself but you're in control, even when you're not, if you know what I mean?"

Dean nodded wondering just how pissed Urban really was.

"Have either of you ever tried coke?" Dean asked tentatively.

"No" said Rod "I wouldn't mind but it's too fucking expensive. I'd rather spend the cash on a big night out or on CD's."

"I've never really fancied it" Urban replied.

"Are you sure? Because I've got some" Dean responded. Rod and Urban both sat up and looked at him.

"You've got some? Why?" Urban asked.

"Yeah, you're a lawyer mate if you get caught you'll be de-barred or struck off or something won't you?" Rod added.

"I've got a mate who had some spare and asked if I fancied trying it. You're only young once so I thought why not and bought some off him. I've got it upstairs if you fancy having a look at it."

"Alright" said Rod "shall we come up to your room?"

"Err no, I'll bring it down here" said Dean quickly standing up.

He ran upstairs and returned a minute or so later with the three paper parcels he'd bought from Yida.

"Fucking hell, how much have you got?" Rod asked.

"Three grams" Dean replied.

"Three grams? That's enough to get an elephant off its tits!" Rod responded. "It's also enough to get you banged up for dealing."

"Well I wasn't intending to keep it for that long. Anyway do you fancy a bit?" Dean asked gesturing to Rod.

"You're the expert mate, after you" Rod replied.

Dean suddenly felt his heart race again. He couldn't put his finger on what he'd liked about taking the coke the previous day but ever since he'd taken it he hadn't been able to get it off his mind. "OK, we need something to do this on" he said standing up and heading off to the kitchen. He returned a few minutes later with a glass chopping board and a meat cleaver.

"I thought it was a mirror and a razor blade that you needed for this?" Urban asked.

"Only if you want to be clichéd about it" Dean responded. He tipped out a small mound of powder onto the chopping board and separated it into three lines using the cleaver. He then took out his wallet, removed a £20 note, rolled it up and snorted one of the lines.

"What's it like?" Urban asked, watching Dean like a wide eyed schoolboy.

"It's fucking excellent" said Dean sitting back on the sofa and feeling a wave of euphoria sweep over him.

"What does 'it's fucking excellent' mean? What does it feel like?" Urban continued.

"It's like that feeling of excitement when you're just about to kiss a girl for the first time, or the feeling of elation when you find out that you've passed an exam, or the sense of joy when your team scores a goal mixed in with what it must feel like to win the lottery" Dean replied with a huge smile on his face.

"So you feel excited and elated? But there's nothing to feel excited or elated about" said Urban trying to rationalise the situation.

"Life" said Dean "that's what there is to feel excited and elated about Urban; life itself."

"Not my life at the moment" said Rod gently patting his swollen eye. "Right then, whizz that stuff over here."

Dean pushed the glass board over to Rod who pulled out a note from his pocket and snorted one of the two remaining lines. He sat back on the sofa and smiled.

"I see what you mean Deano. I think the problem is that I've been looking at this Helen situation all wrong. She's fucking lucky to have me, I mean I could have any bird in the world but I chose her. She's walking a tightrope now though and if she doesn't get her act together then I might just decide to trade her in for a new model. In fact now that I mention it I quite fancy a model for a girlfriend – you know one of those really thin ones with no tits. That'll do for me."

"What a lot of shit" Urban responded. "You couldn't get a bird for about two years before you met Helen."

"It's not that I couldn't get one, I didn't *want* one" Rod replied. "I could've got one like that" he said snapping his fingers "but I'm a free spirit and didn't want to be tied down to any one particular woman."

"Is that why you failed to pull any birds then? Just in case one of them tried to tie you down?" Urban said, laughing.

"I did pull birds. I pulled loads of birds but I just didn't tell you about them. It's private business isn't it, so why would I tell you about all of them?"

"Because you tell us everything else" Urban responded.

"Anyway, are you going to have a toot or not Urban?" Dean asked, eager to get his friend to partake in the drug taking which would enable him to complete the second of Dougie's challenges.

"I'm not sure, it doesn't sound like my sort of thing, especially when I have to sit here listening to the shit that you two are coming out with since you've taken it" Urban responded.

"Come on, you won't know whether you like it or not until you've tried it" said Rod.

"But doesn't it show up in your bloodstream for months? What happens if they decide to introduce random drug testing at work?" said Urban.

"No this is the best thing for that" said Rod. "Pot can be detected for up to six months but coke is gone in a couple of days so you'll be fine."

"Alright then. You know that I'm shit when it comes to peer pressure. But I'm only doing one line" Urban replied. "So how do I do it then?"

"Just snort it up through this" said Dean handing over a £20. Urban leaned forward and snorted up the last remaining line.

"I don't really feel anything" he said. "Hey I love this fucking tune, turn it up" he said referring to the song was playing on the TV. "Did I ever tell you that I used to be in a band?"

Dean glanced up at the hidden camera and smiled as he turned up the volume.

Chapter 14
Week 2 - Sunday

"I feel fucking terrible today mate. I keep thinking that there's something really terrible I've forgotten about and I feel like I'm coming down with the flu" Dean said as he walked into Razor's bedroom.

"That'll be the Charlie. Makes you paranoid the next day and gives you the worst fucking hangover you can imagine. How much did you have anyway?" Razor said as he sat up and rubbed his eyes.

"All of it" Dean responded, opening the curtains and letting the sunshine flood into the room.

"All of it? There was the best part of three fucking grams there Deano, no wonder you feel shit mate."

"It wasn't just me, Rod and Urban had some as well" said Dean starting to feel guilty and disgusted with himself.

"Even so mate, three fucking grams between three novices is a lot of Charlie. How are the other two drugs barons feeling?" Razor asked laughing as he lit his first fag of the day.

"I don't know but if they're feeling anything like I do then they won't be up yet. I think we must have drunk about two cases of beer as well" Dean replied as he dived onto the chaise long in Razor's room.

"Yeah that's one of the other problems, Charlie makes you virtually immune to booze so you can pack it away without any effect, until the following morning that is." Dean nodded in agreement and let out a big sigh. "Anyway mate I take it you got what we needed?" Razor asked referring to the envelope that Dean had been holding since he came in.

"Oh yeah, almost forgot about that" Dean said suddenly remembering why he had come into Razor's room in the first place. He handed over the envelope and Razor took out the three A4 photos. He looked at each in turn and nodded.

"These look like the evidence from some seedy drug bust mate. Best not let these get into the wrong hands. I mean you wouldn't want you mum or your boss to see them would you?" Dean suddenly looked even more paranoid. "I'm just fucking around with you Deano" said Razor.

"You're right though, those photos could really fuck things up for all of us. I'm not sure that this stupid fucking challenge thing is worth it. I mean, Drugs? I've never taken coke before in my life and last night I couldn't get enough of it. When we'd finished it all we started talking about where we could get some more from, like three fucking junkies. Rod was all for heading into town on his bike to see if he could score some from a biker mate of his. We even agreed that we should do it every Saturday night. This is only the second task for god's sake what will Dougie have me doing by the tenth? Human sacrifice? I've done the first two but if the third one is something fucked up then I'm not fucking doing it" Dean said, on the verge of tears.

"Alright mate, calm down. You're just a bit strung out. Last night was a big night so my advice is to go back to bed, get some more kip and things will start to look a lot better" said Razor putting the photos back into the envelope and placing it into his bedside drawer. "Nobody is going to see these snaps apart from me, you and that old solicitor so there's nothing to worry about is there?"

"I suppose not" said Dean getting up and walking over to the door. "Oh, before I forget, the one thing that we did come up with last night that still seems like a good idea today is that we should have a party."

"Great idea. When?"

"Next Saturday night, so put the word out amongst all the women that you know. Right, I'm going back to bed for a bit, I'll see you later."

"Yeah, sweet dreams mate" said Razor with a smile as he opened the drawer to look at the three photos again.

Chapter 15
Week 2 - Tuesday

Daisy was sitting at his desk at work looking out of the window when his mobile rang. He didn't recognise the number but answered it anyway.

"Hello, Colin Day speaking."

"Hi Colin, it's me" said a female voice.

"Oh fuck" thought Daisy instantly *"it's some bird who assumes I know her voice and I've got no idea who she is. I'll just blag it until I can work it out."*

"Hi!" he said in an enthusiastic manner, hoping she'd take it from this that he was pleased to hear from her and give him a hint as to who she actually was.

"You haven't called me" she said, giving him nothing to work with.

"Well, I've been really busy." He still didn't recognise the voice and was hoping to draw some more information from her.

"Busy? Doing what? You must have had a spare five minutes at some point over the past two weeks to give me a call" she said giving him a vital clue.

"Who have I met in the past two weeks? It's Tuesday today. It can't be that bird from last week as I never gave her my number. It must be the one from a couple of Saturdays ago. What was her name? Mel? BINGO!"

"No, *Mel*, I've been seriously busy. I had to move house" he said delighted that he'd remembered her name.

"Move house? You never mentioned that you were moving" she said.

"Yeah it was a bit of a last minute thing, you know the score?"

"No, not really. Who moves house at the last minute? Anyway do you want to fill me in on the details over a drink sometime?"

"Yeah, that'd be great. When are you free?"

"How about tonight?" Mel replied.

"Well, it's a bit short notice but alright then, you're on" said Daisy.

"Oh, just one other thing, is there any chance you could bring a friend along for Heather? I wouldn't normally ask but she's not having much luck with blokes at the moment and it'll be a laugh. Anyone will do, apart from your mate Urban."

"Erm, yeah I think I can sort something out" Daisy responded remembering her dumpy mate and wondering who the fuck he could set her up with.

"Great. Shall we say eight o'clock at the Punch & Judy in Covenant Garden? We'll see you in the basement bar."

"OK, see you there" Daisy said as he hung up. *"Oh Jesus, who the hell am I going to fix that pig up with?"* he thought to himself. He then had an idea. He called up a number on his mobile.

"Hey Urban, have you got Glynn's mobile number?" Daisy asked.

****

Glynn was very nervous when it came to women and it had taken a lot of persuading from Daisy to get him to agree to the double date. He'd arranged to meet Daisy at Covent Garden at six thirty and in order to build up his confidence decided to start off with a couple of beers after work. He hit the bar over the road from his office at two minutes past five and ordered two pints of Stella, one for him and one for his work mate, Graham. They settled into two seats near the bar and started to bitch about how bad things were in the office, how their boss was a complete bastard, how underpaid they were, how they pretty much kept the office afloat and all of the other usual stuff that people in offices rant on about. The Stella flowed freely and the time slipped past rapidly until Glynn suddenly noticed it was almost six thirty.

"Oh fuck" he said to Graham "I've got five minutes to get to Covent Garden."

"But it's your round and you owe me one" Graham replied.

"Right, OK. I'll get them in but then I've got to go" said Glynn nodding to the barman to indicate he wanted two more pints of Stella. The pints duly arrived and Glynn downed his in a oner. "Right, enjoy that mate and I'll see you tomorrow" he said as he left the bar.

"Good luck with the bird" Graham shouted after him as he sipped his new pint.

Glynn jumped into a passing taxi. "I'm running a bit late, mate, so I'd appreciate it if you could get your skates on" he said to the taxi driver after he told him where he wanted to go. The driver nodded in an 'I don't give a fuck if you're late or not' sort of way. As they drove off Glynn suddenly realised he desperately needed a piss. He couldn't remember whether he'd drunk five or six pints of Stella but what he did recall was that he hadn't been to the toilet once. In his semi-inebriated state he calculated it was physically impossible for his bladder to hold six pints of liquid which made him even more desperate to go. Twelve agonising minutes later the taxi pulled up at Covent Garden. Glynn practically threw the money at the driver and bolted into the pub, or more specifically the toilets. He just made it before his bladder muscles collapsed and as he stood at the urinal he decided the relief was one of the best feelings in the world. He then made his way to the bar just in time to see Daisy ordering a pint.

"Hi Daisy, sorry I'm late."

"No worries mate, I was a bit held up at work so I've just got here myself. Did you have to work late?"

"Erm, yeah" Glynn said "but I did manage a couple of beers before coming here."

"Fair enough, right what do you want? Stella?"

"Yeah, great. I'll see if I can grab us a couple of seats" said Glynn as he headed out to the courtyard. A minute or so later Daisy came over and joined him at the table.

"Cheers" said Glynn, as he raised his glass for a clink.

"Cheers" Daisy replied although he felt a bit gay clinking glasses with Glynn as he normally reserved that sort of thing for girls.

"Do you think I look alright?" asked Glynn. "I wasn't sure what to wear, whether to go casual or stick with the suit. I decided that women like men to look smart so I've stuck with the suit, although I'm not too sure about the tie. What do you think? Tie or no tie?"

Daisy started to feel worried that bringing Glynn on the double date was a big mistake. It wasn't even seven o'clock and he was already babbling like a nervous schoolboy at his first school disco.

Why didn't I ask one of the other lads from the house like Razor or Dean? They wouldn't have been too impressed when Heather turned up but at least they would have been a good laugh and Mel would have seen that I hang around with cool, funny blokes thus making me even more cool and funny to her. If Glynn carries on like this they'll spot he's a nerdy desperate twat and will probably both go home before nine o'clock" Daisy thought. He decided that if Glynn was going to be of any use as a wing man he needed to calm him down and boost his confidence.

"Mate, you look absolutely fine but if I was you I'd lose the tie. It might look smart around the office but it looks a bit stuffy on a night out. If you're not sure take a look around, nobody else here is wearing one."

"You're right, thanks Daisy" Glynn said as he rapidly removed his tie and stuffed it into the inside pocket of his jacket.

"Whilst you're at it I'd also undo your top button as well, in fact maybe even the top two buttons" said Daisy, starting to despair at the level of Glynn's nerdishness.

"OK. Anything else?" Glynn asked, as if he was on a crash course in dating techniques.

"Just loosen up and relax. Treat this as if it's just another night out, I mean you've been on dates before haven't you?"

Glynn didn't look at Daisy but stared directly into his pint. "Well, not exactly real dates as such. I mean I have kissed a few girls but I was either too nervous to call them afterwards or when I did they weren't too keen on seeing me again."

"Oh Jesus Christ!" thought Daisy. "Are you a virgin Glynn?" As soon as the words left his mouth Daisy started to feel embarrassed that he'd poised such a personal question to someone he didn't know that well and looked around the bar to make sure nobody had overheard him. Thankfully everybody else was engrossed in their own conversations.

"Erm, well, err, sort, of I suppose" Glynn replied weakly.

"Sort of? You either are or you aren't" Daisy continued, deciding that he may as well finish the investigation.

"Do blow jobs count?" Glynn asked.

"Blow jobs? Are you telling me that you've never had sex with a girl but that you've had a blow job?"

"Yeah. I went out with this girl for just over a year when I was at Uni. We decided that we both wanted to wait until we were married before we had intercourse and agreed to just have oral sex instead. So does that mean that I'm a virgin or not?"

"It means that you've had your pudding before your main course my son" said Daisy raising his glass and clinking it against Glynn's.

"What?" Glynn said feeling confused. A few seconds earlier he'd felt like an inadequate virgin and now Daisy appeared to be saluting that very fact.

"Well respect where respect's due" said Daisy. "I tell you mate if I could meet a bird now and get a blow job off her every night for a year I'd be a happy man. I wouldn't worry about the fact that you haven't nobbed anyone, you'll be fine once you get the chance. In fact if I was you I'd use it as a selling tool. Birds hate to think that a bloke has bedded hundreds of women so if you let it slip that you haven't got off the mark yet they'll be falling over themselves to be the first!"

"Really? I've never thought about it like that. Great! Fancy another before the girls get here?" Glynn said pointing at Daisy's glass.

"Oh yes" said Daisy happy that he'd managed to calm Glynn down and give him an angle for the evening. All he needed now was for Glynn to fancy Heather and he'd be home and dry with Mel.

Glynn returned from the bar with a tray containing two pints of Stella, two vodka red bulls and two packets of nuts.

"I thought I'd get a couple of vodka red bulls in to liven us up a little" said Glynn, who was starting to feel quite pissed.

"Good work fella" Daisy responded as he drained the rest of his pint. "Now tell me more about the Year of the Blow Job."

"Well where do you want me to start?" Glynn proceeded to tell Daisy the whole story of him and his previous (and, to date, only) girlfriend. He'd just finished the part about why they broke up when Mel and Heather arrived.

"Hello big boy!" Mel said as she stood behind Daisy and put her hands over his eyes. "Guess who?"

"Halle Berry?"

"No, better than that it's me" Mel replied removing her hands and giving Daisy a kiss. At the same time Glynn stood up and awkwardly held out his hand towards Heather.

"Hi, I'm Glynn" he said shaking Heather's hand.

"Pleased to meet you Glynn, I'm Heather. Are you always this formal?"

"Only when I meet a beautiful woman" Glynn replied causing Daisy to momentarily close his eyes and cringe.

"Don't worry about Glynn, he's well known for his cheesy one liners" said Daisy.

"Well I think it's sweet, so feel free to ignore him and carry on with the compliments Glynn" Heather replied, poking her tongue out at Daisy. "Right do you boys want a couple of drinks?"

"Two pints of Stella please" Daisy replied before Glynn could come out with anything else embarrassing. The girls headed off to the bar.

Daisy turned to Glynn, "So, what d'ya reckon then mate?"

"She seems really nice."

"Yeah, but do you fancy her? I mean do you want to nob her?"

"Well I wouldn't put it like that but, yeah, she's quite fit and if we get on OK tonight then I'd like to see her again" Glynn replied.

"Fucking excellent!" Daisy said. "I'm really glad that you could make it tonight Glynn."

"So what d'ya reckon of Glynn?" Mel asked Heather as they made their way to the bar.

"Well he looks like a bit of a geek but he seems quite sweet. What I want to know though is how come the mate I get is never as good looking or as cool as the bloke that you end up with?" Heather replied not realising the irony of what she'd just said.

Mel looked at her dumpy friend and replied "I don't know Heth, it's funny isn't it? Anyway do you think you'd snog him?"

"Not yet, but after a few large glasses of Chardonnay I might think about it" Heather said breaking into a giggle.

"Well let's just have a few drinks and see how it goes" said Mel. "If you really don't fancy him within an hour or so I'll ask Colin to tell Glynn to go home."

"OK" Heather replied as they made their way back to the table with the drinks.

"So what do you do for a living?" Heather asked Glynn as she sat down at the table.

"I'm a lawyer, which sounds really boring but it's actually quite interesting and the pay is really good" Glynn responded, desperately trying to put a positive spin on the law profession. He thought when he landed his job with one of the UK's biggest law firms that he'd have women falling at his feet. However he'd soon discovered it had the opposite effect. When he mentioned he was a lawyer it usually caused women's eyes to glaze over and resulted in them rapidly spotting somebody that they desperately needed to talk to over the other side of the pub. As a result he'd decided to try to make it sound a bit more sexy and when this hadn't had the desired effect he'd simply added the fact that he was earning lots of money.

"Really?" Heather responded "so what's interesting about it?"

"Well I get to work with lots of different companies and see how they operate. Last week I was working with a company that makes breakfast cereals and the week before it was in a retail fashion business. I'm aiming to carry on for a few years and then maybe start up my own practice using the experience I've gained from it. What do you do?"

"I'm a lawyer, which sounds really boring but it's actually quite interesting and the pay is really good" Heather replied and they both started laughing.

"Are you qualified yet?" Glynn asked.

"Yeah, last year. What about you?" Heather responded

"I qualified last year as well, so we must have started at the same time" said Glynn getting excited. "I wonder what else we've got in common? Hey you're not a virgin are you?"

"What?!!" Heather replied as Glynn successfully managed to bring the flowing conversation to a grinding halt. He suddenly started to feel very, very pissed. So pissed that he struggled to remember what he'd just said for a second or two as Heather sat staring at him.

"What do you mean by that exactly?" Heather said, virtually spitting the words out. "Are you trying to imply that I'm some sort of slapper? Whatever your mate Urban has said is absolute bollocks!" She stood up and looked like she was about to leave.

Glynn tried to gather his thoughts and come up with something witty to say that would dig him out of this hole and that would have them both laughing and joking again. Unfortunately his brain was full of Stella and vodka red bull and nothing that could save him from public humiliation came to mind so he decided to go for the only option he could muster.

"No, I'm not trying to imply that you're a slapper. I didn't really mean to say that, I mean what I meant to say was, erm. Oh god, look I'm a bit pissed and it's got nothing to do with you but I'm a virgin, OK? Right, there I've said it and now I'm going home." Glynn stood up and in his drunken state started looking on the floor for his jacket, which was hanging on the back of his chair.

Heather sat down. "Glynn, sit down. I'm really really sorry. I thought that you were having a pop at me. I suppose I just feel really embarrassed about what happened with Urban. I didn't realise that, well, you know, you don't really expect to meet anyone in their twenties who hasn't done it yet"

"I have had a few blow jobs though" said Glynn as he sat back down and tried to reduce his embarrassment.

"Well there you go then! Good for you!" said Heather punching him in a friendly fashion on the arm.

"And I've licked a woman's fanny" he continued.

"OK Glynn you can stop there. I get the picture" Heather cut in before Glynn went into any more detail. "I'll tell you what, why don't you get another round of drinks in, you can tell me more about that retail fashion business and we won't mention anything else about you-know-what. Deal?"

"Deal" said Glynn standing up and staggering off towards the bar.

"Where's he going?" Daisy asked.

"To the bar" replied Heather "and I think he probably needs a hand as he seems quite pissed."

"Yeah OK" said Daisy taking the hint that Heather wanted to talk to Mel. He got up and followed Glynn.

"Fucking hell, did you hear that?" Heather said to Mel.

"No we were too busy snogging to hear anything. What did he say?"

"He's only a fucking virgin isn't he?" Heather whispered.

"You what? He can't be. He must be about twenty four or twenty five. There's no fucking way he can be" Mel responded.

"Well he says he is and the way it came out I don't think he's lying" Heather replied.

"Oh my god! What are you going to do then?" Mel asked.

"Well I think he's quite sweet and you don't get too many opportunities like this. It's like a blank canvas isn't it? Let's have a few more glasses of wine and see what happens but tonight could be THE night for Glynn if you know what I mean?" Heather said raising her eyebrows and finishing off her glass of wine.

"Well go easy on him, you don't want to put him off for life!" said Mel as they both started laughing.

Chapter 16
Week 2 - Wednesday

Glynn's head was throbbing and he could feel the blood pumping around his brain. Added to that his mouth was dry as a bone and his tongue felt like it was stuck to the roof of his mouth with superglue. As he opened his eyes he felt a wave of panic sweep over him as he realised he was completely naked and that this wasn't his bed, or his bedroom. He quickly tried to remember what had happened the night before but couldn't recall anything after the pub in Covent Garden. He could just about remember the girls turning up and vaguely remembered being very pissed. He cringed at the thought that he couldn't remember what he'd said to anyone and that he had absolutely no recollection of leaving the pub or coming back to this place, wherever it was. He sensed a presence in the bed alongside him and slowly turned his head to see who he was in bed with. He was initially surprised to see that the person he was in bed with was black and even more surprised to see that it was a man.

"Oh my god! What the fuck have I done?" Glynn thought as he lay perfectly still, petrified that he might wake the bloke lying next to him. He tried to work out if his arse was still intact. He was so cabbaged and hung over that he couldn't really establish whether anything untoward had happened without a physical examination and decided to leave that until he'd managed to escape. He slowly started inching towards the side of the bed and had managed to put one foot on the floor when the guy alongside him started moving.

"Run" thought Glynn as his mind clicked into overdrive and he imagined himself tied to the bed, being butt-fucked all morning. He sprang up and made a grab for his clothes which were scattered over the floor.

"So you're still alive then?" Daisy said, sitting up in bed.

"Daisy? Oh thank god. What the hell are we doing in bed together?" Glynn asked desperately looking for his boxer shorts.

"Well, after the boozer we came back here with the girls. You were getting on really well with Heather…."

"…when you say 'getting on really well' what do you actually mean?" Glynn interrupted.

"You know, you were kissing and cuddling. Don't you remember that?"

"Err, no" Glynn replied sheepishly.

"Anyway me and Mel went to bed leaving you two to it. Then about half and hour later Heather came rushing into Mel's room saying that you'd puked and had passed out in the living room. She didn't want to leave you on your own on the sofa in case you puked again and as she didn't want you in with her the girls decided that the best option would be for me to bunk up with you."

"Cheers mate" Glynn said, nodding gratefully.

"Just as long as you know that you now owe me. I'd just started on the job when you puked so I never even got my nuts off" Daisy replied.

"Well I'm not sure how I can make that up to you but I'll do my best" Glynn replied seriously.

"I'll think off something" said Daisy. "Anyway it's almost eight o'clock and we've got to get to work" he said as he climbed out of bed.

Once they'd got dressed they crossed the corridor to the kitchen. Mel was making toast and Heather was sitting at the table drinking a cup of tea.

"Morning ladies, unfortunately we've got to shoot off to work now" said Daisy.

"OK, give me a call later babe. Maybe we can meet up for a drink tomorrow?" said Mel.

"Yeah, OK" said Daisy heading to the front door. "I'll tell you what, we're having a party on Saturday night, why don't you come and stay over?"

"Great" said Mel.

Glynn wasn't really sure what to do and started following Daisy towards the front door.

"So not even a goodbye then Glynn?" Heather asked.

"Oh yeah, sorry. Bye then" he replied.

"Don't you want my number?" Heather asked.

"Err, yeah. That would be splendid."

"OK, here it is. Give me a call later "she said handing over a scrap of paper with her mobile number on it. "I'm free on Saturday as well if you want me to come to the party."

"Brilliant" Glynn replied enthusiastically.

As Daisy and Glynn headed towards the tube station there was a distinct skip in Glynn's stride.

"You know, I'm actually quite glad I puked last night as it'd be a shame not to remember your first time" said Glynn.

"Yeah, especially as you've waited so fucking long for it" Daisy replied, laughing. "So it looks like the party's going to be a big night for you then mate?"

"I hope so. I really, really like Heather."

"Good, just do me a favour. Don't organise anymore fucking double dates!" Daisy replied with a chuckle.

Chapter 17
Week 3 - Friday

Dean was waiting at lunchtime in the 'All Bar One' pub at Canary Wharf. He was in the process of ordering his second pint when he saw Razor walk through the door and indicated to the barman to make it two.

"Where the fuck have you been?" Dean asked whilst tapping his watch.

"They made me wait for ages. The old boy was there today and wanted to deal with me himself. He was tied up with a client when I got there so I had to wait for twenty minutes before he could see me. Anyway here it is" Razor said handing over the A4 envelope. Dean opened it and took out the letter inside.

"Dear Dean,

So you've managed to get through the first two challenges, well done mate! I thought the last one might prove a bit tricky, with you being a lawyer and seeing as your mates have never really been into drugs but hats off to you that you managed to get it done and hopefully you enjoyed it as well. I thought that this week we could try something a bit different so the third challenge can be summarised by the word:

'THREESOME'

You need to provide photographic evidence of at least two members of the house having sex with the same bird at the same time. Sorry that it can't be two women and one bloke but I thought that would be far too much fun for the bloke.

Anyway, good luck mate and hopefully we'll be in touch again in a week's time.

Your friend,
Dougie"

"Bollocks" said Dean after he finished reading the letter. "Who the fuck are we going to get to do that?"

"Well don't look at me" Razor replied.

"Well we've got the party tomorrow night so maybe we'll get lucky and a couple of the lads will decide to share the same bird" Dean said hopefully.

"At the same time? No fucking way. This is something you're going to have to deliberately set up if it's going to come off Deano."

"What a fucking devious bastard. Why couldn't Dougie just have given me a couple of hundred grand with no strings attached instead of all of this challenge shite?"

"That was Dougie for you. He never took the obvious path in life and he hasn't in death either. So have you got any suggestions as to any birds that might be up for it?"

"Well I had been hoping to meet someone at the party tomorrow. That looks out of the window now.

I'll have to give a couple of birds I used to go out with a bell to see if I can relight some old fires as that'll be the easiest way of ensuring that I get a shag. I'll then just hope that I can persuade her to let one of the other lads join in."

"Ooh, dangerous stuff mate. Never go back to an unexploded firework. You could be letting yourself in for a whole world of pain."

"I haven't got any choice really have I? I don't think I'm likely to pull a bird I've never met before and persuade her to let someone else join in. Jesus, the thought of it is making me feel a bit sick already."

"So who are you going to ask to join in with you?" Razor asked, loving every minute of it.

"You know mate, I've got absolutely no fucking idea. First and foremost I need to find a woman that's up for it with me and I'll just have to see how it goes from there. To be honest I think there's a strong possibility that I won't manage to get this challenge done at all."

"Don't be so negative. If you keep your mind on the amount of money that's at stake I'm sure you'll pull it off" said Razor taking a large swig from his pint.

"Right I need to make a couple of calls to get things moving for tomorrow, so I'll see you later" Dean said as he picked up his jacket. He left Razor finishing his pint, went out and sat on the canal wall. He scrolled through the contacts on his phone.

"Angie, no, she hates me. Claire, not sure she'll be up for it after getting off with her mate while she was in the toilet last time we went out. Debbie? Yeah she'll do for starters."

Dean took a deep breath and pressed the call button. He was desperately hoping to get her voicemail so he could leave a message inviting her to the party without having the embarrassment of having to talk to her. No such luck, it started ringing. *"Shit!"* he thought and considered ending the call but realised it was pointless as his number would now be registered on her phone so she'd know that he'd called. *"Maybe she's deleted my number and won't know it's me"* he thought. He was still thinking about what to do when the phone was answered.

"What the *fuck* do you want?" Debbie said aggressively.

"I don't think she has deleted my number" thought Dean. "Hi Debs, just thought I'd give you a call and see how you're doing?"

"Well I've been doing fine since I gave up waiting for you to call me. 'I'll give you a bell in the week' you said as you left my place that Sunday morning. I wouldn't mind but you'd been there all weekend and then you fuck off and never call me again."

"I lost my phone" Dean replied so weakly that even he didn't believe it.

"You lost your phone? So are you're saying that you didn't have my number? Well how the fuck have you got it now then?" Debbie replied clearly very annoyed.

"Good point" thought Dean. "I've, err, just got it back now."

"You've just got it back now, after three months? Well I'm glad to see that the Met have cracked one of their biggest cases and haven't bothered wasting their time trying to catch rapists and murderers" she replied sarcastically.

As he was treading on very thin ice Dean decided to change the subject. "Anyway, enough of the past, have you got any plans this weekend?"

"This weekend? It's Friday afternoon Dean, it's already the weekend."

"OK, to be more specific have you got any plans for tomorrow?"

"Why?"

"Because I've just moved into a new place and I'm having a party tomorrow night to celebrate."

"…and you're short of girls, so you've been trawling your phone, which you've miraculously just got back today, looking for women to invite. Is that it?"

Dean decided that as the conversation wasn't going too well it was probably best not to reveal that he was actually looking for somebody who he might be able to persuade to not only have sex with him but who would also let one of his mates get involved. "Yeah, that's sort of it" he replied, fully expecting her to cut him off.

"OK then, I'd love to come" she said.

"Really? That's great" Dean said, genuinely surprised. "Look I'm really sorry about not ringing you, I was an idiot but I've now realised that there is something there between us."

Debbie cut his monologue short "I'll come but only if I can bring my *boyfriend*" she said placing emphasis on the final word.

"Boyfriend?" Dean repeated sounding slightly confused.

"Yes, my boyfriend, who calls me when he says he will and who takes me out for romantic dinners and who buys me flowers."

This time Dean cut Debbie short "No boyfriends allowed sorry. Goodbye!" he said and disconnected the call. *"Bollocks"* he thought and started scrolling through his contacts list again. Before he could scroll past 'D' he received a text from Debbie which simply read:

"PRICK!"

Dean deleted the text and continuing searching for another number. He decided that next time it would probably be safer to send an invite by text and see if he received a response before calling. He picked out seven girls' names from his phonebook and sent them all the same text:

"Hi, how are you? Long time no speak. I've been thinking about you a lot recently. I've just moved to Battersea and wondered if you fancied coming to my housewarming party tomorrow night? If you're up for it give me a shout and I'll call you with the details."

He pressed send and considered switching his phone off in case any of the girls called back immediately to unload with a Debbie-style rant but decided instead to screen the calls. Within a minute his phone beeped twice to confirm that he had received two texts. The first was from Jacqui and read:

"Fuck off!"

The second text read:

"Thanks for the offer. I'd love to come but unfortunately I've decided I'd rather have both my eyes poked out with a sharp stick so I won't be able to make it. Mary."

"Fair enough" thought Dean as he deleted both messages. He received two more along the same lines

but the fifth response was from Natalie, a girl that he used to work with and had dated for a couple of months. He hadn't spoken to her for over two years but he had decided to keep her number 'just in case'. The message read:

"Hi Dean, it's great to hear from you after all this time. A lot has happened to me since we last spoke. I got married to Tom Bunner from the pensions department eighteen months ago. After the wedding we moved to Norfolk and we had a daughter, Betty, last year. What have you been up to? Can't wait to hear. Love Nat."

"Married? With a kid? Married to Tom Bunner? Tom Fucking Bunner? That sap? They've called the kid Betty? Betty fucking Bunner? Very lucky escape there" thought Dean as he deleted the text without any thought of responding. He was starting to get concerned when he received responses from the final two girls. The first was from Gill, a Londoner Dean had met in a nightclub a year earlier. They'd dated for a month or two but she was into the whole nightclub scene in a big way and liked to stay out dancing until six am every Friday and Saturday and then go home and have sex all day. He'd packed it in with her because he'd been knackered the whole time and spent the working week trying to catch up on all of the sleep he'd lost at the weekend. Her text read:

"Maybe"

The second text was from Louise, a West Country girl that Dean had met on a seminar through work. She worked for another firm of solicitors and they had gone out six or seven times but the whole thing had fizzled out as they could never seem to co-ordinate their diaries.

She was a classic case of prim and proper goodie-two-shoes girl by day and wild sex crazed maniac by night. Her text read:

"Sounds good but only if I can bring some friends."

Dean sat down to weigh up the two options. Gill was always up for anything and could possibly be persuaded into a threesome. Louise was a bit more reserved and would definitely say no if Dean tabled the idea up front but might be up for it in the heat of the moment. *"So they both might be up for the cup, a score draw so far then"* he thought. He decided to weigh up the potential consequences of inviting them. They were both good looking girls and he would have happily dated wither one of them again. However, if he did go through with the threesome he'd never be able to look at them in the same light again as he'd always be thinking of what happened that night. Therefore he had to pick the one that he would be happy to permanently drop from his phone list and who wouldn't turn into a bunny-boiler after he dumped her. As Louise worked in the same profession there was a chance that their paths may cross again, so he plumped for Gill. He called her number.

"Hello you" she said obviously pleased to hear from him.

"Hi, how's it going?" Dean replied.

"It's going good, thanks. I'm surprised to hear from you after all this time."

"Well I've finally managed to catch up on all that sleep I missed when I was with you and thought it was about time to get back in touch" Dean said turning on the charm. "Are you still out clubbing every weekend?"

"Not as much as I used to but I still get out most Saturdays."

"So you got my text then? Can you make it along tomorrow?" Dean asked.

"What sort of party is it going to be? Will there be many people there?" Gill asked.

"Well there's eight of us who live in the house for starters, so I reckon there should be at least twenty five or thirty people."

"Wow, it must be a big house."

"Yeah, it's quite big. So do you fancy it then? You can come as my date" said Dean wanting to make sure that Gill didn't have any ideas about bringing along a boyfriend.

"Can I now? What makes you think that I haven't got a boyfriend?" Gill said playfully.

"The fact that you replied to my text" Dean replied. "So what do you say?"

"Yeah, alright then, how do I get there?"

Dean gave her the directions to Clapham Junction train station and arranged to meet her at seven thirty. He rang off and his face broke into a smile. *Amazing what you can do when you put your mind to it"* he thought as he headed down into Canary Wharf tube station.

Chapter 18
Week 3 - Saturday

Everything was set for the party. Dean and Glynn had been down to the supermarket and practically bought them out of Stella and Grolsch, both of which had been on a buy-one-get-one-free offer. Glynn had filled the downstairs bath with ice and emptied all of the bottles into it to form a downmarket, but very effective, bottle chiller. Dean had suggested that they all chip in and buy a load of pre-prepared party food from Marks and Spencer but nobody could be bothered to spend all day cooking it so they'd agreed to order fifteen large pizza's once everyone arrived. The living room was stripped of all breakables and the sofas were pushed back against the walls to provide the maximum amount of dancefloor space. The dining room and basement music studio were kept permanently locked and so the main party spaces were to be the living room, kitchen, and conservatory areas. Dougie had wired up the whole house with speakers which meant they could play the same tunes everywhere using one Ipod. Dean had spent almost five hours the night before working on the playlist.

At six o'clock, with everything in place, Dean started the music and set the DVD on his PC to record the events in his room using the digital camera on top of his PC. He headed down to the kitchen where Glynn and Rod were sitting at the dining room table talking about who the expected to turn up.

"So how many birds are we expecting tonight?" Dean asked.

"My bird Heather's coming with Mel, Daisy's bird, Tim has asked some bird that he met last week to come and she's bringing a few mates with her. Razor has lined up a few girls he knows from the East End as well as a few that he works with. How many's that?" said Glynn.

"That's at least ten without the girl that I've invited" said Dean. "Who's this bird that Tim's invited then?"

"Nobody's met her yet. He's being very secretive about her and for some reason only invited her once he found out that Mick wasn't coming."

"How come Mick's not coming?" Dean asked.

"He's playing in a cup final somewhere in Kent and they're having a massive party afterwards so he's going to crash with one of his rugby mates" Rod replied.

"Is Urban bringing his bird?" Dean asked.

"Don't be stupid. He's told her that he's out on a stag night with a bloke from work this weekend. He didn't want her to come as he wants to pull" Rod replied shaking his head.

"He's a fucking nightmare that bloke. Anyway it sounds like we've got enough women then" said Dean. "What time is your bird getting here Glynn?"

"Me and Daisy are meeting them in the pub at the end of the road at seven thirty. We'll probably have a few in there and aim to get back here for about nine-ish."

"What about your bird Rod, is she coming?" Dean asked.

"Err no, she's still thinking things over mate" Rod replied.

"What you mean she's dumped you?"

"Well I wouldn't put it that way Deano but were not looking to book up a summer holiday just yet."

"So you're in the market tonight then?" Dean asked, trying to work out which of his fellow housemates did not have a date for the evening and would therefore be in contention for the threesome. Rod replied with a shrug. "I'll take that as a yes then. Who else is on the pull?"

"Just Urban and Razor I reckon, although you never know with Razor. Knowing him he's likely to be knocking off one of the birds he turns up with."

"What a fucking choice" thought Dean *"a long haired biker or a Brummie bastard who's already got a girlfriend, great! I'd prefer it if it was just me and Gill getting down to it if I had the choice. Still it'll all be worth it in a couple of months' time when I'm sitting on CopaCabana beach sipping cocktails."* Dean was brought out of his dream world by Rod.

"Right we're going down the pub for a couple of looseners, are you coming?"

"Yeah, why not. I'm meeting Gill at seven thirty at Clapham Junction so I've got time for a few beers" Dean responded. The three of them grabbed their jackets and headed out to the pub.

****

Dean was sitting in the corner of the pub finishing his seventh or eighth pint. He looked at his watch and saw it was ten thirty. "Shit" he said as he realised he was an hour and a half late for his own party.

"It's ten thirty, we need to get back to the house" he shouted into Gill's ear to make himself heard above the sound of the DJ's decks.

"Can't we have another one here? It's just getting going and this DJ is great" Gill shouted back.

"Nah, we really should get back there, it's my party and it's bad form that I'm not there yet. Give me a minute whilst I round up the others" Dean replied looking around for Glynn, Rod, Daisy and Urban. He spotted them on the other side of the pub. Daisy was standing with a gorgeous, tall, blonde haired girl whilst Glynn was with a short, dumpy, brown haired girl wearing glasses. Dean headed over and spotted that Rod had just bought another round of drinks, including a tray of shooters. He nipped up behind Rod, snatched one of the shooter glasses and downed it in a oner.

"Oi! We haven't got any spare ones" Rod shouted.

"Well that one will have to be yours then. You can call it my moving in present" Dean replied placing the empty glass back onto the tray. "Right you all need to drink up as it's getting late and we need to be getting to the *'par-tey'*" he said.

"We're just gonna have another one here and then come over" Mel replied.

"Fair enough, but these two are fucking coming with me" Dean said pointing at Rod and Urban. "So neck those pints and let's go."

Rod and Urban downed their pints and followed Dean and Gill out of the pub. As they turned the corner into their road they could hear music blaring out of the open windows of the lounge. Dean looked around to see if any of the neighbours had started to get upset yet and was relieved to see that the two houses on either side of them didn't have any lights on. He opened the front door and went into the hall. The music was so loud that Gill couldn't hear him say "Welcome to my humble abode" and it lost its initial impact after he repeated it twice at the top of his voice. He pointed Gill in the direction of the kitchen and told her to grab them a couple of beers.

Dean walked into the living room. The place was packed full of people dancing, none of whom he recognised. Eventually he spotted Razor sitting on the sofa kissing a very attractive young black girl. Dean went over to the sound control dial mounted on the wall and turned the music down to a more reasonable level which was greeted by a chorus of booing from the 'dancefloor'. He headed over to Razor.

"Who the fuck are all of these people?" Dean asked gesturing to the dancers.

"They're cool man. There all from the boozer we were in earlier. I just asked around to see if anyone wanted to come to a party and they all did" Razor replied with a shrug.

"Of course they fucking did. People like that will do anything for free booze. Well they're your responsibility Razor. If there's any fucking bother or any of them nick anything then you'll have to sort it out" Dean said, clearly pissed off.

"Yeah, yeah, whatever" Razor replied turning back to the girl. "Now where were we before we were so rudely interrupted? Oh yeah" he said and they started kissing again.

Dean headed out of the room to the kitchen, which was also packed. Tim was holding court with three girls; an attractive black haired girl who he appeared to be with and two other girls who were also good looking. On the other side of the kitchen Rod and Urban looked like they were doing their best to chat up Gill. Despite all of the booze he'd drunk Dean couldn't get the word 'THREESOME' out of his mind. Every time he looked at the other blokes from the house he visualised them standing in front of him naked, proudly presenting their erection like an insect in season. The thought made him feel physically sick. He suddenly thought that a great solution would be if Rod, Urban and Gill got it on, leaving him out of it all together. However, left to their own devices the most likely outcome was that Gill would just sleep with one of them which would achieve nothing with regards to Dougie's challenge and would also leave Dean without a shag. He shook his head to try to rid himself of the thoughts and headed over to join them. Gill handed him a bottle of beer.

"You three seem to be getting on alright" he said taking a slug on the bottle.

"Rod was just telling me about his bike" said Gill. "He's offered to give me a ride sometime" she said as she winked cheekily at Rod.

"You can have one anytime Gill" Rod chipped in.

"I'm not sure you'd look that cool riding pillion on a fucking scooter" said Dean shaking his head and laughing.

"A scooter?" Gill said, clearly unimpressed. "You said you had a 1,000cc Kawasaki."

"I didn't actually say that I owned one. A mate of mine has got one and has said that I can borrow it anytime, so the offer is still there" Rod replied trying to hide his embarrassment.

"No thanks, *Scooter boy*" said Gill laughing.

Rod's embarrassment was saved by Tim who came over and introduced the three girls he was with.

"Hi everyone, this is Sam" he said pausing to indicate that she was with him "and these delectable young ladies are Rebecca and Kat."

"Nice to meet you" said Rod, eager to turn the conversation away from the topic of two wheeled transport. Rod and Urban's attention immediately switched away from Gill and towards the two unattached girls they had just been introduced to.

"Fancy a dance?" Dean asked Gill.

"Yeah, alright" she replied and they walked out of the kitchen. As they entered the hallway Gill grabbed Dean by the hand and pulled him close to her against the wall. She kissed him hard and fast and Dean felt his head spin as the mixture of booze and passion kicked in. He suddenly felt a hard lump in his mouth and pulled away. He spat into his hand and looked at the small blue asprin-sized tablet.

"What the fuck's this?"

"What d'ya think it is, it's an 'E'. I've been on one all night and you need to lighten up and get with the groove" Gill replied.

Dean paused for a second, looking at the tablet in his hand. He thought of Dougie's challenge and decided that some chemical stimulation may help.

"Yeah, fuck it" he said, swallowing the tablet and resuming where he had left off kissing Gill.

****

Mick was feeling very, very pissed. He'd just woken up on a train and had no idea where it currently was, where it was going to or which station he had got on at. He looked around the carriage and saw it was full of people who looked like they'd been on a night out, although he could sense that he was probably a lot more pissed than most of them. He decided to stand in order to sober up and in the process of doing so managed to lose his balance and fall head-first into the lap of a young black guy sitting with his girlfriend. Mick mumbled a drunken apology and was pleased to see that the guy didn't want to make more of it. He stumbled his way to the double doors and stood holding on to the metal bar. He was still feeling really dopey and put his face against the bar, which felt pleasingly cold and refreshing. Every time the train turned into a bend Mick's whole body span round the pole until it collided with another part of the train or another passenger (until they eventually all moved away).

After what seemed like an age the train pulled into a station. Mick opened his eyes wide and tried to focus on the station signs. The first couple passed too quickly but he managed to focus on the third which read 'Surbiton'. *"Where the fuck is Surbiton?"* he thought. He quickly decided that wherever it was he'd better get off and try to find a cab before he ended up in Brighton or Southampton or somewhere else that would be impossible to get home from. He staggered off the train and followed the exit signs. He felt like half of his brain had shut down for the evening and that the other half was a thinking in a foreign language. Luckily his body was operating on auto-pilot and Mick hoped that all the years of training it to get him back to his bed would pay off. He suddenly found himself outside the station and was dismayed to see no sign of any taxis. He sat down on the kerb and held his head in his hands. *"I'm fucked"* he thought and starting looking around for somewhere to sleep.

The next thing he knew someone was shaking him and a voice said "Taxi? Hey, you want taxi?" In front of him stood a black guy who once again repeated his offer "You want taxi?" Mick nodded.

"Mate I could kiss you."

"No thank you sir, just taxi" the guy replied in a thick Nigerian accent. "Where do you want to go?"

Mick thought hard for a second and then said "Battersea."

"Thirty pounds" the guy replied. Mick was too tired and pissed to bother arguing and nodded in agreement. "My car is just over there" the guy continued pointing across a wooded patch of grass to where a number of cars were parked. Mick briefly considered that this could be a set up and the bloke might try to rob him. This thought kick-started his brain from sleep mode and he suddenly felt more alert. As they walked across the grass Mick braced himself for trouble but none materialised and they soon arrived at the car. Thirty minutes later the car pulled up outside the house in Battersea. As he stepped out of the car Mick looked at his watch and saw it was just after twelve thirty. As he listened to the music coming from the living room he remembered the party. The taxi ride had brought him back to life a little and as he walked up the path to the front door he thought to himself *"Game on!"*

****

Dean had never felt so good in all of his life. He'd been dancing for what seemed like hours and every song that came on was better than the previous one and captured the moment perfectly. Gill was dancing like a goddess opposite him and he suddenly realised he loved her. They seemed to have a special connection. When he looked into her eyes there was a tunnel of love between them and everything else in the room seemed to melt away. As he looked at her lovingly she spoke to him.

"I really need the toilet" she said and headed out of the room. Dean nodded and continued dancing. He looked around at the other people dancing. He didn't recognise any of them but had an overwhelming urge to hug them all. He turned to the guy dancing next to him.

"Great music eh?" Dean shouted.

"Yeah" the bloke replied. "Do you know whose house this is?"

"It's mine, well sort of anyway" Dean responded.

"Cool. Great house" the guy said.

Dean decided to get another beer. As he walked into the hallway the front door flew open and Mick walked in looking worse for wear.

"Alright Mick, where the fuck have you been?" Dean asked.

"Surbiton."

"Surbiton? In Surrey? I thought you were playing rugby somewhere in Kent?"

"I was, don't fucking ask. Anyway how's the party going? Are there any spare birds?" Mick asked whilst swaying backwards and forwards.

"I'm not sure mate" Dean replied, the mention of birds suddenly reminded him of Dougie's challenge. The 'E' that he'd taken earlier had certainly relaxed him and the thought of sharing around a little love was no longer as abhorrent as it had been. "I'm just about to get a beer?" he said heading to the kitchen.

"Good idea" Mick replied.

Tim's heart sank as he saw Mick. Mick had told him that he was playing rugby in Kent and that there was no way that he would be in any fit state to make it back for the party. Tim knew the sort of state that Mick got into after rugby matches and had felt confident enough to invite Sam to the party. As Mick walked into the kitchen Tim turned his back to him and tried to block Sam's view. If he could avoid her noticing Mick then he could make an excuse and take her upstairs to his room. Unfortunately for Tim, as Mick walked past he patted him on the shoulder and said "Alright Tim my son?" in his strongest Irish accent.

"Hmmm" Tim replied without turning around. Mick suddenly stopped in his tracks and did a double take on the girl that Tim was talking to. He still felt very pissed and couldn't place where he knew her from. As he looked at her she caught his eye and stared straight back at him with a similar look on her face.

"Oh shit!" Mick thought as he suddenly realised that it was Sam, the girl whose purse he had accidentally taken and whose bed he had less than accidentally shat in a couple of weeks earlier.

"You fucking wanker!" Sam screamed. Mick braced himself but was amazed to see her launch her drink into Tim's face. "So you just found my purse by chance then did you? Never heard of a bloke called Mick? You lying fucking bastard. Did you think it was funny? First of all he shits in my bed and then you come round with my purse pretending to be a hero when all of the time it was some sort of set up!" Sam shouted at Tim.

"No, no. It wasn't like that at all. Look I meant to tell you but it sort of came out wrong and then it was too late. There wasn't any masterplan. I came round to return your purse and it just sort of happened. I really like you, please don't be like this" Tim said desperately trying to recover lost ground.

"Well tough shit if you like me or not because I don't like liars" Sam said and slapped Tim hard across the face. She grabbed her handbag and turned to head out of the door. Tim stood there holding his cheek and Mick couldn't help but start laughing. As he did Sam spun on her heals and slapped him even harder than she had just hit Tim. "That's for shitting in my bed" she said. She then slapped him again equally hard "and that is for getting your liar of a mate to do your dirty work for you. I hope you two wankers will be very happy together. I never want to see either of you ever again." With that she walked out of the kitchen and left the house to a rapturous round of applause from Dean, Urban, Rod and Daisy who were all wetting themselves laughing.

"That was one of the funniest things I have seen for ages" said Daisy wiping away the tears of laughter.

"Fucking brilliant lads" Urban followed up however he soon changed his tune as Kat, the girl that he'd spent that last couple of hours chatting up, headed off after her friend. "Looks like I'm off" said Urban waving to the others and as he followed the girl out of the kitchen.

"So how long have you been shagging my bird then Tim?" Mick said, looking pissed off.

"Your bird? Since when was she your bird? The last time you saw her you shat in her bed" Tim replied defensively.

"Well I had her first anyway mate, so if you're happy with sloppy seconds then that's fine by me" Mick said as he opened a bottle of Stella.

"She said you were crap and had a small nob" Tim replied with a smile.

"She must like them small then if she decided to see you again" said Mick laughing. Tim joined in. They clinked bottles to show that there were no hard feelings and started talking about rugby.

With the excitement of the Tim-Sam-Mick love triangle over, Dean took a few moments to assess the situation. In order to pass Dougie's challenge he needed to get one of the other housemates involved. Razor, Daisy and, unbelievably, Glynn all had dates for the night and were out of contention. Urban had disappeared off after one of the girls that had come with Sam, there was currently no sign of Rod (the last time anyone had seen him he was with the other of Sam's mates), so that left Mick or Tim. Dean wasn't convinced that either of them would be up for a threesome if he came out and bluntly suggested it so he decided to try another tack. He decided they'd be much more receptive to the idea if he could persuade them to take one of the 'E's' that Gill had brought with her then. He went to find Gill. She was dancing in the living room and Dean resisted the urge to join her despite the fact that the tune was calling him to dance to it. He grabbed her by the arm and pulled her to one side.

"Have you got any more E's?"

"Yeah babe, why are you coming down already?"

"No, it's just that a couple of the other lads would like one."

"Well I've got four left, two more for us and two spare. They'll have to pay me though, £10 each" she replied.

Dean pulled out his wallet and gave her £20. She fished out a clear plastic bag from her purse and handed him two of the blue tablets.

"Great" he said "I'll be back in a minute."

As neither Tim nor Mick were into drugs Dean knew that it was unlikely that he'd be able to persuade them to take the pills. He therefore decided that he needed to spike something with them so that they wouldn't know that they'd taken it. He thought of putting it into a drink but decided that it would be too obvious as the drink would either look cloudy or have bits floating in it. He headed to the kitchen and looked around for inspiration. After a minute or so he spotted a jar of habanero chillies on the top shelf. Dougie had always been a big fan of spicy food and Dean remembered that he'd told him one night about the habanero chillies he'd brought back from California being in the Guinness Book of Records as the hottest in the world. Tim and Mick were always up for a dare and so he reached up for the jar and took out three of the chillies. They were bright red, bell shaped, about two inches long and looked evil. He grabbed a knife from the drawer and quickly made an incision down the side of 2 of the chillies. He then took the two pills out of his pocket, roughly crushed them with the handle of the knife and stuffed half of the powder into each chilli. He wiped away the residual powder, made a point of remembering which chilli did not have any 'E' in it, placed the three chillies onto a plate and headed over to where Mick and Tim were still talking about rugby.

"Right fellas, I've got a dare for you two" Dean said. "Have you heard of Red Savina habanero chillies?"

"No" Mick and Tim replied simultaneously.

"Well they are the hottest fucking chillies known to man and as I've just found a jar of them I think it is our duty to eat one each."

"Piece of piss" said Mick, "but seeing as you suggested it I think that the honour is yours" he said gesturing for Dean to go first.

Dean wasn't a big fan of spicy food but knew that in order to carry off this scam he'd need to eat one of the chillies. He picked up the chilli he hadn't spiked and held it out in front of him. It looked evil and Dean could feel his eyes starting to water as he closed his eyes and bit it in half. He fully expected all hell to break loose but nothing happened, so he opened his eyes and started to chew the half in his mouth. He was just about to say "Fucking easy" when it hit him. His whole mouth felt like it was on fire, as if he had swallowed a spoonful of napalm. His eyes started to stream, snot started pouring from his nose and he started hiccupping. He held his tongue out in order to gain some relief but that only seemed to make things worse and he started struggling for breath. He ran to the sink, turned on the cold tap and held tongue out under the running water for a full five minutes before the pain started to subside.

Dean stood up and looked at himself in the mirror. His T-shirt was soaking, his eyes were bright red and snot was still streaming from his nose. *"Bloody hell, I look worse after that chilli than I did after all the coke that I did last week"* he thought. He then noticed Mick and Tim were laughing so hard that they were both in tears.

"Right, if you think it's so funny, let's see you fuckers have a go" said Dean wiping away the snot.

Tim stepped forward, grabbed one of Dean's specially prepared chillies, dropped it into his mouth and swallowed it whole.

"That's fucking cheating, eating it whole" said Dean but was stopped in his tracks as Tim suddenly poked his tongue out and started scraping at it wildly with his fingernails. When this had no effect Tim downed a whole of a bottle of beer in one go and then ran to the sink and put his whole head under the cold tap. After a minute or so he came back over to where Dean and Mick were laughing like hyenas.

"Brilliant" said Mick, "that was funnier than Dean."

"Your turn" said Tim sniffing repeatedly.

"No problem, you fucking fannies" said Mick. He picked up the last chilli, dropped it into his mouth, chewed it four or five times, swallowed it and then poked his tongue out to show that he'd eaten all of it.

"Fucking hell Mick, isn't that burning like fuck?" Dean asked looking very disappointed with Mick's reaction.

"Nah" Mick replied "I told you before I've got an iron stomach and my taste buds are fucked so I can eat just about anything."

"Well hats off to you" said Dean who was delighted that neither of them had realised that he had spiked the chillies. "Right, I'm off for a dance."

"Better wipe the rest of that snot off your face first" said Mick laughing.

****

Dean and Gill were still dancing as it started to get light. Mick, who normally hated dancing, had been boogying with them for the last two hours. The only other people in the room were Razor, who was crashed out on the sofa, and Tim who was sitting on the floor in a trance.

"Hey Mick, why don't we leave these two in peace and go up to my room to chill out?" Dean said.

"Alright" said Mick who normally would have ripped the piss out of Dean for use of a phrase like 'chill out' but actually thought it sounded like a great idea.

The three of them headed up to Dean's bedroom. Dean shut the door and put on some music. Gill dived onto the bed and Mick stood nervously fingering through a rack of CD's. Dean joined Gill on the bed and they started kissing. Mick stood transfixed. Usually he would have left them to it but tonight he felt different. There was a feeling of love radiating from Gill and Dean and he had the urge to join them on the bed. They stopped kissing and Gill patted the bed next to where she was sitting. Mick sat down still feeling a little uncomfortable. He stopped feeling awkward when Gill leant forward and kissed him.

Chapter 19
Week 3 - Sunday

Dean felt like he'd been hit by a truck. He was desperate for some water, his head was banging and he felt like his whole body was shaking. As he woke up fully he realised that his body was actually shaking and started to panic. However as he opened his eyes he realised it wasn't him that was shaking but rather the bed. He slowly turned to the side to see that the reason was that Mick and Gill were having frantic sex next to where he was lying. That sight, combined with his drink and drugs hangover, suddenly made him feel even more sick.

"Don't mind me" Dean said sarcastically as he stood up.

Gill and Mick took his advice and carried on. Dean picked up his boxers from the floor, rushed into his en-suite bathroom and, without breaking stride, threw up a mixture of bile and blood. Once the initial wave of vomiting had subsided he slumped onto the floor next to the toilet and placed his cheek against the pleasantly-cool toilet bowl. His head was swimming and although he tried hard to block everything out he just couldn't get the image of Mick and Gill having sex out of his mind.

"All this Dougie challenge shit, it's just not fucking worth it" he thought as he sat on the floor shaking uncontrollably. Once he was sure he'd thrown up everything he had to give he washed his face and listened against the door of the bathroom. The last thing he could face was to see Mick and Gill going at it hammer and tongs on his bed again. As he stood listening he realised that he really liked Gill and would have liked nothing better than to give it another go with her. However that idea was fucked now. He sat down on the toilet, held his head in his hands and started to cry.

"How has everything become so fucked up in such a short space of time? I need to clean up my act. No more booze and definitely no more fucking drugs. I don't take drugs but in the last week I've taken copious amounts of coke, dropped two 'E's' and even spiked two of my friends with the stuff" he thought to himself. *"I'll see what Dougie's next fucking task is and if it's something fucked up then I'm walking out of this nightmare, £2m house or not."*

He could hear Gill and Mick talking in the bedroom and assumed they must have stopped shagging. He opened the door to see them both sitting up in bed as if it was an entirely normal Sunday morning.

"Morning" said Gill grinning "are you coming back to bed?"

"No I'm fucking not" Dean replied abruptly "and I've got loads of things to do today so you'll have to go home soon."

"What makes you think just because you've got things to do that she has to go home? Come on Gill we can go back to my room" said Mick and they got out of bed in silence, scooped up their clothes and walked out.

Dean locked his bedroom door after they left, walked over to the PC and called up the DVD recording of the previous night's events. As he relived what had happened a few hours earlier he felt totally disgusted with himself for manipulating Gill and Mick for his own gain and started to cry again.

Dean snapped out of his self wallowing pity when he heard the screaming and shouting coming from downstairs. He rapidly wiped away his tears and listened to see what was going on. He could tell instantly that this wasn't one of the usual arguments but that something was genuinely wrong. He rushed down the stairs and into the living room. When he arrived he felt his feelings of guilt and self loathing intensify as Glynn looked up at him and said:

"It's Tim, I think he's dead."

****

"Does anyone know whether he took anything last night?" the paramedic asked as he placed an oxygen mask over Tim's face.

"Well he did have a fair bit of booze" said Glynn, but no more than he'd normally have on a Saturday night.

"This looks a bit more serious than a hangover" the medic replied "I mean did he take any drugs? It would really help your mate here if we knew what might be wrong with him."

"No way, Tim doesn't touch drugs. He likes the sauce but never does anything heavier than tequila" said Mick.

Dean looked at Gill who was staring back at him accusingly.

"I think he might have taken an E" Dean said, staring at the floor so that he wouldn't catch anybody's eye.

"An E? Bollocks! Since when does Tim do E's?" Mick replied.

"I don't know but I just think he might have taken an E last night" Dean replied not wanting to admit the truth. He looked at Tim who was lying motionless on the stretcher. On top all of his other angst Dean was certain that he would now face a murder charge.

"Well that's helpful" the paramedic said as he started to wheel the stretcher out to the hallway.

"Will he be OK?" Dean asked, barely able to get his words out.

"Well he's not conscious at the moment so it's really impossible to say. Is anybody going to come with him?"

"I will" Mick and Dean said simultaneously. Mick stared at Dean who, in his paranoid state, was sure that Mick knew he'd spiked Tim with an E.

"I will" Mick repeated assertively and Dean nodded in agreement.

"We'll have to report this to the police, so they'll probably need to speak to you" the paramedic said to Mick.

"Fine" Mick replied "I don't do drugs either."

"I don't get it? Why would Tim take an E? Did that bird he was with give it to him?" Glynn asked as the ambulance pulled away.

"Maybe" Dean replied, sensing a possible escape route from his predicament. "It must have been her sick way of getting even over that whole shitting the bed incident."

"But it was Mick who shat in her bed wasn't it?" Glynn replied.

"What? Mick shat in a girl's bed?" Gill asked.

"Oh it's a long story" Dean replied waving his hand to indicate that it wasn't the time to discuss it. "She might have spiked both Mick and Tim's drinks as Mick wasn't quite himself last night was he Gill?" Dean said raising his eyebrows and looking at her for support.

"Well I've only just met him so I don't know" she replied, refused to play Dean's game.

"Well I've known him long enough to know that he doesn't usually go in for spit roasting" Dean replied.

"I'm going back to bed" said Glynn not wanting to get involved in the discussion.

"Good idea" said Dean. "Shouldn't you be going home now Gill?"

"No, I'm going to wait for Mick to come back" she replied causing Dean to shake his head in disbelief as he headed back to his room.

****

It was just after eight thirty and all the lads were in the living room watching TV when Tim walked in.

"Fucking hell, it's Lazarus!" said Mick laughing.

"Did you miss me then chaps?" Tim asked with a smile.

"You really scared the shit out of us for a while there Tim. It's good to have you back though" Glynn said as he stood up and shook Tim's hand.

"Did they give you the all clear then Tim?" Dean asked, genuinely concerned.

"Yeah, pretty much. They said I was severely dehydrated which, coupled with exhaustion, caused me to lose consciousness. Luckily the blood supply to my brain wasn't cut off at any point so after they stuck me on a drip I was right as rain. They wanted me to stay in overnight to monitor my progress but as they said that there was no permanent liver or kidney damage I decided to sign myself out."

"So have they given you anything to take?" Urban asked.

"No. The doctor told me to lay off the booze for a couple of weeks, but bollocks to that" Tim said sitting on the sofa next to Glynn.

"What about the bizzies?" asked Rod.

"They came and asked me a few questions about where I'd got the E. I told them that some mad bird had spiked my drink and they were fine with that. I think they worked out quite quickly that I wasn't a master drug dealer and that it wasn't worth pursuing."

"Ah well, all's well that ends well" said Dean relieved that he had got away with everything. "Who fancies a beer?"

Chapter 20
Week 3 - Tuesday

"Alright mate, what you up to?" Daisy asked as he walked into Urban's bedroom.

"I'm trying to avoid speaking to my bird. She wanted to come round tonight but to be honest I'm still knackered after shagging that Kat bird from the party all day Sunday so I told her that I was working late" Urban replied as he put down his magazine.

"You're a nightmare mate. I thought you two were meant to be engaged?" Daisy said as he shook his head.

"She is but I'm not" Urban replied with a cheeky smile.

"How does that work exactly?" Daisy asked as he sat at Urban's desk.

"Well, she's looking to get married, settle down, have kids and all that bollocks. I'm looking for a regular shag with a decent looking bird I can take to family weddings and that sort of thing. She was happy to go along with just being a girlfriend for the first year or so but then decided she needed to know where everything was going and said that if we weren't going to get married then she wanted to finish it. As I didn't want to lose her the only option I had was to go for a long engagement. She gets a ring on her finger and the security she was looking for and I get much more freedom to go out and shag other birds, so you could say that it's the best of both worlds really" Urban replied.

"It doesn't sound that good from her perspective" said Daisy.

"Yeah but what she doesn't know won't harm her."

"Unless you catch something off one of those rancid birds you keep shagging. That's what I don't really understand. Charlotte is really fit yet you're happy to shag anything that moves, no matter how ugly. Why is that? I mean surely you'd prefer to make love to a good looking bird rather than some fat moose?" asked Daisy.

"You're looking at it all wrong mate. It's all to do with exploring unchartered waters. An adventurer doesn't settle down in the first place he discovers does he? It might be the most idyllic place on earth and provide him with everything he's looking for but it won't stop him looking to discover new places, even if they aren't as good as the first place. Then one day, after going to all of the other places, he'll finally decide that the first place was the best and go and settle down there. It's like that with me and Charlotte. She might be the best looking bird that I ever shag but I need to try out lots of other birds before I decide that I'm ready to settle down with her."

"That's a beautiful analogy mate. I can see why Charlotte loves you so much now" Daisy said sarcastically. "I hear what you're saying about the thrill of the chase but why do you shag fat pigs and dog-ugly women rather than decent looking ones?"

"I wouldn't say that they were all dog-ugly but I admit that a few have been slightly below average…."

"…you need to include old age pensioners to get an average that low" Daisy interjected with a chuckle.

"Anyway, as I was saying a *few* haven't made the grade but that's the beauty of it when you've got a good looking girlfriend…"

"*Fiancée*" Daisy corrected him with a smirk.

"Are you going to let me finish or not?" Urban asked. Daisy nodded. "Right as I was saying, if you've already got a good looking *girlfriend* then it doesn't really matter if you pick up a bird who's not that good looking as you're never going to see her again and the less attractive ones are more likely to let you shag them and tend to be more grateful."

"So what you're saying is that you go for the ones that you can shag on the night?"

"Exactly. I've got no interest in ever seeing them again so there's no point in pulling some bird who's going to give you a peck on the cheek and her phone number at the end of the night is there?"

"So how many birds do you think that you've shagged?" asked Daisy.

"What, ever?"

"Yeah" Daisy said nodding.

"I dunno. I've never really thought about it. I'll tell you what, throw me that pad and pen and I'll make a list" said Urban. Daisy chucked them to him. "OK then, let's try and do this in chronological order. First of all there was Donna Kelly when I was 16, then her mate Rebecca Dobson two weeks later. After that it was Kim Ashton no actually it was Susan Marley, then Kim Ashton, god what a week that was! Then it was some black haired bird that I met in a club, what was her name?"

"I'll tell you what mate, I'll go and make us both a cup of tea and you carry on" said Daisy as he headed out of the room. Daisy deliberately took his time making the tea and returned ten minutes later.

"How's it going?" Daisy said as he handed the mug to Urban.

"I think I've finished, although I might have missed a couple of birds from Uni that I can't remember" Urban replied.

"Yeah, yeah" Daisy said implying that he didn't believe him. "Let's have a look then." Urban handed over the A4 pad and Daisy sat down at the desk. The list read as follows:

Birds that I've shagged by John (Urban) Lawson:

No	Name	Status	No of times shagged
1	Donna Kelly	virgin	too many to remember
2	Rebecca Dobson	virgin	once
3	Susan Marley	goer	once
4	Kim Ashton	crap shag	once
5	Black haired bird from club	slag	three (same night)
6	Sarah (blonde bird)	goer	twice (same night)

7	Diane Dobson	virgin	once (sister of RD)
8	Claire Peterson	slag	too many to remember
9	Mary Clarke	goer	four (two nights)
10	Natalie (black hair)	goer	twice (same night)
11	Fat Irish girl	slag	three (same night)
12	Posh bird on holiday	slag	twice (same night)
13	Jackie on holiday	goer	ten or eleven
14	Liz Marley	virgin	once (sister of SM)
15	Lesley (black hair)	slag	once
16	Charlotte Burton	virgin	too many to remember
17	Olivia (posh bird)	goer	twice (same night)
18	Fat bird in club toilets	slag	once
19	Scouse bird in alley	slag	once
20	Lisa (Geordie)	goer	four (same night)
21	Black bird in club	slag	once
22	Heather (Glynn's bird)	crap shag	once
23	Kat (from party)	goer	three

"So what d'ya think?" Urban asked as Daisy put the list down onto the desk.

"Twenty three? Fucking hell mate, that's a lot for a bloke of our age" Daisy replied. "I didn't realise that your Charlotte was a virgin when you met her."

"Yeah. She'd been saving herself for 'the one' and I managed to persuade her that it was me. Took me six months to get there though, during which time I managed to shag numbers fourteen and fifteen!" Urban said with a smug grin.

"You're a nightmare mate" Daisy replied with a shake of his head. "Just think, your bird has only ever had sex with you and you've managed to shag seven other birds since you've been going out with her."

"Well they're only the ones I've shagged. I've had a couple of blow jobs as well but I didn't think they merited making the list" Urban replied.

"So when's it all going to stop?" Daisy asked.

"I dunno. Maybe when I'm thirty?"

"Thirty? You're only twenty four now mate. I've a good mind to tell your bird to ditch you myself to save her all the heartbreak" Daisy replied.

"Yeah, but you wouldn't do that as you're a mate" Urban replied with a smile.

"Fancy coming down the local for a couple of pints before closing time?" Daisy asked as he looked at his watch.

"Alright then, but the first round's on you" said Urban as he climbed off the bed.

Chapter 21
Week 3 - Wednesday

The quiet couple of pints had escalated into a full blown session. After heading into town and going to a club it was five thirty before Urban got to bed. He just about managed to make it into work on time but had felt shit all day and by the time five o'clock came around he was dead on his feet. Unfortunately one of the secretaries was heading off on holiday the next day and had organised 'sunshine drinks' for everyone at the pub over the road. Therefore rather than being allowed to head off home as he wanted to Urban found himself with a drink in his hand at five fifteen. He managed a couple of pints but was so tired by the end of the second that he made his excuses and left. Half an hour later he made it back to the house and decided to grab a bottle of water from the fridge before going to bed. As he entered the kitchen Tim was making pasta.

"Alright mate, you look like shit" said Tim.

"Thanks" Urban replied. "Daisy and I ended up in some bollocks salsa club until five o'clock last night so

I didn't get much sleep. I wouldn't mind but there were no decent women in there."

Tim held his finger to his lips and made a 'shhhhh' sound, indicating that Urban should keep his voice down. Urban frowned and gave a shrug to show that he didn't understand.

"Your bird's here" Tim whispered.

"What?"

"Your bird turned up about half an hour ago. She said you'd sent her a text last night asking her to come over tonight. She was really pissed off that you weren't in when she got here."

"Oh fuck" said Urban as he pulled his mobile out of his pocket. He checked his sent box and saw that he'd sent Charlotte a text at five fifteen am, when he was in the taxi home, asking her to come round. "Bollocks" he said, "I was really looking forward to an early night but no doubt she'll want to go out for a meal or something like that. What did you let her in for?"

"Well I was hardly going to turn her away was I?" Tim said as he spooned his pasta out. "Anyway she's in your room so you'd better get up there."

Urban nodded and headed up to the top floor. His door was closed and he could hear Charlotte was listening to Capital Radio as he approached. He opened the door and walked in. Rather than the usual enthusiastic puppy-like show of affection Charlotte usually showered upon him she remained seated at the desk in silence as he entered. Urban was a bit thrown by this reaction but assumed she was just pissed off with him for being late. He walked over to give her a kiss and was surprised when she turned away as he leant in.

"Are you alright?"

"No"

"Is it because I'm a bit late? I'm sorry but Julie at work had arranged these drinks and I couldn't get out of them" Urban said as he took off his suit jacket and hung it up.

"To be honest I couldn't give a fuck that you're late" Charlotte replied, stopping Urban dead in his tracks. Charlotte hardly ever swore and never used the 'F' word so Urban instantly knew something was wrong.

"What's up? Are you late for your period?" Urban asked genuinely starting to get worried.

"No, it's nothing like that. I was just reading this very interesting list that you left out on your desk" Charlotte said as she picked up the A4 pad.

Urban's heart sank and he began to panic as he looked at Charlotte holding the pad in her hands. He desperately racked his brain for an excuse that would get him out of the situation but nothing came to mind. Why hadn't he ripped up the list once he's finished it? Why hadn't he simply put Charlotte at the bottom of the list so that he could explain that he'd been slightly promiscuous before he met her? Why had he written the bloody list in the first place? This was all Daisy's fault.

As everything turned over in his mind at a million miles an hour all he could do was stand in silence staring at Charlotte, like a schoolboy waiting to hear his punishment.

"So I only made it to number 16 on your list then? It's nice to see that you don't know the surname of any of the girls that you've fucked since you met me, that you don't even know the Christian name of four of them, that you have obviously had a party recently that I wasn't invited to and worst of all that you've had sex with Glynn's new girlfriend who you told me was a complete dog." Charlotte said as she burst into tears.

Urban wanted to respond but still couldn't think of anything to dig himself out of his hole.

"Do you need to update this for last night?" Charlotte screamed holding out the list. Urban didn't move. "Well, John Lawson, you can fucking keep your fucking cheap ring and stick your engagement up your fucking arse" she screamed as she threw the A4 pad at him followed by her engagement ring. Urban still didn't move as she picked up in her bag, walked out of the bedroom and slammed the door behind her.

"Fuck" Urban finally managed to say.

Chapter 22
Week 4 - Friday

Once again Dean found himself in the pub at Canary Wharf waiting for Razor to return from Jacobs & Co. After half an hour he finally arrived and ordered two pints.

"How did it go?" Dean asked.

"Yeah, alright" said Razor taking a sip of his lager. "I'll tell you what mate, that Gill is a bit of a sort ain't she? I mean those fucking photos of you and Mick doing the bizz at the same time were top level porn. I think I might have a crack at her some time, on my own of course."

"I think Mick would have something to say about that" Dean replied.

"What is he seeing her now?" Razor asked. Dean nodded. "Is he fucking mad? He's going out with her after you shagged her? No offence or anything Deano but you just wouldn't would you? It's alright for a one-nighter but you wouldn't want that sort of bird as your girlfriend would you?"

"Well I wouldn't but Mick obviously thinks that it's alright given the fact that she seems to have stayed at our house just about every night this week" Dean replied, clearly not happy with the situation.

"Yeah, just think, this time last week she was your bird and now Mick's banging the arse off her every night. It's funny that isn't it?" Razor said smiling to himself.

"No, not really. Anyway did you get this week's envelope?"

"Oh yeah, almost forgot. For some reason there's two envelopes this week" Razor said handing it over the usual A4 envelope together with a much fatter A5 sized one. Dean opened the larger envelope and pulled out the piece of paper inside.

"Dear Dean,

Three down, seven to go. So far so good! I'm not sure if you got involved personally last week or not but I would guess that you did as it was a difficult one to persuade a couple of other chaps to do for you. If you did I hope you enjoyed it. I tried it once but have to say that I didn't really like watching some other bloke shafting the bird I was with. Anyway onto this week's challenge:

'PROSTITUTE'

All you need to do is get a photograph of a member of the house handing over cash and then having sex with a prostitute. As this challenge involves spending some money I've provided a bit of cash for you to use, which Mr Jacob should have given you in a separate envelope. It's entirely up to you how you spend it. If you want to splash out (so to speak) on a classy bird you can use all of it but if you have to bribe one of the lads to do it or just want to keep any surplus cash for yourself, then that's fine as well. The only rule is that you must provide a photograph of whoever has sex with the girl handing over at least £100 in cash to her.

Anyway, good luck mate and hopefully we'll be in touch again in a week's time.

Your friend,
Dougie"

Dean picked up the other envelope that had 'WEEK 4' written on it in large letters. He opened it and pulled out a wad of £50 notes.

"Fucking hell, how much is there?" Razor asked.

Dean counted out the cash. "A grand."

"Jesus, you can get a high class 'tom' for a grand Deano. You'll be able to go to one of those escort agencies that footballers use. You lucky bastard."

"I'm not doing it" Dean replied.

"What d'ya mean? Why not?"

"Why not? Because I don't agree with prostitution, that's why not" Dean responded.

"But what's the difference to pulling some bird in a nightclub, taking her home, having sex and then never seeing her again? Razor asked.

"The difference is that it's consensual" Dean replied.

"It's consensual with a prostitute, it's not fucking rape is it?" Razor replied.

"You know what I mean. If you pull a bird in a club, she goes home with you because she likes you and she wants to, not because you've paid her."

"OK so what's the difference in taking a bird out, spending a hundred quid on a meal, a club and drinks and then nobbing her? It's the same sort of thing. You pay for her night out and she responds by sleeping with you" said Razor.

"It isn't the fucking same at all. She's there because she wants to be. There's no formal contract that she has to sleep with you at the end of the date is there?"

"Not a formal contract but you both know the score. Most blokes would expect to get something back if you've forked out a wedge on a romantic night out" said Razor.

"But it's not the same as paying a bird to have sex with you. Have you ever done it?" Dean asked.

"No, I don't need to pay for it" Razor replied with a smirk.

"That response proves my point. Paying for sex is seen as something that only desperate fuckers who can't pull a proper bird would do and it's one of those stigmas that I don't want to carry with me" Dean replied.

"So do you think any of the other lads will be up for it?" Razor asked.

"I'm not sure. Ideally we could have set someone up by paying the bird in advance and just letting them think that they'd got lucky. But Dougie's a clever bastard as the fact that we've got to get a photo of them handing over the cash scuppers that plan. I think the only way we'll get anyone to volunteer is to bribe them. £500 should be enough to get someone to do it, I mean it's not as if we're asking them to do something they're not going to enjoy is it?" said Dean with a shrug.

****

Dean, Glynn, Urban, Daisy and Tim were in the living room having a few beers and watching women's beach volleyball on TV.

"So what's happening tonight then fellas?" Dean asked.

"I'm seeing Heather" Glynn replied.

"You're seeing your bird again? Urban said in a mock-disgusted tone. "Have you shagged her yet? Did I mention that I nailed her on the first night I met her?"

"Oh yeah, Heather told me about what happened that night. Apparently you're dick is really small and you came really quickly. She then insisted that you slept on the sofa whilst you begged her to let you stay in her room" Glynn replied as Dean, Daisy and Tim starting jeering at Urban.

"Bollocks" said Urban "anyway you haven't answered my question. Have you shagged her yet or not?"

"If you mean have we 'made love' then yes we have thank you for asking" Glynn replied.

"Really? What was it like?" Urban asked.

"Fantastic. In fact now that we've started we can't seem to stop, we're at it all the time" said Glynn with a huge grin.

"Does she take it up the arse?" Urban asked.

"Alright, that's enough about Glynn's bird" Dean cut in before Glynn could respond. "What are the rest of you doing tonight?"

"I was meant to be seeing Charlotte but seeing as she now hates my guts and won't take my calls I've got absolutely fuck all to do" said Urban.

"Me neither" said Daisy and Tim shook his head to indicate that he also didn't have any plans.

"Razor's out with his East End mates tonight and I presume that Mick and Gill are still working their way through the Karma Sutra so it looks like it's the four of us" said Dean.

"Where's Rod tonight?" Urban asked.

"I think he said he was seeing that bird he pulled at the party last week" said Daisy.

"Right I've got to go" said Glynn getting up from the sofa "can't keep a beautiful lady waiting you know."

"That's right" said Urban "but seeing as your bird is a minger there's no rush is there?" Glynn responded to by flicking Urban a V sign as he left the room.

"Hey have any of you lot ever shagged a hooker? Dean said to no-one in particular.

"No" they all replied in turn.

"Would you do it if you had the chance? I don't mean with some skuzzy drug-addict down at Kings Cross but a tasty high class hooker, the sort you see in big budget porn" Dean continued.

"I wouldn't" said Daisy. "For a start there's the risk of catching all sorts of diseases even if you wear a condom, then there's the pressure to perform on demand and finally the stigma attaching to it once your mates find out."

"I wouldn't do it either" agreed Urban. "It's the sort of thing that sticks with you. I'd bet that women would hate to find out that their bloke had ever been with a prossie, even if it was before they met him."

"What about you Tim?" Dean asked hoping that at least one of them would be receptive to the idea.

"Well I think it's alright for someone who's handicapped or something, or if you're fifty and you want to sleep with a twenty five year old bird but not for blokes of our age. I mean we should be able to get birds without having to pay for them shouldn't we?" Tim replied.

"Would you do it if someone paid you?" Dean asked.

"What do you mean? Become a prostitute? Urban asked.

"No, I mean if someone paid you to shag a hooker, would you do it then?"

"Who the fuck is going to pay you to shag a prossie? Urban asked.

"Dougie" Dean replied. "As well as letting us stay here rent free Dougie also left a bit of cash in his will for us to do some dares and the first one is to sleep with a hooker."

"How much cash are we talking about?" Daisy asked.

"£500."

"£500? I thought you were going to say £10,000 or something. Fuck that. It ain't worth it for £500" Daisy responded.

"What about you two?" asked Dean looking at Tim and Urban.

"Nah, not for £500. I'd do it for £5,000 but not £500" Urban replied. Tim merely shook his head to indicate that he wasn't interested.

"What happens to the money if nobody does it?" Urban asked.

"It goes to charity" Dean lied, not wanting to tell them that if nobody did it then they would be evicted from the house and that his potential inheritance would be gone. Just then the living room door opened and Rod walked in.

"Alright Rod, where've you been?" asked Urban.

"Well I was meant to be taking that bird from the party out on my mate's bike but he let me down at the last minute and when I turned up on my scooter she blew me out" Rod replied.

"Hey Rod, would you shag a hooker for £500?" Dean asked.

"I haven't got £50, never mind £500, mate" Rod replied, clearly not understanding Dean's question.

"No, would you shag a hooker if someone paid you £500 to do it?"

"£500? The luck I'm having with birds at the moment I'd shag one for nothing mate!" Rod replied.

"Really?" Dean said getting excited "I'm serious."

"So am I" said Rod. "If someone offered me £500 to do it I'd jump at the chance."

"Great" said Dean "now where are we going to get one from?"

"What?" Rod said, not really understanding what was going on.

"How about the Internet? You can get fucking everything on it these days" Urban suggested.

"Yeah, and it's usually cheaper" Tim followed up.

"Right, let's go and have a look then" said Dean standing up.

"Hang on, what the fuck's going on? I haven't even sat down or had a beer yet and you lot are suddenly off to order me a hooker on the Internet?"

"That's about the size of it Rod" Dean replied as he headed up to his room.

Within a couple of minutes Dean managed to pull up a list of all of the Escort Agencies in London on his PC.

He clicked onto the first website which had some very attractive girls but which disappointingly looked like a genuine escort service rather than an online brothel. After a few minutes searching through various sites he managed to find one that looked seedy enough for him to be confident that it was a guaranteed knocking shop. He pulled out his mobile and entered the number.

"Right then Rod, what do you want?" Dean asked before pressing the call button.

"What do I want? It's not a fucking Chinese takeaway you're ordering" Rod replied.

"It can be, if that's what you want" said Dean smiling. "Fancy a bit of Oriental?"

"Err no" said Rod realising what Dean meant. "Look I'm not sure about this. Can't we just go out for a few beers instead?"

"No we can't. Now, seriously, what do you want" Dean asked again.

"Oh get me a blonde with big tits if you must" Rod replied.

"Excellent choice sir" said Dean as he pressed the call button on his mobile. After a couple of rings the phone was answered by an Eastern European sounding man.

"Is this the right number for an escort?" Dean asked.

"Yes. We have very beautiful girls. What do you want? Black, blonde, Asian?" the guy responded. Dean couldn't help thinking the bloke sounded exactly like he expected a KGB hitman to sound. As a result he started getting worried that he might get ripped off.

"A blonde girl please" Dean replied deciding not to mention Rod's request for big tits.

"It's £500 for two hours or £1,000 for the whole night."

"Two hours will be fine" Dean replied.

"Give me your credit card number and your address" said the guy.

Dean gave the bloke his credit card details and their address.

"Just to check, we are talking about sex here aren't we?" Dean asked.

"Yes, whatever you like" the man responded without any hint of humour. It all started to feel very clinical and Dean was glad that it was Rod and not him who had to perform.

"She will be round within an hour" the bloke said and hung up.

"Right then Rod, she's on her way" Dean said.

"Oh fuck!" said Rod.

****

Dean had never seen anybody voluntarily drink as many bottles of beer in such a short a space of time.

"Rod, calm down mate. The way you're drinking you'd think you were on death row waiting for the chair rather than about to have a two hour romp with some beautiful blonde bird" Dean said trying to settle Rod down. "If you carry on downing those bottles of beer you'll be unconscious before she gets here."

"That's the plan" Rod responded.

"Don't be stupid. Take a step back and think about this. You're going to get paid £500 to have sex with some top bit of totty. In my book that just about makes you a legend" said Dean.

225

"Well I don't feel like a legend in the making. I'm fucking shitting bricks here. It's not like pulling a bird in a club where you're already half pissed and you get time to warm up. This feels cold and calculated. I'm waiting here for some bird to turn up that I've never even seen and when she gets here we're going to have sex. It's weird but the more I think about it the less sexy it sounds. I feel like I'm waiting to take my driving test rather than about to get my rocks off" Rod said, opening another bottle of beer.

"Maybe it will be a bit like taking your driving test" said Urban trying to lighten the mood. "You know, she'll say 'OK sir if you'd like to start your engine, slip your gear stick into first and I'll give you directions from there."

"….and try not to stall before pulling off!" added Daisy as they all broke out into a nervous laugh.

"Hey, that's a good point" said Urban "you don't want to shoot your load too quickly. Why don't you go upstairs and have a wank before she gets here?"

"What if I do that and then can't get it up when she arrives smart arse? I'll look a total prick then won't I? That's why I thought I'd have a few beers so that I can last a bit longer" Rod replied.

They were suddenly interrupted by the sound of the doorbell. All five of them started to panic.

"I'm going to my room" said Urban looking like a small boy who'd been caught out of bed after lights out by his mum and dad. "Good luck mate" he said patting Rod on the back and he ran out of the room.

"Yeah, hope it goes OK mate" said Daisy as he and Tim followed Urban upstairs.

The doorbell rang again causing Rod and Dean's hearts to race even faster.

"I'm not sure I can do this" said Rod who was now visibly shaking.

"You'll be fine mate" Dean assured him. "Oh, one thing I forgot to mention is that you've got to give her £100 in cash before you start."

"But I thought you'd already paid £500?" Rod asked.

"I have but the bloke on the phone made it clear that you've got to give her £100 in cash. It's like a sort of tip I suppose" Dean replied.

"But I haven't got £100."

"Here" said Dean as he pulled out his wallet and handed Rod the money. The doorbell rang for a third time. "Look, we'd better answer the door before she fucks off home" said Dean. "Where do you want to be, in here or your room?"

"Err, in my room I think. Can you let her in, give her a drink and then bring her up in five minutes so that I can tidy up a bit?" Rod asked. He was now pure white with fear and looked more like someone waiting for the results of a brain scan rather than about to get laid.

"No problem mate. You get yourself sorted and I'll get the door" Dean replied, heading into the hallway. As he approached the front door he could see the silhouette of a woman through the glass panel and felt his heart race again. He took a second to compose himself and opened the door. The girl was around twenty years old, very attractive, tall, had blonde hair and, despite the fact that he'd forgotten to specifically ask for them, also had large breasts. She was wearing an ankle length white coat and ridiculously high black stiletto shoes.

"Hi, I'm Dean" he said and opened the door fully to allow her to enter.

"I'm Nina" she replied in a strong Eastern European accent. "So you are looking for a good time Dean, yes?"

"Err, no. Not me, it's my friend Rod. He's upstairs" Dean replied.

"But I was told that Dean has paid for me for two hours. You have paid only for you, not your friend. If you want him to join in it is double" she replied taking off her coat to reveal an extremely low cut, short black dress.

"Yes, I did pay but I just paid for my friend. He doesn't have a credit card" said Dean "so I was doing him a favour by paying for him."

"Why do you not like me Dean? Do you not fancy me? I can show you very good time" she said pulling her skirt up to reveal a red g-string.

"Look, I think you're very attractive and I'm sure you could show me a fantastic time but it really is my friend Rod who'd like to spend time with you today. Why don't I get you a drink and take you up to his room?" Dean replied heading into the kitchen. He grabbed a bottle of beer, opened it and handed it to Nina who'd followed him into the room.

"Do you not have champagne? I only drink champagne" she responded putting the beer bottle down on the worktop.

Dean opened the fridge and spotted that they had a bottle of cheap sparkling wine left over from the party the previous week. He opened it and poured her a glass.

As he did so Urban and Daisy both appeared in the doorway.

"Hi Dean. You never told us you were entertaining tonight. Who's this lovely lady?" Urban asked staring at Nina.

"This is Nina" Dean replied with a sarcastic smile acknowledging the fact that they'd come down simply to see what she looked like. "If you don't mind we're retiring upstairs now" he said, pushing past them both. Nina followed. Dean shot up the stairs and was at Rod's door in a flash. Everything had happened so quickly that he hadn't set up the computer yet and he was therefore eager to show Nina inside and get the PC set up to record all of the action.

"This is Rod's room" he said smiling as he knocked on the door. He waited for a response but there was no reply. "He must just be tidying up a bit" Dean said to Nina and knocked again. Still no reply. Dean opened the door and his heart sank when he saw that there was no sign of Rod.

"Err, he must have gone to the bathroom to freshen up or something. Why don't you wait here while I find him" Dean said gesturing to the bed. He closed the door and ran across the landing to the first floor bathroom, which was empty. He then ran downstairs and into the living room where Urban and Daisy were watching porn.

"Have either of you seen Rod?"

"I thought he was upstairs banging that hooker? That's why we've put this on, as a tribute to him" said Urban.

"Well he isn't and he's not in his room or the bog" Dean replied.

"Have you tried his mobile?" Urban asked.

"Good idea" said Dean pulling his phone out. He called Rod's number and was concerned to note that as it stared to ring in his earpiece he couldn't hear the phone ringing within the house.

"Alright mate" Rod said as he answered. The sound of traffic in the background gave away the fact that he was clearly outside the house.

"Where the fuck are you Rod?"

"Look, I just can't do it mate, £500 or no £500. It's just not me. I panicked when the doorbell went and when you went off to answer it I legged it out of the back door."

"So where the fuck are you now?" Dean asked.

"I'm heading off to meet a few mates of mine at a club. Don't bother waiting up" Rod replied chuckling as he hung up.

"Bastard!" Dean shouted as he heard the line go dead. "Shit! Fuck! Bastard!"

"Hey Deano, calm down mate. What's the problem? The bird has been paid so just go upstairs, tell her what's happened and ask her to go" said Urban.

"Yeah, she's been paid on my fucking credit card and unless someone shags her Dougie's money goes to charity and I'll be £500 out of fucking pocket" Dean lied. "What about you two? You've seen her. She's hot. What d'ya reckon? There's £500 in it for you?"

"We've been through this earlier mate" Urban replied. "It doesn't matter whether she's fit or not, she's still a hooker and it's still paying for sex so I'm not interested."

"Daisy?" Dean asked desperately.

"Nah mate, not my scene" Daisy responded.

"Bollocks" Dean whispered to himself as he headed back upstairs. With all of the others totally against it the only option he had left was to go through with it himself. The alternative was to walk away, lose the inheritance and be homeless by the morning. Reluctantly, he walked into his bedroom, switched on the PC and set up the portable digital camera that sat on top of the screen so that it had a good shot of the bed. *"I thought that things couldn't get any worse than they did last Saturday, but here I am, less than a week later, scraping ever further down the bottom of the barrel"* he thought to himself as he put the blank DVD into the PC. With everything in place he tidied up his bed, cleared away the clothes from the floor and slowly walked over to Rod's room. He opened the door to see Nina lying naked on the bed.

"So it is you after all? "I knew that there was no *Rod"* Nina said in her thick Russian accent.

"Erm, yeah" Dean replied with a nervous smile, "you got me. But this isn't my room, so can we go over to mine?"

"If you wish, but we only have 2 hours and I have been here for twenty minutes already." She bent down and expertly slipped her dress back on. There was no sign of the red g-string Dean had seen earlier. Once she was dressed they took the short stroll to his room. Dean entered first and Nina closed the door with a loud bang making him jump. He turned round to see her posing against the door like a glamour model.

"So then Dean, what do you want to do?" Nina asked seductively.

It was bizarre but Dean had never felt less like having sex in his whole life. All of the constituent parts were in place; he'd had a few drinks, he was in his own bedroom and he had a beautiful sexy woman offering him her body. But it just didn't feel right. He couldn't get the thought out of his mind that it was all just an act on her part and that behind the façade there was a tragic story. He tried to console himself with the thought that she was an ambitious money-minded women with a high sex drive who loved her work and was well paid for it but, in truth, he didn't believe that. He didn't respond to her question but rather took out his wallet, removed £100 and held it out to her.

"What are you doing? You have already paid for two hours. Do you want more?"

"No this is for you to keep" Dean replied not wanting to admit that he was doing it purely for the camera.

"Thank you" she replied placing the money into her bag. She then sprawled herself on the bed. "So what do you want to do?"

"Just the standard stuff" Dean replied.

"OK. Your wish is my command" she replied, standing up and taking off her dress to reveal her naked toned body again. She knelt down and started to unbutton Dean's trousers.

"I'm just going to nip to the toilet. I'll be back in a minute" Dean said.

"Hurry up, I'm getting horny" she replied as she climbed onto the bed.

Dean hurried into his en-suite bathroom, closed the door and sat on the toilet. Usually in this position his erection would have been bursting out of his trousers but this time there was no sign of life in the old fella. Rather than worrying about the moral dilemma of the situation Dean was now concerned that he wouldn't be able to complete the task because he couldn't get it up. He dropped his trousers and furiously started to masturbate. Still no sign of life, in fact if it was possible his nob seemed to be getting smaller. He stood up and caught sight of his reflection in the mirror and quickly looked away, embarrassed for himself. He closed his eyes and decided to try again. He heard the door open and opened his eyes to see Nina standing in the doorway. He genuinely wanted the floor to open up and swallow him. He'd wondered earlier if he could possibly get any lower than shagging a hooker that had been rejected by one of his mates. It had just got a whole lot worse. He had now been caught masturbating by her and worse that than he couldn't even get an erection.

"Hey that's my job!" Nina said laughing which lifted the sense of embarrassment that Dean felt.

"I wasn't sure if the payment covered this" Dean replied, trying to make light of his predicament.

"It covers everything" Nina replied taking his hand and leading him to his bed.

****

Dean lay on his bed staring at the ceiling and wondering what else Dougie had in store for him. His thoughts were broken by Nina.

"So would you like to do anything else? We still have another hour" she said lighting a cigarette.

Normally after sex Dean felt happy, calm, relaxed and at one with the world. This time he felt disappointed, tense and depressed. He felt as though he had sold his body for money and that the whole thing had been an entirely pointless exercise as neither of them had enjoyed it. Nina had put on a good show, making all the right noises and even pretending that he was too big for her at the start, but he knew it was all an act and that she'd have done the same with anyone. He had treated it as if he was doing a job and because of that he'd taken a frustratingly long time to come (at one point he was considering faking an orgasm as he had sufficient photographic evidence but decided that it would have been rude so he carried on out of politeness). Now that it was over Dean just wanted her to go.

"No thanks" he said, as if she was offering him one of her cigarettes. "You can go now." Those last few words sounded harsh and callous and hung in the air for a few seconds like a bad fart.

"Didn't you enjoy it Dean? Did I not please you?" Nina asked, appearing hurt.

Dean was used to giving the junior members of staff at work encouragement but hadn't expected somebody in this field to be looking for positive feedback on their performance. He decided to lie.

"It was fantastic, better than anything I could have dreamed of" he said with as much sincerity as he could muster, "but I'm tired now and would really like to go to sleep."

"Can I see you again?"

"Err, no" Dean replied, shocked at her question "I don't usually do this sort of thing. This was a one off and I'm not looking to make a habit of it."

"I don't mean paying. I mean can I see you again, like boyfriend and girlfriend?"

Dean was genuinely shocked now. It was one thing sleeping with a prostitute but another thing entirely having one as your girlfriend, especially one that all of his mates knew was a prostitute. Before he had a chance to answer she continued:

"This is the first time that I have done this tonight. I do not want to do it again. I am looking for a real job and to have some fun. You seem like a very nice man and I would like to see you again."

Dean's mind returned to the tragic story that he'd concocted in his mind on Nina's behalf half an hour earlier. "Well maybe we could go out on a foursome with a couple of friends" Dean replied felling guilty that he'd exploited her.

"Oh Dean, you make me so happy!" Nina squealed jumping onto his chest and giving him a big hug.

"How can things possibly get any worse than this?" Dean thought as he lay cuddling his newly acquired Russian prostitute girlfriend.

Chapter 23
Week 4 - Saturday

Dean finally managed to get rid of Nina at three am, despite the fact that she'd been extremely keen to have sex again, 'this time as boyfriend and girlfriend' and to stay over. He'd managed to convince her that he was very tired and that he had work in the morning (which was a complete lie). After she'd left he found it impossible to sleep and ended up having two showers to try to make himself feel less grubby and disgusting.

After lying in bed mulling over the events of the evening, he went downstairs and made some breakfast. It was Saturday morning and the rest of the house were either still asleep or not home. He went into the living room and watched Soccer AM. An hour or so later Razor came down.

"Morning Deano, what's the story mate?"

"What does that mean?" Dean replied defensively.

"I mean what's been going on? What did you do last night?"

"Why, what have you heard?" Dean asked, wondering how many people knew already about what he'd done.

"Jesus you're jumpy today. Have you been on the Charlie again? I haven't fucking heard anything. I was just making conversation, that's all."

"Oh right, sorry" Dean replied. He got up and closed the living room door to prevent any other members of the house walking in on their conversation. "It's just that I decided to get the latest of Dougie's challenges out of the way last night and I thought you might have heard what happened."

"Oh yeah" said Razor sitting forward on the edge of the sofa. "So did anyone go for the £500 reward you were offering then?"

"Sort of" Dean replied.

"Sort of? Either they did or they didn't" said Razor looking confused.

"Well Rod said that he was up for it, so I called up this escort agency and paid £500 for this bird to come round to the house."

"Excellent! What was she like?"

"Blonde, big tits, long legs, Russian, you know, that sort of thing" Dean replied, not really wanting to re-live the ending to his story.

"So did Rod nail her?" Razor asked, hanging on Dean's every word.

"No" said Dean shaking his head.

"What, he bottled out?"

Dean nodded in response.

"So what did the bird do then? Wasn't she pissed off with Rod?" Razor asked.

"She didn't have a chance to be as Rod fucked off out the back door when she arrived. A fact I only discovered when I showed her up to his bedroom."

"Shit! What did you do? Did you shag her?" Razor asked almost wetting himself with excitement.

Dean put his head into his hands, nodded and following a deep breath said "yeah."

Razor raised both of his arms above his head in a victory salute and started cheering. "So what was it like? Did you do her up the arse?"

"It was shite mate" Dean responded, refusing to acknowledge the second part of Razor's question.

"Shite?" Razor said looking bemused. "How could sex with a top class Russian hooker be shite? I thought they were paid to do anything you want?"

"You're missing the point. It wasn't that she was crap in bed it was just that the whole thing felt wrong. There wasn't the passion you get with a normal bird. She made all the right noises and did all the right things but it just felt really fake and horribly desperate, if you know what I mean?"

"I can't really say I do" Razor replied as he lit a fag.

"The only way I can describe it is to compare it with a porn film. It's alright to watch it and to fantasise about shagging somebody that's in one but it'd be a different story if you were actually acting in one. I'm sure it'd feel all clinical and not at all sexy. That's what it felt like with that bird last night, everything was technically correct but without any passion or love it was just pointless."

"So did you video it then?" Razor said, suddenly remembering the surveillance cameras.

"Yeah, but you're not seeing it."

"Oh please mate. You didn't let me watch last week's tape of you, Mick and Gill. Oh go on" Razor pleaded.

"I'm still trying to forget about what happened last week. Anyway what have you got planned today?" Dean asked wanting to move the conversation away from his fledgling career as a home made porn star.

"A bungee jump. Are you up for it?"

"A Bungee jump? Are people still doing that?" Dean asked shaking his head.

"There's a couple of Aussie guys I know who work on a building site down the East end who are all into that base jumping shit. The site closes at midday on a Saturday and they've got an agreement with their site manager that they can run a bungee jumping sideline from one of the big cranes, providing that they give him a split of the takings. They're starting it today and charging £10 per jump. The crane is over two hundred feet high. You take one of those cage lifts to the top, walk out to the end of the arm and jump off. Sounds fucking great doesn't it?" Razor said with a huge grin.

"Bungee jumping on a building site? Jumping off a crane over concrete and metal scaffolding? Are you fucking mad? I might think about it for a millisecond if it was over water where you've got a chance of surviving if something goes wrong but not over a fucking building site. What qualifications have these blokes got?"

"As I said they're all into base jumping so they know what they're doing. Apparently they used to do this all the time in Oz. So are you up for it?" Razor asked, relishing the fact that Dean looked nervous just talking about it.

"No I'm not" Dean replied. "I intend to have a very quite day doing fuck all."

"Yeah, I suppose I would as well if I'd been up all night shagging a hooker."

"Fuck off" Dean replied as he threw a cushion at Razor.

A few minutes later the living room door opened and Rod walked in looking very hungover. As he saw Dean he sheepishly said "Alright?"

"You can fuck right off" Dean replied without averting his gaze from the plasma screen.

"Look, I'm sorry mate. I just lost my bottle when it came to the crunch. I thought I could do it but realised I couldn't when you went to answer the door. I'll make it up to you, I promise" Rod said.

"You bet you fucking will" Dean replied.

"So what happened then?" Rod said eagerly awaiting an update.

"Well after we worked out that you had fucked off she went home. I told the bird that she'd had a lucky escape as you were a complete twat with a small dick" Dean said, casting a glance at Razor to indicate that their recent discussion should remain just between them.

"So nobody shagged her then?" Rod said, looking disappointed.

"I'm afraid not mate. You could have, but you shat out" Dean replied.

"What did she look like?"

"A fucking stunner, like all of your dream birds rolled into one. You really fucked up there mate" Dean said.

"Bollocks!" Rod said, looking genuinely annoyed. "Anyway Dean I'm serious, just let me know if there's any thing I can do to make it up to you."

"It's funny you should say that" said Dean smiling and looking at Razor. "What are you doing this afternoon?"

****

Razor, Tim, Mick, Rod and Dean arrived at the building site just after two o'clock. They all had different reasons for being there. Razor had done a number of jumps a few years before and really fancied doing it again. Tim had never done one but had always wanted to. Mick wasn't really bothered about doing one but didn't want to be outdone by Tim. Rod was still feeling guilty about the previous evening and had been press-ganged into it by Dean. Dean had no intention of jumping and had come along just to see Rod suffer.

"Is it supposed to be moving around as much as that?" Rod asked as he looked at the huge crane swaying gently backwards and forwards.

"Yeah, that's totally normal. If it didn't move with the wind it would fall over eventually" Razor replied.

"Since when did you become a fucking civil engineering expert?" Rod asked as they made their way to the site office.

The site office consisted of a large portacabin located at the far end of the site. Inside were four burly surf-dude types who all had shoulder length hair. The largest of the four stood up and introduced himself as they entered.

"Hi guys, I'm Grant. One of you must be Razor?" he said holding out his shovel-like hand.

"That's me" Razor said reaching forward and shaking Grant's hand. The others followed suit. Grant then introduced the others.

"This is Mike, Matt and Jason" he said gesturing to each one in turn. "Now if you guys would like to take a seat I'll run you through everything. As you may already know we're all keen base jumpers and back in Oz we organised weekly jumps off cranes on the local building sites. We thought it would be fun to introduce it in London."

"So is this the first time you've done it here then?" Rod asked, looking petrified.

"Well this is the first week that we've done it here in London but we've done hundreds of jumps before back in Oz so there's nothing to worry about" Grant said with a reassuring smile.

"Well there's no fucking way that I'm going first" said Rod shaking his head.

"Look, what we need to do is weigh each of you to ensure that we use the correct amount of cord. The cord itself is the same stuff that's used to hold down tanks when they're transported on boats and planes and is made of rubber combined with some very strong man made fabrics. The cord is attached to a harness around your legs and will stretch to between three and four times its original size, depending upon your weight. We make a calculation taking into account the height of the crane and your weight and use just enough cord to make it exciting but not dangerous. Any questions?"

"Is there any way the cord can stretch too far and we end up hitting the deck?" Tim asked.

"Not unless we don't like you!" Matt said, causing all four of the Aussies to break out laughing. Razor, Mick, Tim and Dean all smiled and Rod broke out into a cold sweat.

"OK then chaps let's go" said Grant pointing to an old looking set of bathroom scales he'd placed in the centre of the portacabin.

"Not very scientific looking is it" Rod said to Dean.

"You'll be fine mate" Dean replied, loving every minute of Rod's anguish.

One by one all of them, except Dean, stepped onto the scales and had their weight written on their hand in marker pen. The Aussies then waded through masses of cord that was piled in the far corner and pulled out the appropriate one for each of them.

"OK we're ready to rock and roll. Matt and Jason will both do a test jump first and then you guys are up. Who's going to go first?" Grant asked.

"I will" said Razor, much to Rod's relief.

"Have you done this before?"

"Yeah, loads of times" Razor responded cockily.

"A seasoned pro eh? Great. Where did you do it?" Grant asked.

"I spent a summer over in Ibiza and a few of the lads I knew over there set up a jump down at the beach. It was big, much bigger than this one, but after the first couple of times it got a bit dull to be honest."

"Well hopefully this won't be too boring for you Razor" Grant replied sarcastically.

"Only time will tell" said Razor, yawning to add to his bravado.

"Quite" Grant replied as he looked at the other three Aussies and shook his head. "OK let's go."

The four Aussies loaded up with harnesses, ropes and towels and headed out to the foot of the crane. As they all stood looking up, the crane appeared to grow in size and the swaying looked more pronounced than it had done from a distance. As Rod leaned back to see the top he lost his balance and staggered backwards.

"Is this a good time to mention that I don't like heights?" Rod trembled.

"Come on Rod, it'll be a piece of piss" Razor replied slapping him hard on the back.

"OK, we're going up to sort things out. You lot stay here and enjoy the view" Grant said as he got into the small cage with Matt and Jason. Mike remained on the ground whilst the lift made its way to the top of the crane. The group watched as the cage got further and further away before eventually stopping at the top. The three Aussies got out and crawled along the crane's arm until they were positioned directly above the heads of the people on the ground. The group could just about make out that they were attaching the cords to the steel structure. A minute or so later Matt stood up, held both his arms out to the side and dived head-first over the edge. They all watched in silence as he came hurtling down towards them. With around seventy five feet to go the cord started to tighten and he stopped falling with around fifty feet remaining. He then bounced back up to around halfway and after a minute or so of yo-yoing eventually came to a stop. Mike ran over and helped

Matt as Grant and Jason loosened the cord and lowered him safely to the ground.

"Wow! What a rush!" Matt screamed as Mike helped him out of his harness. "It's as easy as that, gentlemen. I must be two or three stone heavier than any of you, so you've got nothing to worry about."

A couple of minutes later Jason came hurtling down, following exactly the same pattern as Matt. As Mike and Matt helped him down the lads realised that it was now their turn.

"I am fucking shitting bricks, look" said Tim holding out his hand to show how much he was shaking.

"I must admit that I'm having a few second thoughts" said Mick. By this stage Rod was so terrified he was unable to speak.

"Come on you fucking pussies, you've seen these Aussie puffs do it, it'll be a piece of piss" said Razor.

"OK chaps, if you'd like to come with me. You two first" said Matt pointing at Razor and Rod.

"Can't one of these two go first?" Rod asked looking at Mick and Tim.

"I'm afraid not mate" Matt responded. "Anyway nobody's jumping yet, we're just getting you all up there first."

Razor and Rod got into the crane's lift with Matt. As it started to rise Rod felt the same feeling of panic he experienced every time he went on a rollercoaster. That desperate desire to get off before it reached the top of the initial climb. However on rollercoasters Rod had always comforted himself with the fact that it was just a ride and that nothing serious would ever happen. This time was different. It felt much more like a real life and death situation. He was riding a lift to the top of a real crane and when he got up there he was going to jump off the side with just an oversized elastic band to save him. He closed his eyes and wished he'd simply shagged the hooker. *"That would've been far less dangerous and much more fun"* Rod thought to himself.

Suddenly the lift stopped. Rod opened his eyes and saw they were at the top. He glanced down at the ground and wished he hadn't. Matt stepped out of the lift and onto the arm of the crane. He held out his hand, helped Razor out and pointed him to where Grant was sitting halfway along the arm. Matt gestured to Razor to drop to his hands and knees and to make his way over to Grant. Very carefully Razor made his way along the steel structure. Matt then turned back to Rod, who was clinging into the inside of the lift as if his life depended upon it.

"Come on man, give me your hand" Matt said.

"I can't" Rod shouted and started crying.

"You have to man, you can't go back now it'll be too embarrassing" Matt replied in an attempt to coax Rod out of the lift.

"I can't do it. Please, please get me back down" Rod replied. Tears were flooding down his face. Matt could see Rod was starting to turn hysterical and decided that the only course of action was to take him back down. He shook his head at Grant and got back in the lift. Rod continued to sob whilst clinging to the cage all the way back down. When they reached the bottom Rod fell out of the cage and started kissing the floor which resulted in Dean, Mike and Jason breaking out into a fit of laughter. Mick and Tim looked at Rod and then at each other and the colour drained from their faces.

"OK chaps, Rod's decided he doesn't fancy it today so it's time for you two to go" Matt said. Mick and Tim made their way slowly into the cage and it started its ascent back up the crane.

"Do you shit out of everything you'll say you'll do Rod?" Dean asked.

"Fuck off" Rod replied weakly, as he wiped his eyes.

Mick and Tim's hearts were racing by the time they got to the top but they both managed to contain their fear and crawl their way over to where Razor was sitting with Grant. Razor was sitting with a harness around his feet, smoking a fag. He looked very relaxed, although Tim suspected he was just as nervous as they were.

"Razor here has been giving me some tips on jumping mate" Grant said to Matt.

"Really, well maybe he wants to fix his own cord then?" Matt asked smiling.

"Err, no thanks. I was just saying that it might be better if you did future jumps from the end of the crane rather than the middle as it'd be more exciting walking to the end" Razor replied.

"Well feel free to walk out to the end and back if you want to" said Matt.

"No thanks. Right, let's get on with it" said Razor.

"OK big man. You're first up" replied Matt.

As Razor stood up the sway of the crane felt much more pronounced than it had when he was sitting down and he grabbed Grant to steady himself.

"Whoah! Don't fucking grab me when we're up here" Grant shouted at him.

"Oh shut up. You're fine" Razor replied. "Now let's get on with this fucking jump, I'm starting to get bored."

Grant nodded to Matt who connected the cord to the harness around Razor's feet.

"OK then Razor, I'll count you in by saying three... two...one...Bungee! Then you jump, OK?" Grant said.

"Yeah, yeah, yeah, I know the fucking drill, let's just get on with it" Razor replied flippantly. Grant shook his head in disbelief.

"OK then, three...two...one...Bung..."

Before Grant could finish the word 'bungee' Matt, who had been checking the cord attached to Razor's harness, stood up with his hands on his head and shouted:

"NOOO!!!!"

Out of the corner of his eye Razor saw Matt stand up and heard him shout but by the time he realised what had happened he'd already leaned out beyond forty five degrees and was unable to bring himself back. He fell forward and over the edge. As he accelerated towards the ground he closed his eyes and braced his body for the impact. During that brief moment he was disappointed that his life didn't flash in front of him. In fact the only thing he could think of as he fell was the word "Fuuuuccccckkkkk!!" Suddenly he stopped falling. He expected the impact to painful but he didn't feel a thing. He then felt himself rising slowly upwards into the air. *"I've obviously left my body now and so I can't feel any pain"* he thought. However just as suddenly he started falling back to earth again.

He opened his eyes and realised he wasn't dead and was actually still attached to the bungee cord. He looked down and saw Mike and Jason pissing themselves laughing. He glanced up and could just about make out Grant and Matt waving and although they were too far away to see for sure he was confident they were also laughing.

"Did you enjoy that big man?" Mike said as he helped Razor down.

"You fucking bastards! I thought I was fucking dead for a minute there" Razor replied.

"Well you were getting a bit cocky so we thought we'd treat you to a bit of Aussie humour mate."

"You fuckers" said Razor. He looked over at Dean, who was killing himself laughing. Rod still looked terrified and hadn't even broken out into a smile.

Mick and Tim both completed their jumps without any hitches or practical jokes and they all headed over the road to the nearest pub.

"I'm still fucking shaking" said Razor as Dean handed him a pint.

"That was the best £10 that I never spent. Your face was a picture" Dean replied.

"Talking of pictures, I'm looking forward to this week's offering" said Razor referring to the photo of Dean and the hooker from the previous evening.

"Touché" Dean replied as he took a long drink from his pint.

Chapter 24
Week 4 - Tuesday

"This is all your fucking fault" Tim said to Mick as they sat in the waiting room of the Sexually Transmitted Diseases Clinic.

"How is it my fault? I never gave that fucking bird anything. She gave it to me" Mick replied.

"Maybe, but if you hadn't decided to shit in her bed and then nick her purse then I wouldn't have met her would I" said Tim in an aggressive whisper.

"I only told you to go round and give her the purse back. I don't remember at any point instructing you to shag her" Mick said shaking his head.

"Well I'm just saying that if you hadn't asked me to take that purse round to her then I wouldn't be here now."

"And I'm just saying that if you can't control yourself then you deserve everything that you get, including lumps on your dick!" Mick replied with a chuckle. "Anyway I should be the one who's pissed off as you seem to be forgetting that you nicked my fucking bird."

"She wasn't actually your bird was she? Or was the shit in her bed your way of marking your territory?" Tim replied with a smirk.

Before Mick could respond a nurse appeared with a clipboard. "Mr Smith?" she shouted out. Both Mick and Tim stood up. She stared at them with a disbelieving look. "Have you brought a urine sample?" They both nodded. "OK can you take it over to the main desk and a doctor will be with you shortly. Tim and Mick picked up their rucksacks and walked over to the desk.

"When we phoned we were asked to bring a sample and the nurse has just told us to give it to you" Tim said as he opened his bag. The receptionist nodded. Tim rustled around in his bag, pulled out a small pill vial filled with his urine and handed it over whilst Mick was still fiddling with the clasps on his bag. Mick eventually got his bag open and slapped a jumbo sized jar of Nescafe, filled with around a pint of dark brown urine, onto the counter. The receptionist stared wide-eyed at the jar.

"Is that alright" Mick asked.

"Well there is certainly plenty of it" the receptionist replied with a surprised look as she picked up the enormous glass jar.

"Well they told us to bring our first urine of the day and mine's always a big one" Mick replied looking pleased with himself. "That was the only thing that I could find that would hold it all."

"We just need a sample, to test" the receptionist replied with a smile.

"Oh right" said Mick starting to turn red as he looked at the tiny plastic pill bottle sitting on the counter in front of Tim. "I'll just take a seat" he said as he scurried back to the seating area. Tim, who was now pissing himself laughing, followed him.

"You could have fucking told me that they only wanted a some of your first piss of the day" said Mick whose face was now bright red.

"I did" Tim replied. "Did you wash that jar out?"

"Yeah, I gave it a rinse, why?"

"Because the liquid was dark bloody brown. I bet when they do the tests your caffeine levels will be off the scale. They'll probably rush you straight in for some sort of emergency operation" said Tim crying with laughter.

"Fuck off" said Mick who was relieved to see that the nurse was coming back.

"Mr *John* Smith?" she said looking at both of them.

"That's me" Tim replied.

"Follow me" she said and walked towards a small room on the right hand side of the corridor. "Please take a seat. The doctor will be in to examine you in a few minutes" she said and closed the door, leaving Tim alone in the room. The room was plastered with posters about STD's, all of which carried graphic close up photos of infected genitals. As Tim caught sight of a picture of a giant penis covered in scabs his groin started to feel extremely itchy and he started scratching it. At that moment the doctor entered. To his horror the doctor was not only a woman but an extremely attractive woman. He stopped scratching and tried to look casual as he stood up and offered his hand. The doctor sat down without shaking it.

"Hello Mr Smith I'm Doctor Jackson" she said. "Your notes say you've developed some lumps around the base of your penis. Is that correct?" Her manner was assertive making her even more attractive to Tim.

"That's right" Tim whispered as he cleared his throat in an attempt to combat his embarrassment.

"OK, if you can just drop your trousers and shorts I'll take a quick look" the doctor said as she put on a pair of rubber gloves.

Tim stood up, slowly unbuckled his belt and pulled down his trousers to reveal his penis which disappointingly looked much smaller than he was hoping it was going to.

"OK, can you point out the infected area" the doctor said as she pulled her chair nearer to him.

"Erm, it's just there" Tim said pointing at a group of lumps, the size of peppercorns, clustered at the base of his penis.

"And how long have you had them?"

"About a week. It started getting really itchy and then these lumps appeared" Tim said as he remained standing in front of her with his trousers around his ankles. As he looked down at the hot female doctor inspecting his penis the phrase *"Go on, you know you want to"* flashed into his mind, but he managed to restrain himself enough not to actually say it out loud.

"OK, you can get dressed again now *Mr Smith*" she said sitting back on her chair. "The condition you have contracted is Genital Warts, which is one of the most common STD's."

"I don't really understand how I've picked it up as I always make sure I wear a condom" said Tim.

"Unfortunately Mr Smith warts are passed on by skin contact and so if your partner has the condition then you can pick it up simply from touching their skin. It is entirely feasible that the condom has ridden up a little and exposed the base of your penis, thus allowing the condition to infect that area."

"Is it treatable?" asked Tim.

"Yes. I'll give you a prescription for a spray which freezes the warts so that they dry up and disappear. You must keep the area dry as much as possible and refrain from any further sexual activity until they have cleared up. You can get dressed now."

"Oh right" said Tim, realising that he was still standing with his trousers around his ankles. "How long will it take to clear up? Will they be gone by the weekend?"

"Well everybody is different but they should certainly have cleared within two to three weeks."

"That's not too bad then is it? Tim replied, trying to make light of his condition. As he buckled his belt back up he decided to make the most of the situation. "Would you like to come out with me?" he asked with a cheeky smile.

"Excuse me?" the female doctor replied.

"Would you like to come out with me for dinner or a drink?" Tim said boldly.

"I don't think that would be appropriate."

"Oh come on, it'll be fun. Why not?" Tim said jovially.

"I'll tell you why not *Mr Smith*. Firstly I am your doctor and doctor-patient relations are strictly forbidden and secondly, unless you have forgotten, this is a clinic for people who have sexually transmitted diseases and is therefore not the sort of place that I am looking to meet a boyfriend."

"Right, I see. Well if you change your mind my mobile number is on the form" Tim muttered, trying to hide his embarrassment. The doctor looked at him with a withering glare. "Thanks then, I'd better be off" Tim said as he moved towards the door.

"Hang on a minute Mr Smith. There are a number of other STD's going around at the moment and whilst you're here we should really check to make sure you don't have any other problems" the doctor said as she opened a drawer and pulled out a thin glass rod around twelve inches long. "I just need to slip this down the middle of your penis to check."

"Actually I'm feeling a lot better now thanks so I won't trouble you any further" Tim replied as he bolted out of the door.

"Another one ask you out Sally?" the nurse asked as she entered the room and saw Doctor Jackson sitting with the glass rod in her hand.

"Yep" she replied. "You know I just don't know where these blokes get their balls from. They come in here riddled with disease and expect me to swoon and fall at their feet. I tell you the next bloke that asks me out whilst I'm inspecting his warty dick is definitely going to get this shoved down the end of it. Who's next?"

"Would you believe it's another Mr Smith?"

"OK, send him in" Doctor Jackson replied.

A minute later Mick appeared at the door. As soon as he saw that the doctor was an attractive woman he stood up a little taller and started to straighten out his crumpled shirt. "Hello, I'm Mr Smith" he said, "Peter Smith. Now what is a fine looking girl like yourself doing working in a place like this?"

"Here we go again!" Doctor Jackson thought to herself as she put the glass rod down, ignored Mick's offer of a hand shake and gestured for him to sit down.

Chapter 25
Week 5 - Friday

"This is fucking great stuff Deano" said Razor who, despite sitting on a packed Jubilee line train, was inspecting the photo of Dean and Nina from the previous Friday evening. "At least you know that if the law thing doesn't work out you've got a fall back career as a porn star."

"Very funny, now let's put that away before the whole carriage sees it" Dean replied grabbing the photo out of Razor's hand and putting it back into the envelope. "I've got a meeting this afternoon so I can't hang around today."

"Me neither" Razor replied "I'm having a beer with some new candidates this afternoon."

"More beers? Your job just seems to be a constant stream of beers with potential new candidates" Dean replied shaking his head.

"I know, it's great isn't it?" Razor responded with a smile.

"Anyway we're here now"" said Dean as they pulled into Canary Wharf station.

Dean bought a copy of the Evening Standard and headed to All Bar One for a pint whilst Razor walked to the offices of Jacobs & Co. Razor returned twenty minutes later.

"I'll tell you what Deano, I reckon I'm in with that receptionist bird."

"Really?" Dean replied sounding as uninterested as he possibly could.

"Yeah, every week she seems to be wearing skimpier tops and getting more and more flirty. She's gagging for it."

"Ever thought that the reason she's wearing skimpier clothes is that it's now summer?" Dean replied without looking up from the paper.

"Don't talk bollocks mate. I'm telling you she's bang up for it."

"Anyway, on a less important note did you get this week's envelope?" Dean asked sarcastically.

"Envelopes" Razor corrected him as he reached into his bag and pulled out two envelopes. They looked similar to the ones from the previous week, a thin A4 envelope and an A5 envelope around an inch thick. Razor placed both envelopes onto the table in front of them.

"Oh fuck, what now?" said Dean looking at the A5 envelope and guessing it was filled with cash. He picked up the A4 envelope and pulled out the letter.

"Dear Dean,

Congratulations on another successful week. So far, so good, you're now 40% of the way there. I don't know if you did the deed yourself or paid someone else to do it for you but either way it's nice to know that someone's having a good time with my money even after I'm dead. Anyway, onto this week's challenge:

'BISCUIT GAME'

I'm not sure if you know what this is but if not let me explain. As the previous two challenges have been based around shagging birds I thought I'd mix it up a bit this week and introduce everyone's second favourite pastime; masturbation! The Biscuit Game is something I heard about from an old public-school friend of mine who went to an all-boys' boarding school. Apparently when the lads in the dorm used to get bored a group of them would play it late at night. All you need to play is a digestive biscuit (the bigger the better, for reasons that will become obvious) and a group of deranged perverts. The rules of the game are simple. The group sits in a circle and the biscuit is placed on the floor in the middle. Each participant then gets their cock out and starts wanking themselves off. The aim of the game is to come as quickly as you possibly can and when you do you spunk all over the biscuit. The last member of the group to come is the loser and his forfeit is that he has to eat the biscuit! I must admit that I never tried the game myself but it sounds like a hoot doesn't it? So your challenge this week is to get a photograph of at least three members of the house playing the game. I'm aware that this is without doubt the most difficult challenge to date as nobody in their right mind is going to want to play so I've arranged for Mr Jacob to provide more cash for you to use to bribe people to do it. Once again it's up to you how you spend it and if you decide that the task is impossible then you can keep the lot but as you know you will then forgo your inheritance and you will all need to move out by the end of the week.

Anyway, good luck mate and hopefully we'll be in touch again in a week's time.

Your friend,

Dougie"

"Dougie was always a sick mother-fucker" Razor said as he lit a fag.

"I've been humiliated enough already, there's no way that I'm getting involved in some stupid fucking wanking circle at my age" said Dean as he scrunched the paper into a ball and threw it onto the floor. "The whole thing is definitely a non-starter this time."

"Calm down there fella, don't be too hasty" said Razor seeing that Dean looked serious. "Let's not forget the bigger picture here. Remember what's at stake and what we're playing for in this game. I agree this task is a fucked-up sick one, but let's have a look at how much cash Dougie has given us and think about whether we can do it." Razor said as he picked up the A5 envelope and tipped out the bundle of £50 notes onto the table.

"Fucking hell Razor, be a bit more discrete" said Dean as he scooped up the notes from the table and started counting them. "There's about £2,500" Dean said still looking unimpressed.

"£2,500? Fucking hell Dean you can get somebody shot for less than that. I'm sure that we can get a couple of the lads to have a quick wank for that sort of money."

"Maybe, but we need three people in order to succeed" Dean replied staring at Razor "and there is no fucking way on earth that I'm doing it."

"Let's just see how it goes" Razor replied as he put out his fag and took a sip from his pint.

****

"So how long have you been seeing Mel now mate?" Urban asked Daisy as he handed him a pint of Stella.

"Must be about five or six weeks now I suppose."

"So would you go as far as to use the 'G' word yet then?" Urban asked.

"I'm not sure about that, but I do really like her."

"So have you seen much other action since you've been seeing her?"

"To be honest I haven't even thought about it" Daisy replied.

"Fucking hell mate, it must be serious. Do you *love* her?"

"I dunno. I might do." Daisy said, surprising himself with his response.

"You might do?" Urban exclaimed. "After five weeks? Fucking hell mate this is serious. You want to put down that pint right now, get yourself round to her place, get out your pipe and slippers and live happily ever. Looks like I need to find a new pulling partner."

"All I'm saying is that I really like her, there's nothing wrong with that is there?" "Nothing at all mate. In fact I haven't been to a good wedding for ages" Urban replied with a laugh.

"Oh fuck off and get me another Stella" Daisy replied as he finished his pint.

Two hours and six pints of Stella later they found themselves in a very packed late night Soho bar-cum-club.

"What time is it Urban?"

"Twelve thirty mate, why?" Urban replied as the barman delivered the two double vodka red bulls he'd just ordered.

"It's just that Mel sent me a text earlier saying she was now at home and that if I finished up early enough then I could go round there" Daisy replied sheepishly.

"Look around you mate. It's wall to wall totty in here tonight and things are just getting started. I need a good wing man if I'm going to be engaging any of these ladies in crossfire so there is no fucking way you're going home."

"I was just saying in case you were feeling tired or anything like that."

"That's what these fuckers are for" Urban responded as he handed Daisy his double vodka red bull. "Now, what d'ya reckon on those two birds over there" he said gesturing towards two girls sitting on high stools along the opposite wall. The two girls in question were slim, attractive, were both wearing short skirts and cropped tops which showed off their pierced belly buttons. One was tall with long straight blonde hair and had a tattoo of a dolphin on her left shoulder. The other was smaller, had brown hair cut into a bob and had a thin Celtic armband tattoo on her right arm. Daisy nodded to acknowledge that he thought that the girls were OK.

"Right, we're both footballers" Urban said as he took a large gulp from of his drink.

"What? Can't we just have another couple of drinks and go home? I'm not interested in pulling" said Daisy.

"No we can't. Just because you're all loved-up doesn't mean that we have to stop talking to girls does it? OK then, as I said we're both footballers."

"Footballers? That'll never work. Some birds are into their football. They might rumble us" Daisy responded shaking his head.

"No they won't. We don't say that we play for Arsenal or Chelsea or anyone like that. We're both in the first team at Brentford; they'll never fucking know anyone there. Right I'm left back and you're centre forward, OK?"

"But I usually play at the back, you know sweeper" Daisy responded.

"Look it's only a make-believe bollocks story, you can play wherever the fuck you want. If it makes you happy you're the sweeper then. All we need to do is make sure that we're consistent OK?" Urban replied. "Now let's go over and say hello." Daisy reluctantly nodded his agreement and they walked over to where the girls were in deep conversation.

"Excuse me ladies, but do you mind if we join you?" Urban asked politely.

"Yes we do" the blonde replied abruptly and returned to their conversation.

"Alright, fair enough. How about you let us buy you a drink if I can make you laugh? If not then we'll go away? That's got to be a reasonable request hasn't it?" Urban replied.

"OK, you've got thirty seconds" the blonde responded as she stared at Urban, as if daring him to make her laugh.

"OK, although I have to say that you do look like a tough audience" Urban said as he laughed and glanced at Daisy. Both girls stared at him expressionless waiting to hear what he had to say.

"Right, a bloke goes up to a girl in a club and asks if she'd like to dance. She gives him a filthy look and replies dismissively 'not with you' to which he responds 'Oh, I'm sorry love you must have misheard me, I said you look a right fat cunt in that skirt!'"

Urban waited apprehensively for a moment before both of the girls burst out laughing. "Right then, what can I get you to drink?" he asked.

"Vodka red bull" the blonde replied and the brunette nodded to indicate that she wanted the same. Urban and Daisy shot off to the bar and returned with the drinks a couple of minutes later.

"So you like my joke then ladies?" Urban asked.

"Well I don't like people using the 'C' word but I have to admit that it was quite funny" the brunette replied. "My name's Amy."

"I'm Urban and this is Daisy" Urban replied, shaking hands with both girls. The blonde introduced herself as Chloe.

"Urban and Daisy? What are your real names?" Amy asked.

"My name's John and he's Colin but everyone calls us Urban and Daisy. It's a long story, don't ask" Urban replied.

"I won't" Amy responded as she shook her head and laughed.

"So what do you lads do for a living then?" Chloe asked, directing her question towards Daisy to indicate she was interested in him rather than Urban. Urban braced himself for Daisy's response. He didn't want to face another evening explaining that accountancy was actually quite cool and gave him good career prospects. Girls in their early twenties weren't interested in career prospects. They wanted a good time and to meet someone interesting. Accountants simply didn't fit the bill.

"It's a bit embarrassing really" said Daisy, causing Urban to wince. "We both play football."

"Football?" Chloe responded looking like she didn't believe a word of it. "I don't recognise either of you. Who do you play for?"

"Brentford" Daisy replied, "that's why it's a bit embarrassing."

"How much do you get paid playing for Brentford then?" Chloe asked.

"Nothing like the big boys unfortunately" Daisy replied. "With win bonuses you can pull in a decent six figure salary though."

"So how come you're out on the piss tonight? Haven't you got a game tomorrow?" Chloe asked, still looking unconvinced.

"No, the season's over now so we've got six weeks off. It's a bit like being back at school again" Daisy replied, thinking on his feet.

"So what sort of crowds do you get at Brentford then?" Chloe asked, in an attempt to catch Daisy out.

"Not huge, usually about four or five thousand but we can get double that for a big match" he said starting to get into the part.

"Do you get a lot of female admirers then?"

"Not one's that you would want" Daisy responded, laughing. "It's usually football mad grannies with beards or twelve year old girls. Nobody hot like you" he said leaning forward and touching her arm. Chloe didn't flinch and he could sense that things were going well. "Another drink ladies?" Daisy asked and they both nodded.

Chapter 26
Week 5 – Saturday

Daisy could feel his brain throbbing, he felt hot, his mouth was bone dry and worst of all it tasted of garlic, which made him desperate for some water. He opened his eyes and was surprised not to see the familiar sight of the ceiling in his bedroom. It wasn't that his ceiling was particularly remarkable, in fact he'd have struggled to describe it in detail to anybody, but it was the comforting sight that he recognised when he woke up every morning. The strange ceiling above him brought the events of the previous evening flooding back to him, as if he was flicking through scenes of a movie on DVD. First there was bar where he and Urban had started talking to the two girls, then there was the dancing, then the kissing, then the kebab (obviously with lashings of garlic sauce), then the taxi, then the calm of the girl's bedroom and finally the frantic sex. Having brought himself up to speed on where he was he took a deep breath and glanced at his watch; seven thirty. He calculated that he'd had three hours sleep, at most. *"I need to get out of here"* he thought.

Daisy quietly swivelled around and sat up on the side of the bed which caused his head to spin. The girl in bed next to him showed no sign of movement. She was either in a deep sleep or was pretending to be asleep and waiting for him to go to avoid an embarrassing conversation. Either way Daisy didn't care and just wanted to leave. He suddenly had a flashback of the 'footballer' blag he and Urban had pulled and decided it was definitely time to leave as he didn't want to face any awkward questioning on that topic in the cold light of day. As he stood up he glanced briefly at a framed photograph on the bedside table. He looked around the floor for his clothes but before he spotted them he suddenly did a double take back to the photograph. He stared at it for a few seconds in disbelief. There was nothing extraordinary about the photo itself, a shot of two girls in graduation gowns with their arms around each other. However the thing that caught his attention was that the girl he had just spent the night with, Chloe, was standing with her arm around Mel, his girlfriend.

Daisy put his hands on his head and stood silently in a blind panic. His initial instinct was to grab his clothes, get out of the house and disappear. The problem with that plan was that he really liked Mel and he had no idea who this girl Chloe was. She was obviously very close to Mel and he couldn't take the risk of accidentally bumping into her when he was out with Mel, or worse still being invited round to her place for dinner. After thinking it through for a minute he reluctantly decided to grab the bull by the horns and wake Chloe. She was facing away from him with the duvet wrapped around her. He gave her a shake and her slow, confused response indicated to him that she had actually been asleep rather than faking it.

"Hi you" she said blinking the sleep away from her eyes. "Did you sleep OK?" She sat up and looked at herself in the mirror mounted on the opposite wall. "God I look a right state, that's what happens when you don't take your make up off before going to sleep."

"Yeah, I slept fine thanks" Daisy replied, wondering how best to broach the subject of her friend.

"So what are you doing today?" Chloe asked. "Not playing football, it's the close season" she said with a grin, referring to their conversation the previous evening.

"Yeah, I wasn't entirely truthful about the football thing" Daisy said wanting to gauge her reaction to this first piece of negative news.

"I know" she said "but I fancied you anyway so I thought I'd play along with your little game. So what are you doing today? Have you got plans or do you fancy grabbing lunch somewhere?"

"Err, it might be a bit difficult today" Daisy replied feeling flattered that Chloe wanted to spend more time with him but desperate to raise the issue of Mel. He decided to take the easy option and picked up the photo. "Who's this?" he said nonchalantly.

"That's my best friend Mel. We met at Uni and have been best mates since. She was out with us before we met you last night. She's seeing this new bloke that she's mad about and went home when we went to the club as she was hoping he would go round. Why, do you fancy her? Everyone does" Chloe replied as she rubbed her eyes.

Daisy was now shitting himself and immediately started worrying that Mel might turn up to see Chloe any minute. He desperately wanted to get dressed and get out of the house but knew that he had to bite the bullet. "Err, yeah she's very attractive" he mumbled. "Look, there's no easy way of saying this so I'll just come out with it. I'm Mel's new boyfriend, the one you said that she's mad about" he said, suddenly realising that he was standing in front of Chloe stark bollock naked. He grabbed the bed sheet and pulled it across him to protect his modesty.

"What? You can't be. He's called Col…." She stopped mid sentence, closed her eyes and put her head into her hands. "Oh fuck!"

"Oh fuck is right" said Daisy sitting down on the bed. "So what are we going to do about it?"

"Well firstly I'm going to do this" Chloe said as she slapped him hard across the face. "You are a lying, conniving, cheating bastard and you don't deserve someone like me or Mel" she said, starting to cry. "I just went out looking for a bit of fun last night and end up sleeping with my best friend's new boyfriend. How unlucky is that?" she said to herself shaking her head.

"I know, you're right, I'm sorry. But I do really like Mel and if we can keep this to ourselves I promise you that I won't ever do anything like this again" pleaded Daisy.

"How am I meant to believe that? All you've done is lie to me since I met you. 'No I don't have a girlfriend. I'd love to take you out next week. Did I mention I'm a professional footballer?"' Chloe said mimicking Daisy's voice.

After wiping away her tears and sitting in silence for a couple of minutes she continued. "Even though I think you're a complete bastard Mel is happier at the moment than she's been for a long time and I don't want to be the one to spoil that. So I won't say anything to her about last night as long as you promise not to."

"I promise" Daisy replied sincerely.

"If I hear about you stepping one foot out of line I will tell her straight away what you are really like, do you hear me?"

"Loud and clear" said Daisy. "From now on I'm going to be the model boyfriend."

"I severely doubt that. Anyway, fuck off out of my room. I never want to see you again, you bastard" she shouted as she rolled herself back up in the duvet.

Daisy gathered up his clothes and rapidly got dressed. He closed the bedroom door and headed for the front door. He stopped for a second and tried to remember if Urban had come back to the flat with them. He couldn't remember but decided that if he was still there he could find his own way home. *Why didn't I just go round to Mel's when I was going to? This is all Urban's fault making me talk to those birds"* he thought as he left the flat and walked off in search of a tube or train station.

****

"If we're going to persuade anyone to play this stupid fucking game it's got to be tonight" Dean said to Razor as they sat having a pint on Saturday afternoon.

"If everyone is a bit pissed up they might do it for the cash."

"True" said Razor "then again I wouldn't do it for any amount of money. It's sick and perverted if you ask me."

"Well just as well that I'm not asking you then isn't it?" Dean replied. "What are you doing tonight anyway?"

"I'm meeting up with a Lapdancer I got off with on Wednesday night" Razor replied.

"Where did you meet her?"

"In a fucking lapdancing bar, stupid" Razor responded.

"What? You're going out with a bird that you've already paid to take her clothes off? Isn't that a bit like paying for it?"

"Well you'd know all about that wouldn't you?" Razor replied with a grin. "Hey, talking of that have you seen that bird again yet?"

"No I fucking haven't. She keeps leaving voicemails on my mobile saying that she really needs to see me and that she loves me. It's got to the point where I feel sick every time the bloody thing rings" Dean replied.

"Why did you give her the number if you didn't want her to call?"

"Oh you know what it's like, I felt a bit guilty on the night and all that."

"No, I never feel guilty about birds. Love 'em and leave 'em, that's my motto" Razor replied as he lit the fag that had been hanging from his mouth for the past thirty seconds.

"I thought your motto was 'Live fast, die young and have a good looking corpse'?"

"Yeah, that as well" Razor responded nodding his head. "You can have more than one motto you know".

"Can you? I thought a motto was meant to be a mission statement. How can you have more than one?" Dean asked.

"Because I'm a man of many missions" Razor replied with a grin. "Anyway stop changing the subject. Who do you think might be up for this stupid fucking game of yours?"

"Well Urban, Mick and Rod are always brassic so I'm hoping they'll do it for the cash. If they don't then it looks like I'll just be getting £2,500 of Dougie's cash rather than the house" said Dean.

"Well, good luck. I've got to shoot off to see a man about a dog. Hope it all goes well, although I must admit I'm not really looking forward to seeing the photos from this week" Razor said as he stood up and finished his pint.

Dean finished his drink and headed back to the house. Urban was sitting in the living room watching football.

"Alright mate, is anyone else around?" Dean asked.

"I haven't seen anyone but I've only just got in myself" Urban replied, looking very pleased with himself.

"Oh yeah? Did you pull last night then?"

"I certainly did" Urban responded.

"Did you get a shag?"

"Not *a* shag, three shags" Urban replied holding up three fingers on his right hand to emphasise the point. "Two last night and one this morning just before I left."

"Sounds like you're getting over the split with Charlotte alright then" Dean said rhetorically. "I must admit that I've always been a big fan of the morning-after shag. You don't have any of the 'will she let me?' worries that you have before you first get your end away, you're more sober than you were the night before so you enjoy it more and you can last for ages as you've already shot your load once or twice during the night and your body is still full of ale. In fact, now that I'm thinking about it, I reckon the morning-after is one of the best shags."

"You're so right. I was like a stallion this morning mate. I could've gone for hours. In fact it was going on so long I considered faking it at one point, but I decided that would have been just wrong so I managed to get there in the end" Urban replied.

"You're so considerate Urban. Have you ever faked it?" Dean asked.

"Not on a proper shag" Urban replied "I have occasionally on those pointless ones at four o'clock in the morning when you're so pissed that your nob's like a piece of wood and you know you're never going to come. What about you?"

Dean thought back to the previous Saturday evening when he had considered doing exactly that with Nina. The thought made him feel a bit depressed. "No, I've never faked it. My view is that at least one of you should enjoy it if your going to bother having sex so I always make sure that I do" he said as they both started chuckling. "So what are you up to tonight, are you seeing this bird again?"

"Nah, I don't think so. When she was pissed up last night she was talking about going out on a double date with her mate and Daisy, but all hell seemed to break loose this morning between those two for some reason so I think it's all off."

"What? Did Daisy shag her mate?"

"Well I think so, but as I said they had a massive barney this morning and he left their flat before me. I haven't seen him since to see what it was all about."

"I thought he was getting serious with that Mel bird he brought to our party?" Dean asked.

"Yeah, he is. Maybe he told the bird this morning that he's seeing someone and she freaked out. Who knows? Anyway what are you doing tonight?"

"I've just picked up another one of those cash dares from Dougie's solicitor so I was going to see if anyone fancied giving it a go" Dean said hoping to reel Urban in by dangling the bait.

"Is it as fucked up as the one from last week?"

"Nah, it's got nothing to do with shagging or anything like that. This one's more of a lads' party game" Dean replied, once again stretching the truth.

"Sounds alright" said Urban "How much cash are you talking about? I'm skint at the moment and could do with some extra dough."

"£750 each."

"£750? I could do with a bit of that. Count me in. What do I need to do?"

"All will be revealed later."

"Well whatever it is it can't be as humiliating as shagging a hooker. I don't blame Rod for shitting out of that one" Urban replied, still unaware of what had actually happened that night.

"Hmmm" Dean responded, feeling sick as the images from his evening with Nina came flashing back into his mind. "Anyway, if you see any of the other lads and they fancy earning a bit of easy money make sure you tell them to hang around the house tonight" Dean said, as he got up and headed to his room. As he walked up the stairs he looked at his mobile and saw that he had three new texts and three missed calls, all from Nina. He went into his room, sat on his bed and deleted the messages without reading them. *"Fucking hell Dougie, what other shit have you planned to get me into?"* he thought as he lay back on his bed.

****

Dean was woken by Daisy banging around in his room at about seven pm and decided to have a chat with him about the bird he'd pulled with Urban. However, after the first few comments Daisy appeared extremely touchy and Dean decided to change his tack from taking the piss to calming him down.

"We've all done it mate. It's a well know fact that it's physically impossible for a bloke in his twenties to remain faithful, you only need to look at Urban to see that. He had a gorgeous girlfriend but just couldn't stop himself shagging other birds. It's all to do with excess testosterone so it's not really your fault it's down to Mother Nature" Dean said.

"I know you're trying to make me feel better but just leave it, OK?" Daisy responded aggressively. "I really like Mel and I've fucked up big time so I just want to put it behind me and the less people that know about this the better."

"Whatever you say" Dean replied as he left Daisy's room. He wondered why he was being so touchy. They'd all made a few mistakes along the way but as long as only the boys knew about it you were safe. Nobody would let slip, that was the lads' code, so Dean couldn't understand Daisy's reaction. *"Probably just feeling a bit guilty about it just now"* he thought.

A few minutes later Daisy left and Dean assumed that he was off to Mel's place. He wasn't the only one seeing his woman that night. Annoyingly for Dean, Mick and Gill were still hard at it, mainly in Mick's room which was directly above Dean's bedroom. Dean couldn't work out whether Gill was doing it just to piss him off and to get her revenge for the threesome incident or if she really liked Mick. Either way it was highly tedious, and slightly frustrating, to see her constantly wandering around the house in her underwear or in Mick's T-shirts. It was also a constant reminder of one of the low points in Dean's life.

The final member of the house who had a date that night was Glynn, who was seeing his bird for what seemed to Dean like the 100th consecutive night. Dean didn't have a problem with the fact that Glynn had a girlfriend, but what did irritate him was that Glynn insisted on going through the age-old routine of seeking Dean's opinion on his outfit before going out.

"What about this one?" Glynn asked as he stood in a beige linen suit and a bright open neck orange shirt. It was the third outfit he had showed Dean already.

"Are you going to a 1970's fancy dress party?" Dean asked as he stared in amazement at Glynn's latest choice.

"No, we're going for a meal at a new restaurant that's just opened in the West End. Heather's mate knows the sommelier and he's managed to get us a table. Apparently loads of celebrities have been seen there so I want to look a bit flash" Glynn responded refusing to acknowledge Dean's continuing sarcasm.

"Flash, yes. A twat, no" Dean replied pointing at Glynn's attire.

"So you think this is a bit over the top?" Glynn asked.

"That's one way of putting it" Dean replied returning to the pages of FHM.

"Right, don't go away, I'll be back in a minute" said Glynn as he disappeared back to his room.

"Can't wait" Dean whispered to himself.

Glynn returned five minutes later in a pair of brand new jeans that had rips and holes all over them, and a yellow Sex Pistols 'God Save the Queen' T-shirt which also had a couple of designer rips in the side.

"Tann aaahh!" Glynn said flamboyantly holding out his hands as if he had just performed a magic trick.

"Where the fuck did you get that from?" Dean asked shaking his head.

"There's a new place opened down the Kings Road. It's not cheap but they've got loads of really cool gear" Glynn replied.

"So why didn't you buy any of it?" Dean replied, astounded by Glynn's outfit.

"Very funny" Glynn replied. "Seriously though, what do you think?"

"Well, you'll certainly get noticed. In fact if it is a celebrity hang out it wouldn't surprise me if you made it into the tabloids as everyone will automatically assume you must be famous if you're dressed like that" Dean replied sarcastically.

"Honestly? Right I'm going with it then" said Glynn oblivious to the fact that Dean was taking the piss. "I bought it especially for tonight but I just wanted to see what you thought. Thanks Dean" he said as he disappeared back to his room.

"I'd love to see that sommelier's face when he arrives at the restaurant" thought Dean laughing to himself as he carried on reading his magazine.

****

By ten thirty they'd already drunk their way through two cases of beer and were getting a bit lively. Tim and Rod were sat on one sofa whilst Dean and Urban were on the other. They'd been playing drinking games for the past hour or so. As usual, Rod was doing really badly which meant he'd drunk a lot more than the rest, by way of forfeit.

"What are the fucking rules of this game again?" Rod asked as the others shouted at him to down the rest of his bottle for getting it wrong again.

"It's very simple" Dean replied. "As we've told you about twenty times already, all you need to do is say the name of a famous person. The next person has to take the first letter of that person's surname and use it to name another famous person whose Christian name starts with that letter. If I say George Bush, you take the

'B' of Bush and could then say Brad Pitt. You then take the 'P' of Pitt and say Paul McCartney, and so on."

"So what was wrong with Mickey Mouse?" Rod asked.

"Mickey Mouse doesn't exist, he's fictional and you can't have anyone that's fictional or dead. So by using a fictional name you lost and you have to down the rest of your beer" Dean replied.

"This is a shit game" Rod replied as he drank the remainder of his bottle.

"No, it's just that you're shit at it" Urban replied laughing. He was getting bored of watching Rod constantly downing his beers and decided to change the subject. "So Deano, what's this fucking dare that Dougie is offering £750 for?"

"Oh yeah, I almost forgot. Would any of you lads like to earn yourselves an easy £750?" Dean asked directing his question to Tim and Rod.

"Not if it involves shagging another hooker" Rod replied.

"What d'ya mean another one?" Tim responded. "You never actually shagged that one last week did you?"

"You know what I mean" Rod replied gesturing to Dean to continue.

"No, it doesn't involve any hookers, or dwarves or donkeys or anything like that. This time it's more of a lads' drinking game."

"Well if it's anything like this one I'll be shit at it" Rod replied, laughing as he opened another bottle of beer.

"No, I think you'll be quite good at this one actually, it's just up your street" said Dean chuckling to himself.

"So stop spinning it out and tell us what it is then" said Urban.

"It's called the 'Biscuit Game'" said Dean.

"Oh, fuck off! Not that shit!" Tim shouted, shaking his head.

"Do you know it?" Dean asked.

"Yeah a few of the fucked up older boys used to make the younger kids do it at my school while they all watched. It's a game for fucking benders" said Tim.

"What does it involve?" Urban asked.

"It's a group wanking game" Tim continued. "You all sit in a circle wanking over a biscuit. Everyone spunks onto it and the last one to come has to eat the fucking thing!"

"Oh fuck off!" Urban said staring at Dean. "You said that this one was a fun lads' game. What sort of twisted sense of fun have you got?"

"I know it's fucked up, but think of the money" Dean replied.

"How much did you say it's worth?" Rod asked.

"£750 each" Dean replied.

"Well there's no way I'm ever doing it" said Tim. "Too many bad memories" he continued, making the rest of them think that maybe he'd been one of those young boys he'd referred to.

"I'll do it for a grand" Urban said bluntly.

"No, Urban, it's not worth it" Tim cut in.

"Shut up, Tim" said Dean.

"Look Tim, you might come from a rich family that can bail you out whenever you need it, but I don't. I've got credit card bills coming out of my arse, student loans that I'm trying to pay off and I've just met a new bird. £1,000 will go a long way to giving me a bit of breathing space at the moment" Urban replied.

Dean quickly calculated that if he had to pay two of the lads £1,000 each to do it then he'd have to join the game himself as he only had a budget of £2,500 to play with. His only other option was to fail the challenge and lose the chance of getting the house. He therefore quickly resigned himself to his fate. "What about you Rod? Will you do it for a grand?" Dean asked consoling himself with the fact that he'd still make £500 out of it.

"Well, I could get rid of the scooter and buy myself a half decent bike for a grand" Rod replied. "Yeah, OK. But only on the basis that it goes no further than this room."

"Agreed" they all said together.

"It's not really something to brag about is it?" Urban said, expressing all of their thoughts.

"OK then, where do we start?" Rod said.

"Well I'd like to start by seeing the cash" said Urban.

"OK. Hang on here while I go and get it" Dean replied directing his comment specifically at Rod, who smiled in return.

"Don't forget the biscuit!" Urban shouted after him but nobody laughed and the word 'biscuit' seemed to hang in the air.

Dean returned a couple of minutes later, having made sure that the PC was set up to record their exploits.

In one hand he had an A5 envelope stuffed full of cash and in the other a packet of plain digestive biscuits.

"I don't like digestives" said Rod laughing nervously. "Haven't you got any chocolate ones?"

"Or Hob Nobs? Wouldn't they be more appropriate?" Urban followed up.

"Right, there's £1,000 each for you two here. I'll keep it on me just in case either of you bottle out" said Dean looking directly at Rod.

"I can't watch this. If you don't mind, I'm going to my room" said Tim excusing himself.

"Yeah, I can't imagine that it's going to be much of a spectator sport" said Rod. "Definitely better to play than watch."

"Not if you lose" Tim said seriously.

"Right then let's get started" said Dean placing a biscuit onto the floor and sitting on the edge of the sofa.

"After you big man" said Urban. Dean looked at Rod for support but found him staring straight back at him.

"OK then, but you two had better join in" Dean replied as he started to unbuckle his belt. "Just think of the money" he continued. He dropped his trousers and took his limp penis in his hand. Despite the fact that there didn't look to be any sign of getting an erection he started 'thrashing the bishop' anyway. "Don't forget" he said, without looking up from the job in hand, "the last one to come has to eat the biscuit."

As that thought registered with both Urban and Rod it caused a flurry of activity. They both frantically unbuckled their trousers and pulled their pants down. Dean was disturbed to see that Urban had a semi and

Rod had a full on erection. *"Am I the only one not turned on by this shit?"* he thought as he watched his two friends start masturbating furiously in front of him.

Thankfully Dean had worked out from the angle that if he sat with his back to the camera it would not be possible to see his penis, so he knew that he didn't need an erection for the purposes of the photo. All he needed was for the other two to look good enough to convince Razor and he could stop the game. *"That's good enough"* he thought as he imagined the photo and shouted "Stop!"

"What?" Urban said, slightly out of breath "Oh you've made me lose concentration now, that's cheating!"

"Stop!" Dean repeated. "You can both have your £1,000 anyway" he continued but the last part of the sentence was drowned out by Rod shouting "Geronimo!" as he shot his load over the biscuit.

"Right then you fuckers, let's see you eat that little lot" said Rod looking very pleased with himself as he held up the sodden digestive.

"Didn't you hear what I said?" said Dean who had zipped up his trousers and was staring at Rod like a naughty schoolboy.

"No, what?" Rod asked as he tidied himself up.

"I said that you can have the money anyway. We don't need to complete the game. Under the rules it was sufficient just to start it" Dean replied.

"Hang on a minute, rules are rules" said Rod. "You two have got to go head to head and the loser has to eat this fucking biscuit" he continued looking very pissed off. He suddenly realised what he was holding in his hand and dropped it onto the floor.

"I'm afraid not" said Dean "and there is no fucking way that I'm even touching that biscuit, let alone eating it.

"Me neither" said Urban laughing. "That's got to be the easiest £1,000 anyone has ever made!"

"You fucking pair of wankers!" Rod said. After a few seconds thinking about what he'd just said they all burst out laughing.

Dean gave the two of them their money and headed up to his room. He checked the DVD and was happy that he had a good enough still photo to satisfy Razor and therefore complete the task. *"Five down, five to go"* he thought to himself as he put the photo into the A4 envelope. *"Surely Dougie can't come up with anything more fucked up than this though."*

Chapter 27
Week 5 – Wednesday

"Where the fuck have you been?" Tim asked as Urban walked into the living room in his suit.

"I've been to work. Where do you think I've fucking been at five thirty on a Wednesday afternoon?" Urban replied as he flopped onto the sofa. "Why what's your fucking problem?"

"If you remember we've arranged to play golf tonight. We're due to tee off in half an hour so we need to get a move on" Tim replied.

"Oh fuck, you're joking aren't you? I thought that was tomorrow?" Urban said. "I'm ready for bed not eighteen holes of fucking golf."

"Well you're the one that's been giving Mick and Razor the big one for the last week about how we're going to thrash them so you're not getting out of it. You've got five minutes to get your stuff together" Tim said looking at his watch.

Urban slowly picked himself up off the sofa and made his way to his room. When he got to his bedroom he cut himself a large line of coke, just to give himself a boost of energy and by the time he came back down to the living room a few minutes later he was literally bouncing with energy. "Right then, let's get on with it then" he said. "Where's Mick and Razor?"

"They went up fifteen minutes ago so they could have a go on the range" said Tim. "I said that we'd see them up there."

"So are Mick and Razor any good then?" asked Urban as they got into Tim's car.

"Both of them played a bit when they were younger but haven't played much recently so I'd imagine they'll be a similar sort of standard to us" Tim replied.

"Speak for yourself" said Urban who, boosted by his line of coke, now fancied himself as a bit of a player.

"I suggest that you keep the cocky statements under wraps until we've played a few holes" said Tim.

When they arrived at the course Mick and Razor were practicing on the putting green next to the first tee.

"You don't want to bother practicing your putting Razor, it's the ten shots that you'll have had before you get onto the green that you want to worry about" shouted Urban, much to the annoyance of the other golfers who were quietly waiting to tee off.

"Drive for show, putt for dough" Razor replied with a smile as Urban joined him on the practice green.

"Don't give me any of that clichéd nonsense" said Urban. "All I know is that me and Tim are going to give you two a good spanking. So how much are you guys prepared to lose today then?"

"Well it was going to be five quid per head but if you're that confident why don't we make it a tenner?" Razor replied.

"I'd be happy to play for more but I suppose a tenner is OK. It'll be the easiest money that I'll make today and will taste even sweeter knowing that it came from you two" Urban said as they made their way up to the first tee. The tee was set back into a cutting of trees so they left their golf bags and trolleys at the front of the clearing where everyone was queuing and walked back to the tee box.

"Well then, if you're so confident you can have the honour" said Razor gesturing to Urban to tee off first.

Urban stepped forward and put his ball on his tee. "Watch and learn gentlemen" he said as he addressed the ball. He looked around and saw a group of eight blokes standing near to their bags, waiting to play. As he thought about them watching him he suddenly started to feel really nervous. He took a practice swing with his driver, dug a divot of grass out of the floor and received an ironic cheer from Mick and Razor.

"We're watching and learning" Razor shouted making Urban feel even more nervous. He took a deep breath pulled back his club and swiped at the ball. It flew off the heel of the club and shot at a hundred miles an hour towards where the eight blokes queuing were standing. All of the blokes started to duck as Urban finally managed to shout "Fo…." before the ball smashed straight into his own golf bag and ricocheted off into the bushes. Urban heard the raucous laughter behind him and turned to see Tim, Mick and Razor bent over double.

"Still watching and learning" said Razor as he wiped away his laughter tears.

"Oh fuck!" Urban said as he ran towards his golf bag. Some of the blokes queuing were also wetting themselves laughing whilst the rest were shaking their heads and mumbling things like 'someone that shit shouldn't be allowed to play.' Urban quickly unzipped the pouch where the ball had struck his bag and pulled out his mobile phone. The ball had impacted directly onto the screen causing it to shatter and the phone showed no sign of life. "My phone is totally fucked" he shouted to the others, holding it up. This produced another round of hilarious laughter from his playing partners and more tutting and head shaking from the blokes in the queue.

"Looks like it's down to you on this hole partner" Urban said to Tim as he walked back to the group. As they saw Urban approach with another ball in his hand the other three ran over to their bags and brought them next to where they were playing, out of Urban's firing line.

"Oh, ha ha!" Urban said. "Even the pro's hit a bad shot now and then you know?"

"We're just watching and learning" Razor replied with a smile. Urban responded with a shake of his head.

Tim stepped forward, put down his ball and cracked a perfect drive down the middle of the fairway. Mick strode up and after a couple of practice swings played a similar shot to Tim. It was then over to Razor.

"No pressure big man!" Urban shouted as Razor set himself up on the tee. He took a long drag on the cigarette he'd just lit and flicked it out to the side so that he could continue smoking it after he'd played his shot. The wind took the lit cigarette and, rather than land on the grass, it went straight into his golf bag. Razor dropped his driver and ran over to his bag, which now had smoke billowing out of it. He quickly tipped it upside down causing all of the clubs and a handful of balls to scatter over the tee. The cigarette eventually came out and Razor stamped it out. He looked round to see Mick, Tim and Urban applauding.

"We're watching and learning" Urban shouted with a smile. Razor looked over at the blokes who were queuing and saw they were all shaking their heads. He then returned to the tee, picked up his driver and topped his ball about fifty yards along the floor. Urban followed him and played a similar shot which ended up about seventy yards from the tee. They picked up their bags and made their way past the ever-growing queue of blokes.

"Looks like it's going to be a slow one today" said Razor to the queue with a smile as he topped his next shot another fifty yards along the floor.

Chapter 28
Week 6 - Friday

Dean and Razor found themselves in the now familiar lunchtime surroundings of All Bar One at Canary Wharf. They ordered a couple of pints and sat at their usual table. Dean handed over the envelope containing the photo of the 'Biscuit Game' that he'd refused to allow Razor to look at on the tube. Razor immediately opened it and pulled out the A4 photo.

"That is fucking sick Deano. I never had you down as a fudge packer but the camera doesn't lie" said Razor as he sat staring at the photo of Urban, Rod and Dean sitting in a circle masturbating. "Look at Rod he's got a full on stalk-on and actually looks like he's enjoying it. Unbelievable."

"You know exactly why I did it so don't start giving me any shit. If you were in my shoes you'd have done the same. In fact you should be thanking me as if I don't get through all of these fucking challenges then you'll get fuck all money from Dougie's will as well" Dean replied, taking a sip from his pint.

"Oh don't get me wrong Deano, I'm pleased that you've done it and all that but there's no way that I would have done any of the shit you've done over the past couple of weeks, money or no money. So who won then, or more importantly who fucking lost and had to eat the biscuit? Urgh, I genuinely can't think of anything worse that having to eat Rod's spunk!" Razor said holding out his tongue and pretending to gag.

"Look, just shut up and get that photo over to the old boy. I want to see what Dougie's got planned for me this week" Dean said, changing the subject.

"Alright, I understand that it must be hard to talk about it, what with the taste still practically fresh in your mouth. It's meant to be salty isn't it? Anyway when you're ready to talk I'm all ears, just remember that" he said, as he finished his pint and headed off.

Razor returned around twenty minutes later with two new envelopes. "Oh fuck" said Dean as he saw Razor holding up the fat A5 envelope.   "You know what that means don't you?"

"Yep" Razor replied, "more shit that nobody wants to do for free."

Dean ripped the top off the A4 envelope and pulled out the letter inside.

"Dear Dean,

Well, well, well! The fact you're reading this means that you managed to persuade two sick fuckers to join you in a group wanking session. It just shows you what people will do for money doesn't it? I suppose congratulations should be in order; I just hope that you didn't lose and if you did that you haven't picked up any nasty diseases! Anyway I thought it was time to move

*away from sex and onto a different type of challenge
this week. As they say in show business it's time to:*

'BREAK A LEG'

*Or an arm, it's up to you really. The challenge this
week is to see how much pain someone is prepared to
endure for money. You need to persuade someone in the
house (or if you wish you can do it yourself) to volunteer
to have their arm or leg deliberately broken by another
member of the house in return for a cash payment. It's
as simple as that. You need to get photographic evidence
of the act and Mr Jacob will once again provide you
with a pot of cash. It's up to you how you distribute
the money and you can keep all of it if you decide not
to take on the challenge but the usual forfeit rules will
then apply.*

*Anyway, good luck mate and hopefully we'll be in
touch again in another week's time.*

Your friend,

Dougie"

"Break an arm or leg? This is starting to get fucking
stupid. I mean that's not just something you can wake
up in the morning and forget about is it?" Dean said
shaking his head. "We'll need a lot of fucking cash to
persuade anyone to do it. How much is there?"

"Looks like there's about five grand" Razor said as
he counted out the money.

"Do you think anyone will go for it?" Dean asked.

"I dunno. It's a lot of money but it's a big fucking
ask. I mean it takes a couple of months to get over
something like that doesn't it?"

"Well it depends on how bad the break is" Dean
replied. "I broke my leg playing footie at school and it

still gives me jip now from time to time. However aside from the financial side of things there's also the moral issue. I've managed to convince myself over the past few weeks that I can put all these sex games behind me as a bit of harmless fun, but deliberately breaking someone's arm or leg for money, that's barbaric isn't it? I'm not sure I'm that comfortable with it."

"Well you'd better get comfortable quickly Deano as you've only got a week to sort this thing out" Razor replied as he finished his pint.

"I know" Dean replied as he sat staring at the pile of cash in front of him.

****

Mick looked at his watch. It was just after eight pm. He'd had every intention of going out for 'just one beer' after work but three hours after his first pint he was onto his seventh, or maybe even his eighth.

"I've got to go" he said "I was meant to meet my bird and some of her mates in Islington at seven thirty."

"Give her a ring and tell her you'll meet her later, or better still tell her to come round to yours with a takeaway" said Mick's work colleague Ronnie.

Despite the circumstances that had brought them together (which they never discussed) Mick was really keen on Gill and tried to see her as much as he could. If he'd been asked to make a rational decision on what to do on a Friday evening, spend time talking about banking with all the boring fuckers from the bank or have a few drinks and rampant sex with Gill, it would have been a no-brainer. However the perspective was slightly different when he was half pissed, stuck in a pub on the other side of town and in the middle of a discussion about the order in which he would like to nob all of the women who worked in the bank.

"Anyway, you can't leave yet, I've just bought you a new pint" Ronnie continued.

"OK, I'll have one more but then I'm definitely going" Mick replied as he drained his remaining half pint so that he could start the pint Ronnie was holding out for him. One of the problems of drinking in a round with the office crowd was that they all had to drink at Ronnie's pace which meant everyone quickly got very pissed.

"So are you going to ring your bird or not then? You'd better check in otherwise she'll be getting worried" said Ronnie sarcastically. "I never imagined that you were one of those under-the-thumb types Mick. It just goes to show that you never know."

"Fuck off" Mick replied, taking the bait. "I'm not under the thumb, it's just that I'm really late."

"Late for what?" Sharon, one of the secretaries, asked as she joined the conversation.

"He's meant to be meeting his bird" Ronnie said dismissively.

"I didn't know you were seeing someone" said Sharon. "Why didn't you tell me?"

"I'm not really seeing anyone, it's just a girl I met recently at a party" Mick lied. Sharon was the stereotypical Essex girl - blonde hair (peroxide), all over tan (fake), and a big personality. She brightened up otherwise dull days for the men at the bank with her short skirts, revealing tops and high heels. She had a reputation as a man-eater and Mick had always had a bit of a thing for her. Even though things were going really well with Gill he couldn't bring himself to admit to her that he had a girlfriend in case it spoiled his chances, especially as it looked like Ronnie was trying to use Gill as an angle to pull Sharon.

"So should I be worried or not?" Sharon asked as she flicked her long hair over her shoulder and batted her eyelashes at Mick. Mick suddenly forgot all about Gill and the fact that he was already almost an hour late.

"It depends what you're worried about" Mick replied as he put his arm around Sharon's waist and laughed. To both his surprise and delight she didn't move away, but allowed him to leave his arm where it was as she laughed along with him.

"Shouldn't you be getting off now?" Ronnie asked, changing his tune as he saw Sharon becoming receptive to Mick's advances. "You don't want to keep that lovely *girlfriend* of yours waiting any longer do you?"

"Ah, fuck her. She'll be OK, she's with her mates anyway so it doesn't really matter if I turn up or not" Mick replied. He felt pissed enough to make an unprovoked attempt to pull Sharon but the fact that Ronnie was now sniffing around her made him even more determined to have a go. "Right, who's up for a black sambuca?"

"Too right!" Sharon responded. Ronnie nodded his approval to Mick's suggestion.

"I'll come with you" Sharon said as Mick pushed his way to the bar. As she followed him through she put her hands on his hips, causing Mick to instantly forget all prior arrangements that he had for the evening.

Chapter 29
Week 6 – Saturday

Mick woke up with a start. For a few seconds he had no idea what day of the week it was. All he knew was that he had a raging hangover and was sweating like a bastard. As he opened his eyes he noticed that he was still wearing the suit and shoes he'd worn to work the previous day. As he tried to blink himself awake he was pleased to note that he'd made it back to his bedroom and that there was nobody in bed with him. However his thoughts suddenly turned to Gill. He closed his eyes and winced at the fact that he'd stood her up, especially as it had been the night when he was due to be vetted by her mates. The thought sent his head spinning and he put his hands over his face to make himself feel better. It didn't work. He looked at his watch, saw it was six thirty am and decided it was too early to do anything about the situation. The best thing for him to do was get undressed, get into bed and get some proper sleep, as opposed to the alcohol fuelled coma that he had just experienced.

Mick sat up on the bed and noticed that there was no sheet, duvet or pillows and that the mattress was completely bare. He looked around the room and saw that it was also completely barren, no clothes, CD's, no posters on the walls; nothing.

"Have we been burgled?" Mick thought as he tried to get his head around the situation. *"Strange that they've taken fucking everything though."*

He got up and walked out of the bedroom. The corridor was also completely stripped and as he walked through into the bare living room he suddenly realised that he was in his old flat in Hackney.

"What the fuck am I doing here?" Mick thought as he started to panic. The last thing he could vaguely remember about the previous night was being in a cab on his way home. He walked back into the bedroom and as he looked at the open window he had a flashback of shinning up the drainpipe. He looked down at his suit trousers, which were covered in all sorts of shit, and sat on the bed to collect his thoughts. When he'd lived in the flat he'd lost his keys more times than he cared to remember. Tim could never be relied upon to wake up and let him in so Mick permanently left his window open so that he could shin up the two stories and let himself in. Mick concluded that he'd been so pissed that he'd switched into autopilot, told the taxi driver to take him to Hackney by mistake and then climbed in through the window.

"Fucking lucky that no-one else has moved in since we moved out" he thought as he decided it was time to leave. He walked down the corridor to the front door, took a final glance around the flat, turned the lock and

pulled the door. It didn't budge. Mick looked at the lock and realised it had been double locked with a key. He rummaged around in his pockets, pulled out his keys for the house in Battersea and desperately tried to unlock the door. After a futile couple of minutes he gave up and slumped to the floor.

"FUCK!" he shouted in frustration, "why am I so fucking stupid?" He briefly thought of Gill and the alternative Saturday morning he should have been having with her, curled up together in bed.

He walked back into his old bedroom and looked down out of the window. He had climbed up the drainpipe at least ten times, but it had always been when he was pissed and had no fear. He'd never had cause to climb down before. The drop from the window was around fifty feet, more than enough to cause him serious injury if he fell. As he looked down he felt a wave of nausea sweep over him and started to feel dizzy. He steadied himself, took a deep breath and slowly climbed out onto the window ledge.

The drainpipe was an old heavy-duty cast iron pipe around eight inches thick. Mick had never given it a second thought before but he now wondered how old it was and how secure the fittings were. He stood up on the window ledge and stared at the drainpipe for a minute or so. It was only two feet away from the window and he'd never had a problem reaching across in the past but it was easier reaching out for a large flat ledge than a round pipe. He shuffled to the edge of the window ledge and leaned across to the pipe. He grabbed it with his right hand and followed up with his left. He still had both feet on the window ledge and was now positioned at a diagonal angle staring down at the pavement below. From this position the drop looked far worse than it had done when he was looking out from the safety of the bedroom. He briefly considered going back and trying to kick the door in but decided that it would probably be more difficult to get back onto the window ledge as the majority of his weight was now resting on the drainpipe.

Mick closed his eyes and swung his legs onto the pipe. The momentum of the swing caused him to start sliding down and he slipped about five feet or so, ripping the knee on his right trouser leg in the process. Just as he thought that he was about to plummet all the way to the bottom he came to a stop as his feet landed on one of the fittings holding the pipe to the wall. He opened his eyes and took a deep breath whilst continuing to cling to the pipe for dear life. All of the excitement had caused him to break out into a cold sweat and he started to feel really sick. He composed himself and gradually started inching his way down the pipe. Eventually, after what seemed like an hour but was probably more like ten minutes, he got to the bottom and gratefully stepped off onto pavement. He looked back up the pipe and wondered why he'd never realised just how high the window was before. As he stood looking up he felt a hand on his shoulder.

"May I ask what it is that you are doing sir?"

Mick turned round to see four uniformed police officers and two police cars.

"Well, it's quite a funny story really" he replied laughing to himself.

"Oh good" the officer with his hand on Mick's shoulder replied "as I haven't had a good laugh for ages" he said without any hint of humour in his voice. "Probably best if you tell it to us down the station though" he continued as he pushed Mick towards one of the cars.

"I'm fucked" thought Mick as he got into the back of the squad car.

They arrived at Stoke Newington Police Station five minutes later. Mick had been secretly impressed that the police officers had felt the need to turn on the sirens and drive at breakneck speed. *"Must be a slow morning"* he thought.

After giving his name and details to the guy on the front desk he was taken to an interview room and given a cup of coffee. Fifteen minutes later the two policemen who'd driven him to the station came in to interview him.

"So then Michael, can you tell us exactly what it was that you were doing this morning?"

"Well, it all started when I went for a couple of drinks after work last night" Mick said jovially. As neither of the policemen appeared to be amused he decided to cut the banter and stick to the facts. "Anyway I ended up staying longer than I'd wanted to and, to be honest, I probably had a couple of beers too many. I've recently moved house but after all of the beers I sort of forgot about that and ended up going back to my old flat. I must have shimmied up the drain pipe and climbed in through the open window as I woke up on the bed fully clothed this morning." As the words left his mouth he realised they sounded totally ridiculous to anyone who wasn't used to drinking themselves stupid every Friday night.

"So why didn't you just let yourself out this morning?"

"I would've but the door was locked from the outside so the only other thing I could think of was to climb back down the drainpipe" Mick replied.

"OK. We'll need to check with the owner of the property to get him to verify your story"

"Great" said Mick, relieved that his nightmare was coming to an end.

"However, before we can let you go we need to ask you a few questions about the stains on your trousers."

Mick looked down at his suit trousers and, for the first time, noticed that his groin area was covered in white stains. He suddenly had a flashback to the previous evening and had a vague recollection of a frenzied sex session with Sharon in the ladies toilets of the pub. He felt the colour drain from his face.

"Right" was all he managed to say.

"So would you like to tell us how you got them?"

"Erm, it's private, actually" Mick replied, shrugging his shoulders.

"I'm afraid that's not a good enough answer Mr Brady. You need to tell us what happened or we may need to arrest you."

Mick now started to feel like his nightmare was never going to end. He should have been tucked up in bed with Gill now but all because he'd gone for a quick beer after work he was now being interrogated and on the verge of being arrested, which would probably mean that he'd lose his job.

"OK, I had a few beers and I think I ended up having sex with one of the girls from my office in the toilet of the pub."

"You *think* that you had sex with one of the girls from your office in the toilet of a *pub*?"

"Yeah" Mick replied weakly.

"And is this something that the people from your office do on a regular basis?"

"No" Mick replied.

"Will the lady in question verify your story?"

"Well I'd rather that she didn't have to "Mick replied with an embarrassed smile.

"Well you'd better hope that she does. If she doesn't then it could be much more serious for you. If you're not 100% sure what happened how can you be 100% sure that it was consensual?"

Mick suddenly started to feel really sick. He was now facing a potential rape charge on top of breaking and entering. In addition he had the mother of all hangovers and it was highly likely that he no longer had a girlfriend. As he was taken back to the cells Mick couldn't believe that a few quiet drinks after work could turn his life upside down so quickly.

"It's all that fucker Ronnie's fault. If it hadn't been for him I'd have made it to Islington and had a really great evening with Gill and her mates" he thought to himself as he sat in his cell.

A few hours later, after the police had received verification of Mick's stories from firstly an amused former landlord and secondly a very un-amused Sharon, Mick was released without charge. As he left the police station he switched on his mobile and saw that he had twelve missed calls and five texts, all from Gill. He didn't have the stomach to listen to the voicemails but checked the final text. It simply read:

"Go fuck yourself!"

"Quite" Mick thought to himself as he made his way to the tube station.

****

Dean woke up feeling decidedly groggy. His throat was dry and his head sore but on the plus side he was in his own bed, alone (although at two thirty the night before he'd seen that as a negative), he still had all of his possessions and was relatively confident that he hadn't upset anyone. Overall therefore he should have been happy and content with the world but his demeanour was anything but.

The previous evening he'd met Tim and Rod for a few beers. Rod was still on a high after trading in his scooter and using the £1,000 he'd earned from the Biscuit Game to buy himself a second hand Ducati Monster. Rather than his usual denim jacket he'd turned up in full biker leathers and kept them on all night (despite the fact that they'd walked to the pub) hoping that his new bike would provide him with new-found pulling power. It didn't. Dean had asked both Tim and Rod if they would consider allowing him to break one of their limbs in exchange for £5,000. Now that he had his new toy Rod didn't want to be off the road for a month. Additionally he'd broken his arm when he was a kid and that it had been the single worst experience of his childhood and he wasn't prepared to go through it again for any money. Tim had never broken anything in his life but as he didn't need the money he wasn't interested in starting now.

Given their response Dean had undertaken an assessment of the rest of the lads. Glynn was too conservative and would never agree to do something like that. He didn't know Daisy that well but didn't think he'd be interested. Mick could be a mad bastard at times but played rugby at a high standard and Dean wasn't sure he'd want to jeopardise the one thing he was really passionate about for the sake of £5,000. The most obvious candidate was therefore Urban. He was always skint and had just done the biscuit game for a grand. Urban would do most things for money but if he couldn't persuade him to do it then Dean knew his last resort was to get one of the lads to break his own arm in order to keep the dream of the inheritance alive. The thought made him feel depressed and he pulled his duvet on top of him.

Just as he was drifting into a pleasant dream-like state Dean was woken by banging and shouting from Mick's bedroom. After listening to the racket for a minute or so he went upstairs to check what was going on. Mick was sitting on the floor in his dirty, ripped suit surrounded by mounds of clothes, photos, paper and an assortment of general shit.

"What's going on Mick?"

"I've just had the single worst night of my life" Mick replied as he looked around at the chaos he'd just created.

"Has something happened between you and Gill?"

"Yeah, she's finished with me."

"Why?"

"Just because I went out from work, got pissed, stood her up in front of her mates, shagged a secretary from work in the bogs of a pub, broke into my old flat, got arrested for breaking and entering and then got held in the cells on suspicion of rape"

"Fucking hell, women are so unreasonable" Dean replied shaking his head. "Didn't you explain that it wasn't your fault?"

"Well I would've but it was such a busy night that I sort of forgot to call her" Mick replied with a shrug.

"Oh well, I'm sure when you tell her that it was all down to the booze she'll understand" said Dean as he walked over and patted Mick on the shoulder.

"Yeah, you're right. I mean it wasn't as if anyone died was it? What's all the fuss about?" Mick replied with a weak smile.

"That's the spirit. Get yourself cleaned up and give her a call. I'm sure she'll be delighted to hear from you" Dean said as he left Mick to sort himself out. As he closed the door to Mick's room he shook his head and whispered to himself "Fucking mental!"

****

Mick made his way back from the bar with the drinks. Despite the fact he'd been asked to get a different brand of alcohol by each of the lads he'd decided that it was far too difficult to remember who wanted what and had simply bought four pints of Stella and four shots of tequila. He arrived back at the fruit machine and presented the tray of drinks.

"Where's my bottle of Budweiser?" Rod asked.

"I'm not fucking wasting money on half pints of American piss. Be a real man and have a pint of Stella" Mick replied gesturing for Rod to take the glass off the tray.

"Did you get me a pint of Fosters?" Tim asked.

"No" Mick replied as he gestured to Tim to take one of the remaining pints.

Dean looked at the tray and picked up the pint nearest to him without bothering to ask about the Guinness he'd asked for.

"And get those fucking tequila's down your necks as well" said Mick nodding at the four shooter glasses that were sitting untouched on the tray.

"Do we have to? It's only six o'clock" Rod protested.

"Yes you fucking do" Mick replied as he downed his shot. Reluctantly the other three picked up the shooter glasses and downed the contents. Mick then picked up his pint and downed it.

"Right, whose round is it?" he asked with a wild look in his eyes "and why are you wearing biker leathers when you're not on your bike Rod?"

"Because women love them" Rod replied to which Mick responded with a 'wanker' gesture.

"I'll get you one Mick" said Tim. "What do you want?"

"A Stella and a tequila" Mick replied. As Tim walked to the bar both Dean and Rod stood looking at Tim shaking their heads and mouthing "no tequila." Tim responded with a nod.

"So, did you speak to Gill then Mick?" Dean asked.

"I tried to but she wasn't answering her mobile. I left a couple of voicemails saying that I'd been caught up at work and couldn't get away but she hasn't called me back."

"Fuck her" said Rod who had no idea what had happened the previous evening. "If she can't be bothered to take your call then she's not worth it mate. I'd bin her."

"I think she's already binned me to be honest" Mick replied as Tim returned and handed him another pint of Stella. "Worse than that though, that bird from the office left me a voicemail saying that somehow everyone in the office knows what happened with her in the boozer last night."

"Nightmare" said Dean "I bet you're not looking forward to going in on Monday morning?"

"You can say that again. I don't even like the bird. She's quite fit but she's a right loudmouth and is at the root all of the office gossip. In fact, thinking about it, it was probably her that told everyone" Mick replied.

"Told everyone what?" Rod asked.

"That he nobbed her in the pub bogs last night" said Tim.

"I though you said you were working late?"

"Oh get with the fucking programme Rod. That's just a cover story. Nobody works late on a Friday night. He was out getting pissed and shagged some other bird" said Dean.

"Right, well it seems fair enough that your bird has binned you then" Rod said to Mick, who responded by dipping his fingers in his pint and flicking lager into Rod's face.

"What was that for?" Rod asked as he wiped the Stella out of his eyes.

"For being insensitive" said Mick sarcastically.

"Anyway, that's enough talk about Mick's love live" said Dean "have you seen those two over there?"

On the other side of the bar were two attractive blonde girls sitting at a table, drinking pints of lager.

"Right, who's with me?" Mick asked, chomping at the bit.

"What happened to being depressed about losing your bird?" said Rod.

"What bird?" Mick replied.

"OK, I'm in" said Tim. "Which one d'you want?"

"I'm not bothered mate, they both look alright to me. Let's just see how it goes" Mick replied as they walked over to the girls.

Mick was the first to arrive at the table. The two girls were engrossed in conversation and didn't notice him until he sat down on one of the spare seats.

"Evening ladies, I'm conducting a survey on behalf of the Ministry for Agriculture, Fisheries and Food and was wondering if I could ask your opinion on one of the current hot political topics?" Mick said seriously. Neither of the girls responded but simply sat staring at him. "Good. Right, the big question is 'Grapes with seeds in them, what's the point?'" For a second there was still no response from either of the girls and Mick considered getting up and walking off but suddenly they both started giggling. Mick was unsure what they were laughing about until one of the girls leaned forward.

"I'm sorry. We are Swedish. We didn't understand you. Can you please repeat?"

Mick's heart skipped a beat. To meet two blonde, pint-drinking, attractive Swedish birds was one of his all time fantasies. Before he could say anything Tim joined them.

"Hi I'm Tim" he said holding out his hand.

"Hello Tim. I am Maja and this is Astrid" the more attractive of the two girls said.

"And I'm Mick" said Mick also offering his hand.

"So, Mick. What were you saying? Something about grapes?" Maja said.

"I'm doing a survey for the government, which is technically meant to be just for British people but as Sweden is part of the EU your opinion should still be valid. Do you have grapes with seeds in them in Sweden? If so, what's the point? Someone has gone to the bother of inventing grapes without seeds so why do people still sell ones with seeds? Who in their right mind prefers to eat a grape with seeds rather than one without? It's just madness" Mick said trying to remain official-looking whilst taking a gulp out of his pint of Stella.

"You're funny" said Maja laughing.

"Can I get you two ladies a drink "asked Tim noticing that they'd almost finished their pints.

"Yes please. Two pints of Stella, thank you" Maja replied.

"Thank you god" Mick whispered to himself whilst fighting back his tears of joy.

****

"Fucking slag!" Mick shouted as he flung open the living room door.

"Evening Mick" said Dean, who was sitting on the opposite sofa watching 'Scarface' on the plasma screen. "What happened to your Swedish bird?"

"She's got a fucking boyfriend hasn't she?" Mick slurred. "She could have fucking mentioned that when I first went over to speak to her so that I wouldn't have wasted four fucking hours chatting her up. I mean why did she think I was talking to her?"

"Maybe she thought you were just being friendly and welcoming her to our country?" Rod, who was lying on the floor, said sarcastically.

"Fuck off" Mick replied. "It was obvious that I was trying to get into her pants and she sat there knowing all along that there was no chance. I should have got the money back from her for all of those pints of Stella I bought."

"Where's Tim?" Dean asked whilst continuing to watch the plasma screen.

"He's upstairs with the other fucking bird now. I wouldn't mind but *she* was meant to be mine and we switched halfway through the evening because I didn't think she was up for it. By rights it should be me who's upstairs with her now, not that public school nonse."

"Oh well, at least you've got us and we love you" said Rod handing Mick a bottle of beer.

"So what did you lads get up to then?" asked Mick as he took a large slug from the bottle and sat down.

"We talked about birds and football, got pissed, got blown out a couple of times and had a kebab on the way home. The usual stuff" Rod replied.

"Sounds great" said Mick sarcastically. "What are we doing here? We should be out sowing wild oats."

"I think you sowed enough wild oats last night to last a whole lifetime" Dean replied.

"Good point" said Mick as he took another large swig from his bottle. "So where's everyone else?"

"Glynn and Daisy are seeing their birds. Urban is seeing that bird he just met last week Razor is behind the sofa unconscious" Dean said whilst continuing to watch the screen.

"What?" said Mick. He kneeled up on the sofa and saw Razor lying fully clothed and comatosed on the floor. "What the fuck's the daft twat doing down there?"

"Dunno" Dean replied. "He was there when we got back from the boozer. I've no idea why he didn't go to bed."

"Are you just going to leave him there?" Mick asked.

"Well you can take him to bed if you want to, but he looks happy enough to me" Dean replied.

"Good point" said Mick as he lay back down on the sofa.

"Anyway Mick, I've got a little proposal for you."

"Oh yeah, what's that then?"

"You know that Dougie left a number of dares in his will for us to do for cash? Well I've just been given the latest one by the solicitor and it pays £5,000."

"Jesus Christ! Five grand? What have you got to do for that? Assassinate the Pope?" Mick said laughing.

"No, the challenge is to let someone break one of your arms or legs."

"You're fucking joking aren't you? Who in their right mind would do that? Five grand is nowhere near enough for that sort of thing. What happens to the money if nobody does it?" Mick asked.

"It goes to charity" Dean lied.

"Ah well, at least it'll go to a good cause then" Mick replied as he finished his beer and nodded to Rod to pass him another one.

Dean had been thinking about the situation all night and had come up with a fall back plan. "Fair enough then, but instead of £5,000 how do you fancy making £1,000?"

"It depends what I have to do. If it involves breaking a finger or a toe or something stupid like that you can fuck right off."

"No, it doesn't involve breaking any of your bones, in fact quite the opposite" said Dean with a wry smile.

"Go on" said Mick, intrigued.

"Well, under the terms of the dare we can do whatever we want with the money as long as a limb from someone in this house gets broken. I was thinking that that we could pay you £1,000 to break someone else's arm and give the rest of it to the person whose arm get broken" said Dean.

"I don't get you" said Mick. "Who would agree to do it for £4,000 rather than £5,000? They'd have to be fucking mad."

"Or unconscious" Dean replied as he jumped onto the sofa Mick was on and peered over the back at Razor.

"Oooh, I dunno about that" said Mick as he shook his head. "Razor will go fucking mad when he comes round."

"Yeah but he'll be £4,000 better off though won't he and it'll heal up before he knows it. Anyway you can always say it was my idea."

"Alright. Call it two grand and I'll do it" said Mick.

"You're on" Dean replied. "What are you going to do it with?"

"I dunno, have you got a crowbar or something?"

"Funny you should say that, but no" Dean replied sarcastically.

Rod, who'd been lying on the floor watching the events unfold suddenly sprung into action. "Leave this to me chaps" he said as he got up and ran out of the room. He returned a few minutes later.

Rod was a martial arts film fan and, unbeknown to the other members of the house, had a secret collection of weapons. He carefully laid them out on the sofa for Mick and Dean to inspect.

"Right these are called nunchaku and were one of Bruce Lee's favourites" he said pointing at a pair of black wooden sticks joined at the top by a metal chain. "These are tonfa and have been used by all the greats" he said pointing to a pair of wooden nightsticks "and this is a bokken which is the preferred weapon of choice for Ninja Warriors" he said pointing at a lethal-looking long wooden stick. Dean and Mick looked at the implements one by one and then at each other in a slightly uneasy fashion.

"Are these legal?" Dean asked.

"They are if you're a registered martial arts expert" Rod replied.

"You're not though are you?" Dean asked.

"No, but I bought them off a bloke who is" said Rod. "Anyway Mick, if it was me I'd go for the tonfa as they are made of really hard wood, are easy to use and will easily break someone's arm."

"Right" said Mick apprehensively. "Well give us it then."

Rod handed over one of the tonfa and Mick practiced by whacking the sofa a couple of times.

"OK, let the dog see the rabbit" said Mick as Dean pulled back the sofa. "Which arm does he wank with?"

"I think he writes with his right hand so probably best to go for the left arm" Dean replied.

Without any hesitation Mick leapt forward and brought the stick crashing down onto Razor's left arm. It connected just below the wrist and made a loud crack. Mick used so much force that the top of the stick left a visible indentation in the wooden floor. The cracking sound was instantly replaced by a stomach-wrenching scream as Razor regained consciousness and opened his eyes. After a second or two his eyes closed again and he slipped back into a state of unconsciousness. Mick, Dean and Rod all stood staring at Razor's arm, which now had a noticeable kink where Mick had struck it.

"What do we do now?" Mick asked.

"I think it might be a good idea to get him to the hospital" said Dean.

"It's got fuck all to do with me" said Rod.

"Me too" said Mick "you never said anything about having to clear up afterwards for my two grand Deano, so it's over to you now son."

"Fucking great" said Dean as he pulled out his mobile and dialled a taxi.

****

Tim showed Maja into his room and closed the door. He looked around and wished he'd tidied up a bit before he'd gone out. From where he was standing he could see an assortment of T-shirts, jumpers and dirty boxers strewn across the floor but worst of all was the collection of used tissue paper lying next to his bed. Thankfully Maja asked if she could use the toilet and he directed her to the bathroom across the landing, which gave him a minute or so to clean up.

Maja returned a couple of minutes later and sat on the corner of the bed. In the bright lights of his room she was still attractive but looked really drunk. Tim was feeling decidedly randy and the last thing he wanted was for her to start puking or to pass out.

"Would you like a drink?" Tim asked.

"Just water please" Maja replied weakly.

"Are you OK?" Tim asked.

"I have a sugar deficiency but will be OK in a minute" she said.

"Right. I'll go and get us a couple of drinks and will be straight back" Tim said as he left the room and headed to the kitchen. He could hear Mick and Dean talking in the living room but decided not to pop in for a chat as his main priority was getting back to the lovely Maja. He grabbed a couple of bottles of beer for himself and a glass of tap water for Maja. He ran back up to his room, taking two stairs at a time, and bounded back through the bedroom door.

"I wasn't too long…." he stopped mid sentence as he saw Maja lying unconscious on the bed. *"Oh fuck"* he thought. He sat down and lifted her up by her head and shoulders.

"Maja, wake up! Are you OK?" Tim shouted as he gently slapped her face. She was still breathing but showed no sign of coming round. He continued slapping her face and tried sprinkling water on her. After a few minutes he started to get concerned that she wasn't showing any sign of waking up and the words 'Sugar deficiency' started swimming around in his head. He picked up her handbag and emptied it out onto the bed. Along with the usual stuff (lipstick, make up brushes, mirror, purse etc) around fifty sachets of sugar spewed out onto the duvet. *"Oh fuck!"* Tim thought as he looked at the mountain of sugar. *"Sugar deficiency, is that diabetes? Do you give someone sugar if they pass out or is that going to kill them? Fuck! Fuck! Fuck!"* he thought as he started to panic. He decided to get some help.

"Don't go anywhere" he shouted as he ran out of the room. He sprinted downstairs and burst into the living room. "Do any of you guys know anything about diabetes?" Tim blurted out before he stopped in his tracks. For a second he stood staring in bewilderment at Mick, who was holding what looked like a truncheon and standing over Razor, who looked to be dead. Rod was standing next to him, holding a variety of other weapons in his arms, and Dean was shouting into his mobile. Tim looked at the three of them and for a moment forgot about his own emergency upstairs.

"What the fuck's going on here?"

"Err, Razor's had an accident" Rod replied.

"A fucking accident? It looks anything *but* accidental to me. What the fuck are you doing with all those things?" Tim asked pointing at Rod's armoury. "Anyway, bollocks to all that. Do any of you know anything about diabetes?"

"I know a bit about it, my grandma was diabetic" said Rod as he dropped the weapons back onto the sofa. "Why? I thought you were shagging that Swedish bird?"

"Well I was going to but she's passed out and I can't wake her up. The last thing she said to me was something about a sugar deficiency and she's got millions of packets of sugar in her bag. What do you think I should do?"

"Just shag her anyway" said Rod who started to laugh at his own joke but quickly stopped when he saw that Tim not amused.

"I'm not fucking around here Rod. She's in a bad way."

"OK, OK. If she's diabetic it sounds like she's having a hypo, which means she hasn't got enough sugar in her blood. As she's unconscious she won't be able to eat anything so you'll have to give her a warm sugary drink to bring her round" said Rod.

"Right, let's go then. We can talk about this fucking mess later" Tim said as he pointed at Razor.

Tim and Rod ran up to his bedroom. Maja was still flat out on the bed, exactly where Tim had left her. Rod took the glass of water, refilled it with warm water from the bathroom and emptied ten or eleven packets of sugar into it. He handed it to Tim who started pouring it into Maja's mouth. At first most of it dribbled down her chin and onto the bed but after four or five attempts she swallowed some of the liquid and started showing signs of life.

"Thanks Rod, I'll take it from here" said Tim.

"Are you sure, I don't mind taking over" Rod replied hopefully.

"Rod, fuck off!" Tim responded.

"Fair enough" said Rod as he headed back down to collect his weapons from the living room.

****

Razor started to regain consciousness in the taxi. As he opened his eyes he immediately winced with pain and let out a groan.

"Aaaahhhh, fuck.......my arm" he mumbled.

"It's all right mate, you've had an accident but we're on our way to the hospital and they're gonna sort you out" said Dean.

"Just help me" said Razor who looked like he was about to pass out again.

They pulled up at Accident and Emergency at Chelsea and Westminster hospital a few minutes later. Dean ran into the department, grabbed a wheelchair, put Razor in it and wheeled him to the front desk.

"If you would like to take a seat a doctor will see you as soon as possible" the receptionist said once she had taken Razor's details from Dean.

"Any idea how long that might be?" Dean asked politely.

"Take a look around" she said "unless it's life threatening all of these people need to be seen before you."

319

Dean looked around the waiting area. It resembled a scene from a zombie movie. Everywhere he looked there were pissed up people, covered in blood and plodding around making moaning sounds. Occasionally one of the zombies would start shouting for no apparent reason at one of the others, the staff or at nobody in particular.

"Is it always like this?" Dean asked feeling slightly concerned for his safety.

"It is on a Saturday night" the receptionist replied.

Two hours and much groaning later Razor was finally seen by one of the doctors.

"It looks like you have broken your arm Mr Peach."

"I could have told you that" Razor replied through clenched teeth.

"We'll need to send you for an X-Ray to see how bad the break is."

"OK then, let's go" Razor replied.

"You'll need to join the queue" the doctor said, with a smile.

Another hour later Razor's arm was finally put in a cast and he was allowed to leave. Razor and Dean waited for their taxi in silence.

"You fucking bastard Dean" Razor said once they were in the cab.

"What d'ya mean? It wasn't anything to do with me" Dean said, unable to stop himself laughing.

"You know that technically under Dougie's rules you haven't completed this week's challenge. As Dougie's Appointed Representative for the will I have to volunteer to join in the challenges, so I could tell the solicitor that you haven't actually completed it this week" said Razor.

"Oh fuck off Razor. If you do that then you won't get your £500,000. You stand to make almost as much as I do from the will but so far it's been me that has had to go through all the shit. You've done fuck all, so it's about time you pulled your weight. The doctor said that it was a clean break and you should recover fully so stop fucking whinging."

"I'm still going to get you back though Dean. Mark my words" said Razor as he turned away and looked out of the window.

They got back to the house around five am and found Tim sitting up in the living room watching TV.

"Did you manage to get that Swedish bird sorted out?" Dean asked.

"I certainly did" Tim replied "I shagged her twice before she got a taxi back to her hotel!"

"That's not quite what I meant" said Dean shaking his head in disapproval as he headed off to bed.

Chapter 30
Week 6 - Wednesday

Tim was up and dressed by six am. He closed the door to his room, crossed the corridor and knocked quietly on Mick's door to wake him up. He then went down to the first floor and gave Rod's door a knock.

"Come on Rod, we've got to get going if we're going to be there in time" he whispered, in an attempt to avoid waking the rest of the house.

Rod sat up and looked at his watch. *"What am I doing getting up at six o'clock on a day off work?"* he thought to himself as he climbed out of bed and looked around the floor for his clothes. "This had better be worth it Tim" he shouted.

"Just hurry up" Tim whispered back "we need to get going in ten minutes." As he couldn't hear any sign of activity from upstairs Tim headed back up and gave Mick's door a second knock.

"I heard you the first time, you fucker" came the response from within the room.

"Does that mean that you're up then?"

"What are you, my fucking mum?" Mick shouted. "Yes, I'm fucking up now" he said as he opened his bedroom door and stood there in a shabby pair of Y-fronts.

"Well you'd better put something a bit more respectable than those on, unless you want to be arrested for indecency" Tim replied pointing at Mick's choice of underwear.

"Ha fucking ha! With wit like that you should be on the telly" Mick said as he pushed past Tim and headed into the bathroom.

Fifteen minutes later they were all in Tim's car heading for the countryside.

"Is that coat new?" Tim asked as he admired Mick's beige trench coat.

"It certainly is. It's Armani, this shirt is Paul Smith and these boots are Patrick Cox. All courtesy of Dougie's will and Razor's arm of course" Mick replied with a grin.

"Great idea wearing new clothes on a day's shooting at a farm" said Rod, who was sitting in the back of the car.

"I've brought a change with me for when we get there, you prick" Mick replied without turning around. "Anyway I didn't recognise you without those fucking biker leathers that you've had glued onto you for the past week. Have they managed to weave their magic with the ladies yet?"

"Fuck off" Rod replied. "So what's the score with this shooting lark then Tim?"

"Well, this is the time of the year that rats and other vermin start to become a real nuisance for farmers as they eat the crops and steal food from the animals. A few years ago a school friend of mine, Roger, and I came up with the idea of offering a free extermination service. We visit all of the local farms with our shotguns and go around looking for rats, rabbits, foxes or any other types of pest. When we find them we blow them away. It works for the farmer as they get to keep things in check for free and it works for us as it's a blast, quite literally" said Tim.

"So what do you do with the carcasses?" Rod asked.

"We generally keep the rabbits. My mum cooks up a good rabbit stew and the feet make for good souvenirs. If we get a fox, which is quite rare in daylight, we'll keep its tail but the rest of it and anything else we shoot goes onto a huge bonfire at the end of the day. The smell is awful but it's quite satisfying to watch it burn."

"It all sounds like a right laugh" said Rod. "I've never shot a real gun before. I've had a go on those rifles at funfairs but they're not really the same are they? Have you ever shot anything Mick?"

"My old man had a shotgun when lived in the countryside. We used to fuck around with it when we were kids until my brother shot the neighbour's cat. I haven't shot anything for at least ten years though."

The conversation stayed on gun related topics for the next hour or so until they turned off the road and came to a stop at a huge set of gates. Tim lowered his window and pressed the call button. An extremely posh voice answered and the gates opened to reveal a private gravel road. After a couple of hundred yards they came to a huge manor house, which looked like a miniature version of Buckingham Palace.

"Fucking hell, is this where you live Tim?" Rod asked.

"It's where my parents live."

"Jesus Christ look at the size of it!" Rod continued. "How many bedrooms does it have?"

"I'm not sure" Tim replied. "Not all the rooms are used as bedrooms upstairs so I've never really counted."

"Yeah, we've got the same problem with our house back in Dublin" Mick said sarcastically. "We're forever losing count of the number of bedrooms. In fact people have been known to go missing for days at a time."

"Very funny" Tim replied with a smile. "Anyway we're here to do some shooting not to admire my folks' house."

They piled out of the car and were met by an elderly lady in an apron.

"Hello boys, would you like some breakfast before you head off?" she asked.

"That would be great Clarris" said Tim. She smiled and headed back into the house.

"Do you call your mum Clarris?" Rod asked, looking a bit confused. "I know your posh but that's a new one on me."

"Clarris isn't my mum, she's our housekeeper" Tim replied.

"Keep up Rod" said Mick patting him on the back as they made their way into the house.

They'd just finished eating the full English breakfast that Clarris made for them when they heard a car horn outside.

"That'll be Roger" said Tim as he stood up. They all headed out to see a tall, brown haired guy standing in a flat cap, green tweed jacket, brown cord trousers and a pair of wellies. Despite being dressed like an old farmer he was leaning against a bright red Porsche Cayenne.

"Hi Roge" said Tim as he gave him a firm hand shake. "Did you bring the spare guns with you?"

"Oh course" Roger replied, sounding like a member of the Royal family. He opened the boot to reveal four shotguns.

"Great, let's get a bit of practice in" said Tim, as he grabbed a couple of them.

They headed round the back of the house to an area of the garden that had obviously been used for shooting practice before as the ground was covered in shot-up tin cans and empty cartridges. Tim placed ten of the cans onto a fence. He picked up one of the guns, loaded it, took aim and fired, sending one of the cans flying backwards off the fence.

"It's as easy as that" he said looking at Rod and Mick. "All you have to remember is that it's not a single bullet but hundreds of pieces of shot that come out of the barrel. Therefore if you shoot at something it's better to move the barrel in a sweeping motion across the target. That way the shot will spray out over a wide area and you've got more of a chance of hitting whatever it is you're aiming at. Right then, who's first?"

"I'll have a go" Rod said eagerly.

Tim reloaded the gun and carefully handed it to Rod. "Now Rod, before you do anything you must always make sure that the barrel is pointing away from you or anyone else you're with."

"I'm not fucking five years old Tim" Rod replied as he took the gun from Tim. It let out an enormous "BANG!" as it fired into the ground two feet in front of him. "Fucking hell, that trigger's a bit sensitive isn't it?" Rod said, laughing nervously.

"That's what I mean" said Tim as he snatched the gun back out of Rod's shaking hands. "As I was saying, never point the gun at anyone and never put your fingers near the trigger unless you're ready to fire it. Now, shall we try again?" he asked looking at Rod like he actually was five years old.

"OK" Rod replied, rather less eagerly. Tim reloaded the gun and handed it slowly back to Rod. This time Rod held his trigger finger on the handle and waited for Tim's instructions.

"OK Rod, put the handle into the muscular part of your shoulder" said Tim.

"Or in your case, the fatty part where the muscle should be" Mick cut in, laughing.

"Are you sure that you want to start taking the piss when I've got a loaded shot gun in my hand?" Rod asked smiling.

"The way you shoot, I'm happy to take my chances" Mick chuckled.

"Anyway" said Tim, cutting across the banter, "place your cheek onto the handle so that you can see right the way along the barrel. When you've lined up your target, squeeze very gently on the trigger. Don't jerk it otherwise the gun will rise up and you'll miss."

"OK" said Rod. He put the gun up to his shoulder, crouched down like a sniper, put his cheek onto the handle, closed his left eye, lined up the tin can and pulled the trigger. The shotgun let out another almighty "BANG!" and Rod fell backwards into a puddle, causing the other three to break down in hysterical laughter.

"Sorry Rod, I forgot to say that it carries a bit of a kick when you fire it" said Tim still laughing at Rod's effort.

"And we're not actually in a combat zone so you don't need to crouch down before you shoot. The enemy is that tin can and it can't see you whatever you do" Mick added whilst continuing to piss himself laughing.

"It's a bit late for all this advice now isn't it?" Rod said as he picked himself up and wiped the mud from his jeans. "Anyway did I hit it or what?"

"No" the other three said simultaneously.

After another half an hour's practice Rod finally started hitting the can, providing he was standing near enough.

"Just wait until you see the whites of the rats' eyes and you'll be fine" said Roger, assuring Rod that he was ready to go.

"Rats haven't got any whites in their eyes have they? Aren't they pure black?" Rod asked seriously.

"You know what I mean old bean" Roger replied patting him on the shoulder.

Annoyingly for Rod, Mick managed to hit the tin can with every one of his first three shots.

"It's like riding a bike or shagging a fit bird, you never forget the technique" he said cockily to Rod as he handed the gun back to Roger.

"What would you know about shagging fit birds?" Rod asked.

"A lot more than you do that's for sure" replied Mick. They headed back to Roger's car. They set off down a country lane and soon arrived at the first of the farms. Roger went to see the farmer and returned a few minutes later.

"OK guys, I've cleared everything with Mr Woodcock, the farm manager. There have been a lot of rats about recently and he thinks there's a nest in the barn. All of the livestock are out grazing at the moment so we're free to wander around the barn and shoot anything that moves."

"Except for us" Tim added looking at Rod.

"Very funny" Rod replied.

"OK let's go" said Roger as he opened the boot to get the guns out. He handed each of them a gun and filled his pocket with cartridges. Rod followed suit, stuffing as many cartridges as he could into all of his pockets.

"Fucking hell Rod, we're not going into a combat zone you know" said Mick shaking his head.

"You might not be, but I am" said Rod in a failed attempt at an American accent. "My whole family was killed by rats and today it's payback time!"

"Shut up!" Mick replied. "Your mum and dad live in a semi-detached house in Leeds."

They walked over and entered the barn. The place was huge and reeked of animal dung. Other than the piles of cow shit there were huge piles of hay and very little else of interest.

"Why don't you and Mick go up to the loft area whilst Rod and I have a look down here?" Tim said to Roger.

"OK" Roger replied, gesturing to Mick to follow him upstairs.

Tim and Rod started sorting through the piles of hay. Tim brushed the hay to one side with his boot whilst holding his gun ready and loaded on his arm. Rod copied Tim's stance and movement and slowly started to move a pile of hay in front of him to one side. He held his breath, expecting hundreds of rats to run out and attack him, but was relieved to see that there was nothing there. He continued brushing through the hay and soon started to get bored.

"Is this whole thing a wind up Tim? I bet there aren't even any…..AAAAARRRRRRGGGHHH!!!!!!" Rod screamed as he came face to face with a rat that was large enough to be mistaken for a small cat. He dropped his gun, turned and ran back towards the entrance of the barn. Tim, who was standing around six feet away saw the events unfold and as Rod started running he fired.

"Got the bastard!" Tim said as he stood triumphantly over the remains of the rat. He turned to talk to Rod but couldn't see any sign of him in the barn. Mick and Roger ran down the stairs to see what had happened.

"What was it?" Mick shouted.

"A rat, and a fucking big one" Tim replied.

"Where's Rod?" Mick asked as he ran over to Tim to inspect the evidence.

"I'm not sure. He saw the rat, screamed and ran out of the barn just before I shot it" said Tim laughing.

At that point Rod sheepishly came back into the barn. "Did you get it, Tim?"

"Yeah, don't worry. It's safe to come back now you big Jessie!" Mick said.

"That's easy for you to say. Did you see the size of that thing? It was the size of a fucking cat and it looked at me like it was about to pounce" said Rod tried to justify his actions.

"Does lambkins need a cuddle?" Mick said adopting a baby voice and putting his arm around Rod.

"Well let's just see how you get on when you come face to face with one of those bastards" Rod replied as he pushed Mick away.

"Right that's enough chatting. Well done for finding the first one Rod" said Roger

"And for running away like a girl" Mick added.

"Look, let's just get back to finding some more shall we?" Roger said as he nodded at Mick to follow him back upstairs.

They stayed in the barn for another hour. The silence was periodically broken by the sound of shotgun blasts, usually followed by a bout of cheering and high fives. It soon became very competitive on both an individual basis and between the two 'teams'. At the end of their session Tim had bagged seven, Roger five, Mick three and Rod none.

"I was fucking unlucky there" said Rod explaining his poor performance as they gathered at the barn entrance. "There were at least four that I'm sure I hit but they still managed to get away."

"Do you think that they were wearing bullet proof vests or were they just super rats that are immune to gun shots?" Mick asked sarcastically. "Although that first one you found, the one you ran away from, seemed to die pretty easily when Tim shot it. Strange that."

"Oh fuck off Mick. Anyway there were a lot more of them upstairs than downstairs so it was easier for you" Rod replied.

"Ladies, ladies!" Tim cut in. "We've still got another two farms to visit so there'll be plenty more opportunities. Let's clear up here and head off."

They grabbed the two bags of carcasses, headed back to Roger's car and set off for the next farm. The story there was similar to the first farm and as they set off for the third farm Tim led the way with seventeen kills, Roger was just behind with fifteen, Mick was up to eight and Rod was still on zero, despite the fact that he had probably fired more shots than the other three combined.

"Let's face it Rod, you're just shit at shooting mate" Mick said taunting him.

Rod was completely pissed off. He'd always considered himself to be good at most sports and had assumed he'd pick up shooting easily enough. He refused to acknowledge Mick's comment and sat sulking in the back of the car, determined that he was going to break his duck at the last farm. When they arrived Roger and Tim went into the farmhouse to speak to the farm manager.

"How are you Eddie, old boy?" said Tim.

"I'm good, thanks for asking" Eddie replied. "I take it that you're here for your annual shoot up? I thought I'd be seeing you sometime soon."

"Yeah. We've brought a couple of friends with us, if that's OK? One of them can shoot a bit but the other's a hopeless city boy, although he's harmless enough" said Tim.

"No problem at all. We've seen a lot of rats around here this year so it'll be good to have a couple of extra guns on the case. In fact, now that you're here you could do me a favour. We've got an old bull up in the fields. He's lost his fertility and we need to get rid of him so that we can bring in a new bull. The vet can't make it out here for another week and I was wondering if you lads could do me a favour and bump him off. He's harmless so there's no danger and as you've both been brought up around farms I'm sure you know where to shoot him to make it quick and painless. He's in the field next to the barn, you can't miss him really" Eddie said as he lit a cigarette.

"It'd be a pleasure" said Tim. "Anyway we don't want to keep the other boys waiting all day, so is it OK if we crack on?"

"Fire away" said Eddie as he took a sip from his cup of tea.

As they walked back down the corridor to the front door Tim turned to Roger. "Are you thinking what I'm thinking?"

"That we could have a bit of fun with the boys?" Roger replied.

"Absolutely" said Tim and they both broke out into a smile.

Rod and Mick were standing in silence when the other two got back to the car.

"What's wrong with you two?" Tim asked.

"He's sulking about not being able to shoot a barn door from two paces" said Mick smirking.

"We'll see" Rod replied.

"OK then, we've cleared everything with the farm manager so we're good to go. Grab some ammo and let's get amongst it" said Tim as he opened the car boot.

The four of them loaded up, with Rod taking enough cartridges to kill a herd of elephants. As they made their way towards the barn, Tim suddenly stopped at the adjacent field.

"You know what Roge? I'm getting a bored of just shooting rats. I fancy having a go at something a bit bigger" said Tim. Before Roger could respond Tim ran over to the gate, hurdled it, ran up to the bull that was tethered in the field and shot it in the head. Mick and Rod watched in silence as the bull slumped to the floor. Tim turned to face them and stood with his shotgun held high above his head in both hands cheering like a triumphant warrior

"Now you're fucking talking!" Rod shouted and took off before Roger had time to let him in on the joke. He ran over to the field next to the one the bull was in, jumped the gate, ran over to the herd of cows and shot two of them in quick succession at point blank range. They both dropped down dead instantly. Rod raised his gun above his head and copied Tim's victory stance.

"Take that you fuckers!" Rod shouted, as he jumped up and down next to the two dead cows. "You see what you get when you mess with me!" He was still jumping up and down when Tim came running over and chinned him.

"Ow!" Rod said, holding his chin as he picked himself up off the floor. "What the fuck was that for?"

"For being a fucking prick!" Tim replied staring incredulously at the two dead cows.

"What d'ya mean? I was just following your lead" said Rod looking angry and confused.

"It was a fucking joke" said Tim shaking his head. "The farmer asked us to do him a favour and kill the bull. We thought it'd be a laugh to see the look on your faces. I never expected you to go on a fucking killing spree."

"Oops" said Rod laughing nervously. "Do you think he'll know it was us if we just fuck off?"

"Well he won't need to be Sherlock fucking Holmes to work it out when he finds two dead cows lying around in his field with gun shots wounds in their heads will he?" Tim said, still flabbergasted by Rod's actions.

"True" said Rod, "how about if we hide the bodies? Maybe we could bury them or stick them in the back of Roger's car?"

"Rod, each of these cows weighs over six hundred kilos. There is no fucking way that we could move them. Anyway don't you think that they know how many fucking cows they've got on a farm?" Tim replied.

"So what are we going to do then?"

"Well I'll have to go and see Eddie, tell him what a prick you are and then ask him how much it will cost to replace these two cows" said Tim who was obviously less than happy.

"You've got to admit that it is a bit funny though Tim?" Mick said laughing as he and Roger came over to inspect the damage. "I think you've found your forte Rod. If we can just find a farm that's being harassed by gang of rogue cows then you might be in with a chance of beating us on the kill count today after all."

Rod allowed himself a quick chuckle. Tim looked like he was about to chin him again before he finally broke into a smile. "You're a fucking nightmare Rod. I can't take you anywhere" he said shaking his head. He nodded to Roger and the two of them headed back in the direction of the farm house.

"I don't think I'm really cut out for this shooting lark" said Rod, as he rubbed his jaw. "I'll tell you what though? If we're measuring kills by total weight I reckon I've spanked all your arses, even if you include Tim's bull."

"Shut up and get back in the car before the farmer comes out and decides to kick your arse" said Mick.

"For once Mick, I think you're right" said Rod as they headed back to Roger's car.

Chapter 31
Week 7 - Friday

Once again Dean and Razor found themselves in the All Bar One at Canary Wharf on Friday lunchtime. However, unlike the previous occasions, there wasn't the usual jovial banter between the two of them. Razor had his left arm in a bright purple cast from his elbow to his wrist. He'd still felt pissed when the cast was applied and although coloured casts were meant to be just for children he'd persuaded the doctor that it would be amusing to let him to have one. However, in the cold light of day, it looked totally ridiculous and as a result he made sure it was covered up wherever he went.

"Do you want a pint mate?" Dean asked as they approached the bar.

"I can't. I'm on fucking antibiotics, thanks to you."

"Oh yeah, I forgot" Dean replied. "How is the arm?"

"Well, the pain wakes me up every time I move in the night, it aches like fuck during the day and this cast is beginning to itch like a bastard, but apart from all of that it's fine" Razor replied sarcastically.

"Look you can't go on all the time like you're the only one that's had to do something you'd rather not have done for this fucking Dougie inheritance thing. Over the past few weeks I've had to have a threesome with Mick, shag a hooker and watch Urban and Rod wank off in front of me. None of that has been particularly enjoyable I can tell you."

"Yeah but this is fucking different isn't it?" Razor said holding up his cast.

"Not really. At least it's just physical pain. In a few weeks time it'll have totally healed up whereas I'll still be regretting fucking up a second chance with Gill, I'll still have the fact that I paid someone for sex on my conscience and I'll never be able to eat a digestive biscuit again for as long as I live" said Dean.

"Whatever" Razor replied. "Right let's see the fucking photo then."

Dean handed over the envelope containing a still shot of Mick hitting Razor's arm with the nightstick. Razor pulled it out and stared at it for a couple of seconds.

"That fucking cunt Mick did this? I'm going to make him pay as well" said Razor clearly very annoyed.

"Don't be such a big kid" said Dean. "We're not in junior school now Ray. You'll see that there's three grand in that envelope along with the photo. That's your cut of the money the solicitor gave us for the challenge. Mick didn't want to do it so I had to pay him two grand to persuade him. Take the money, spend it on whatever makes you happy and stop all this childish bollocks about getting revenge."

"Alright, I'll drop it for now" said Razor counting out the cash. "But if you try to rope me into anything else that Dougie sets up I promise you that I'll get somebody to break both your fucking legs."

"I guarantee that you won't be included in any more of Dougie's challenges. I wouldn't have included you but I was desperate and the fact that you were already anaesthetised just seemed like too good an opportunity to pass up."

"OK" Razor said offering out his right hand which Dean shook firmly. "I'll take this over to the old boy and will be back before you know it."

He returned twenty minutes later and handed two envelopes over to Dean. Dean opened the A4 envelope and pulled out the letter:

"Dear Dean,

Congratulations mate! You've already made it much further than I expected you to. I thought the last challenge might have stumped you but obviously not. I'm not sure if you're reading this with one of your arms or legs in plaster or if you managed to persuade some other poor fucker that it was worth five grand to have a limb broken, but either way you've been sharp enough to handle the curve ball I dealt, you so well done. Anyway I think this week it's time to go back to our favourite topic of sex but this time with a twist:

'SHEMALE'

The challenge this week is for you to set up one of the lads on a date with a transsexual – i.e. someone that looks completely like a woman but has still got a cock. In order to successfully complete the challenge the individual involved must not be told that it isn't a real woman (some of them look that good, believe me) and you need to produce a photo of them kissing their date passionately. They don't have to take it any further and actually shag them (that would be too sick, even for me). They only exception to this is that if you fail to set somebody up and decide to take on this challenge yourself you WILL need to go all the way (as you are aware of the he-she surprise). Once again I've arranged for Mr Jacob to provide some cash as these 'girls' don't come cheap (especially the pretty ones) and you might feel that you need to bung whoever you set up a bit of cash afterwards to make sure that there are no hard feelings. If you decide not to take on the challenge the you can keep the cash but obviously you will then all have to move out of the house by the end of the week.

Anyway, good luck mate and hopefully we'll be in touch again in another week's time.

Your friend,
Dougie"

"Ladyboys? The dirty fucking bastard" said Razor. "That'll be a delicacy that he picked up from all those holidays he had in Thailand I'll bet."

"I'd go fucking mad if someone set me up with a trannie on a date and I didn't find out until it was too late. This is the sort of thing that you could fall out permanently with somebody about" Dean said, shaking his head.

"It'll be a piece of piss. All you need to do is set one of the lads up on a 'date', wait for them to bring the trannie back to the house, watch the events unfold live on your PC and, once you've got a shot of them snogging go into the bedroom, break it up. Whoever you pick doesn't even have to know that it wasn't a bird" said Razor.

"But where the fuck are we going to find a ladyboy to set someone up with?" Dean asked.

"The fucking Internet, brains. You can get escorts of all shapes and sizes so I'm damn sure we'll be able to find a few blokes dressed as women" Razor replied.

"It's not a fucking pantomime dame we're looking for. We need to get someone that'll be able to fool one of the lads into thinking they're a hot bird. Let's see how much cash we've got to play with" said Dean wiggling his fingers towards the A5 envelope. Razor threw it to him. "There's about five grand in here" Dean said as he flicked through the notes.

"Well you should be able to get a fucking good looking bloke for that sort of money" said Razor.

"You know what, Razor? I reckon that providing we stay in control this challenge could turn out to be a bit of a laugh and we might even be able to make a profit from it. All we've got to do now is work out which poor fucker we're going to set up" said Dean as he downed the remainder of his pint.

****

"What's going on?" Dean asked as he walked into the living room to find Urban, Rod and Daisy huddled around the coffee table, giggling like girls.

"Nothing" Urban replied as they all sat upright, looking guilty.

"Come on, what the fuck were you doing?" Dean asked as he sat down on the end of the sofa.

"Do you *promise* not to say anything?" Urban asked.

"Go on then. What is it?"

Urban leaned forward, looking excited. "Well, you know that Glynn has been seeing his bird for yonks?"

"Her name, as you well know, is Heather" Dean replied.

"Well he's meeting her mum and dad for dinner at some posh restaurant in town tonight."

"What's so exciting about that?" said Dean taking a swig from a spare bottle of beer on the table. "Are you getting excited that you might have a wedding to go to or something?"

"Don't be fucking stupid" Urban replied, "I haven't finished yet. It just happens that on the same night that he's meeting her mum and dad, Daisy here has obtained a supply of Viagra tablets."

"What the fuck's that got to do with Glynn meeting Heather's mum and dad?" said Dean looking bemused as to where the conversation was going.

"We thought it'd be a bit of a laugh to crush up one of the tablets, spike a bottle of beer with it and get Glynn to drink it before he heads off to dinner" said Urban with a huge smile on his face.

"That's wicked" said Dean shaking his head as he looked at Rod, Daisy and Urban, all three of whom were grinning like Cheshire cats. "Does it definitely work? Have you tried any of them Daisy?"

"I haven't but a few of the blokes at work have. They said it makes your dick turn to steel and that you have a hard on for ages" Daisy replied.

"How long?" asked Dean.

"You seem to be very interested Deano. Have you been having trouble getting it up lately?" Rod chipped in, as he laughed at his own comment.

"Yeah, ever since I watched you beating your meat in my face" Dean replied.

"What?" Daisy asked looking both confused and concerned at Dean's comment.

"Nothing. He's just pissing around" Rod replied quickly.

"How long the effect lasts for depends on how much you take" Daisy continued. He pulled three blue tablets out of his pocket and held them out in the palm of his hand. "These little babies are the Rolls Royce of Viagra, the strongest you can get. They affect different people in different ways but one of the blokes at work had a hard on for twelve hours after taking one."

"Twelve hours? Fucking hell his nob must have been killing him after that" said Rod as he put his hands over his groin and pulled an expression of mock-pain.

"Yeah, that's the problem" said Urban looking at the tablets "they make your nob stay hard for longer than your brain wants it to. So if your lady wants to keep going she can, whether you like it or not!"

"So what you're saying is that there's no chance of rolling over and going straight to sleep after shooting your load then?" Rod said.

"Well by the sounds of it you won't be able to roll over at all" said Dean laughing.

"And you definitely won't be able to go to sleep" Urban added.

"Yeah, what's the difference between light and hard?" Daisy asked rhetorically. "You can sleep with a light on!" he said as they all fell about laughing, more at the thought of spiking Glynn rather than his joke.

"So have you spiked the bottle of beer yet?" Dean asked.

"Yeah, you're drinking it" Urban said as he continued laughing.

"What? You're fucking joking?" exclaimed Dean as he threw the bottle onto the floor.

"Yes, I'm joking, we're just going to do it now" said Urban with a shake of his head. "Why don't you go up and see Glynn and then bring him down here for a beer before he goes out."

"Oh I'm fucking Judas now am I, bringing him to the slaughter?" Dean said, pissed off that he had fallen for Urban's joke.

"Just go and fucking get him" said Urban. "Right Daisy, give us one of those tablets then" he said as he pulled out the rolling pin he'd hidden under the cushion when Dean had entered the room.

Dean headed upstairs to Glynn's room. Glynn was standing in the far corner of the room wearing a black pin-striped suit, white shirt and red tie. He was looking at himself in a full length mirror and turned round as Dean entered.

"What do you think?" Glynn asked.

"Fine, if you're going to a funeral" said Dean shaking his head. "So I hear you're meeting Heather's mum and dad tonight?"

"Yeah, we're going for dinner at the Ritz. Her mum and dad are really rich and dead posh. It's going to be a nightmare. I need to leave shortly but can't decide what to wear. Do you think this is too formal?"

"Yeah, why don't you wear that beige linen suit that you've got?" Dean asked, whose plan was to get Glynn to wear the thinnest trousers that he owned.

"Do you think so? I thought it might be a bit too casual?"

"No I think it'll work well. It's a suit, so it's still smart but it's more relaxed than a dark work-suit. Go with that and an open necked shirt and you can't go wrong" Dean said reassuringly.

Glynn quickly got undressed and put on the beige linen trousers. He reached for the bright orange shirt he'd worn previously with the suit.

"Not that fucking shirt, you tit" said Dean. "Go for the white one that you've just taken off, then you'll have a laid back summer look."

"OK" said Glynn as he put on the outfit. "What do you think?"

"Perfect. Right let's go and grab a drink with the boys downstairs before you head off" said Dean.

"Alright, but it'll have to be quick as I need to leave soon" Glynn replied.

"It'll just be nice for everyone if you can squeeze one in" said Dean patting Glynn on the back as they headed downstairs.

Rod, Urban and Daisy were all sprawled on the sofas watching VH2 on the plasma screen. As Glynn walked in all three of them immediately checked out what trousers he was wearing.

"Hey, I like the threads Glynn" said Daisy as he winked at Dean.

"Yeah, you look hot tonight mate" Urban added.

"Here, have a beer mate" said Rod as he thrust the specially prepared bottle into Glynn's hand.

"Cheers lads. You don't usually bother commenting on what I'm wearing though" Glynn replied looking confused at their interest.

"Yeah, but tonight's a special night isn't it? You want it to go just right so we're just doing our bit as mates to help out" Urban lied.

"Thanks lads. It's good to have a bird but it's great to have mates like you lot" said Glynn as he took a large swig out of the bottle.

****

After watching Glynn finish the bottle of spiked beer Dean went up to his room. He switched on his PC, typed the words 'transsexual escort in London' into Google and clicked on search. He was amazed to see there were literally hundreds of websites that matched the criteria. Tentatively he clicked into the first website and launched the photo gallery. He was amazed to see that all of the 'women' pictured on the sight were either naked or scantily clad and that the majority of them were gorgeous. *This has got to be a wind up. There is no way that these birds are blokes"* he thought to himself as he stared at the screen. *"I'll bet they just post these photos to lure people in and when they turn up it does actually turn out to be a bloke in drag."*

After scouring through numerous websites he picked out one with the best looking 'women' and called the number.

"Hello. I'm, errm looking for a couple of escorts for tomorrow night" he said nervously.

"You need to be a bit more specific love. Are you looking for female, male, straight, gay or trans?" the female voice at the other end of the phone replied brusquely.

Dean felt himself go red and lowered his voice to a faint whisper. "I'm, err, looking for trans?" he said hoping that meant ladyboys.

"Pre or post op?" she replied casually.

Dean paused for a second and considered hanging up. "What's the difference, exactly?"

"Well to put it bluntly, love, do you want one with a cock or without a cock?"

"Errm, both with, please" Dean replied not really believing the words that had just come out of his mouth.

"Fine, where are you based, love?"

"London."

"OK, just let me have a look who's available for tomorrow night. Right, you've got a choice of Jemma, Gloria, Nikita or Chantelle."

"Errm, are their pictures on the website?" asked Dean.

"Yes, all of our girls are on there."

"Hang on a second" said Dean as he clicked into the photo gallery. He scrolled through the photos and came to Jemma first. She was pictured wearing a bikini, had model good looks, long blonde hair and looked every inch a woman. Dean put his face up close to the screen to see if he could detect a bulge in the bikini bottoms but couldn't see anything. *"Bloody hell"* he thought *"this is really scary, not only do they look like women, but they look like really hot women!"* He clicked onto the next photo, which was of Gloria. She was also gorgeous, had long dark hair, was wearing stockings and suspenders and had her (rather large) tits out. "Errm, Jemma and Gloria will be fine" he mumbled into the phone, still not really believing that these photos were of two blokes.

"OK. It's five hundred pounds for each girl for the evening but that only covers the cost of their time and companionship. If you want anything more you'll have to discuss it with the girls and pay them direct."

Dean paid the thousand pound charge with his credit card and arranged to meet the 'girls' at Clapham Junction station at nine o'clock the following evening. After he hung up he looked at the photos of Jemma and Gloria on the website again. *"Either this is a wind up or we are going to be out with the two best looking 'birds' in Battersea tomorrow night. Probably best not to get too pissed though"* he thought as he headed back down to the living room. As he walked in Rod, Urban and Daisy were all still lying on the sofas.

"I wonder what Glynn's up to now?" Urban said, laughing.

"He's probably so randy that he's trying to shag Heather's mum" Rod replied.

"Ooh, can you imagine what she looks like? Heather's no oil painting but add another thirty years on top. Not worth thinking about really" said Urban

"Yeah but I bet the way Glynn's feeling he'd be happy to shag her dad" Daisy said laughing.

Dean though this was an appropriate point to cut into the conversation. "Hey, are any of you boys free to go on a date tomorrow?"

"Who with" said Rod, showing interest.

"Well I met this Russian bird at a lapdancing bar last week. She wants me to take her out and asked if I could bring a friend along. I think her mate is a lapdancer as well so she's guaranteed to be hot."

"Sounds brilliant, what's the catch?" Rod asked sensing that it sounded to good to be true.

"There's no catch mate" Dean lied. "About 9 o'clock tomorrow night OK?"

"Cool!" Rod replied.

****

As Glynn came out of the tube at Green Park he felt decidedly strange. Unusually the tube had been absolutely packed full of fit women. A very attractive girl had sat next to him and the smell of her perfume had really started to turn him on. So much so that he'd actually asked her what brand it was, which was completely out of character for him. Unfortunately she'd taken his innocent question to be some sort of lame chat up line, got up and walked off to the other end of the carriage without responding. After she'd got off he'd noticed two Brazilian-looking girls sitting opposite him who were also really hot. Before he knew what was happening he was fantasising about a threesome with both of them and suddenly realised he'd started to get a lob-on.

At first it was just a lazy-lob, the size and consistency of a raw sausage. However, even though he'd tried to quell it by thinking non-erotic thoughts, it had got firmer and firmer until it was fully erect and more like the consistency of a fully cooked sausage that was bursting at the seams. Initially he'd tried to disguise it by crossing his legs and positioning it along his thigh but that became more difficult as it got bigger and he finally had to resort to casually placing his right hand over his groin to press it down onto his leg. Getting off the tube had been a nightmare as the linen trousers he was wearing provided no resistance against the now monstrous erection. The tube was really busy and in order to avoid poking somebody in the back with his throbbing penis Glynn had resorted to keeping his right hand over his groin as he stood up and got off. Initially he tried to pretend that he was merely wiping something off his trousers but he soon gave up the act and resigned himself to the fact that he would just have to look like a pervert until he got out of the tube station. The alternative was to walk along the platform with a tent pole sticking up inside the front of his trousers.

Once he was out in the open air he nipped into one of the side streets to sort himself out. He thrust his hand down the front of his trousers to try and reposition his tackle so that it would be less obvious to passers by. As he put his hand into his pants he was disturbed to feel that his nob felt rock hard. It wasn't merely erect, as it normally was when he had sex with Heather, but genuinely as hard as a rock. It was also throbbing like he had never felt it before, as if a new pint of blood was being delivered into it every few seconds. The act of touching it made matters worse and he quickly decided to abort the repositioning exercise, just in case there was a minor eruption which, given the colour of his trousers, was his worst case scenario. As well as the swelling in his trousers he also started to feel very hot and his skin felt itchy. He looked at his watch and saw it was ten past eight. He was already ten minutes late for dinner and as he couldn't wait for nature to take its course he decided to go. As a last resort he grabbed the waistband of his boxer shorts and pulled it from his left hip towards his right, causing the shorts to twist across the front of his body. In turn this pulled his erection diagonally across his stomach and made it look as flat as it was ever going to under the circumstances.

He slowly started walking across the road to the Ritz. With every step he could feel his erection trying to break free and his boxers inching their way back to their normal position. He started taking smaller steps, which seemed to help but caused him to almost get run over as he was now in the middle of the road. Unable to run to the other side he merely waived at the drivers who had screeched to a halt in front of him and who were all beeping their horns and making rude gestures towards him. By the time he eventually got to the doorway of the Ritz hotel a small crowd had gathered, watching his progress as if it was street theatre. As he walked up to the entrance the doorman opened the door, tipped his hat and gave him a wink. Glynn immediately felt self conscious and convinced himself that the guy knew he had a raging erection that was desperately trying to get out of his flimsy trousers.

Glynn walked into the lobby and Heather, who was with a well dressed older lady, waved to him from the bar on the other side of the huge atrium. He looked down at his crotch hoping to see an improvement but could feel that the stalk-on was showing no sign of subsiding yet. He slowly walked towards them like a catwalk model, deliberately crossing his legs over his crotch with each step. After what seemed like an eternity and a few close shaves he made it to the relative safety of the bar and sat down with his legs firmly together.

"Hi" said Heather as she gave him a peck on the cheek. "This is my mum, Glenda. Mum this is Glynn" she said gesturing between the two of them.

"Very pleased to meet you" said Glynn as he shook her mother's outstretched hand.

"Likewise" she replied in her extremely posh accent.

"Is your dad not coming?" Glynn asked.

"He went out to see what all the commotion was outside" Heather responded.

"Commotion?" asked Glynn starting to feel self conscious again.

"Yeah, we heard car brakes screeching, horns beeping and a crowd had gathered outside. Daddy thought there might have been an accident and as he's a surgeon he went to see if he could be of assistance" said Heather taking a sip from her glass of champagne.

"Oh" said Glynn desperately hoping that her father hadn't got there in time to see him crossing the road.

"Here he is" Heather said pointing to a grey haired gentleman wearing a dinner suit and dickie bow. Glynn looked down at his beige suit and open necked shirt and silently cursed Dean for persuading him not to wear his pin striped suit.

"Sorry to miss you when you arrived old boy, but there was a bit of a palaver outside and I thought they may have needed me. It had all cleared up by the time I got there but the doorman told me that it was just some mad exhibitionist who demanded that the traffic stop for him. Call me Miles" said Heather's father as he offered out his hand.

"Nice to meet you Miles" said Glynn trying desperately to think of a different conversation topic.

"Probably a vagrant or one of those homosexuals, London's full of them" Heather's mum said flippantly.

Ordinarily Glynn would have picked her up on either topic and tackled her bigoted views, but on this occasion he decided that he had bigger things to worry about to let it go.

"So Glynn, Heather tells me that you're a lawyer? Some of my best friends are barristers" Miles said taking a drink from his whisky tumbler.

"I'm not actually a barrister I'm more on the corporate side" Glynn replied.

"Oh well, not to worry. I'm sure that it's still very interesting" Miles replied. "Anyway I think our table is ready" he continued as he waived at a waiter on the other side of the room.

Glynn was hoping that meeting Heather's mum and dad and sitting down would have calmed things in his boxers but he could sense the fires were burning stronger than ever. As he stood up he quickly yanked his boxer shorts around again, pinning his nob to his belly in the process. He then waited for everyone to start walking to the table, intending to follow behind them. Unfortunately Miles insisted on waiting for him so that the men could walk together. He gingerly made his way to the table desperately hoping that his erection didn't bring the conversation to a sudden halt. Eventually they arrived at the table which was surrounded by a hoard of waiters. There appeared to be one for every single aspect of the meal. Glynn was helped into his seat by the chair waiter and as he sat down a rather attractive female waitress elaborately unfolded a napkin and attempted to place it onto his lap. Glynn anticipated her move, was able to grab it from her hand to avoid any unnecessary embarrassment and carefully placed it onto his lap. He then pulled his seat as far forward as it would go to ensure that his 'old fella' was safely under the table and out of sight.

"You know Glynn, my favourite part about the Ritz is that after dinner the band comes on and we can all have a nice waltz together" said Glenda as she broke her bread roll.

Glynn's heart sank at the thought of dancing as he placed his hand under his napkin and checked on his still-throbbing penis.

"That'll be nice" he said trying his best to look pleased as he picked up his menu and he encountered his second nightmare of the evening. All of the dishes were written in French with an English translation. However, the English version was equally difficult to understand. He looked at the first three starters on offer, which were (in English) 'Ravioli of Oyster, Lasagne of Langoustine and Ballotine of Foie Gras.' *"Why don't they tell you what the fuck any of this stuff actually is?"* he thought as he started to feel even hotter and his skin started itching even more. All of a sudden things took a turn for the worse when he felt Heather's hand on his leg. He looked at her out of the side of his menu, gave her a pleading look and shook his head to indicate that he wanted her to stop. In response she gave him a wink and dragged her finger nails along his thigh. As soon as her hand started to move Glynn felt his erection move into another gear.

His penis started to throb even harder and he could sense that ejaculation was not too far away. A feeling of blind panic came over him as he looked at Heather, then her mother and finally her father. Knowing that he only had seconds to avert imminent disaster he flung his chair back, mumbled "I need to go to the toilet" as he stood up and bolted off. He managed to get to the toilet door, which was thankfully out of sight of the table, before the inevitable ejaculation started. As he finally made it into the cubicle the ejaculation was into its dying throws. He unbuckled his trousers and pulled open the waistband of his boxers to inspect the damage. It looked as if somebody had poured a pot of glue into his shorts, and a big pot at that. Glynn grabbed some tissue paper and started mopping it up. He'd cleared up the worst of it when he suddenly realised that it had totally soaked through the front of his boxers.

"Oh please god no!" he thought as he bent down and pulled his trousers up from his ankles. Glynn's worst fears came true as he inspected the front of the beige linen garment to reveal a dark wet patch the size of a tennis ball. *"Shit, shit, shit, shit, shit!"* he thought as he stood staring at the sticky wet patch. *"Right, there's only one thing for it"* he thought as he sat on the toilet seat, pulled off his shoes and whipped his trousers off. He opened the cubicle door, walked over to the bank of sinks on the other side of the room, turned on the cold tap and thrust the groin area of the trousers under the running water. Just as he started scrubbing the offending area Glynn felt a presence behind him and froze. *"If this*

is Heather's dad I'm fucked" he thought as he turned round. Behind him was the toilet attendant.

"Can I help you with that sir?" the attendant asked with a genuinely large smile on his face.

"Err, no. I'm fine thanks. I'm just trying to clean some mayonnaise off my trousers, thanks" Glynn replied with a less than genuine smile.

"OK sir" the attendant replied still grinning from ear to ear. Glynn then became very conscious of the fact that he was standing opposite the guy in his boxer shorts with a full erection. He hadn't given the erection a second thought since he'd entered the toilets as the normal form was for it to deflate rapidly once he'd ejaculated. However, for some reason, it hadn't moved an inch despite the fact that it had emptied the contents of his scrotum all over the inside of his trousers. He looked down at his boxers with the tent pole inside and then back at the attendant.

"Errm, could you give me a minute?" Glynn said politely.

"No problem sir" the attendant replied allowing himself a chuckle as he returned to his seat near the door.

Glynn finished scrubbing his trousers and looked around for a hand drier. The toilet area was decorated in a highly ornate fashion, however the style was straight out of the 1900's and there were no hand driers in sight.

"How do you dry your hands?" he shouted to the attendant hopefully.

"Use the hand towels provided sir. Each one is made of the finest Egyptian cotton and only used once" he replied.

"Fuck" Glynn said to himself as he held up his trousers. The entire front patch from the waistband to ten inches down the leg was totally soaked. He picked up a hand towel and started trying to dry them but it had no impact on the wet patch. He thought back to his exit from the table and was convinced that Miles would be coming to check he was alright at any second. As he still had a raging hard on he decided to head back into his cubicle. It proved to be a timely move as a few seconds later he heard Miles' voice.

"Glynn? Are you in here? Is everything OK? Did a young guy come rushing in here a few minutes ago?" Miles asked the attendant.

"Oh please don't say anything about washing the trousers or, worse still, the erection!" Glynn thought as he rapidly put his trousers and shoes back on.

"I think so sir" the attendant replied giving Glynn just enough time to tie his laces, reposition his penis as best he could and rush out to the sink before Miles could see him. He quickly turned the tap on full blast and thrust his hands under the water so that it diverted the majority of it out of the sink and onto him. "Whoa! Oh no!" he exclaimed theatrically as Miles came around the corner and into the main part of the toilets.

"Glynn. I thought that was your voice. Are you alright old bean? The ladies were starting to get a bit worried and sent me to find you."

Glynn remained facing the sink with his back to Miles. He looked at him in the mirror as he replied.

"Well I was fine before this happened" he said turning to reveal the water he'd just sprayed dripping off his suit.

"Oh bad luck old boy" said Miles grabbing a hand towel and handing it to Glynn. "That's one of the problems of wearing light trousers eh? Shows up all the spits and spots!" he said laughing. Glynn joined in laughing, relieved that the tension was broken.

"I had a curry last night and my stomach's been playing up all day today" Glynn said pointing at the cubicle to explain why he had rushed away from the table.

"We've all been there old bean" Miles replied. "I did a six month stint over in India when I was a medical student and spent half my time on the kazi."

"Well I think I'm over the worst of it now so hopefully I'll be OK for the rest of the night" said Glynn patting his stomach gently.

"Great. Well let's get back to the table, the ladies will be wondering what we're up to" Miles said laughing and patting Glynn on the back. As they passed the attendant he winked at Glynn, who pulled a relieved expression in response.

Chapter 32
Week 7 - Saturday

"What did you say these bird's names are?" Rod asked as Dean handed him another pint.

"Jemma and Gloria?" Dean replied as he took a sip from his drink.

"And which's one's mine?"

Rod tended to go for biker chicks or Goths so Dean had decided he would prefer the brunette. "Gloria" he replied.

"Gloria? She sounds like someone's mum. Where did you say she's from?"

"I'm not sure but I think she's Russian" Dean lied.

"But she's definitely hot and up for it?"

"Yeah. I haven't met her but apparently she's gagging to meet a nice English boy" said Dean as he subconsciously patted his trouser pocket to make sure the five grand was still there.

"Have you shagged yours yet then?" Rod asked.

"Err, not exactly" Dean replied, careful not to say anything that he might regret once Rod found out the truth about the 'girls'. "She was bang up for it but I got a bit too pissed and passed out."

"I must admit I'm shitting myself" said Rod as he downed half of his new pint. "I've never been on a blind date before and I think it's worse knowing that the bird is bang up for the full monty. I need something a bit stronger than this" he said heading to the bar. He returned a couple of minutes later with two pints and two vodka red bulls. Rod handed Dean his drinks and downed the vodka red bull in one go. "That's what you need, gets you in the mood and gives you stamina to go all night" said Rod placing the empty glass down on the table next to where he was standing. Dean started to feel a guilty about setting Rod up with a transsexual and downed his drink.

Two hours, six pints of Stella and five vodka red bulls later Dean looked at his watch and saw it was ten past nine. "Oh fuck, we're late" he said to Rod indicating that he needed to drink up. They both finished their pints and headed out of the pub.

"I feel a bit pissed" Rod said as the crossed the Road and made their way to Clapham Junction. As they approached the station they could see two tall, stunningly attractive women standing outside, wearing black cocktail dresses.

"Fucking hell, is that them?" Rod asked, excitedly.

"Yep" Dean replied amazed that the 'girls' actually looked like their photographs.

"I think I've died and gone to heaven. Good shit like this never happens to me" said Rod almost crying. Dean felt even more guilty but the thought of his future playboy lifestyle ensured that he kept up the pretence.

"Hi Jemma" said Dean as he gave the blonde 'girl' a peck on the cheek and prayed she wouldn't give away the fact that they'd never met before. "This is Rod" Dean continued.

"Hello Rod. I'm Gloria" said the dark haired girl in a strong Eastern European accent. She held out her hand and Rod smiled as she shook it enthusiastically.

"I thought we could go for a few drinks and maybe grab a bite to eat later if that's OK with you two?" Dean asked rhetorically. Both of the girls smiled and nodded and they set off to the pub they'd just left. Once there they grabbed a table and as the girls settled in Dean and Rod headed to the bar.

"Fucking hell Deano, they're hot and I mean fucking hot. Did you see the way that every bloke in here was staring at us as we came in? We'll be like a couple of celebrities around here if we start knocking-off these two on a regular basis. I'll tell you mate this is going to be the best night of my life" said Rod as he started jumping up and down with excitement.

"I hope so mate" Dean replied still feeling guilty that there was one very important thing he had omitted to mention about the 'girls'. "Shall we get ourselves a couple of cheeky shooters to pep us up a bit?"

"Yeah, go on then" Rod replied. "We should probably get a couple for them as well, just to make sure they're in the mood. Get six tequilas and we can down two at the bar and then have one with them at the table as well."

"OK. Can I have two pints of Stella, two glasses of dry white wine and six tequilas please?" Dean asked the barmaid. She served him the drinks and, after slamming the first two tequilas, they headed over to the table with the drinks.

"So I believe that you ladies are both lapdancers?" Rod asked as they sat down.

Jemma looked at Dean who was made a subtle nodding gesture.

"Yes" she replied. Gloria followed up by placing her hand on Rod's leg and wiggling suggestively. "Would you like me to dance for you now Rod?"

"Not just yet, but definitely later" he replied taking a large gulp out of his pint. "So where are you girls from?"

"I am from the Ukraine and Gloria is from Moldova" Jemma replied taking a sip of her wine.

"That's nice" Rod replied having no real idea where either country was. "And how long have you been in London?"

"Almost three months" Jemma replied. "We were brought over by a friend who knows the woman who runs the agency."

"What agency?" Rod asked.

"The place that gets them jobs in the lapdancing clubs mate" Dean cut in before either of the girls could reply. "Anyway, I'm sure that you don't want to be talking shop all night. Where do you girls live?"

"Near to Kings Cross station" Gloria replied.

"Fucking hell, you don't want to stay there. It's really seedy, full of drug addicts and prostitutes" said Rod. "You want to move somewhere round here or Islington, somewhere a bit more trendy."

"But Rod, it is very expensive in these places and we do not have much money. The place we stay is very cheap. It is provided for us and lots of girls from our countries stay there, so it is not too bad."

"It sounds nice" said Dean insincerely, wishing he'd chosen a different topic to talk about.

The conversation bumbled along in a similar awkward manner for the next hour or so. Rod or Dean asked various inane questions that they weren't really interested in hearing the answer to and the girls provided them with answers which revolved around the fact that they were either foreign or that they had no money. This slightly tedious routine was made bearable by two factors. The first was that they were all drinking heavily (Rod and Dean had passed the double figure mark for pints of Stella) and the second was that Jemma and Gloria were stunningly attractive and very flirty with it. As a result both Dean and Rod got more pissed and horny as the night went on.

Rod eventually went to the toilet and, despite the fact that he was also bursting to go, Dean remained at the table. As soon as Rod was out of sight Dean asked the one question he'd been desperate to ask all night.

"So the lady on the phone said I should talk to you directly if we want anything more than just a drink?" Dean asked nervously.

"Yes darling" Gloria replied. "If we are interested then it will be one thousand pounds for us to stay the night with you."

"And are you interested?"

"Yes. You're both nice boys" she replied fluttering her eyelids. Jemma smiled to acknowledge her agreement.

In order not to cause any suspicion from Rod, Dean knew that he'd have to pay both of the girls to ensure that they both came back to the house. He'd already set up the PC to record the events in Rod's bedroom and his plan was to wait until they paired off and then tell Jemma to leave. Once he had recorded evidence of Rod kissing Gloria he would go into Rod's room and stop him before things went too far. Dean pulled out the wad of cash from his pocket, counted out a thousand pounds under the table and handed it to Gloria.

"It's one thousand pounds each" she said looking at the remaining pile of money in Dean's hand.

"Fucking hell, that's a bit rich isn't it?" Dean replied.

"Well, we are very special girls aren't we?" Gloria replied with a smile.

Dean knew that he didn't have time to argue as the whole deal would be over if Rod came back and saw him handing over the money. He quickly handed over another thousand pounds and stuffed the remainder of the cash back into his pocket.

"Oh, one other thing" he said "this is a surprise birthday present for Rod so can we keep both the financial side and your special secret to ourselves?"

"No problem" Gloria replied as she put the money into her handbag.

****

When they got back to the house Rod and Dean were both feeling very pissed. None of the other lads were around and they decided to have a bottle of wine with the 'girls' in the living room. Dean and Jemma sat on one sofa and Rod and Gloria grabbed the other. Dean noticed that Rod and Gloria had been holding hands on the way back from the pub and as they sat down Rod put his arm around Gloria's shoulder. Dean couldn't get the thought that Gloria was actually a man out of his head and the guilt of setting Rod up started to kick in again. To help him put it out of his mind he poured himself a large glass of wine and gulped it down.

"Take it easy" said Jemma. "We've got all night to get through" she said running her index finger under Dean's chin and smiling seductively.

Dean's head was swimming and the room started to spin. He knew that Jemma wasn't a real woman but every time he looked at her he couldn't help fancying her more and more. He blinked hard and shook his head to try to sober himself up. It didn't work and only made the room spin even faster. He looked over to Rod who was now necking with Gloria and had his right hand on her breast. Dean suddenly decided that the deception wasn't right and that he should tell Rod the truth. However, as he lurched forward he found himself unable to speak. He was so pissed that all he could do was watch as Rod thrust his tongue down Gloria's throat and started to lift his leg across hers. Dean suddenly felt Jemma's hand on his thigh and turned to look at her. She started to spin round the room as well and he fell back onto the sofa. He felt Jemma's breath on his cheek and her long blonde hair on his face and everything went black.

Chapter 33
Week 7 - Sunday

Dean found himself in that pleasant twilight zone he occasionally entered when he woke from a deep sleep; not quite asleep but definitely not awake. He felt at peace with the world, in fact he felt more than at peace, he felt positively great. There was a warm feeling all over his body, a sort of aura of happiness. As he started to drift into a more conscious state he realised that this state of delirium wasn't just in his mind but also involved physical pleasure. As he opened his eyes, the hangover that started to seep into his brain was outweighed by the fact that under his duvet someone was giving him a blow job. For a few seconds he lay back and enjoyed the experience, revelling in the pleasure of the situation. Then the realisation of who was in bed with him hit him like a truck. He pulled back the duvet and saw Jemma vigorously sucking away on his nob. Appalled, he sat up quickly, intending that the action would remove his penis from her mouth. Unfortunately she had a really tight grip on it with her right hand which meant it remained in her mouth but was now bent forward at an acute angle.

"Whoa, whoa, whoa!" Dean shouted as Jemma finally relinquished hold of his erection.

"What's wrong darling? Don't you like it?"

"I don't want any of this" Dean replied looking at Jemma's body as she sat up. She was naked apart from a thong, which Dean was extremely grateful she was still wearing. She looked like a Playboy model, huge breasts with a tiny waist, and for a second he considered allowing her to carry on. Then he thought of the dark secret within the thong caused his resolve to harden and his dick to soften.

"You didn't complain last night" said Jemma as she put her hand on his leg and gave him a cheeky smile.

"I was very drunk and don't remember any of that" Dean replied feeling sick to the stomach. "I want you to go now."

"Are you sure you don't want me to suck it again? Or maybe you would like to suck mine?" Jemma said standing up.

"No way, you fucking pervert. Now get out of my room, please" he said, adding the please as he felt disappointed with himself for calling her a pervert, especially as he had specifically ordered, and paid for, a woman with a penis.

Clearly upset at what he had said, she picked up her clothes and started to get dressed in silence. Dean grabbed his boxer shorts from the floor and pulled on his jeans. Once she was fully clothed he opened the door and took her out onto the landing. Dean was disturbed to hear talking and giggling coming from Rod's room but decided it was best not to interrupt. He showed Jemma downstairs to the front door.

"I'm sorry that I called you a pervert."

"It's OK honey. You're the one that paid a thousand pound to sleep with me, so who's the real pervert?" Jemma replied with a flick of her hair. She then spun round on her stilettos and walked off down the path.

After he closed the door Dean ran back to his room and straight into the shower, where he stayed scrubbing his penis for the next half an hour.

****

It was a full two hours later that Dean heard Rod and Gloria emerge from Rod's bedroom. Dean felt dirty, guilty and disgusted with himself for getting so drunk that he'd allowed a man into his bed, even if it was a very attractive man that actually looked like a woman. However, worse than that he felt unbelievably guilty that he'd set Rod up with what was, in his mind, effectively a male prostitute. When he'd planned it all the previous day he'd fully expected there to be fireworks when Rod found out about Gloria's 'surprise package.' Dean thought Rod would firstly go ballistic with Gloria and then secondly with him. In fact he'd prepared himself for the possibility of Rod chinning him and had decided that if he did he'd take his punishment fair and square without fighting back as he had done such a shitty thing to a mate. He hoped that the three grand he had left over from Dougie's money would be sufficient compensation for Rod to forgive him.

What Dean hadn't expected was that Gloria would spend the whole night and most of the following morning in Rod's bed. Dean had been thinking about what could possibly be going on and had come up with three theories:

1. Nothing had happened. Like Dean, Rod had simply been too pissed to do anything and had passed out, therefore not actually discovering that Gloria had a penis.

2. Heavy petting. Maybe Gloria had said that she didn't put out on a first date and they'd only gone as far as kissing and cuddling.

3. Rod was a raving homosexual who had spent the night happily sucking away on Gloria's cock.

Dean was desperately trying to believe that the truth lay in theories one or two, however he couldn't get theory three out of his mind. If Gloria had left during the night then he may have believed that Rod had passed out or that nothing had gone on, but the fact that she was still around in the morning did not bode well for Rod's heterosexual credentials. In Dean's experience if a girl stayed the whole night then it was an odds on certainty that you would shag her again in the morning. In fact he considered it positively rude not to.

There was, of course, a simple way of finding out the truth as to what had gone on. Dean switched on his PC and booted up the DVD he'd set to record the events in Rod's bedroom the previous night. He forwarded through all of the blank footage, recorded whilst they had been in the pub, and got to the point where Rod and Gloria entered the room. Rod was obviously very pissed as he staggered in holding Gloria's hand. Dean couldn't help laughing as Rod proceeded to fall over the corner of his own bed, pulling Gloria onto the floor with him. However, Dean stopped laughing as they started necking on the floor and Rod put his hands all over Gloria's boobs. Dean couldn't bear to watch in real time and forwarded the footage. He saw the events unfold four times quicker than they had in real life. After a lot of rolling backwards and forwards on the floor, Rod and Gloria eventually made it up onto the bed where they continued rolling around and necking. Then Gloria stood up and disappeared out of sight of the camera. When she returned she was wearing just her bra and thong and had a tube of what looked to be some sort of lubricant in her hand. Dean stopped forwarding and watched in real time. Rod proceeded to take off all of his clothes, except for his boxers, and lay face down on the bed. *"Oh, here we go, let the pillow biting commence"* thought Dean as he braced himself for the worst.

However the lubricant turned out to be massage oil and Gloria began to give Rod a massage. Dean forwarded the footage again and watched as Gloria ran her hands all over Rod's back, turned him over and eventually started to give him a blow job. As Dean had more than enough to satisfy Dougie's challenge he paused the footage and sent a copy of the blow job to the printer. He then stopped the DVD and turned off the PC, unable to watch what else Rod and Gloria had got up to. He lay down on his bed, curled up into the foetal position and started to cry. *"This whole thing is not fucking worth it. I'm destroying everyone's lives, including my own, just for the sake of money"* Dean thought to himself as he lay on his bed feeling as low as he'd ever done in his whole life.

His depression was broken by a knock on his door.

"Hey Deano, are you in there?" Rod shouted from the hallway.

"Err, yeah. Hang on a second" Dean replied as he sat up and made sure it wasn't obvious he'd been crying. He opened the door and Rod came bounding in like an excited puppy.

"So how did you get on then?" Rod asked, grinning like a madman.

"What d'ya mean?" Dean replied.

"With Jemma, you nobhead. How did you get on? Did you shag her?"

The fact that Rod had used the word 'her' rather than 'him' confused Dean and left him unsure as to how much Rod could actually remember about the evening. "Err, no I didn't mate. I was too pissed. I just passed out."

"Again? What about this morning? Didn't you shag her then?" Rod asked looking shocked.

"Err, no. She had to leave early so she didn't have time" Dean lied. "What about you then mate? Did you do the bizz?"

"Pretty much" said Rod with a beaming smile.

"Pretty much?" Dean replied. "What does pretty much mean? Did you shag her or not?"

"We did everything except for shagging. It was her time of the month so she wouldn't let me near her snatch but she sucked me off a couple of times and I even had a tit wank" he said bursting into a delirious fit of laughter.

"Right. So you didn't get your hand down her pants at all then?"

"No, she wouldn't let me. I said that I wasn't squeamish and didn't mind a bit of blood but she was having none of it and said that we should wait until she was feeling a bit more feminine" Rod explained.

"That could be quite a long wait" thought Dean. "So are you seeing her again then?"

"Well she said she was a bit busy this week but would give me a call once her diary frees up. I've got to fucking see her again though Deano as they were the best blow jobs that I've ever had, different fucking gravy!"

"Yeah, they do say they give the best blow jobs" Dean replied without thinking.

"Who?" Rod asked looking confused.

"Err, Moldovans" Dean said trying to cover up his absent minded comment.

"Do they? I've never fucking heard that. Still, after last night I can't disagree" he said rubbing his groin to emphasis the point.

"Quite" Dean responded looking at his watch. "Anyway the boozer's open. Fancy a spot of Sunday lunch?"

"Too right. I'll tell you mate I think I might have fallen in love. After what you did for me last night I think the food's on me" said Rod springing to his feet.

"You wouldn't say that if you knew the truth" Dean thought to himself as they headed out of his room.

Chapter 34
Week 7 - Wednesday

Daisy and Mel were in the local DVD rental store looking for a movie. Daisy looked at the myriad of covers laid out in front of him and immediately wished he was in the pub with the boys.

"Why do you use this crappy store instead of Blockbuster?"

"Shhh! Keep your voice down" Mel whispered nodding in the direction of the two eighteen year old spotty geeks behind the desk.

"It's not as if they own this bloody place is it? I'm sure they don't give a monkey's arse whether we go to Blockbuster or not" Daisy replied, whispering to keep Mel happy.

"Well I do. I don't want large American Corporations taking over all of my local stores. If I wanted to live in a soulless place like America I'd move there. I want to support local businesses that give the area character and make it different to every other town in the UK.

So that's why we're not going to Blockbuster" Mel said, drawing a metaphorical line under the discussion.

"But the choice is crap here. I can never find anything I want, they never have the latest titles and you have to actually bring the DVD's back into the shop rather than posting them through a letterbox" Daisy replied. Before Mel could respond the shop was filled with the sound of familiar classical music and Daisy looked up at the screen above his head to see the opening titles to Star Wars. He looked over at the two geeky assistants.

"Good choice dude" the spottier of the two said to the one with the greasier hair as he gave him a high five.

"May the force be with *you*" the greasier one replied. The spottier one then made a "vooooom" sound and held out his hands as if holding an imaginary light sabre.

Daisy looked at the bloke who was standing in front of the desk with his girlfriend, waiting patiently to be served. The bloke looked back at Daisy and shook his head in despair. Daisy scanned around the rest of the shop. The population consisted of three other couples, two groups of teenage girls who were giggling and screaming and three blokes on their own, two of whom were looking at the martial arts section whilst the other was hovering around the top shelf porn section whilst pretending to look at the 'International Films.' *"Jesus Christ, when did I become one of these sad fuckers?"* Daisy thought. His thoughts were broken by Mel's voice.

"OK, here's my short list" she said and handed over three DVD boxes. Daisy looked at them. The first was a cartoon about a bunch of animals that had the word 'HILARIOUS' written in large letters along the top of the box, the second was a true life story about a family coping with an autistic child and the third was the usual girl-meets-boy-girl-loses-boy-girl-marries-boy-in-the-end chick flick. Daisy stared at the three boxes in his hands and started to lose the will to live.

"Are these really the best three films in here" he asked.

"No, but I've given you a selection of different types of film. The Disney film is meant to be really funny" Mel replied.

"I'm not watching a cartoon on a Saturday night" Daisy replied handing her back the box "and I'm definitely not watching that, it looks really depressing" he said handing over the true life story box.

"It's supposed to be uplifting" Mel replied indignantly as she took the two boxes from him and put them back on the shelf. "So are we going for this one then?" she said snatching the last remaining box out of Daisy's hand.

"If we have to" Daisy said, as he resigned himself to his fate. "Unless you fancy an Action Thriller?" he said hopefully.

"No, I think this will be just perfect. It's meant to be really funny, I think you'll like it" she said heading off to the counter. Daisy followed her, like a condemned man heading for the gallows. Mel handed the box over to the spotty assistant who looked at it and said "Good choice!"

"You see, I told you it was a good one" Mel said to Daisy.

"He's said that to every single person who has taken a film out since we've been in here. Even the pervie bloke who rented all those porn films" Daisy replied shaking his head.

"Well maybe they were particularly good ones" Mel responded.

Spotty handed over the film and Daisy breathed a sigh of relieve as he made it out of the shop.

"Shall we nip in for a quick beer before we head back?"

"Well I did say to Heather we'd be straight back" Mel said, meaning 'no'.

"Oh come on. Glynn will be round soon so she won't mind" he said pulling her by the arm.

"OK, but only a quick one."

The pub next to the DVD store was a female friendly chain that served food and had flowers on each table. Daisy was surprised to see that it was full of small groups of women and made a mental note to go back there if he ever finished with Mel. He ordered a couple of drinks and they sat down at a table near the window.

"Oh, I forgot to mention, it's Heather's birthday a week on Friday so we decided to have a party to celebrate. Can you invite all of the guys from your house to come as we need some eligible men to be there" she said taking a sip from her glass of wine.

Whenever he was with Mel, Daisy's mind was never far away from the horrendous incident with Chloe. The merest mention of 'meeting a friend' would cause him to break into a sweat. His heart sank at the mention of the word party, this was his worst possible nightmare.

"So who'll be coming to this party" he asked trying to appear casual as he took a sip from his pint.

"All my friends are coming. Let's see, there's Claire, Diane, Lorraine, Chloe and Catherine. Oh, I can't wait for you to meet Chloe, she's such a scream. I think you two will get on like a house on fire" she said excitedly.

"Great" Daisy said as sincerely as he could muster and immediately starting thinking up reasons why he wouldn't be able to go to the party.

Chapter 35
Week 8 - Friday

Dean arrived at Canary Wharf slightly later that usual. Razor was already in situ, reading the Evening Standard and drinking a pint.

"Alright Razor? You don't seem to have been around much this week mate, what have you been up to?" Dean asked as he sat down opposite him with a pint.

"I've been getting some much needed TLC from a bird I met last week. I told her I broke my arm in an ice climbing accident so she thinks I'm an all action hero" Razor replied.

"There you go. I told you I was doing you a favour" Dean replied pointing at Razor's cast.

"I wouldn't go as far as to say that. I'm still pissed off about it but I've decided to use it to my advantage. It's my USP!"

"USP?" Dean asked.

"Unique Selling Point" Razor continued looking very pleased with himself. "Anyway, have you got the photos of you shagging some bloke then?"

"Not quite. In fact they're not of me at all, they're of Rod" Dean replied.

"I never knew he was an arse bandit" said Razor taking a drink from his pint. "Let's have a look then."

Dean handed over the A4 envelope and Razor pulled out a photo of Rod getting a blow job from Gloria.

"What's this" asked Razor looking confused. "He's meant to be shagging a bloke not some fit bird."

"That is a bloke" Dean replied.

"Look, I think that I know a bloke when I see one and there is no fucking way that is a bloke" Razor responded as he continued staring at the photo.

"I thought you might say that" said Dean as he pulled a few folded up pieces of paper out of his pocket and handed them over. "The first page is a print off of the Transsexual Escort website that I found 'him' on and the other two pages are pictures of 'him' along with a biography. Checkout the website for yourself if you don't believe me."

"So this is definitely a bloke?" Razor said as he looked at the pictures of Gloria in disbelief.

"I'm afraid so" Dean replied.

"Fucking hell. You'd never know would you? I mean imagine if you met him in a club when you were pissed up. It'd be a fucking nightmare when you got home and got down to it" Razor said still staring at the picture of Gloria in her underwear and shaking his head. "So at what point did Rod find out it was a bloke?"

"He didn't" Dean replied.

"What? How did he not realise he was in bed with a bloke?"

"She gave him some cock and bull story about it being the time of the month so it was blow jobs all the way" said Dean smiling.

"The poor bastard. Wait till I tell him tonight" said Razor looking highly amused.

"No mate, don't tell him. He's all giddy with excitement that he had a night of passion with a really fit bird and keeps going on about how he loves her. He doesn't know I had to pay her a grand to spend the night with him."

"Or that she was a he?" Razor added.

"Exactly. I've got some cash left over from the money that Dougie provided last week, so how about I give you a grand and we keep this just between you and me?

"You spoil all of my fun but alright then" Razor said reluctantly. "Right I'd better get this over to the old boy" he said putting the photo of Rod back into the envelope and heading for the door. He returned around fifteen minutes later and handed two envelopes over to Dean. Dean ripped open the A4 envelope and took out the letter inside.

"Dear Dean,

So far so good mate. With seven down and only three to go you must be starting to think that you can see light at the end of the tunnel. Well don't start counting your chickens just yet as I can assure you that the last few challenges are going to be by far the toughest. I don't know how much you've been sharing things around between the housemates but I'll take this opportunity to provide you with a timely reminder that one of my key rules is that every housemate must take part in at least one of the challenges. Therefore if anyone hasn't done one yet you should start thinking about including them in the fun. Anyway, last week's action gave you, or one of your friends, a chance to explore sex with a member of the same sex and this week's challenge is along the same lines but slightly more extreme:

'BLOW JOB'

This week really is a test to see just how far someone is prepared to go for money. You have to persuade someone in the house (or obviously you can do it yourself) to voluntarily give a blow job to one of the other house members. I've arranged for Mr Jacob to increase the amount of cash available for this one as I'm aware that it is absolutely disgusting and makes me sick even thinking about it. Once again it's up to you how you spend the money and you can keep all of it if you decide not to take on the challenge.

Anyway, good luck mate and hopefully we'll be in touch again in another week's time.

Your friend,

Dougie"

Dean scrunched up the letter and threw it onto the table without saying a word.

"Hang on a minute. Don't you want to see how much money's on offer?" Razor asked waving the A5 envelope at Dean.

"Firstly, I don't give a shit how much money there is on offer and secondly it looks like there's fuck all anyway as there's nothing in the envelope" he said referring to the fact that the A5 envelope was not bursting at the seams with cash as it had been in previous weeks.

"Just fucking open it before you make any final decisions" said Razor throwing the envelope at Dean. Reluctantly Dean picked it up and took out the single piece of paper within.

Dear Mr Williams,

As part of the Last Will and Testament of Douglas Forsythe Mackenzie I am hereby irrevocably instructed to transfer the sum of £20,000 (Twenty Thousand Pounds) to a bank account of your choice. Please advise me of the sort code and account number that you wish the monies to be transferred to, no later than seven days from the date of this letter.

Yours Sincerely,

Peter Jacob

Partner

Jacobs & Co

"Twenty grand? Fucking hell" Razor exclaimed.

"Well at least I'll have a bit of cash at the end of all this shit then" said Dean as he put the letter back into the envelope.

"What? You're not even going to think about it?"

"Don't be fucking stupid. I'm going to call it a day and keep the twenty grand, so you'd better start looking for somewhere else to live" Dean replied.

"Twenty grand is a fuck of a lot of money though Deano. It's a big ask but for that sort of cash one of the lads might just decide it's worth sucking someone's cock for five minutes" said Razor.

"Would you do it?"

"No fucking chance and you can count me out of your calculations as I've still got this fucking thing" Razor replied waiving his cast at Dean. "But I wouldn't have wanked myself off in front of you either so it doesn't mean that someone else won't. I mean we are talking serious money here Deano."

"OK I'll put it to the group and see if there's any interest but if not then we're all out of that place this time next week" said Dean.

"The other thing you should remember Deano is that house is worth at least a two million quid and whilst twenty grand is a decent wedge you ain't gonna be able to retire on it. That playboy lifestyle you've been talking about won't last for long on twenty grand."

"I know" Dean replied as he took another sip of his pint and thought about the harsh reality of working for another forty years.

Chapter 36
Week 8 - Saturday

"You've got to give it a go mate. You've come this far and just give up now" said Razor who was sat at the desk in Dean's room smoking a cigarette.

"I've given it a lot of thought overnight Razor and I should have put a stop to all this weeks ago. The humiliation and degradation simply isn't worth it for the sake of a few quid?" Dean said as he sat up in bed, nursing his usual Saturday morning hangover.

"But it's not just a few quid is it? It's two million fucking quid. Surely it's worth doing anything to get hold of that sort of money? How many normal lads in their twenties have that sort of opportunity? Unless you're born into money or you're a fucking computer geek whiz kid it just doesn't happen. If you walk away from this now you'll regret it for the rest of your life Deano. There are people out there who'd kill their own grandmother for a few hundred quid and you're gonna throw the towel in just because you don't want to do something that will last for five minutes and you can forget about. This is the chance of a lifetime and if you give up now then you're a fucking idiot" said Razor as he stubbed out his cigarette on the sole of his shoe and threw the butt out of the window.

"Yeah, well you would say that wouldn't you? If I chuck it all in now you lose out on your chance of half a million quid as well don't you?"

"That's true and I must admit I'll be gutted if I miss out on the money, especially as I've still got this fucking thing to remind me of my contribution" said Razor holding up his purple cast. "I've literally given my left fucking arm to get us this far and all you've had to do was a bit of coke and have a bit of kinky sex, all of which you'll have forgotten in a few weeks time when you're sunning yourself on some desert island."

"I hear what you're saying Razor but I'm finding the side effects of all of this hard to live with. Urban has been acting very strange since I forced him to take that coke, Mick is fucked up over the Gill thing, you've got a broken arm and Rod's in love with a fucking man. It's just not right."

"If you feel so bad about it all why don't you give them all a share of the money once it's all over? That way you can come clean, tell them why you did everything and bung them a few quid to say sorry. I'm sure there won't be any hard feelings and it'll ease your guilt" Razor replied.

"Maybe, but I still don't think that anyone will go for this blow job thing" said Dean taking a sip from his mug of tea.

"Dean, you've got twenty fucking grand to persuade them to do it. Most of these lads are up to their ears in debt and that sort of money goes a very long way. All you need to do is ask, no harm in that" Razor said lighting another fag.

"Alright then, let's run through who could possibly be a maybe. I think the absolute non-starters are Glynn, Tim and Daisy. I've known Glynn long enough to be sure he wouldn't do it, Tim was disturbed by the whole biscuit game thing and doesn't need the money and Daisy seems keen on that Mel bird he's been seeing and doesn't look like the sort of bloke that would be interested in doing something just for the cash. That leaves Mick, Rod and Urban. I think Mick would chin me if I asked him so it looks like the shortlist is Rod and Urban, unless you fancy getting involved?" Dean said raising his eyebrows and looking at Razor.

"No thanks" Razor replied. "You have, of course left one other person off your list, you."

"I've told you, I'm not fucking doing it" Dean replied angrily.

"And I've told you not to be so hasty and to think about the end game. Anyway I've got to go as I'm seeing my old dear today. I'm out with a few old school mates tonight so I'll probably catch up with you tomorrow. Good luck tonight and, although I'm not one to betray someone's confidence, if I was you I'd make sure that Urban is around if you want to get this challenge completed.

"What does that mean?" Dean shouted but Razor was already on his way downstairs and didn't respond.

****

"Where is everybody?" Dean asked Urban, who was watching porn in the living room.

"I'm not sure" Urban replied without taking his eyes off the screen. "I heard Tim and Mick go out really early this morning as the noisy fuckers woke me up banging around. Mick finds it impossible to talk in anything less than a shout."

"Oh yeah" said Dean nodding "Mick's rugby team are playing in a tournament today and he's roped Tim into playing for them."

"Is Tim any good?" Urban asked.

"Yeah. He was captain of the first team at Uni until he knackered his knee. It still gives him a bit of jip so he doesn't play regularly any more but I think he's still pretty decent. Where's Rod?"

"He's gone to watch Mick and Tim" Urban replied, still glued to the screen.

"But he doesn't like rugby does he?"

"No, but he likes drinking copious amounts of beer and Mick promised him there would be loads of female rugby groupies there watching so he decided to go on the pretext that he might get a shag out of it."

"Let's hope not" Dean replied with chuckle. "Isn't it a bit early for this?" Dean said pointing at the screen.

"It's never too early or too late for good porn mate. Maybe it's just that you're getting too old and sensible" Urban replied.

"Maybe" Dean replied with a nod. "Razor's out with a few of his old school mates tonight and I'm guessing that Glynn and Daisy are out with their birds, so that just leaves you and me mate. Do you fancy going out on the pull?"

"Yeah, alright. I'll tell you what, just between you and me, I've got some top notch coke upstairs. We could have a couple of snifters before we go out if you fancy it?" Urban said sitting up and looking excited.

"Coke? When did you start buying coke?" Dean asked.

"I really enjoyed the buzz it gave me when we did it a few weeks ago, so I asked Razor if he could sort me out with some. It's fucking wicked mate" he replied.

Dean was concerned at how animated Urban had become since he raised the topic of coke but was more concerned about what Urban had just said about Razor. "Did you say that Razor bought it for you?"

"Yeah. Razor knows a few geezers who seem to be able to get it really easily. It's not cheap but it's fucking good stuff. In fact I really fancy a toot now we're talking about it" he said as he jumped up off the sofa and headed out of the room.

Dean sat down and thought about what Urban had just said. He was confused. Razor had been really cagey with him when he needed to buy coke for Dougie's challenge and had said that he 'might know a few people'. He'd then made Dean go with him to a dodgy housing estate in Mile End and take coke in front of the dealer. However it now seemed Razor was happy to score coke for Urban without any of the rigmarole Dean had been put through. Something just didn't stack up. Urban returned a minute later with a clear plastic sandwich bag full of white powder.

"Fucking hell Urban! How much have you got?" Dean exclaimed as he got up and closed the curtains.

"I gave Razor all of that £1,000 you gave me last week to get me some. I dunno how much there is by weight but I can tell you that there's plenty" said Urban laughing.

"So did Razor make you go with him when he bought it?" Dean asked, wanting to see if Urban had been to the same place in Mile End.

"No."

"Do you think he's skimming some off for himself?"

"Probably, but I don't really care as it's nice to know I can get more whenever I want it" Urban said as he poured out some of the powder and started to separate it into two lines with his bank card.

"So how long have you been buying it from him?"

"It started just after that Saturday night when we did it with Rod. I went out for a few beers with Razor and he mentioned he could get me some off a mate of his. Since then he's been getting it for me on a regular basis. His mate seems really cool as he's happy to run a tab for me" said Urban as he snorted the first line he'd set up.

"Really?" Dean said looking even more concerned as Urban handed him the rolled up twenty pound note.

****

"So why do they call you Urban?" the blonde girl asked as she took a sip from her wine glass.

"Because I know a lot of stories which are all totally true but people like Dean here are so small minded they think they're urban myths" Urban replied, teeing her up.

"Like what?" she asked, falling head first into his trap.

"Well, let me see" he said theatrically, "oh yeah, there's this bloke I know who works in the kitchen in a big hotel in London and he knows this lad who works there who bats for the other side."

"Who what?" asked the girl.

"Bats for the other side, you know, he's gay. Anyway this lad hasn't actually ever done the full monty if you know what I mean" said Urban looking at the girl with a knowing look on his face.

"No. What do you mean?" she replied with a blank expression.

"Which hotel did you say your friend works in?" the blonde's friend asked.

"Fucking hell, this is hard work" thought Urban biting his lip. He looked down at the blonde girl's breasts, which were bursting to get out of her ripped, cropped T-shirt, and managed to regain his composure. "It doesn't matter which hotel, OK?" he said curtly to the black haired girl and returned his attention to her blonde friend. "When I say he hadn't done the full monty I mean he hadn't had penetrative sex, you know up the bum."

"Aaaahhh!" both girls screamed and burst out giggling. Urban looked at Dean and gave a brief shake of his head.

"Anyway, as I said this lad hadn't done the full monty and so one night he decides to see what it feels like by using a coke bottle, one of the old fashioned glass ones. He smears a bit of butter over the top end of the bottle and starts pushing it in an inch at a time before pulling it out again. He soon gets it going so that he's got three quarters of the bottle going in and out of his arse. He decides to go for one big push to get the whole thing in there but as he does so the angle he's got the bottle at causes all of the air to be forced out, creating a vacuum inside. The pressure of the vacuum sucks the whole of his bowel inside out and into the bottle so he's then standing with the bottle hanging off the end of his arse with his innards trapped inside it. He's in total agony but doesn't want to make a sound in case someone comes and finds him so he panics, grabs a pair of scissors from the work top and cuts through his innards to get the bottle off" said Urban as he took a drink from his pint and watched the horror unfold on the girls faces.

"Ho my god! What happened to him? Was he OK?" the blonde girl asked.

"I dunno. My mate never really told me what happened after that. I think he went to hospital and was alright" Urban replied.

"That's why it's total bollocks" Dean cut in. "If it was genuinely a true story you'd know exactly what happened to him afterwards."

"It is fucking true" Urban responded.

"Well it's a horrible story. Thanks for the drink but we're got to go now" the blonde girl said.

"What? It's only nine thirty" Urban replied. "Don't you want another?"

"No we're meeting our boyfriends down the road" the blonde replied as she picked up her bag and headed towards the door.

"I think you scared them off with your story" Dean said to Urban as they watched the girls walk away.

"Oh well, fuck em. Their loss" Urban responded. "Right, hold my pint, I'm off to the bog".

When he returned Urban was literally bouncing up and down and it was clear that he'd used his toilet break to treat himself to a pick-me-up. "Right, there's a couple of other birds, let's get over there" he said as he walked off towards them before Dean could object.

"This time, try to avoid any stories about blokes sticking things up their arses" said Dean placing his hand on Urban's shoulder as he hurried after him.

****

On a normal night the amount of alcohol Dean and Urban had consumed would have put them in casualty at Chelsea and Westminster hospital. However the equally large amount of cocaine they'd also consumed enabled them to stay coherent and to keep drinking. Urban looked at his watch and saw it was ten to two, which meant he still had ten minutes left to pull. Despite the fact he'd failed to pull during virtually continuous attempts over the previous six hours the coke gave him never-ending confidence as he stood on the edge of the dance floor looking for a suitable candidate. Dean was standing with him but the time for hunting in pairs was over. *"In the last chance saloon it's every man for himself"* Urban thought as he scoured the remaining dancers for a semi-reasonable looking girl. Disappointingly the only people left on the dance floor seemed to be recently formed couples (i.e. that had met in the club at some point over the past couple of hours and who were trying to prove that they'd actually come to the club to dance rather than pull) or blokes who felt the need to advertise the fact that they were desperate by dancing together.

Just as Urban was about to give up and go home he spotted a girl standing on her own on the other side of the dance floor. On a normal day Urban would have scored her as a three or four out of ten and wouldn't have bothered making the effort. But this wasn't a normal day, he was now in the last chance saloon with his beer goggles well and truly strapped on and therefore she was more than acceptable. On top of that she was obviously extremely pissed which made her an even more desirable catch at that time of night.

"Give me five minutes" Urban said to Dean as he strode over to where the girl was leaning against a rail.

"Hi, I'm Urban. I couldn't help noticing that you're on your own" he said flashing her a friendly smile.

"I'm with my mates" she slurred back in a northern accent.

"Are you?" Urban said, looking around. "Are you sure they haven't left without you?"

"I'm with my mates" she repeated as she looked for them across the dance floor.

"What do they look like, your mates?"

"Yes" she replied, looking like it was a real effort to speak "I'm with my mates."

Urban considered walking away and trying to find a girl that was a bit more coherent, but had to abandoned those thoughts as the music stopped and the lights came on. In the subdued lighting of the club the girl had looked mysterious and sultry but all mystery and sultriness were wiped away by the harsh lighting. Urban turned and gestured to Dean to join him.

"What's going on?" Dean asked as he came over.

"This girl is totally fucking hammered and seems to have lost her mates."

"I'm with my mates" she repeated.

Dean looked at her and decided she wasn't in any fit state to have a conversation with. "So?" he said with a shrug.

"We're going to help her out and see if she can find her mates outside" Urban replied grabbing the girl around the waist and walking towards the exit.

"Since when did you become a fucking Samaritan?" Dean asked.

"Just doing my bit for society" Urban replied with a smirk.

When they got outside they joined the throng of other people milling around outside the club. Most of them were kissing each other goodnight, exchanging phone numbers or looking for cabs.

"Can you see your mates anywhere?" Urban asked. The girl slowly looked around, blinking every ten seconds as if operating in slow motion and eventually shook her head. They waited until the majority of people had disbursed but there was still no sign.

"Where do you live?" Urban asked, making sure he spoke slowly.

After a few seconds thinking about what he'd said the girl finally replied; "Ealing."

"Ealing? That's fucking miles away" said Dean.

"What are you doing in Battersea if you live in Ealing?" Urban asked.

"I'm with my mates" she replied once more which caused Dean to shake his head in despair.

"Just stick her in a cab mate and let's go home" Dean said as he walked towards the kebab shop.

"We can't do that. She'll never get a black cab at this time of night and we can't put her into a dodgy mini cab in the state she's in."

"Less of the 'we.' She's your problem mate. Fuck all to do with me" said Dean.

"Right, let's get a kebab and see if your mates turn up" said Urban to the girl as he half carried her into the kebab shop. Inside it was almost as lively as it had been in the club and it appeared that every single bloke who'd failed to pull had migrated there. As Dean joined the back of the queue two pissed-up blokes at the front started arguing. This was soon followed by some pushing and shoving.

"Why is it that you would never dream of eating a kebab during the day but after ten pints of lager people are so desperate to get one that they're prepared to fight each other?" Dean asked Urban as the bloke at the front of the queue pushed his donner kebab into the face of the bloke he was arguing with and they started trading blows.

"Beats me" Urban replied. They continued to watch as more people joined the melee. Order was restored when a police car stopped outside, switched on its siren, waited for the fighting to stop and then sped off.

"Two donners please mate with lots of chilli sauce" Dean said as the man behind the counter shouted "who's next." Dean caught sight of his reflection in the mirror opposite, didn't like what he saw and quickly looked away, abandoning any thoughts he was harbouring of trying to chat up anybody in the shop. A minute later they had their kebabs and were outside the shop. The girl was now literally falling asleep on her feet and needed to be propped up by Urban.

"So what are you going to do with her now mate?" Dean asked as he picked out a handful of the grey meat.

"We'll have to take her home with us and see if she sobers up. If not she'll have to crash at our place til the morning" Urban replied.

"Oh, I getcha!" Dean replied shaking his head.

"No, it's nothing like that. I'm a man of honour" Urban said as he threw the grated cabbage and carrot from his kebab onto the floor. "I thought I said no salad?"

"I forgot" Dean replied as they started the walk home. By the time they'd finished their kebabs the girl was totally out of it and was a complete dead weight. Dean reluctantly helped Urban to carry her by placing one of her arms over his shoulder. When they got into the house Urban carried her into the living room and dropped her onto one of the sofas.

"What now then mate? Fancy a beer?" Dean asked.

"Yeah. I'm still totally wired so I can't go to bed yet" Urban replied.

Dean went to the kitchen and grabbed a couple of beers. When he returned Urban was watching one of the music channels.

"So what are you going to do with her then?" Dean asked as he looked at the prostrate girl lying on the sofa.

"Just leave her here I suppose" Urban replied as he took a swig from his bottle.

"You can't leave her here mate. If one of the other lads comes in pissed up and finds a comatosed bird in the living room they'll think that Christmas has come early. Why don't you stick her in your room, then come back down and finish your beer."

"Yeah, you're right. It'd be a bit ironic if I brought her back here to protect her from the ravages of unsavoury characters only for her to be molested by one of the unsavoury characters that lives here" Urban replied laughing. "Give me a hand then" he said as he picked her up. She seemed to have got even heavier but they managed to get her up the stairs and onto Urban's bed.

"She doesn't look too bad now that she's on my bed" said Urban raising his eyebrows.

"I thought you were a man of honour?" Dean said shaking his head.

"I will be tonight, but tomorrow's a different day. I'm sure she'll be grateful when she wakes up and finds out that I made sure she got home safely" Urban replied with a cheeky smile.

They closed the door to Urban's bedroom and headed back to the living room.

"Stick the porn on mate" Urban said as he threw himself onto the sofa and grabbed his bottle of beer.

"Why is it that after a failed night on the pull blokes feel the need to watch porn in the company of other blokes?" Dean asked as he chucked the remote control to Urban.

"Because it's fucking great" Urban replied smiling smugly. "Why, don't you like it? Are you gay or something?"

"Well you might say that two blokes watching a porn film together could be construed as more of a gay statement than not watching it" Dean replied.

"Shut up" said Urban as he pulled the bag of coke out of his pocket. "Fucking hell mate, we've got through a fair bit of this tonight" he said as he poured some of the powder onto the table.

"How much money are you out to Razor's mate for?" Dean asked bringing a more serious tone to the conversation.

"Not too much" Urban replied as he prepared to snort the powder.

"Seriously mate, how much?"

Urban took a large toot of the coke, closed his eyes and sat back sniffing. "About five grand, but it's cool as I'm hoping to get a good bonus from work soon which should clear it" he eventually replied.

"Five grand? Fucking hell Urban you're meant to be saving money by living here rent-free not clocking up debts of five grand." For the first time that night Dean thought about Dougie's challenge and the twenty grand that he'd been given. "How would you like to make an easy ten grand?"

"Is this another one of those stupid fucking dares from Dougie's will? What do I need to do this time, eat my own shit?" Urban replied.

"No. You need to give me a blow job" Dean replied, looking deadly serious.

"Fuck off!" Urban replied shaking his head. "I bet there's no money and you just want me to suck you off. I knew you were a fucking bender!"

"I'm being deadly serious Urban. I can't show you the cash this time as the money's been transferred directly to my bank account but I give you my word as your friend that I will put ten grand straight into your account on Monday if you do it."

"Why can't you suck me off?" Urban asked. "I'll do it that way."

Dean thought for a second. The previous day he'd decided categorically to walk away and give up on the whole inheritance thing. However since then he hadn't been able to get the thought of losing the money out of his head. He'd been thinking over what Razor had said; that he'd forget how he got the money once he was living the millionaire's lifestyle. After all of the alcohol and coke he'd had Dean decided he never wanted to work again and the prospect of taking a blow job from Urban didn't seem too bad, although he still didn't really fancy giving him one.

"Hang on a minute" Urban said "why don't we just say that we did it and keep the cash anyway?"

"Because I need to produce photographic evidence" Dean replied.

"What? I don't remember you taking photos when we did that fucking stupid biscuit game" Urban said, looking confused.

"Dougie installed a hidden camera in this room, it's up there in the sensor for the alarm" Dean said pointing at the small white box in the corner of the room. "It's connected to the computer in my bedroom so that I can record things on DVD. I then print off the photos and present them to the solicitor as proof that the dare has been completed."

"Cool" said Urban. "So, are you going to do me? I'm happy to let you for ten grand."

Dean closed his eyes and focussed on the thought of packing in his job, touring the world and meeting lots of gorgeous women. He eventually opened his eyes and simply said "OK." He then went upstairs, set up the PC and walked back into the living room was just in time to see Urban snort another huge line of coke.

"So it's definitely ten grand then mate?" Urban asked.

"I give you my word that you'll have it in your account on Monday."

"I think you might need some of this" said Urban pointing to the mount of coke on the table.

"I think you're right" Dean replied, as he cut up a fat line with Urban's bank card and then snorted the lot. "Right, let's get this over with."

Urban stood up, unbuckled his belt and simultaneously pulled down both his jeans and his boxers to reveal his flaccid penis.

"I'm glad to see you're not aroused by this but I think you need to make a bit of an effort for the camera" Dean said and he turned away so that he wouldn't have to watch.

Urban started working on his limp penis but after a couple of minutes of furious masturbation there was still no sign of any action.

"Do you want me to stick the porn back on?" Dean asked trying not to laugh.

"I don't think there's any point mate. I'm either too pissed or too coked up. We'll have to go back to the original plan and I'll do you" Urban replied looking very unhappy as he pulled his trousers back up.

"OK" Dean said as he stood up and dropped his trousers. After a minute of playing around he managed to get his penis semi-erect. "Right that'll do" he said nodding to Urban.

"So it's definitely ten grand then?" Urban asked again as he took a long drink from his beer bottle.

"Definitely mate. I don't want to do this anymore than you do" Dean replied.

Dean stood at an angle he knew would work well for the camera and nodded to Urban, who came over and knelt in front of him.

"That fucking stinks" said Urban as his face got near to Dean's penis. "What have you been doing with it?"

"Fucking pissing out of it" Dean replied laughing at the absurdity of their conversation. "Right you only need to do it for about ten seconds so that we've definitely got the photo."

"OK, but you never know you might like it" said Urban laughing nervously. "OK then here goes" he said as he closed his eyes and put Dean's penis into his mouth. Dean also had his eyes closed as he didn't want a visual image of Urban giving him a blow job forever engrained in his mind. For the next ten seconds or so they both remained motionless, as the seconds passed by like hours. Just as Dean was about to say "that's enough" they were interrupted by the sound of the living room door flying open.

"What the fucking hell is going on here?" Rod said as he stood in the doorway staring at the pair of them.

"It's not what it looks like mate" Dean replied as Rod turned and ran up the stairs. Dean started to run after him but tripped over his trousers, which were still around his ankles.

"So not even a thank you? Well that's the last time you get a blow job from me Dean Williams, I'll tell you that for nothing! And next time wash your fucking cock before you ask someone to put it in their mouth!" Urban shouted to Dean who by that time was running up the stairs after Rod.

Chapter 37
Week 8 - Sunday

Emma woke up with a start. She knew instantly she wasn't in her own bed. *"Oh Jesus, where the fuck am I?"* she thought as she looked around the bedroom. She thought hard and tried to remember how she'd got there. Her last memory was of the bar that she'd met her friends in. They'd planned to go on to a club but she couldn't remember whether she had made it there or not. She could feel the presence of somebody in bed with her and decided to establish whether she'd had sex or not. Slowly she put her hands down under the duvet and was relieved to feel that she was still wearing her knickers and bra. She decided to get up and go without waking whoever it was in bed next to her. As she attempted to slip silently out of bed the man next to her spoke.

"Morning. How are you feeling today?" he asked in what sounded like a Brummie accent.

She turned and looked at him, hoping his face would trigger memories of the previous evening. He wasn't her type at all. She normally went for trendy, dark skinned, handsome types. This guy was pasty faced, not particularly good looking and had long centre-parted hair.

"I'm feeling a bit rough actually" she replied with a polite smile.

"Do you remember anything about last night?" he asked.

"Not really" she replied, truthfully. "I was out with a few of my girl friends but I don't remember anything about coming back here."

"I met you in the Grand where you were on your own. You kept going on about your mates but we couldn't find them so we came back here."

"So did anything happen?" Emma asked trying to appear casual.

"Well, you were all over me and practically begging for sex but I said that it wasn't right doing it when we were drunk and that we should wait until the morning" he replied.

"That was very honourable of you."

"That's the sort of guy I am, always looking to do the right thing. Anyway by my reckoning it's morning now" he said looking at his watch.

"So?" Emma replied with an innocent smile.

"So I've got you a present" he replied.

"What is it?"

"This" he said pulling back the duvet to reveal his erect penis.

"But it's not wrapped" Emma replied. "Who gives a girl a present without wrapping it?"

The guy looked confused for a second and then smiled. "How rude of me, hang on a second" he said as he reached into his bedside drawer, rustled around for a few seconds, pulled out a condom, opened it and put it on. "I'll tell you what, the anticipation of putting one of these on before you're about to have sex with someone for the first time is one of the best feelings in the world. You can almost feel the electricity and sense of excitement. OK then, it's now fully wrapped" he said as he sat up on his pillow and proudly showed off his condom-covered erection.

"That's nice, but I've already got one of those so I don't need another one thanks" Emma said as she stood up and pulled on her trousers.

"What?"

"I said, I've already got a boyfriend, so thanks for the offer but no thanks" Emma replied smiling as she picked up her bag. "Thanks for helping me out last night and everything but I've got to go. Which way is the nearest tube?"

"But what about this?" he said pointing to his erect penis.

"I'm sure you'll think of something to do with it" Emma replied with a smirk as she opened the bedroom door and walked out.

Urban quickly grabbed his jeans and made after her. He ran down the stairs just in time to see her standing in the doorway of the living room asking for directions. As he rounded the corner he saw she was talking to Rod.

"I'll walk you to the station if you like" Urban said, trying to sound cool and casual.

"I wouldn't go anywhere with him love" said Rod. "When I got back here last night I walked in to find him with a bloke's cock in his mouth!"

"He's talking shit" Urban said as he started turning bright red.

"Whatever," Emma replied as she headed to the front door.

"Can I see you again?" Urban asked.

"No. Goodbye" Emma replied as she closed the door behind her.

Urban decided not to embarrass himself further by going after her.

"So did you shag her or were you too busy getting it on with Dean?" Rod asked.

"Dean explained all that to you last night. You know perfectly well what we were doing it for" Urban replied. "And for your information yes I did shag her, twice" he lied.

"You must have been pretty shit then as she didn't seem to want to know you at all this morning" Rod replied as he returned to the sports pages of the News of the World.

"Oh, she was just feeling guilty this morning as she's got a boyfriend" said Urban.

"I believe you mate, thousands wouldn't" Rod replied sarcastically without looking up from the newspaper.

"Anyway, I'm going back to bed" Urban responded as he went back upstairs. When he got back to his room he took off his jeans and realised that he was still wearing the condom. *"Oh well, waste not, want not. Might as well have a posh wank"* he thought as he climbed back into bed.

Chapter 38
Week 8 - Wednesday

"Hey, have any of you ever used sex toys?" Urban asked as he brought the tray of pints over to the table that Rod, Tim and Mick were sitting at.

"What? Where did that come from?" Rod asked as he picked up his pint.

"I pulled this really fit bird last night and she was desperate for me to use a vibrator on her" Urban said with a huge smile on his face.

"You pulled a bird last night? Where did you meet her?" Rod asked.

"I went to this lapdancing bar in Soho and paid for a private room. The birds all thought I was loaded so they were falling over themselves to take me home" Urban replied.

"A fucking private room? That must have cost you a fortune" said Tim as he took a sip from his pint.

"Two grand, but it was worth every penny" Urban replied with a cheeky smile.

"Is that how much you got paid for sucking Dean's cock?" Rod asked. Urban responded by flicking him his middle finger whilst taking a drink from his pint.

"Anyway, as I was saying, when we got back to this bird's place she whipped out a vibrator and got me to use it on her" Urban continued.

"What was it like?" Tim asked.

"Well she seemed to really enjoy it" said Urban smiling "although she didn't like it as much when I tried to stick it up her arse later on" he continued with a chuckle. The rest of them broke out into a ripple of laughter.

"I once went out with a bird that was into all of that sex toy stuff" said Rod. "She had loads of vibrators, some of them were really big and you had to really work hard to get them in her. The only problem then was that her fanny was like a wizard's sleeve when it came round to shagging her."

"Yeah, but to be fair a polo mint feels like a cave when your dick's as small as yours" said Urban laughing. Rod responded with a pretend belly laugh.

"She had one of those rampant rabbits that's got a second part. I thought it was supposed to go up her arse but it turned out that you're meant to use it on her clit. She really liked it when I used that, although you had to make sure that you cleaned it each time otherwise it honked the next time you came to use it!" Rod said laughing. "She also had a set of those love balls which she used to put in before we went out to the pub. She'd then sit there drinking, having orgasms every twenty minutes or so."

"Can you imagine if they had something like that for men? We'd all be asleep in the pub after an hour!" Tim said with a chuckle.

"It was quite handy though as by the time we got home from the pub she was sopping wet and gagging for it so I never needed to bother with any of that foreplay nonsense" said Rod taking a sip from his pint.

"Have you ever tried one of those virtual pussies?" asked Urban.

"Virtual pussy? What the fuck's that?" said Mick.

"It's like a male equivalent of a vibrator. You stick your dick into it and it vibrates and moves as if you're on the job."

"No but it sounds great" Mick replied laughing. "Where can I get one?"

"I tell you what would be great, if they created a blow up woman that had one of those virtual pussies built into it. You'd never have to leave the house again" said Rod.

"Except to buy cleaning fluid" Tim added.

"I tried a blow up woman once at Uni" said Urban. "I ordered it on the internet and was really excited when it turned up. It was a top of the range one modelled on some blonde American porn star and had real hair, even on the pubes. I was living in the hall of residence at the time and the porter gave me this huge box that had been delivered. I didn't have a bird so I raced back to my room to have a go at it. I started blowing it up but it turned out to be six foot tall and by the time I'd finished I was too fucking knackered to be arsed shagging it!" Urban said breaking down in laughter. The rest of them joined him. "Anyway I put her in my bed and then went out for a walk. For some stupid reason I was feeling a bit nervous when I came back to my room. I got undressed and got down to business. The only problem was that I'd blown her up too much and she was rock hard, like one of those lilos you get on holiday. So I let a bit of air out which made it feel much better although the fact that she wasn't fully inflated meant that every time I pulled my nob out her head deflated to about half the size and then re-inflated when I pushed it back in which was a bit off-putting. Anyway once I'd come I felt really disgusted with myself and decided to get rid of her. I waited until it was really late and left her in the common room in front of the TV. I then heard the next day that this lad who lived in the same Hall as me had come in pissed up, taken her back to his room and shagged her. He was bragging to his mates the next day about how realistic it was as her fanny was all wet. He ended up leaving Uni when he found out that the reason she was so wet was because I'd shot my load into her earlier that day."

By this stage the other three lads were crying with laughter.

"Anyway these sex toys may be alright for a laugh but you can't beat the real thing so let's finish these and get to a club, I'm paying" said Urban.

"Agreed" the other three said simultaneously, as they downed the remainder of their drinks.

Chapter 39
Week 9 - Friday

As it was sunny Dean grabbed a table outside the pub and sat down with his pint to wait for Razor. He put the A4 envelope, containing the photo of him and Urban from the previous Saturday, down on the table in front of him. Since Rod had caught them in the act he'd taken every opportunity to make homophobic jokes and remarks. Dean accepted there would be a bit of friendly banter over something like that but the amount of money involved seemed to annoy the rest of the house and some of the ribbing had started to get quite vicious. Dean felt embarrassed and degraded over the incident and the constant reminders were really starting to get to him. As he sat looking at the envelope he wished Dougie had never included him in his will and that he could just go back to leading his normal life. But, of course, that was impossible. If he walked away now the fact that he'd lost the opportunity to inherit the money would eat him up for the rest of his life. Every time he had a bad day at work or received a bill he couldn't afford to pay he'd be thinking about that money. As he stared at the envelope he decided Dougie had stripped him of any remaining dignity he had and made a positive decision to finish the ten challenges and get his hands on the money. His thoughts were broken by Razor.

"Do you want another one?" Razor said pointing at Dean's glass. "What do raving homosexuals drink anyway?"

"I'm fine thanks" Dean said nodding towards the half full pint sitting in front of him and ignoring Razor's second comment.

"So have you got it then?" Razor asked looking excited.

"Look, you know what the photo shows so don't make a big deal of it" Dean said as he handed over the envelope. Razor ripped it open and pulled the photo out.

"Fucking hell, you've got a hard on and Urban really is sucking you off!" he said as he held up the photo. "Oh my god, you've got your eyes closed and look like you're enjoying it!"

"Keep your fucking voice down" Dean replied, as he snatched the photo out of Razor's hand. "You know exactly why we did it so don't try making it into something it isn't."

"All I know is that it is a photo of you with your cock in another bloke's mouth which can only mean one thing in my mind" said Razor with a broad grin on his face.

"Anyway, shouldn't you be going?" Dean said as he handed the photo back to Razor.

"Watch my pint then" Razor said as he took a sip from it, placed it on the table and headed off in the direction of the solicitors' offices.

A quarter of an hour later he returned and threw two A4 envelopes onto the table in front of Dean. "Here you go, Gaylord" he said. Dean glared at him without responding as he opened the first envelope and pulled out the contents.

"Dear Dean,

The thing that I personally always hated about money is that when there is too much of it around people change and start doing things they wouldn't normally do. It's like a disease, it eats people up and becomes all consuming. That's why I never told you or any of the other lads about my money as I knew it would change the way you acted towards me and I wanted everyone to like me for who I was not how much money I had. The fact that you're reading this is a bit of a disappointment as it means that you and a friend or two of your close friends have committed a homosexual act, purely for money. Who would have thought before all of this began that any of your mates would consider turning to male prostitution? It just proves that people will drop their principles and abandon their morals providing the price is right. Do you agree? Well let's put my theory to the test in the most extreme way possible This week's challenge can be summarised simply by the word:

'DEATH'

This is the big one Dean. I don't care how you do it but in order to succeed with this week's challenge one of your housemates must be dead by this time next week. As this is potentially something you could end up in prison for the rest of your life for organising you don't need to produce photographic evidence this week as it would be too incriminating. Instead you just need to ensure Razor can verify that one of the group is dead which should be fairly straightforward to do. I've arranged for Mr Jacob to substantially increase the amount of cash available and it's up to you how you spend it (you can use it to pay for professional help if you need to). If you decide not to take on the challenge then you can keep the money that Mr Jacob gives you and walk away with a free conscience. Finally I would remind you that to successfully complete all the challenges you need to make sure that every housemate was involved in at least one challenge.

Anyway, good luck mate and this time I hope that we won't be in touch again in another week's time, although obviously you'll lose everything if we're not.

Your friend,
Dougie"

As soon as Dean finished reading the letter he put it down on the table without saying a word. He opened the second envelope and took out the piece of paper inside.

Dear Mr Williams,

As part of the Last Will and Testament of Douglas Forsythe Mackenzie I am hereby irrevocably instructed to transfer the sum of £100,000 (One Hundred Thousand Pounds) to a bank account of your choice. Please advise me of the sort code and account number that you wish the monies to be transferred to no later than seven days from the date of this letter.

Yours sincerely,
Peter Jacob
Partner
Jacobs & Co

Razor read the letter over Dean's shoulder. "A hundred grand, fucking hell Dean!"

"Yeah, it's a decent pay off. I think I'm going to use it as a deposit on a flat" Dean replied as he placed the piece of paper back into the envelope.

"What? Aren't you even going to think about it?" Razor asked.

"Think about what Razor? About killing one of my mates for the sake of money? Are you fucking insane?"

"But it's more money that you can imagine. It'll set you up for life. You'll never have to work again and you'll be able to have any bird in the world that you want. This is the sort of chance that everyone would give their right arm for" Razor said with a smile as he held up his purple cast.

"That's an interesting phrase, 'set you up for life.' It would set me up but the trade off is that one of the other lads in the house has to give up his life for me to get it. Don't tell me that you'd even consider it?"

"I don't know Dean. All I'm saying is that it's a lot of fucking money" Razor replied.

"And how much is someone's life worth?" Dean asked as he finished his pint.

****

"So who's going to be at this party then Daisy?" Mick asked as he came into the living room.

"Well it's Heather's birthday but from what I can gather she hasn't got many friends so it's mainly going to be Mel's mates that'll be there" Daisy replied.

"Have you met any of them? Are any of them fit?" Mick asked.

Daisy immediately thought of the morning he'd woken up in bed with Chloe and started to feel sick at the prospect of seeing her at the party. "Yeah I've seen a couple of them, they're alright."

"Is that a polite 'alright' that you'd say to Mel if she asked you or a proper 'alright' that you'd say to the boys? I mean just to be clear and set a benchmark I think Heather is a minger" said Mick.

"Agreed. Mel's mates are proper alright, much better looking than Heather. You'd probably shag most of them" Daisy replied closing his eyes to try to blot out the fact that he *had* actually shagged one of them.

"So what time does it start?" Mick asked.

"Everybody's meeting in the boozer round the corner from their place between eight and nine thirty and then it's back to the house."

"Great. I haven't been to a good house party for ages. How are we getting there?" Mick asked.

"We've ordered one of those people carriers to pick us all up at eight."

"Fuck, I'd better start getting ready then" said Mick as he looked at his watch and saw it was seven thirty.

By seven fifty-five all of the lads were gathered in the living room drinking beer and watching porn.

"Lads, we're going to a fucking party. Can't we have some music on to get into the mood?" Dean asked as he gestured towards the screen.

"We are getting into the mood. Bollocks to dancing I'm going to this party to get laid" Mick replied.

"Anyway, just because you prefer blokes to women doesn't mean that we have to stop watching straight porn" Razor chipped in.

"Yeah, if you don't like it why don't you go and suck Urban's cock again whilst we're waiting for the taxi to turn up?" Rod followed up.

"Oh fuck off" Dean replied. He was sorely tempted to respond by telling Rod the truth about Gloria but decided to keep it subtle. "Have you heard from Gloria yet Rod?" he said as he winked at Razor.

"No. I've left a few messages on her mobile but she hasn't called me back. I was hoping to take her to this party tonight but I think she must have a bloke on the go or something." Dean looked at Razor who was now almost crying with laughter but managed to contain it enough so that Rod didn't notice.

"Glynn, why don't you sit down? You're making me feel fucking anxious standing there" Tim said to Glynn, who was standing at the window looking out from beneath the curtains.

"I just don't want to miss the taxi" Glynn replied.

"Look I know that it's Heather's birthday and you're a bit nervous about being the boyfriend of the hostess but constantly looking out of the window is not going to make the taxi arrive any quicker" said Tim shaking his head.

"Right, it's here" said Glynn turning away from the curtains and pulling his tongue out at Tim.

They all piled into the people carrier and set off for Islington.

"Oh, who's fucking farted?" Urban asked as he pulled the front of his T-shirt up over his nose.

"Aaarrgghhh, that's fucking rancid" said Daisy as he also pulled up his T-shirt. Everyone else in the vehicle (apart from the driver) then followed suit apart from Rod who was crying with laughter.

"That was a fucking peach!" Rod said as he wiped away his tears.

"If you think that was good listen to this" said Mick as he sat up on one cheek and let out a long fart that sounded like somebody tuning up a trombone. Rod and Urban couldn't help laughing at the sound.

"You can't beat a good fart for comedy value" said Rod but suddenly put both of his hands over his nose as the smell hit him.

The remainder of the half hour journey followed the same pattern with contributions from all of them except for Glynn, who spent the whole time shaking his head and saying "disgusting" under his breath. By the time they arrived at the pub the majority of them had their noses permanently under their T-shirts and the inside of the people carrier reeked of rotten eggs and cabbage. Tim threw open the side door of the vehicle and stumbled out onto the pavement.

"Fucking hell, you can almost see the fumes from those farts billowing out of the van" Tim said as he sucked up the fresh air.

"I am never getting into an enclosed space with him again" Daisy said pointing at Rod.

"Imagine being stuck in a space ship with him?" Urban chipped in. "Apparently the increase in pressure makes you break wind all the time. It's lucky you didn't become an astronaut Rod as you'd have probably ended up getting your air supply mysteriously cut off on a moon walk one day."

"I feel like I had my air supply cut off in that fucking van" said Daisy, still holding his nose with his finger and thumb. "Is it safe to breathe yet?"

"Right I've paid the driver and you all owe me four quid. For some reason he said he's not available to pick us up later. I can't think why" said Glynn.

"It'll take a week to fumigate that thing" Mick said pointing at the van as it drove off.

"To be honest I think he'd be better off ripping out all of the upholstery and starting again" Rod added.

"I don't need a lift home anyway as I'll be spending the night at some bird's house" said Razor as he lit a fag.

"Look, are we going to stand here all night or are we actually going to get on the beer?" Dean asked.

The pub was an old fashioned local London boozer, split into separate bar and lounge areas. As the bar areas tended to still be frequented mostly by men they made the assumption that the girls would be meeting in the lounge and headed in through that door. It was Friday night and the place was packed. There were a few small groups of locals dotted about but the vast majority of the people were young trendies who had moved to the area since it had become one of the fashionable places to live in London. Daisy looked around and eventually caught sight of Mel, who was standing with a large mixed group in the far corner. He tried to catch her attention but she was engrossed in conversation with some bloke. The music was really loud so he tapped

Urban on the shoulder and pointed over in the direction of where she was standing. Urban did the same to Rod and the signal was then passed down the line. As he made his way over Daisy thought about the prospect of being introduced to Chloe by Mel and took a couple of deep breaths. After pushing his way through the throng of people he eventually made it to where Mel was standing. She was still in deep conversation and didn't notice him so he grabbed her from behind and kissed the back of her neck. She let out a huge squeal, turned around, threw her arms around his neck and gave him a kiss on the lips.

"Hello you! I was just telling Keith here all about you" she said pointing at the bloke she was talking to. He was white, around six foot tall, had the build of a rugby player and a trendy haircut. Despite the fact that he didn't know him Daisy took an instant dislike to him.

"Hi, nice to meet you" Keith said in a public school accent as he held out his hand.

"Likewise" Daisy replied shaking Keith's hand.

"Right, I'm going to get another round in for the girls so can I leave you two to have a little chat for five minutes?" Mel said as she disappeared off into the crowd.

"It's Daisy isn't it?" asked Keith. Daisy nodded. "I've heard a lot about you from Mel."

"All good I hope?"

"Mostly" Keith replied trying to be funny but failing to amuse Daisy. Under normal circumstances Daisy would have happily walked off and left Keith on his own.

"So how do you know Mel then?" Daisy asked in order to keep the conversation going until Mel returned.

"We went out with each other for a while but it didn't work out and now we're just good friends" Keith replied.

"Fucking great" thought Daisy *"I'm only here five minutes and she's already introduced me to one of her ex boyfriends. I knew there was something about him that I didn't like."* "So why did you break up?" Daisy asked, now genuinely interested in what Keith had to say.

"Just one of those things, really. I was crazy about her but she said she didn't want anything too heavy and needed a bit of space. Then the next thing I know she'd started seeing you" Keith replied.

"So this was quite recent then?"

"We split up about six months ago but, as I said, we're both over it now and are just mates" said Keith taking a drink from his beer bottle.

"Anyway mate, it was nice to meet you but I've got to get a beer" Daisy replied as he patted Keith on the shoulder and headed over to where the rest of the guys were congregated.

"Who's your mate?" Urban asked as he handed Daisy a pint of Stella.

"He's no fucking mate of mine. Would you believe it's one of Mel's old boyfriends? Who fucking invites their old boyfriend to a party when they're going out with someone else?" Daisy replied as he took a long drink.

"Fucking birds mate, that's who" Urban replied. Every bird I've ever been out with has still been in touch with all their old boyfriends and always wanted me to meet them. What's the fucking point of that? The main reason you get to know a bird is because you're attracted to them and you want to shag them. So when you take that part of the relationship out of the equation it's time to call it a day. It's like meeting someone you used to work with. As you don't have work to talk about anymore the conversation dries up after about five minutes. It's the same with birds. If you're not going out with them anymore the majority of things that you used to talk about – what to do at the weekend, planning a holiday, meeting their friends, family etc - are all off the table as discussion topics and so the whole fabric of the relationship is undermined and not sustainable in my view."

"You're right mate. I like Mel and I get on really well with her. If she was a bloke I reckon she'd be a mate of mine but she isn't and an important part of our relationship is that we have sex. If we finished things would change and I wouldn't want to stay friends as not only can you no longer be intimate with her but you've also got to stand there whilst she gets intimate with some other bloke. All that staying friends bollocks is not for me and it winds me up that she's invited him here. It's almost like she wants to parade the fact she's had sex with someone else in my face."

"What are you two talking about?" Dean asked as he joined them.

"Ex-boyfriends" said Daisy.

"More specifically, one of Mel's ex boyfriends" Urban added.

"What has she invited one to the party? Why do girls insist on doing shit like that? It's hard enough meeting all of her mates and trying to be the perfect boyfriend without having one of her old flames to contend with. Why don't you get Tim to knock him out?" Dean said as he took a drink from his pint.

"Oh yeah, that'd go down well wouldn't it? The first time I meet her friends one of my mates chins her ex? No I'm just going to ignore the fucker and get on with it" Daisy replied.

"Right, enough talk about ex boyfriends. It's a party so let's get things going by getting on the tequila" said Dean as he headed off to the bar.

****

"Come on you lot, we need to get over to the party. It's gone ten thirty and everyone else left about an hour ago" Daisy said to the rest of the lads.

"Parties never get going until the pubs have closed Daisy mate, so chill out and have another black Sambuca" said Tim as he handed him a small shooter glass filled to the brim with an ominous looking black liquid.

Daisy took the glass from Tim and downed it. "Look, I promised Mel that we'd follow her over as soon as we'd finished our drinks. We've had at least another two pints since then. Can we finish these ones and get over there?"

"Alright mate, if you insist. But let's just get one last round of shots in before we do" Tim replied as he headed off to the bar. He returned a couple of minutes later with a tray of shot glasses filled with clear liquid, which he handed out to everyone. Once they all had one in their hand Tim counted down "Three, two, one, go" and they all downed the drink.

"What the fuck was that?" Rod gasped as he grabbed his throat and started gagging.

"Fuck me, that's hot" Urban followed up.

"It's chilli vodka!" Tim exclaimed looking very pleased with himself, "it burns a bit doesn't it?"

"It's fucking horrible!" Razor said as he made a spitting gesture.

"Right, can we go now?" Daisy asked, looking impatient as he made his way to the door. They followed him out and were soon all gathered outside on the pavement.

"Shouldn't we get some booze? There's an off license over there" said Dean pointing over the road. Dean, Tim, Urban and Rod all ran over to the shop whilst the others waited for them outside the pub. A few minutes later they emerged carrying a case of beer each.

"Fucking hell, do you think you've got enough?" Daisy asked sarcastically as they got back over the road.

"Mate, you can never have too much lager at a party and this stuff was on special offer" Rod replied as he dropped the twenty four cans he was holding onto the floor. "It's fucking heavy though."

"Is Mel putting any food on Daisy? I hope so 'cause I'm fucking starving" said Mick as they made their way to Mel and Heather's flat.

"I think Heather has sorted out some posh grub from Marks and Spencers or somewhere like that. That's why Glynn left the pub early, to help her cook it."

"Well there'd better be some left or there'll be trouble" said Mick.

In the pub Daisy had deliberately and successfully managed to avoid being introduced to any of Mel's friends. She'd got caught up in various conversations and he'd taken the opportunity to quietly slope off with the lads. However as he approached the front door of the flat the feeling of dread he'd been carrying with him ever since Mel mentioned the party reached it's peak. As he rang the front door bell his imagination started to run riot and he could feel himself breaking out into a sweat. He imagined a nightmare scenario inside, where Chloe was telling Mel how it wasn't her fault as she didn't know who Daisy was. As the scene gathered momentum in his mind Daisy briefly considered making a run for it. Before he could the front door opened. It was Heather and to his relief she greeted him with a broad smile.

"Hi guys, we were just about to send a search party out for you lot."

"Happy birthday Heather" Daisy said as he kissed her on the cheek.

"Yeah, happy birthday" said Urban "we've brought you a present. I hope you like it" he said holding out the case of lager he was carrying.

"Great" Heather replied sarcastically whilst doing her best to avoid eye contact with Urban. "Anyway get yourselves in here, there are loads of girls dying to meet you" she said as she headed back up the stairs to the party.

As soon as those words had left Heather's lips all of the lads made a rush for the door which resulted in a drunken rugby scrum as they all tried to be the first in. Daisy was at the front holding back the mass of bodies and as he made an attempt to climb the first step a hand came through the melee of arms and legs and pulled his foot back, which caused him to nose dive onto the stairs. This had the effect of collapsing the scrum and left them all seven of them in a pile at the foot of the stairs. As they writhed around they were interrupted by a female voice:

"I guess that you lot must be Daisy's friends then?"

The majority of the writhing and scrumming stopped instantly. Daisy, who was lying face down with his head pressed against the first step, managed to free himself enough to raise his head.

"That's right. I'd offer to shake hands but as you can see I'm a bit tied up at the moment" Daisy said trying to push Mick, who was lying across his back, off him.

"I'm Claire and this is Diane."

"Great. I'm Daisy and these are my very mature friends" he said trying to catch his breath. He finally got Mick off him and managed to stand up.

"We've been looking forward to meeting you and your friends all week" Claire replied with raised eyebrows as she stepped over Rod and Urban who were still grappling with each other on the floor like two five year olds.

"Don't mind those two, they're a bit simple" said Daisy with a smile as he kicked Urban to get him to stop.

By now most of the other lads had picked themselves up and started trying to look cool in front of the girls.

"After you ladies" said Razor pointing the way upstairs.

"OK, but only if you promise not to rugby tackle me" Diane, who had her hair in a short black bob and was wearing a cropped white top and short denim skirt, replied.

"That'll come later darling" Razor replied as he gave her a wink.

They all stood and watched as Diane and Claire made their way up the steep staircase.

"Nice arse" Dean said to Tim.

"Which one?" Tim replied.

"Both" said Mick as he put his arm round both Dean and Tim's shoulders and held out his tongue.

"Down boy!" Dean replied. "Let's get a few of these beers down us before we start sharking on the ladies."

"Good call" said Mick as they all headed up the stairs to the flat.

At the top of the stairs was a long hallway with five doors running from it, two of which were open and three were closed. The living room, at the far end of the corridor, was packed full of bodies and had music blaring from of it. Daisy led the way and walked straight through the door next to the living room and into a large open plan kitchen-dining room. The lights had been turned down and there were around ten or twelve people in there. Daisy spotted Glynn on the far side of the room preparing some food.

"Oi oi saveloy!" Daisy said as he patted Glynn's shoulder.

"Hi Daisy" Glynn replied. "Where have you been mate, Mel's been looking for you for ages."

"You know what this lot are like" Daisy replied. "It took me all my time to get them here now. So what's cooking then masterchef?"

"There's tonnes of stuff in the front room already but I'm now doing all of the hot stuff. It's just a matter of sticking it all in the oven really but it takes time getting it all out of the packets"

"Well you're doing a great job mate. You'll make somebody a lovely wife one day" said Daisy as he grabbed a couple of cold vol au vents that Glynn was laying out on a tray. Glynn responded with a sarcastic smile. Daisy grabbed a can of beer and decided it was time to run the gauntlet and find Mel. He pushed his way past the mass of bodies blocking the doorway to the kitchen and went into the front room. The lighting was much dimmer than the kitchen and it took him a few seconds to spot her. She was sitting at the other end of the room with three girls. *"Time to grasp the nettle"* he thought as he walked over. Mel had her back to him and didn't see him come over. He waited for a break in her story to say hello which resulted in an awkward couple of seconds where he was standing behind her like an eavesdropping stalker. Mel continued her story, oblivious to Daisy's plight until one of the other girls looked up and said "Can we help you?"

"I'm Daisy" he said with a smile, hoping desperately they weren't discussing what a bastard he was. The group immediately burst into a chorus of delighted squeals and shrieks and Daisy knew he was on safe ground. Mel turned round, gave him a kiss and a big hug. He sat down and joined the group to face his first interrogation.

"So how long have you two been an item? What do you do for a living? Are you well paid? Do you have a car? Where do you live? Have you bought yet? Have you got any nice friends?" were just some of the questions that he fielded before Mel took him away on the pretence of meeting some of her other friends.

"That wasn't too bad was it?" Mel asked as she dragged Daisy into her bedroom.

"No, not at all. Are all of your friends here?" Daisy asked, knowing perfectly well that he'd so far avoided his dreaded meeting with Chloe.

"Everyone apart from Chloe is here. She sent me a text saying she's at a leaving do with a few of her friends from work and will hopefully make it along later. Anyway that's enough talking, get you trousers off and let's make this a party to remember" she said.

"Oh well, if you insist" said Daisy as he unbuckled his belt.

****

Despite the fact he was completely pissed Razor had managed to follow up on his earlier good work in the stairwell and found himself passionately necking with Diane. His head was spinning from all of the booze he'd drunk and he had no idea how long they'd been kissing but it felt like a long time. In fact if he'd taken time to analyse their entire relationship he'd have worked out that ten per cent of their time together had been spent talking and the other ninety per cent kissing, which classified as the perfect balance in any relationship for Razor. However he wasn't thinking about that at the moment, all he was concentrating on was firstly trying to get his hands on her breasts and then moving on to bigger and better things.

Dean and Tim were sat at the other end of the sofa Razor and Diane were lying on.

"How come he always seems to pull really fit birds?" Dean asked.

"I'm not sure. I think it must be his earthy Cockney charm they're attracted to" Tim replied as they sat staring at the action. By now Razor had his hand up the front of Diane's cropped top.

"Do you think she's wearing a bra?" Tim asked.

"No chance" Dean replied. "If we're lucky we might get a flash of tit in a minute."

"Do you think this is a bit perverted?" Tim asked.

"Err, yeah, probably. Let's give it another couple of minutes and then see if there's any action in the kitchen" Dean responded, still transfixed by Razor and Diane.

"Agreed" said Tim nodding.

Their enjoyment was suddenly spoiled by Rod who dived over the back of the sofa and landed on top of Razor.

"Let's have a threesome" Rod shouted as he wrapped his arms and legs around Razor.

"What the bloody hell's going on?" Diane shouted as she tried to get up but found she was now pinned to the sofa by the combined weight of Razor and Rod. She managed to free herself enough to push both of them off the sofa and onto the floor. Rod had his arms and legs wrapped around Razor and was clinging to his back.

"Give us a kiss then Razor" Rod shouted as they rolled around the floor together. Both of them were very pissed and despite being initially disappointed by Rod's intervention Dean and Tim were now pissing themselves laughing at Razor's predicament. Diane sat upright on the sofa, adjusted her clothes and looked very annoyed. Razor was desperately trying to get up off the floor but Rod had him in a vice like grip and showed no sign of letting go.

"Rod, get the fuck off me before I kill you" Razor shouted.

"Go on then" Rod replied, with a drunken laugh.

Razor tried to free himself by rolling around but it just made Rod cling on tighter and laugh even more. After three full cycles of Razor threatening to kill Rod and then failing to break free Diane got up and walked off. Dean and Tim took this as the sign that their fun was over and that it was time to intervene. They got up and eventually separated the two of them, although it took all of their strength to get Rod off. Once they'd freed Razor all four of them sat on the floor.

"What just happened?" Razor asked.

"What do you mean?" Dean replied.

"I mean what's been going on for the last hour or so? Was I doing something? I'm fucking hammered" Razor said looking very disorientated.

"Do you remember pulling that bird?" Tim asked.

"What bird?" Razor replied.

"It doesn't matter" said Tim shaking his head.

As Tim and Dean stood up they noticed that Rod was now unconscious.

"He's fucked" Dean said as he stood over Rod. "We'd better stick him in a cab home."

Dean and Tim picked up Rod's prostrate body and carried him out of the room. Razor sat back on the sofa.

"What about Razor?" Tim asked.

"He'll be OK. He's cabbaged but at least he's still conscious" Dean replied as they carried Rod to the top of the stairs. "Shall we just chuck him down?"

"Nah, I think we owe him for the comedy value of wrestling Razor."

"Alright then" said Dean as they made their way down the stairs. When they got outside they propped Rod up against the wall and Dean called a cab. Once he'd finally managed to persuade the cab driver to take Rod Dean headed back to the party. It was just after midnight and the party was now in full swing. Dean spotted Daisy, Urban and Tim talking to Mel and three other girls and headed over to join them.

"Did the cabbie take him alright then?" Tim asked.

"Yeah. I bunged him an extra twenty quid, just in case he puked."

"You should have just left him where he was" Tim replied. "It would have been cheaper."

"Nah, he's was liability. He either would have puked everywhere or woke up and decided to wreck somebody else's chances of pulling like he did with Razor" Dean replied.

"Talking of Razor, have you seen him?" Tim said pointing over to the sofa. Dean turned round and saw that Razor was now writhing around on the sofa with a blonde girl.

"Fucking hell, how does he do it? Twenty minutes ago he didn't know where he was or that he'd even been necking with Diane for the past hour and now he's managed to pull another fit bird. Unbelievable!" After a few seconds watching Razor in action a smile appeared on Dean's face. "So where's Diane then? Has she seen them yet? That should make for good spectator sport when she does."

"I'm afraid not mate. After the incident with Rod she got all upset and went home so he's in the clear."

"It's just not fair is it? Here we are, two good looking, eligible bachelors, who can remember what they were doing half an hour ago and none of the girls want to know. Yet Razor drinks himself into a stupor and he's got women throwing himself at him" Dean said, shaking his head as he took a long drink from his can of lager.

"I know. Maybe that's where we're going wrong. We're not drinking enough" Tim replied. "I'll go and see what I can rustle up from the kitchen. "

As Tim headed off to find more booze Dean turned to the rest of the group. Daisy was in the middle of telling a story to Mel and one of her friends whilst Urban was having a one to one conversation with the other girl. The girl had very long hair, was wearing a floral print dress, had a variety of facial piercings and overall looked a bit of a hippy. Urban had managed to corner her off in such a way that it was clear he was trying to pull her and obviously didn't want anyone else joining the conversation. Dean went over and put his arm round Urban's shoulder.

"Alright mate? How's it going?" Dean said with a broad grin.

"We're in the middle of a conversation actually" Urban replied with a look that indicated he wanted Dean to fuck off.

"You don't get rid of me that easily" Dean thought as he continued smiling. "Really? What about?"

"It's private" Urban responded, giving Dean another dirty look.

"Oh" said Dean, trying to look hurt by Urban's reply. Luckily the girl fell for Dean's ploy.

"No it isn't" she said causing Urban to give Dean a drop-dead stare.

"You were telling me that if somebody gets so drunk that they pass out then you can make them piss and shit themselves by placing their hand into a bowl of warm water" the girl continued.

"Oh not that bollocks? Did he mention why we call him Urban?" Dean said, shaking his head.

"Yeah, he said that it was because he's a modern day Urban Warrior who's fighting a crusade against the waste and destruction of the capitalist society."

"Is he?" Dean replied trying not to laugh. One of Urban's many chat up techniques was to try to morph himself into his target's ideal boyfriend. He'd obviously decided that an anti-capitalist-Urban-warrior fitted the bill this time.

"Why isn't that the real reason?"

Urban's death stare suddenly changed into a begging please-don't-scupper-my-chances look. Dean briefly considered telling the girl that Urban was actually an accountant who was very much part of the capitalist society but decided that he'd had enough fun at Urban's expense.

"Yeah, that's exactly it. Anyway must move on, got to work the room and all that!" Dean said as he turned to talk to Daisy and Mel. They were standing talking to another girl who wasn't stunning but was certainly attractive enough for the time of the night. She had shoulder length brown hair and was wearing a short black dress that made her look quite sexy. Daisy was telling a story and Dean waited for him to finish before joining the three of them. The two girls suddenly broke into laughter and Dean took that as his cue to join the discussion.

"I see the big man is keeping you both entertained" Dean said as he stepped into their circle.

"I could listen to his stories all day" said Mel putting her hand onto Daisy's forearm.

"Hi, we haven't been introduced. I'm Dean, one of Daisy's friends" he said offering his hand to the brown haired girl.

"Nice to meet you Dean, I'm Lorraine" she replied with a friendly smile.

"So do you girls know who that is then?" Dean asked pointing at the girl lying underneath Razor on the sofa.

"Oh yes, that's Claire. She's terrible. She got no shame" Lorraine replied shaking her head.

"Well I hope she knows what she's letting herself in for with Razor, he's got the morals of an alley cat" said Dean.

"You could say the same about Claire. It sounds like they're ideally suited" Lorraine responded.

"Does she know that he was with Diane earlier tonight?" Dean asked.

"Oh yeah. I was standing with Claire watching the two of them. She just doesn't care" Lorraine replied.

"So have you got any more mates who don't care once Razor has finished with Claire then Mel?" Dean asked smiling.

"Well the only one of my friends who's wilder than Claire is my best friend Chloe. She's mental. She's meant to be here but for some reason she hasn't turned up and her phone's switched off" Mel replied.

"She's probably pulled some bloke and gone back to his place" Lorraine said.

"Whatever the fuck she's doing, thank Christ she's not here" thought Daisy as he tried to think up a different topic of conversation. Dean saved him the bother.

"How long have you lived here Mel?"

"Just over six months. Heather and I used to live with a couple of other girls but one moved in with her boyfriend and the other decided to go travelling so we had to get a smaller place" Mel replied. "Why, do you like it?"

"It seems really familiar, like I've been here before. Do you know who used to live here before you?"

"No idea. Anyway if you'll excuse me I need the loo. I'll be back in a minute." Mel said as she headed off to the toilet.

"So do you two live together?" Lorraine asked directing her question at both Dean and Daisy.

"Yeah. It's an interesting story really. A guy I used to be mates with died a couple of months ago. We didn't know it but he turned out to be loaded and owned a big house in Battersea. As part of his will he's letting eight of us stay there rent free for six months, which has been quite a laugh so far" Dean replied.

"Cool. So is it a nice house then?" Lorraine asked.

"Yeah, it's the dogs bollocks" Daisy cut in. "It's got plasma screens, state of the art kitchen, conservatory, en-suite bedrooms, the lot."

"Sounds great. I'd love to see it" said Lorraine looking at Dean flirtatiously.

"I'm sure that can be arranged" Dean replied with a cheeky smile.

Their conversation was suddenly stopped by a number of shrieks and screams over the other side of the room. Dean looked over and saw Mel hugging two girls in the doorway.

"Oh here's Chloe and Catherine. I'd given up on them turning up at all. They must be really pissed by now" said Lorraine.

"Oh fuck!" thought Daisy as he watched the girls finish hugging.

Mel led the two girls over to where Daisy, Dean and Lorraine were standing. She arrived with a beaming smile on her face.

"They've made it! This is Catherine" Mel said gesturing towards the black haired girl "and this is my best friend in the whole world, Chloe" she said gesturing to the blonde haired girl. "This is Dean and this gorgeous hunk is Daisy."

Daisy looked at Chloe and held his breath. She looked different to how he remembered her and he could see she was really pissed. Catherine stepped forward and gave Dean a kiss on the cheek and then did the same to Daisy and Lorraine. Chloe didn't move a muscle. She stood staring at them as if she was trying to work something out. Daisy started to panic and could feel his heart beating faster and faster.

"Are you OK Chloe?" Mel asked as she looked at her friend who remained motionless with a thoughtful expression on her face. Chloe suddenly lunged forward and slapped Dean hard across the face. Daisy, who had froze the moment he saw Chloe move, expecting the blow to be aimed at him, was confused.

"What the fuck was that for you psycho bitch?" Dean shouted as he rubbed his face.

"Don't you remember?" Chloe said indignantly and slapped him again, even harder than the first time.

"No I fucking don't" Dean shouted "and don't do that again or you'll get one back."

"It's for puking on my fanny!" Chloe replied with an annoyed look.

This time it was Dean's turn to stand motionless with a thoughtful expression. After a few seconds his face broke into a smile and he let out an embarrassed laugh. "Oh" he said "was that you?"

"Yes, that was me!" Chloe replied still looking very annoyed.

"Hang on a minute, you shat on me! That's much worse than puke" said Dean as his memory started to slowly come back to him.

"Maybe, but you started it and I thought that was a fitting way to end it" Chloe replied.

"What the hell are you talking about" said Mel looking very confused.

"Do you remember the last party you had, a couple of months ago? Well I met shithead here in a pub that night and brought him back here. I think you were in bed with someone by the time I got here" Chloe said, deliberately looking at Daisy to make him feel jealous. "Anyway we started to get it on and this prick decided to go down on me before throwing up all over my minge. It took me fucking ages to get all those bits of carrot out of my pubes. Anyway he passed out on the spot so I decided to take my revenge by leaving a little present on his chest" Chloe said looking pleased with herself.

"I knew I'd been here before" said Dean nodding. However he wasn't pleased with himself for long as Mel stepped forward and gave him a hard slap.

"What the fuck was that for?" Dean asked holding his now bright red cheek.

"You stuffed your shitty T-shirt behind our radiator didn't you? It drove us mad trying to work out where the smell was coming from. It was two weeks until we found it. You're disgusting!" Mel said as she stormed off.

Daisy was about to breathe a sigh of relief when Chloe slapped him. "Don't think you've got away with anything either" she said. "With friends like him I've a good mind to tell her what you've been up to right now."

"Do what the fuck you want Chloe, but just remember that she's supposed to be your bestest friend in the world" Daisy replied. "Come on Dean let's get out of here."

Dean was unsure what Chloe meant but decided this wasn't the time to ask and followed Daisy. Mel's ex-boyfriend Keith, was standing talking to another bloke by the door, had watched the whole episode unfold and gave Daisy a smug smile as he approached. Without breaking stride Daisy chinned Keith who fell backwards into a stack of CD's and spilt his drink over himself. Daisy was already on his way down the stairs as Dean walked past Keith's mate.

"What can I say? He's a bit wound up" Dean said with a shrug as he headed after Daisy.

****

Glynn found himself alone in the kitchen. He wasn't really a fan of house parties and wanted to get some of the washing up done before he went to bed. The party was into its final throws and most people were either in the living room or had gone home. Glynn had Coldplay blasting out of the stereo as he washed up and didn't notice two blokes come into the room until one of them turned off his music and put on some hard-core rap.

"Hey, do you mind? I was listening to that" Glynn said as he turned around from the sink.

"I don't give a fuck if you were listening to it" said the guy standing over the stereo. "We're listening to this now, like it or lump it" he said as his friend started rolling a spliff on the kitchen table.

Glynn didn't recognise them but he knew their type. They were the sort of blokes you see playing pool in a rough pub or who sit on the back seat on the top deck of the bus and intimidate the rest of the passengers. Despite not being a fighter Glynn had a principle of never bowing down to bullies and refused to be intimidated.

"Who invited you two?" Glynn asked guessing that they had gatecrashed the party.

"Who invited you?" the chav next to the stereo replied as he turned up the music so loud that it started to distort.

"Right, can you both leave now please" Glynn said as he moved to turn down the stereo. The chav next to the stereo grabbed his arm and twisted it behind his back causing Glynn to bend forward in pain.

"Not such a big man now are you?" he said as he twisted Glynn's arm further, causing Glynn to cry out. His cries were drowned out by the blaring music. "Right, let's make this piggy squeal" he said nodding to his mate to close the kitchen door.

The chav continued twisting his arm until Glynn was lying face down on the floor. He then kicked Glynn four or five times in the ribs. Between his cries of pain Glynn pleaded with them to let him go and protested that he hadn't done anything.

"Tough luck mate, you were just in the wrong place at the wrong time" said Glynn's tormentor as he rolled him over onto his back. Glynn made a brief attempt to stand up but abandoned it after another couple of kicks to the ribs. "Stay right there you fucker, I've got a little present for you" he said as he unzipped his flies and started pissing on Glynn's head. Both of the chavs started laughing and the second one decided to join in. As he stepped forward and unzipped his flies the kitchen door opened. Oblivious to what was going on Mick wandered in looking for more beer. As soon as he saw what was going on he lunged at both of the chavs and brought all three of them crashing to the floor and into the pool of piss.

"This has got fuck all to do with you fat man" the first chav said just before Mick punched him hard in the mouth. Mick hit him again and was just about to deliver a third blow as the second Chav, who had managed to squirm free, hit Mick over the head with one of the kitchen chairs. Unlike the movies the chair didn't break into pieces but gave off a loud thud as it bounced off Mick's skull and knocked him flying. Mick tried to stand up but was still dazed by the impact of the chair and staggered backwards, landing on his arse next to the cooker. The chav Mick had punched got up holding his bleeding mouth.

"Right then fat man, you fucking deserve this" he said as he pulled out a butterfly knife and flicked it open. "I'm going to give you a Chelsea smile" he said smiling to reveal his blood soaked teeth. As he stepped forward the blade was kicked clean out of his hand by Tim who had heard the commotion and had come to investigate what was going on. He swiftly followed up with a headbutt to the face and the first chav dropped to his knees. The second chav made a break for the door but as he ran Tim grabbed him from behind and smashed his head against the kitchen table, causing him to drop motionless to the floor.

"Right, what the fuck's all this about?" Tim asked as Mick made it up onto his feet.

"These fucking bullies decided to give me a kicking and then piss on my head" said Glynn as he stood up holding his ribs. "Mick came in and helped me out but that fucker hit him with a chair" Glynn said, giving the unconscious chav a kick in the ribs.

"Look mate we don't want anymore trouble" the first chav, whose face was covered in blood, said as he stood up.

"Oh, you don't want anymore trouble? You're happy to disfigure someone for life when you're on top but as soon as it goes the other way you want to stop. Is that it?" Tim asked with a hard stare. The chav didn't respond. "It's lucky for you that we're decent blokes and don't think that knifing someone is acceptable. Now get your mate and fuck off!"

"You can fucking leave that where it is" said Tim as the chav started to bend down to pick up his butterfly knife. He did as Tim said, helped his disorientated mate up and made his way to the doorway.

"Just one more thing" said Mick as they stopped in the doorway. "This!" he said as he punched the first chav in the side of the head which caused it to crash into the second chav's face and they both fell over. They picked themselves up and made their way out of the flat.

Urban appeared in the kitchen where Tim, Mick and Glynn were now all sitting. "What's going on?"

"Glynn's been kicking off again" said Mick holding a bag of frozen peas on the back of his head.

"Typical!" Urban replied as he grabbed another beer.

Chapter 40
Week 9 - Saturday

As Urban came round he quickly realised he wasn't in his bed. He realised this without even opening his eyes as he could feel he wasn't actually in a bed at all. In fact he was outdoors, lying on wet grass. He sat up and started to feel very sick as he looked around. He was totally alone in some sort of park he didn't recognise. He looked at his watch and saw it was five thirty. His jeans were wet through from the morning dew and as he started walking he tried to remember what had happened the previous evening.

He remembered the party and could vaguely recall that there had been some sort of kick off involving Dean, Daisy, Mel and some other bird. The main reason he could remember the argument was it had killed his chances of pulling the hippy he'd been talking to all night as she'd then gone off to console Mel. After that he vaguely remembered some sort of fight, snorting a few lines of coke and scoring some pot off a bloke at the party. The last thing he could remember was going outside to have a quick spliff.

He put his hand in his pocket to check he had everything and a familiar sinking feeling hit him as he realised he didn't have his wallet or his mobile phone. As he continued walking he spotted a bloke walking his dog.

"What's the best way to Battersea mate?" Urban asked.

"Battersea? Your best bet's a taxi. You're in Islington which is north of the river. Battersea's on the south side, miles away from here."

Urban ignored the bloke's unhelpful comments and continued walking down the road having no idea whether he was walking in the right direction or not. *"Right, that's it. I'm definitely packing in the booze and drugs after this. Next weekend I'm getting a take away, staying in watching telly and going to bed early"* he thought to himself as it started to rain.

****

In another part of town, Elephant and Castle to be precise, Rod found himself in a similar situation to Urban. He could vaguely remember being in the boozer and then at the party but had no idea how or why he left. The next thing he remembered was being woken up by a very annoyed taxi driver and being dumped onto the pavement. He'd tried to walk home but as he had no idea where he was, he'd given up and crashed out on a bench by the side of the road. He'd stayed there until ten minutes ago when a police car had pulled up and warned that he would be arrested if he didn't move on. He was now wandering around a huge roundabout looking for a signpost to Battersea. He eventually managed to find one for Clapham and set off in that direction. As he passed an old woman out walking her dog he looked down at his T-shirt and saw it was covered in dried puke. He gave her a half hearted smile as she crossed the road to avoid him. On top of his vicious hangover he felt totally disgusted with himself. *"If I manage to get home in one piece after this I'm finished with alcohol for good. What's the point if you can't remember anything that you've done anyway?"* he thought to himself as he tried to muster up enough energy to get home.

****

As Razor opened his eyes he was surprised to see there was a girl lying literally right next to him. She was so close in fact that the tip of her nose was actually touching the end of his. Razor looked at her and had absolutely no idea who she was. He could vaguely remember talking to (and possibly kissing?) a black haired girl the previous night but didn't remember even seeing this blonde girl at the party. He was lying on the inside of a sofa, up against the back, so it was going to be difficult to get up without waking her. He decided to give it a go but unfortunately his face was stuck to the artificial leather and the noise it made as he peeled away from the plastic caused the girl to wake up.

"Hi" she said breaking into a smile and kissing him on the lips.

"Morning" Razor replied hoping she wouldn't ask him any difficult questions like 'what's my name?' or 'do you remember last night?'

"How are you feeling?"

"Thank god, something I can answer" Razor thought. "Fucking terrible" he replied as he sat up fully.

"Are we still on for today?"

"Oh bollocks" thought Razor *"I knew it couldn't last. I can either blag my way through and end up spending all day with her or admit that I can't remember a thing and go home for a kip."* He looked at the girl's pretty face and ample bosom and decided to go for the first option. "Yeah, absolutely!" Razor said having no idea what she was talking about. "I'll obviously need to go home and get changed first though."

"That's OK. It doesn't start until four o'clock anyway."

"What doesn't start until four o'clock?" Razor thought starting to think that maybe the second option would have been a better choice.

"You don't remember do you?" the girl said shaking her head and hitting him playfully on the arm. "You agreed to take me to the matinee showing of Les Miserables."

"Les Miserables" Razor thought. *"That piece of shit musical? No bird is hot enough for me to spend my Saturday afternoon watching that crap surrounded by a coach load of old age pensioners."* "Oh fuck!" he said "I've just remembered, I've got to help my brother move house today."

"Really?" she said looking crestfallen. "But you promised."

"I know. I'm really sorry but it's on all the time so we can go and see it next week. Anyway I have to go" he said standing up.

"Don't you want my number?"

"Yeah, of course" Razor replied as the girl picked up her bag and took out a piece of paper. She scribbled something on it and handed it to him. The note said 'Call me, love Nikki' and had a mobile phone number written on it.

Razor was relieved to see that she'd written her name on it. "Thanks Nikki" he said smiling "I'll definitely give you a call."

"My name's not Nikki" she said with a stern look on her face "and I've got no interest in fucking Les Miserables."

"What?" Razor said looking confused.

"I knew you were so hammered that you wouldn't remember a thing you said last night" she said looking angry. "All that shit about me being your perfect woman and wanting to wine and dine me. I knew it was all bollocks."

"Ah well, what can I say? I was pissed" Razor replied as he scrunched up the piece of paper and threw it on the floor. "It's your loss though love and by the way I haven't even got a brother" he said as he walked out of the room. He closed the door just in time to hear something heavy bounce off it. *"Best just go home and have that kip after all"* he thought as he made his way down the stairs and out of the flat.

****

Dean woke up early on Saturday morning. As he lay in bed the memory of the incident with Chloe the previous evening came back to him and he closed his eyes to blot it out. On the way home in the cab Daisy had told him the whole story about his unfortunate one night stand with Chloe. Dean felt genuinely sorry for Daisy as he could tell that he really liked Mel. However the fact of the matter was that not only had he cheated on her but that he'd actually done it with her best friend. Even though Daisy didn't know who Chloe was at the time it wasn't something he and Mel were going to be able to laugh off over a glass of wine. It would always be one of those things Daisy would have hanging over him whilst he was going out with Mel, even if they got married and spent the next fifty years together. Dean's advice had therefore been for Daisy to cut his losses, finish with Mel and put the whole thing down to experience. Conveniently that scenario also worked well for Dean as he didn't want to be reminded of the whole puke-shit fiasco by Chloe every time he bumped into her at a night out with Daisy and Mel.

Dean got out of bed, went to his desk, unlocked the draw and pulled out a brown A4 envelope. He tipped out the contents and looked at the various photos that scattered over the desk. They were copies of the photos he'd provided each week for Razor to give to the solicitor. For the past two weeks Dougie's letters had made a point of reminding him that to complete the terms of the will he had to make sure every one of the housemates was involved in at least one challenge. Dean hadn't really focussed on who'd been included until now. He looked through the photos in the order of the challenges and noted down who'd taken part. It soon became obvious to him that everyone in the house had been involved in at least one of the challenges apart from Glynn.

Dean sat and looked through the photos again and again hoping to prove himself wrong. *"Why didn't he get involved in the party tricks or the drugs?"* Dean asked himself as he picked up the latest letter from Dougie which had the word 'DEATH' written in large bold letters at the top. *"Firstly I don't want to be responsible for Glynn's death and secondly I don't want to go down for twenty years for murder"* Dean thought as he sat staring at Dougie's letter. He sat forward and pulled out the letter from Mr Jacob advising him of the £100,000 that was due to be transferred to him. *"A hundred grand is better than a poke in the eye, but it's not going to give me a playboy lifestyle"* he thought. *"There must be some way that I can do this."*

A few minutes later he picked up his mobile and scrolled through the list of names in his address book looking for a number he hadn't rang in a long time. He finally found the name 'Moonie' and pushed the call button. It rang a few times before a surprised voice answered.

"Well, well, well. Dean Williams! Long time no speak. How the fuck are you mate?" Moonie said in a strong Scouse accent.

"I'm doing alright mate. Still living in London and all that but things are going well."

"So do you ever make it back up North these days? You must have a bird as we haven't seen you down the Stack in years mate" said Moonie.

"Does everyone still go there? Jesus I bet they've still got the same pool table and dartboard haven't they?"

"Oh yes. A weekend wouldn't be the same if it didn't start with a few games of pool down the Stack. Anyway I'm sure you didn't call to ask if the local pub was still open, what can I do for you?"

"Don't take this the wrong way but you know a few dodgy people don't you?"

"Yeah, you could say that there are a few characters knocking around up here" Moonie replied laughing.

"Well, is there any chance you know someone who could get me a gun?" Dean asked. There was a pause for a second whilst the word 'gun' hung in the air.

"A gun? Are you in some sort of bother mate? If you are just say the word. I can get a few of the boys together and we'll come down and sort things out for you."

"No, it's nothing like that. I just need a gun, really quickly" Dean replied.

"What type of gun do you need? A handgun or something a bit bigger?"

"I'm looking for a handgun but I need it within the next few days" said Dean.

"Leave it with me and I'll call you back" Moonie said as he rang off.

An hour later Dean's mobile rang. He saw it was Moonie.

"Any joy then mate?" Dean asked as he answered.

"I've had to call in a few favours but I've managed to track down a bloke I know who can sort you out. It's not going to be cheap though, he's looking for a grand for the gun and some ammo."

"Great" Dean replied. "How soon can he get it?"

"He's got one right now so if you can get your arse up here we can get it from him today" Moonie replied.

"Right, I'll jump on the next train to Liverpool. Can I stay at yours tonight as I don't really want to leave a gun at my mum and dad's place whilst I'm out on the piss."

"No problem mate. I'll round up a few of the lads and make a night of it. See you later."

"Yeah, looking forward to it" said Dean as he put down his mobile and immediately started packing his rucksack for his overnight trip up North.

****

Moonie picked up Dean from Lime Street station, Liverpool, in his convertible M3.

"Fucking hell Moonie, you're doing alright for yourself aren't you?" Dean said as he climbed into the passenger seat of the car.

"Not bad mate. This is on one of those monthly lease deals so it doesn't actually cost that much. Still the birds don't know that and I'm happy to let them think I'm rolling in it" he replied with a wink.

"So what's the score then? When are we going to see this bloke?" Dean asked.

"Well if you've got the cash with you I'd rather go and do it right now" Moonie replied. "The pub we're meeting him in is a bit mental and you don't really want to go over to that part of town too late as everyone will have been on the piss all day and it can get a bit nasty."

"I've got the money, it's in my bag" Dean replied patting the bag on his lap.

"OK, we'll head over there now then" said Moonie as he spun the steering wheel round causing the car to do a sharp U turn.

"Where are we meeting him?"

"In a pub in Toxteth"

"Toxteth? Oh fuck."

"Exactly. That's why I want to get over there as soon as possible" said Moonie.

Five minutes later they pulled up outside a run down old pub that had metal shutters instead of windows.

"Is this the place?" Dean asked looking concerned. Moonie nodded. "What's going on with the windows? It looks like it's been shut down."

"They got smashed so often by the regulars that the landlord decided to replace the glass with metal sheets. As well as being more practical they also provide the added benefit of making the pub dark inside so you never know whether it's night or day, which is helpful for trade. It also makes it more difficult for the bizzies to do any surveillance so it means that a lot of dodgy business gets done in there. Hence why we're here" Moonie said with a smile.

As they got out of the car two scruffy looking lads aged about ten years old came up to them.

"Mind yer car mister?" said one of them.

"OK, I'll sort you out when I get back" Moonie replied.

"Hasn't your car got an alarm and an immobiliser to stop people nicking it?" Dean asked as they walked towards the pub.

"Yeah, but neither of them will stop those little fuckers from slashing the tyres will they?" Moonie replied with a smile as he pulled open the front door of the pub.

Despite the fact that it was three o'clock in the afternoon Dean and Moonie were hit by a wall of smoke and blaring music as they opened the door. Inside the place was really dark and absolutely packed. At one end of the pub was a huge screen showing horse racing and at the other were two dartboards and a group of old men playing dominoes. The only women Dean could see were the barmaids, both of whom looked like they had a fair bit of mileage on the clock. All of the blokes in the pub could be split into two distinct categories. Unhealthy looking fat blokes, with huge beer bellies and unhealthy looking skinny blokes, who looked like they hadn't eaten for a week. Dean guessed that they all followed the same sort of lifestyle, spending all their time drinking lager and eating lard but that the skinny ones either had fast metabolisms or, more likely, were doing some type of drugs.

"Let's get a drink" said Moonie.

"Good idea" Dean replied.

As they stood waiting to be served a dodgy looking scrawny bloke whose hands were covered in home made tattoos came up to Dean holding six or seven carrier bags.

"Hey mate, do yer wanna buy some meat?" he said in a thick Scouse accent.

"What?" Dean replied, unsure whether 'meat' was slang for some type of drug.

"Do yer wanna buy some fucking meat?" the bloke repeated as he pulled a leg of lamb out of one of the bags and slapped it onto the counter.

"Err, no thanks" Dean replied.

"Wot about a watch?" said the bloke pulling out a handful of watches from another bag. "They're all fucking designer names like. All nicked so they're dirt cheap, la" he said as he thrust the watches under Dean's nose.

"No thanks Knockoff mate" Moonie said as he handed Dean his pint.

"Well if ya change ya minds lads, I'll be sitting right over derr" Knockoff said as he headed back to where he'd been sitting.

"Fucking hell, who buys meat in a pub?" Dean asked as he followed Moonie through an archway and into a back room with two pool tables and that was even smokier than the bar area.

"I told yer mate, you can buy fucking anything in here. Why would you bother to go to Tesco's when you can get everything you need cheaper from the pub?" Moonie said laughing and shaking his head. He then waved at a bloke who had a shaved head and was sitting in the far corner wearing a Nike track suit. "Right, he's here so let's go and see him, get it over with and get the fuck out of here."

The two of them walked round the pool tables and headed over to the table where the bloke was sitting alone. He was in his mid forties and was one of the skinny variety of unhealthy looking blokes. Dean guessed that his physique was definitely down to drugs rather than metabolism.

"Alright Quiggo lad?" Moonie said as he sat down. "This is my mate Dean, the one I was telling you about earlier."

"So you want a gun then la?" Quiggo said, as he picked up a spliff from the ash tray in front of him and took a drag. Dean decided that brevity was probably the order of the day and nodded his response. "Right, I've got three different ones here, la. I've got a Glock, a Beretta and a Smith and Wesson" he said as he pulled a leather bag from under his seat and put it on his lap. "The Glock and the Beretta are both automatics which are the ones you want if you need to fire off a load of ammo quickly. But if you want something that'll really shit people up I'd go for the Smith and Wesson. It looks like an old fashioned cowboy gun but it'll take someone's head off from a hundred yards" he said laughing.

"What ammo have you got to go with them?" Dean asked.

"How much do you need, la?" Quiggo replied with a smile. "Are you looking to take out a load of people or something? I've got a full clip for both the automatics and a bag of bullets for the magnum, all of which should be enough for whatever it is that you want to do."

"And are they all clean?" Dean asked "I don't want one that's been involved in anything dodgy."

"What the fuck do you think this is? I suppose you're looking for a fucking warranty and a twenty eight day money back guarantee as well are you? I was told you needed a fucking gun at short notice, so take it or fucking leave it, la. Simple as that" Quiggo said, clearly agitated.

"Sorry mate. I was only asking" Dean said quickly attempting to calm the situation.

"Well fucking don't ask, la. That's how people get into trouble round here, asking too many fucking questions" Quiggo replied as he gave Dean a hard stare.

"I'll take the Smith and Wesson and all of the ammo" Dean replied.

"Good choice, la. Have you got the money with you?" Quiggo asked. Dean looked at Quiggo sitting with a bag that contained three guns on his lap and suddenly felt vulnerable having so much money on him. He pulled the envelope out of his pocket and handed it over to Quiggo, who quickly counted it. He then smiled, pulled out the Smith and Wesson revolver and pointed it at Dean's head.

"Now, why don't you two fuck off whilst you've still got the chance" he said with a crazy look in his eyes. Dean froze on the spot. He could feel his heart beating rapidly and sweat forming on his forehead. He wanted to get up but was unable to move. He sat staring at the gun until Moonie suddenly burst out laughing.

"Fuck off Quiggo, you cunt" Moonie said, playfully punching Quiggo in the stomach.

"What did I tell you eh? Scares the fucking shit out of people this gun doesn't it?" Quiggo said to Dean, who was still frozen with fear.

"Too fucking right" Dean managed to say as he continued staring down the barrel.

"Well just remember that before you go and stick it into someone's face" Quiggo said smiling "and if you get caught don't bother telling the bizzies where you got the gun from otherwise the next time you see me stick a gun in your face I won't be fucking around.

OK?" Quiggo said as he handed the gun to Dean. Dean nodded as he put the gun in his jacket pocket. Quiggo then handed over a plastic bag of bullets.

"Right, let's go" said Moonie standing up.

"What, are you lads not going to stay for a game of pool?" Quiggo asked.

"Haven't got the time Quiggo, mate. Gotta see a man about a dog if you know what I mean?" Moonie replied as they both walked off.

When they got outside Moonie paid the two lads sitting on the bonnet of his car and they sped off. "Right, let's get that thing stashed and then get on the ale" Moonie said to Dean.

I couldn't agree with you more" said Dean as he sat with his hand in his jacket pocket holding the gun.

Chapter 41
Week 9 - Sunday

Dean got back to the house late on Sunday and headed straight to his bedroom. He closed and locked his door before unzipping his bag and taking out the gun. The wooden handle was fantastically smooth and the metal barrel made the gun feel reassuringly heavy. He released the safety catch, flicked the barrel out to the side, and then flicked the gun to the opposite side which caused the barrel to click satisfyingly into place. Dean liked the look of the gun in his hand. It made him feel powerful and he stood in front of the mirror and practiced pulling it out of his jacket pocket. His playtime was broken by a knock on his door.

"Are you alright Dean?" Glynn asked as he tried to open the locked door.

Dean put the gun back in his bag and threw it into the bottom of his wardrobe.

"I'm fine, mate" he replied as he unlocked the door.

"It's just that you disappeared without a word yesterday, your mobile has been switched off and you didn't even say hello when you came in just now."

"I had to go up north at short notice. There was a bit of a family crisis but it's all sorted now" Dean replied.

"Oh right. Well as long as everything's OK" said Glynn, obviously disappointed that Dean didn't want to talk about it. "Have you had any tea? I've made a chilli if you fancy some?"

"Yeah, great" Dean replied as he followed Glynn down to the kitchen to help him with the food.

"So where did you get to yesterday Deano?" Razor asked as Dean came into the front room and handed him a plate of chilli and rice.

"I had to go up north to sort out a bit of family business" Dean replied, being deliberately evasive.

"Not another one of your relatives banged up for burglary that needed you to bail them out?" Razor replied with a chuckle.

"Something like that" Dean replied. "Has anyone got plans for Thursday night?"

"I'm meant to be going out on a work do" Daisy said.

"Yeah, I've got some work thing on as well" said Urban. "Why? What's happening?"

"I've got a bit of a surprise for all of you" said Dean. "So if it's possible to cancel your arrangements do it as it's going to be a night to remember" he said with a smile and put a spoonful of chilli into his mouth.

Chapter 42
Week 9 - Thursday

Dean was upstairs with the gun. Unlike the other times he'd taken it out of his bag he didn't caress and play with it but simply stared at it as it lay on the bed next to him. *"Here we go then Deano. This is the big one. There's no turning back now"* he thought as he put the gun back into the bag and headed downstairs.

The rest of the lads were watching football on the plasma screen as he walked into the living room.

"Right then Deano, put us out of our misery. What's the story?" Urban asked.

"OK. As you might have guessed it's another one of those dares from Dougie's will. This time everyone who takes part gets ten grand each" said Dean. A buzz filled the room and everyone looked excited.

"So have we all got to shag a troop of hookers or something?" Rod asked. "I'm definitely up for it this time, so bring em on."

"No it's nothing like that. All we've got to do is play a load of party games. Everyone who plays every game through to the end gets ten grand" said Dean.

"Do any of the games involve wanking?" Urban asked, prompting puzzled looks from a few of the lads.

"No" Dean replied.

"Piece of piss then" shouted Urban. "You might as well give me my ten grand now!"

"The rules are that we have to play each game for exactly an hour each" Dean said as he disappeared out of the room. He returned a few seconds later with a case of lager and dropped it onto the coffee table. "Right, the first game is Rod's favourite, the drinking name game."

"Oh fuck, I'm shit at this" said Rod. "I might as well just down all those cans now and save everyone the bother."

"It's the usual rules, the first person to go names a famous person. The next person takes the first letter of that person's surname and must use it for the first letter of the next person's Christian name. You can't use any fictional characters, anyone who is dead and you can't repeat any names that have already been said. OK? Right Rod, you can start" said Dean.

"OK. Errm, give me a minute" said Rod looking panicked.

"Come on Rod, just name any famous person, it's not hard" said Urban shaking his head.

"Yeah, it's easy when it's not your go" Rod replied. "Erm, OK, John Lennon" he said with a grin.

"He's dead" Urban shouted, "down that can!"

"I fucking hate this game" said Rod as he downed his first can of beer.

Three hours and numerous cans of beer later most of the lads were pissed. Rod had proved to be consistently bad at all of the drinking games and had downed at least ten cans of beer. They were currently playing 'Fuzzy-Duck" which involved everyone repeating the words 'Fuzzy-Duck' in sequence until somebody said 'Does he?' when the direction reversed and everyone then had to say "Ducky-Fuzz." Dean got up and left the room just as Rod said "Duzzy-Fuck" for the third time in a row which resulted in him holding his head in his hands as the rest of the lads to broke out into another round of cheering.

Dean went up to his room and closed the door. He opened the wardrobe, put the bag on his bed and took out the gun. He put one of the bullets in his pocket, placed the gun inside the waistband of his trousers and headed back downstairs. As he entered the living room he heard Rod say "Fucky-Duzz" followed by "Oh fuck off" and another round of cheering. Dean walked into the middle of the room, took the gun out from his waistband and pointed it at Glynn's head. Instantly the cheering stopped and the room fell totally silent. Glynn looked petrified as he sat staring at the gun.

"Right, that seems to have got everybody's attention" said Dean as he turned the gun away from Glynn.

"Is that fucking real?" Urban asked.

"Yep. It's real alright" Dean replied. "This gentlemen is a Smith and Wesson 357 magnum, immortalised by Clint Eastwood in the Dirty Harry films. I can now reveal that the main event for tonight's festivities is a game of Russian Roulette."

"Russian Roulette? Fuck off. Drinking games are fair enough but I'm not fucking playing that" said Daisy.

"The rules of the game are as follows" said Dean ignoring Daisy's outburst. "The chamber of this gun holds eight bullets. One bullet is placed into the chamber which is then spun randomly. You place the gun to your temple and fire. If nothing happens you get ten grand. Everyone gets one go each and as there will be seven empty chambers there is an 87.5% chance that you will be OK. We spin the barrel before each go so the odds are the same for everyone. So what do you say fellas? Are you man enough to do it?"

"Let's see you go first then big man" Razor replied.

"OK" said Dean. They all sat in silence as he held the gun out in front of him, released the safety catch and flicked open the barrel. He took the bullet from his pocket, held it up so they could all see it and deliberately placed it into the second hole on the left. He then carefully put the chamber back into the gun and gave it a precise spin. The spinning sound was the only noise in the room and after a few seconds it came to a stop and Dean pulled back the hammer and put the gun to his temple. Time stood still as they sat transfixed, all desperately wanting to look away but equally unable to stop watching. Dean closed his eyes and squeezed the trigger. Everyone's heart was in their mouth as the pistol gave off a loud click, revealing that the chamber was empty.

"There you go. It's as easy as that. The quickest ten grand that you'll ever make" Dean said as he opened his eyes and put the gun down on the table. "Who's next?"

Nobody moved until Tim stood up. "I'll give it a go." Dean was surprised that Tim was the first to volunteer. He'd expected one of the lads that needed the money to step forward. As Tim obviously didn't need the cash Dean guessed this was something he'd been secretly wanting to try for some time.

"Are you sure?" Dean asked as he picked up the gun.

"Absolutely" Tim replied.

"OK, do you want me to put the bullet in and spin the barrel or do you want to do it yourself?"

"I'll do it" Tim replied, taking the gun from Dean. He pulled back the catch, released the chamber and tipped the bullet out into his hand. He then placed it into one of the empty slots, put the chamber back into the gun and gave it a long spin. "Wish me luck" he said as he put the gun to his temple. He took a deep breath, pulled the trigger. The room was once again filled with the sound of a loud "Click" as the hammer fired against the empty chamber. Tim let out the breath he'd been holding.

"That is fucking scary shit" he said as he put the gun back down on the table. "It might be the quickest ten grand, but it's definitely the scariest."

After thirty seconds of silence Mick was next to stand up. "If that fucking Jessie has done it I suppose I'll have to" he said pointing at Tim. Dean picked up the gun and held it out to Mick. "Can you sort it out for me Dean, I'm shaking like a bastard."

"No problem" Dean replied as he opened the gun, showed the bullet to everyone, closed it and then gave it a precise spin. He held the gun out to Mick who stared at it for a few seconds before taking it from him.

"This is fucking madness" Mick said as he held the gun in his hand. "Dougie was a mad bastard. Only he could come up with something this crazy as a way to distribute his money. Ah well, here goes nothing" he said as he whipped the gun up to his head and pulled the trigger in one rapid movement. Once again the tension was broken by the sound of the metallic click as the hammer of the gun struck the empty chamber. "Thank Christ" Mick shouted as he handed the gun back to Dean. As he did so Urban got up and announced that he was going to the toilet. When he returned a minute later he seemed much more animated and Dean guessed he'd boosted his confidence with a bit of coke.

"Right then, let's fucking have it" Urban said as he stepped forward and took the gun off Dean.

"Do you want me to sort it for you?" Dean asked.

"No need" Urban replied as he put the gun to his head.

"Hang on!" shouted Dean, "you haven't spun the…"

His words were cut short by the sound of the gun as Urban pulled the trigger.

Chapter 43
Week 9 - Thursday

"You stupid fucking cunt!" Dean shouted as he stood staring at Urban.

"What's the fucking problem?" Urban replied as he handed back the gun.

"The problem is that you never spun the barrel and as the previous chamber was blank you only had a one in six chance of that chamber being empty rather than a one in seven" Dean replied shaking his head.

"But I'm alright, so it's no big deal and I do believe that you now owe me a cool ten grand."

"Right, after that potential fiasco, who's next?" Dean asked holding out the gun. He looked round the room.

"Don't look at me. I wouldn't do it for a million pounds" said Daisy shaking of his head.

"The way my luck's going tonight I think I'll give it a miss as well" Rod added.

Dean looked at Razor who said nothing but simply shook his head. That just left Glynn.

"How about you then Glynn? What about living on the edge for a change?" Dean asked as he held the gun out.

"I don't think so" Glynn replied. "All this macho bullshit is not really my scene."

"How about if I up the ante a bit? Seeing as these three have bottled out" Dean said pointing at Daisy, Rod and Razor "I'll add their money to yours so that you get forty grand for doing it? How about that?"

"Forty grand? That's not fair" Urban shouted. "I'll fucking do it again for that!"

"You've had your go, Urban, so shut it!" Dean shouted back without looking round at him. "So what do you say Glynn? Just think what you could do with forty grand. It'll make for a nice little deposit on a place for you and Heather" he said, knowing perfectly well that this would be prize bait as Glynn and Heather were already talking about getting a place together.

Glynn sat thinking for a few seconds before standing up. "Right, I'll do it for forty grand" he said as the rest of them started clapping and cheering. Despite the huge amount of money on offer Dean was still shocked that Glynn had agreed to do it. Dougie's statement about people abandoning their morals if the price was right came back to him. "Can you sort it out for me Dean?" Glynn asked as Dean held the gun out to him.

"No problem" Dean replied as he flicked open the barrel and tipped out the bullet. This time he deliberately placed the bullet into the fourth chamber on the left, closed the gun and gave it a precise spin. By the time Dean handed him the gun Glynn had turned completely white and his hand was shaking with fear. "You'll be fine mate" Dean reassured him as Glynn took the handle of the gun in his hand.

"God, I'm really scared" said Glynn as he stood looking at the gun. "Seven to one are pretty good odds though" he said as he raised the gun to his head. He closed his eyes and pulled the trigger.

'BANG!!!!!'

All seven spectators froze in shock as the gun let out an almighty blast and Glynn's body dropped to the floor. They all remained motionless as they sat staring at Glynn's lifeless form.

Daisy was the first to move. "This has got fuck all to do with me" he said as he got up and ran out of the room. Despite the severity of the situation Rod, Mick and Urban all followed suit shortly afterwards.

"What are we going to do Dean?" Tim shouted as he stood up and starting pacing backwards and forwards as he stared at Glynn's body.

"Firstly we've got to be calm otherwise we're all fucked" Dean said quietly. "Secondly we've got to get him out of here. I know somewhere where we can go that nobody will find him. Can we use your car Tim?"

"Err, yeah, of course" Tim replied as he started to regain his composure.

"Can you give us a hand getting the body in the car Razor?" Dean asked as he got into position to lift Glynn's arms.

"I'm afraid not lads. I don't really want to be part of this. Why don't you just call the police Dean and tell them what happened? You didn't force him to do it so you'll probably only get charged with owning a gun without a license" said Razor.

"No chance" Dean replied. "If I get done for anything I'll be struck off and will lose my job. I think we should stash Glynn's body somewhere until I've worked out what to do. Tim, I promise on my mother's life that if you help me I won't tell anyone you were involved." Tim nodded his agreement to Dean's proposal.

Dean grabbed Glynn's arms and Tim took his legs.

"Fucking hell, he's really heavy" said Tim as they lifted Glynn.

"It's a dead weight, isn't it?" Dean replied. Nobody laughed.

Razor watched as Dean and Tim carried Glynn's body out to Tim's car and dumped him onto the back seat. He continued watching until the car had sped off into the night. Once it was out of sight he closed the front door, smiled and whispered to himself "I love it when a plan comes together."

Chapter 44
Week 10 - Friday

It was a gloriously hot day and Razor had a skip in his stride as he made his way to the pub near Canary Wharf station. He got himself a pint and grabbed a table outside where he could oggle the scantily dressed secretaries who were out on their lunch breaks. After ten minutes he was surprised to see Dean appear from the tube station. Dean spotted him and headed over.

"I wasn't sure if you were going to make it today after what happened last night" Razor said as Dean sat down opposite him.

"Well I've come this far so it seemed stupid to walk away now" Dean replied, looking around to make sure nobody could hear what they were saying.

"You look like shit mate. I take it you haven't been to work this morning?" Razor said gesturing to the jeans and T-shirt Dean was still wearing from the previous night.

"Funnily enough, I haven't" Dean replied with a sarcastic smile. "You probably wouldn't look your best either if you'd had the sort of night I have" he continued.

"So where did you take the body?" Razor asked.

"Keep your fucking voice down" Dean whispered angrily. "All you need to know is that everything is cool for the time being, so let's just get this last challenge over with and we can then sort out what to do in the longer term. Have you been to see Jacob yet?"

"No, I was waiting for you to turn up. I didn't think there was any point going if you didn't" Razor replied.

"Well I'm here now so get your arse round there. I'll mind your pint" Dean said as he picked up Razor's glass and took a long drink from it. Razor got up and headed off in the direction of the solicitors' offices.

It was a full half an hour before Razor returned.

"Where the fuck have you been?" Dean asked as Razor sat down.

"As we didn't have photographic evidence I had to sign a statement that I'd personally seen the challenge completed before the old boy would release the final letter" Razor replied as he picked up a full pint from the table.

"You did what?" Dean exclaimed. "What the fuck did the statement say you saw?"

"Don't worry. All it said was that in my role as Personal Representative for Dougie's will I was fully satisfied that the terms of week nine's challenge had been met, that's all."

Dean sat in silence for a minute or so, thinking things over. "Did you get it then?"

"Yeah, here it is" Razor replied as he pulled the folded up A4 envelope out of the inside pocket of his suit and chucked it onto the table.

"Is there another one as well?" Dean asked as he picked it up. Razor shook his head.

"No cash on offer this week, let's hope it's something fucking easy then" Dean said as he opened the envelope and pulled out the letter in side. Razor pulled his chair round so he could also read it.

"Dear Dean,

The fact that you're reading this letter disappoints me enormously as it means that you have either killed one of your close friends or (knowing you to be a smart boy) have cleverly engineered their death through some sort of elaborate plan. Either way I really don't know how you'll be able to live with yourself. You may end up rich at the end of all of this but the question you have to ask yourself is 'was it worth it?' I spent a long time planning the terms of this will and I always believed that week nine would be the key test of what type of man you really are. In my view if you passed week nine then you would actually fail to be the man I hoped you were. Initially therefore I had decided that week nine would be a trap and that if you passed the challenge (and brought about the death of one of your friends) then you wouldn't get the house and vice versa

However, after giving it a great deal of thought I decided to stick to the original agreement as the guilt you'll carry with you forever will be punishment enough and will make you realise that money doesn't bring happiness. Therefore, providing you complete the final challenge, you will still receive the house and everything in it.

In some ways I suppose I should really be congratulating you on your achievements. I honestly never thought you'd make it this far but hats off to you for perseverance Dean. As you'll have spotted there's no money on offer this week, the main reason being that this week's challenge is more of an experiment. You don't have to have kill anybody (sorry to keep bringing that up or even have sex with someone you don't want to. The final challenge can be summarised simply by the word:

'SÉANCE'

I want you to gather the remaining members of the house (obviously not the dead one) and have a séance to see if you can contact me on the other side. I was involved in a séance once and it frightened the shit out of me so much that I vowed never to do it again. When I was alive I always believed in the spirit world and now that I'm dead I want you to see if there's any truth in it. If there is I'll let you have my final message from beyond the grave. If it's all just bollocks then enjoy my house and the rest of your life.

Take care.
Your friend,
Dougie"

Dean finished reading the letter and put it back into the envelope.

"A séance?" Razor said. "That should be a laugh. Have you ever done one?"

"I did a Ouija board with a few mates at Uni once. We all thought it was one of the others pushing the glass with their fingers but shat ourselves when the glass carried on moving across the board once we'd all taken our hands off it. I'm really not into all of that occult, spirit world stuff. It scares the shit out of me" Dean said taking a long drink from the pint they were now sharing.

"Yeah, but it's a piece of piss compared to some of the other challenges isn't it, so we're home and dry and in the money" said Razor taking the pint back from Dean.

"I suppose so" Dean replied. "Let's try and do it tonight so that we can get this whole thing put to bed. I'll have a look on the internet when I get back to the house to see what we need to do for a séance. I'm not sure if it'll work but if it does I'll be interested to hear what Dougie's final message is" said Dean as he finished the pint.

****

"A séance? Are you fucking mad?" Urban shouted at Dean. "It was only last night that Glynn died in that room and you want to hold a séance to speak to the dead tonight? Well you can count me out."

"Look mate. It looks like everyone is going to move out this weekend after what's gone on, so it'll be a good way of getting closure on all the things that have gone on here over the past few months" Dean replied.

Urban stood staring at Dean, remembering some of the things that had happened between them since they'd moved in. "I'm still trying to forget most of those" he said with a serious look on his face. "Oh and don't think

I've forgotten that you owe me £10,000 from last night. I need that money" Urban said looking desperate.

"Don't worry, you'll get your money. Will you do this séance thing then? It'll only take half an hour and you can then fuck off and do whatever you want" Dean asked.

"OK, I'll give you half an hour and that's it" Urban replied.

"Great. We're aiming to do it at eight o'clock so I'll see you in the living room then."

Dean worked his way around the rest of the housemates and had similar conversations with them. Dean sold it to them all as the last united act of the house. He was secretly pleased that everyone was intending to move out as it would save him the bother of having to ask them to leave before he sold it. All of the lads were freaked out by what had happened to Glynn the previous night and wanted to get away from the house but eventually they all agreed to take part.

Dean sat in front of his PC researching how to conduct a séance he sat back and thought about the fact that he was almost at the end of the ten weeks. For a moment he was able to put all of the mental ghosts and nightmares out of his mind and allowed himself to think about the money. He opened up a new browser page and typed in the words 'dream holiday.' From the results he selected a website showing luxury breaks in Martinique. *"That's where I'm going to be this time next week"* he thought as he clicked through various photos of sandy beaches, palm trees and enormous villas. After half an hour of fantasising he returned to his research.

By eight fifteen all of the lads were gathered in the front room.

"So where's your crystal ball then Dean?" Urban asked as he came in and sat on the end of the sofa.

"Very funny" Dean replied sarcastically. "OK, I don't know that much about all this but I've done a bit of reading up and I reckon I've got the basics covered. Firstly we all need to sit on the floor around a table. They all stood up, pushed the sofas against the walls and reluctantly sat in a circle on the floor.

"Do we have to do this? This floor is fucking filthy and these pants are clean on" said Daisy who was wearing a pair of light coloured trousers that he intended going out in later.

"Just sit down and stop whinging, it'll be over before you know it" Dean replied. "OK, we now have to select a medium and unless you have any objections I thought I'd take on that roll."

"How come you get all the good jobs?" Urban chipped in.

"Shut up Urban. Right, as medium I have to do all of the talking so if we do manage to make contact with Dougie don't start shouting things out. The next thing we need to do is charge a candle by passing it around the group" said Dean as he picked up a large white candle from the table and passed it to Razor. Razor passed it onto Rod and it made its way round the group and back to Dean. Dean got up, drew the curtains and turned off the lights, plunging the room into darkness. He then lit the candle, which filled the room with an eerie flickering light.

"Woooahh!" Urban said imitating a ghost noise.

"Right, the next thing we need to do is join hands" Dean said sitting back in the circle

"Oh, here we go, next it'll be 'you now need to get your cocks out'" said Rod.

"Shut up and try to be serious for a minute Rod. Right if we can all join hands" Dean said. Reluctantly they all joined hands, although not without protests from Urban and Rod who seemed to be particularly reluctant to hold each others. "OK we now need to do a few breathing exercises. You all need to breathe in slowly through your noses, hold it for a second and then breathe out slowly through your mouth." Dean showed them the way and they all followed suit. "Now we all need to clear our minds so that they're totally blank.

"Shouldn't be too difficult for you Rod" Urban said as he gave Rod a dig in the ribs.

"Fuck off you bell end" Rod replied as he pushed Urban over.

"Look, children, can we leave this until later? I'm sure we'd all like to get this over with and get out on the beers" Dean said. "OK if we can all hold hands and start the breathing exercises again. The next thing we need to do is a chant, so repeat after me 'Douglas Forsyth Mackenzie we ask you to commune with us and move amongst us.'" Dean repeated the chant a couple of times and eventually they all joined in. After a minute or so nothing had happened and most of the group stopped chanting.

"I knew this was a bollocks idea" said Mick. "Let's just get down the boozer."

"Hang on. It said on the website that if you don't get a response from the chanting you should ask for sign, like a knocking noise of something. Can we give that a go? If it doesn't work then the first round is on me" said Dean.

"I still think it's all bollocks but let's give it a try and then get down the pub before all the decent birds are taken" Mick replied.

They all joined hands again and resumed the previous chant, to which Dean added 'Spirit, if you are with us, please knock once.'" Nothing happened. As they repeated the chant for a third time they suddenly heard a loud knocking noise.

"What the fuck was that?" Daisy asked looking freaked out. "Was that one of you lot pissing about? If it was it's not funny. Was it you Urban?"

"No, I swear to god it wasn't me" Urban replied also looking freaked out.

"Let's try it again" said Dean with a serious look on his face. They all joined hands and as they chanted the 'please knock once' part again there was a loud knocking noise. The room fell deadly silent.

"Spirit? Knock once if you are Douglas Forsyth Mackenzie" said Dean. They waited in silence for a response and almost jumped out of their skins as they heard another loud knock.

"If you have a message for us, please knock once" Dean continued. Again there was silence followed by a loud knock. Dean looked around, unsure how to continue. "Knock once if you can you give us the message now and twice if it will come to us in another form" Dean said looking around the group with shrug. They waited in silence until another single knock followed. Dean looked around the circle for inspiration but none was forthcoming. In desperation he looked up at the ceiling and said "Spirit, I don't know what it is that you want to tell me or how I'm going to understand you. Please give me a sign."

Suddenly the living room door flew open, blowing out the candle and throwing the room into total darkness. They all sat motionless, too scared to move or even breathe, until a voice filled the room.

"Do you understand me now?" boomed Dougie's voice.

Chapter 45
Week 10 - Friday

Dean sat in the pitch black room frozen with fear. His eyes darted around the darkness expecting to see Dougie's ghostly image appear but he saw nothing. The room was totally silent and Dean wondered whether the others were still alive. He'd never felt so terrified in all of his life and his heart was beating so fast he thought he was about to have a heart attack. What happened next didn't help.

"I said do you understand me now?" Dougie's voice boomed out again. Dean tried to respond but his throat was so dry that he couldn't get his words out. After a couple of attempts he managed to clear his throat and simply said "Yes."

"Good, because I want all of your friends to hear what a cunt you are" Dougie's voice continued. The room was suddenly illuminated as the living room light came on.

"OH FUCK!" Dean shouted as he sat staring at Dougie's figure standing in the doorway. The other lads let out a variety of screams, yells and cries of disbelief.

"I told you not to mess with this shit" said Urban. "Now we're all going to fucking die thanks to you" he said as he started to cry.

"No you're not" said Dougie as he stepped forward and sat down on the sofa. Everybody was transfixed but nobody said a word. "Don't worry lads, I'm not a ghost. In fact I'm not even dead" he said as he looked at each of them.

"What do you mean you're not dead?" Dean said.

"Exactly that. I didn't fall in the Thames that night, I didn't drown and I'm not dead" Dougie said with a cold smile. "Anyway before I answer any more questions I'd like you all to watch a short film that will reveal what has really been going on for the past couple of months."

The group sat motionless in silence as Dougie nodded at Razor who stood up and put a DVD into the player. A recording of the first night in the house when they'd all played party games flashed up onto the plasma screen. As Dean looked at the screen he closed his eyes and shook his head, as he realised what they were all about to be shown.

"Hang on a minute, that's me. What the fuck's all this?" Mick asked as he stared at the plasma screen which showed him draining the contents of his stomach with a tube.

"That's a very good question Mick" Dougie replied as he pulled a fat cigar out of the top pocket of his shirt and lit it. "The first thing you should all know is that Dean here has been recording all of your actions for the past few months. He set up secret cameras in this room and each of your bedrooms so that he could record all of the things you've done."

"You what? You've been recording me having a wank in bed? You fucking pervert!" Mick shouted at Dean.

"He's recorded stuff that's a lot more incriminating than that" said Dougie picking up the remote control and forwarding the DVD. He stopped the footage at a scene in the living room showing Urban and Rod snorting cocaine.

"Whoa" Urban shouted. "You fucking taped us taking coke? What the fuck else have you got?"

"Everything" Dougie replied with another disturbing smile.

"Oh fuck" Urban muttered as he sat down on the sofa.

"Why the fuck did you record this?" Rod asked, pointing at the screen.

"There's a very simple answer to that question Rod. Money" Dougie replied before Dean could respond. "Your friend Dean here has done things that you wouldn't believe over the last couple of months in order to get his hands on a pot of money. Not only has he abandoned any self respect that he might have once had but he's also set up every single one of you in his greedy pursuit of cash. The 'dares' that he said I'd set in my will were actually given to Dean as part of a bigger game plan. He was told that if he successfully persuaded you lot to complete all of the 'dares' then he would be given this house as part of the will. As the 'dares' became more extreme so did his greed and his desire to get his hands on the cash, as you'll see if you keep watching" Dougie continued as he forwarded the DVD to the next scene.

They all sat, watching in silence, as the location of the footage changed to Dean's bedroom. Mick covered his face as the seedy threesome he'd shared with Dean and Gill unfolded on the screen.

"You deliberately set that up? You fucking wanker!" Mick shouted at Dean.

"Not just that Mick, but in order to get you in the mood he spiked you with ecstasy" said Dougie. "Oh, and he also spiked you Tim, that's why you ended up in hospital." Tim stared at Dougie but said nothing.

Dougie forwarded the DVD to the footage of Dean with Nina the prostitute.

"So you did fucking shag her? Rod shouted. "You said she went straight home after I left. You lying bastard." Dean gave a shrug in response and said nothing.

Dougie forwarded the DVD and stopped again at the biscuit game. Both Rod and Urban put their hands over their eyes to hide their embarrassment as they looked away.

"What the fuck's this?" Mick asked. Nobody replied as they all watched in horror as Rod and Urban started masturbating on the huge screen. Dougie waited until the moment that Rod ejaculated before forwarding the DVD onto the next piece of action. He stopped the DVD as it switched to the scene in the front room when Mick broke Razor's arm.

"This is the only one I'm not embarrassed about" said Dean flashing Razor a false smile. "You're obviously in on all of this so I'm fucking glad it ended up being you that got done. Just out of interest how did you get copies of all of this?"

"When Dave set everything up he rigged a second PC in my room so I had a copy of everything you recorded, it was a piece of piss really" Razor replied with a smug grin. "And if it makes you feel any better my arm has healed up just fine and I'm getting this thing off next week" he said as he held up his purple plaster cast.

Dougie forwarded the DVD and the next scene was of Rod and Gloria necking in Rod's bedroom.

"What's this all about?" Rod asked looking confused. "What's so fucking great that you need to record me getting a blow job?"

"That's a very interesting question Rod. Would you like to answer him Dean?" Dougie asked. Dean shot a deadly stare at Dougie before looking down at the floor and closing his eyes. "No? Oh well, I'll tell him then shall I? The woman that Dean introduced you to that night wasn't the friend of a girl he met at a lapdancing bar. In fact it wasn't a woman at all. It was a transsexual prostitute that he paid to sleep with you on camera."

"A fucking what?" Rod shouted, standing up.

"A transsexual, which means that 'she' was originally a man and that 'she' still had a fully functioning penis" Dougie replied.

"You set me up? You fucking cunt!" Rod shouted as he ran over to Dean and punched him in the face. They fell in a bundle on the floor and after a few seconds of wrestling Dean managed to pin Rod down.

"Fucking calm down Rod, I'll tell you exactly what this is all about once this prick has finished his stupid fucking film show" said Dean as Rod eventually stopped writhing.

"I am seriously fucking pissed off with you Dean" Rod said as he stood up and gave Dean a hard stare.

"And so you should be Rod. He's tricked you into becoming a homosexual" said Dougie mixing things up as much as he could.

"You can fuck off as well" Rod replied as he sat back on the sofa.

Dougie flicked the DVD forward to the next scene which showed Dean and Urban taking coke together in the living room.

"We've already seen this one Dougie" Mick shouted.

"Just wait" Dougie replied as they all watched the events unfold and Urban started giving Dean a blow job.

"Oh turn this fucking shit off before I end up killing somebody!" Urban shouted at Dougie.

"Hang on, there's only one more to go, and as it's a big one it'd be a shame to miss it" Dougie replied as the game of Russian roulette appeared on the screen. They all watched in silence as each of them took their turn with the gun. Most couldn't watch as Glynn stepped forward for the last fateful attempt. As soon as the sound of the gunshot and Glynn dropping to the floor filled the room. Dougie switched off the screen and stood up.

"So gentlemen, you have just seen that your so-called mate Dean has set you up and sold you all down the river over the past few months just for the sake of a few quid. This is the bloke who claims that mates are the most important thing in the world to him and that he'd do anything for anybody. But as soon as there was a quick buck to be made he dropped all of his principles and was happy to stitch up his mates and become a liar, a drug pusher, a pimp, a pervert, a homosexual and a murderer" Dougie said letting the last word hang in the air for dramatic effect. "I'd ask each one of you to think about what this mercenary has done to you."

"Tim he secretly drugged you in an attempt to get you to join in a sordid threesome with some drug addict bird. He did the same to you Mick, with worse consequences, and also persuaded you to deliberately break one of your mates' arms. Rod he got you to take coke, to wank off in front of him on camera and to have sex with a transsexual. Urban he got you to wank off on camera, give him a blow job and most damaging of all got you hooked on coke. I don't need to remind any of you what he's done to Glynn. All of this has been driven by his desire to get rich at all of your expense. I would ask you all to consider very carefully whether you really want to be friends with somebody like Dean Williams. I know I fucking don't."

Dean, who had decided to let Dougie's finish his performance, now stood up. "Have you fucking finished yet?" He received a nod from Dougie in response. "OK then, can I ask you what the fuck all this is really about?" Dean said looking to Dougie for an answer.

"Don't you get it yet Dean? It was all a set up. I arranged for someone to make the call your mum with the news of my death as I knew I could rely on you to pass it on to everyone and ensure they all turned up for the funeral. I paid the crematorium to put on a remembrance service for 'my old friend Dougie.' As it was just a remembrance service they didn't ask any difficult questions or need a body and I knew that you lot would all be too shocked to know the difference. I then got a few of the boys from back home to come down for an all expenses paid piss up and asked them to pretend it was my funeral for a laugh. All of that was a piece of piss. The only tricky part was setting up the solicitor. Luckily enough there was a lot of spare office space down at Canary Wharf so I hired a fully furnished office for a month and paid an old boy actor I know to pretend to be a solicitor. After that I made sure the terms of the will determined that it was only Razor who could go to see the solicitor so that I didn't need to keep paying for the offices. In fact he never went to those offices again but used to come and meet me on Friday lunchtimes. We used to have a pint and a good laugh at the photos you provided each week before he'd head back with the next humiliating ruse that I'd thought up for you. To be completely honest I never thought you'd make it all the way through the ten weeks. I kept upping the ante hoping you'd jack it in but you kept surprising me with your greedy desire to get your hands on my money."

"Well I take my hat off to you Dougie, you had me completely fooled all the way along. I take it that I won't be getting the house then?" Dean asked.

"No, you get fuck all!" Dougie replied shaking his head and smiling.

"What about the story about you being a wealthy musician? Is that bollocks as well?" Dean asked.

"No, that part is actually true. I wrote a jingle in about five minutes when I was twenty and entered it into a competition for young musicians. It was picked up by an insurance company and luckily enough they're still using it today and pay me a royalty fee every time the ads are broadcast on telly and radio anywhere around the world" Dougie replied toking on his cigar again.

"I'm really pleased for you" Dean replied sarcastically, "but I still don't understand why you've gone to all of this effort. I thought we were mates?"

"We *were* mates. Past tense" said Dougie as he blew a large smoke ring. "You haven't been a real mate of mine for a long time Dean. All of this was designed to bring you to your knees."

"But I still don't see why?"

"You don't really need to ask that do you Dean?" Dougie replied.

"Oh don't tell me you're still trying to blame me for what happened to your sister? I thought we'd cleared all of that up?" Dean said shaking his head.

"Did you really think that just because you were young and decided that you needed to fuck other women that I'd let you get away with destroying my family? Blame you? Of course I fucking blame you. You killed Sarah just as much as if you'd given her those pills yourself. She loved and adored you and gave you everything. What did you do in return? You repaid her by breaking her heart and destroying her spirit. Before she met you she was full of life and the most beautiful person I have ever known. After you'd finished with her she was just an empty shell. All the life had been sucked out of her and she lost the will to live. Forgive you?" Dougie said with an ironic laugh "I just said that to put you at ease. You know what they say about keeping your friends close but your enemies closer. I wanted you to believe I'd forgiven you but I never have and I never will. I've just been biding my time waiting for the right opportunity to fuck you over and I think I've done quite a good job don't you?" Dougie said his face distorted through a combination of anger and grief.

"So are you pleased with yourself then?" Dean asked as Dougie took another long drag on his cigar.

"Yeah, I am actually. It doesn't bring Sarah back, nothing will, but the fact you've now got your best friend's blood on your hands and that you won't have any friends left after all of this has finished makes me feel that we're close to being even. For the first time in years I'll be able to sleep soundly at night again, knowing that I've avenged Sarah's death."

"So if I'm so fucked, what's to stop me coming after you. I mean I've still got the gun" Dean said starting to get angry.

"Don't be a fucking idiot all of your life Dean. You can keep what's left of the money you were given by Razor and I'd suggest you leave it at that. I've given a copy of the DVD to my solicitor, who is under full instructions to send it to both the police and to the partners at your law firm if anything should happen to me. Even the most simple minded copper should be able to work out a link back to you and I don't think your firm would be too happy if they knew what one of their up and coming solicitors gets up to in his spare time, do you?"

"You've got it all worked out haven't you, you bastard?"

"I should hope so I've been planning this for almost a year" Dougie replied.

"So that's it then? I just slope off now and you live happily ever after?"

"Something like that" Dougie said with a smirk. "If I was you I'd make sure you dispose of Glynn's body good and proper as I don't want to be implicated in any of that shit when they find him."

"Don't worry about that, I've got it all sorted" Dean replied, standing up. "So does anyone fancy a last pint with me before I go?"

Mick and Rod both deliberately avoided Dean's eye and stared at the floor. Urban was the first to speak.

"I might be able to forgive you for what you've done to me, after all you paid me for most of it, but I can't believe you persuaded Glynn to take that loaded gun and to shoot himself. He didn't want to do it but you made it virtually impossible for him to say no. I bet you even set up the gun so the bullet landed in the chamber when it was his go. He was your best mate and you effectively killed him just so you could get your hands on this house. I'm never going to be able to forget that Dean. The trust between us as mates has gone and I just don't think we can be friends any more."

The rest of the group nodded to indicate they agreed with Urban's sentiment.

"Looks like your little plan has worked a treat then" Dean said to Dougie as he made his way to the living room door. Dougie said nothing but continued grinning.

"Right, I'll be back tomorrow to collect all my stuff" said Dean.

"Don't bother. You're out of here as of now. I'm getting all of the locks changed. I've arranged for a group of removal men to collect all of your stuff. It will be delivered under your name to self storage facilities in Clapham tomorrow" Dougie replied.

"Great" Dean said sarcastically as he stood in the doorway. "Well I have to say that you got me good and proper Dougie, fair play to you for that" he said as he held his hand out for a final handshake. As Dougie stood up and he reached out to shake Dean's right hand, Dean caught him in the eye with his left fist. Dougie fully expected Dean to go out swinging and threw himself at him, sending them both sprawling backwards into the hallway. Dougie was bigger than Dean and also more adept at fighting and had Dean in a headlock before he could hit him again.

"Let me go you fucker and fight me like a man" Dean shouted.

"I'd fucking kill you" Dougie shouted "so just fucking leave it Dean."

"What else have I got to lose?" Dean said as he struggled to get free from Dougie's grasp.

"Your fucking teeth for a start" Dougie said, laughing at his own joke. Dean also started laughing and stopped struggling. "Are you going to calm down if I let you go?"

"Yeah" Dean replied and Dougie released him from the headlock.

"Look Dean, you've still got your job and you've made a bit of cash out of all this so why don't you just fuck off whilst you still can? From my point of view we're now even so let's just leave it at that" said Dougie. "By the way good shot" he said holding his hand over his swollen right eye.

Dean said nothing. He picked himself up from the floor looked at each one of the lads, who were now all crowded into the doorway of the living room, opened the front door and walked off down the path.

Dougie stood and watched Dean go. He then turned to the rest of them. "Sorry chaps but I'm moving back in as of now so you'll all need to move out tomorrow morning."

"I suppose we should all start packing then" Daisy said.

"Fuck that. After all this excitement I need a drink. Let's get down the boozer" Urban replied. They all nodded in agreement and made their way out of the front door, leaving Dougie and Razor behind in the house.

Dougie made a call on his mobile. "Donnie, it's me. It all went pretty much to plan so I didn't need to call you for help. Can you arrange for one of the boys to come round and change the locks tomorrow morning."

"Are we still on for that trip to Ibiza then big man?" Razor asked as Dougie put away his phone.

"Oh yeah" Dougie replied. "I promised that you'd get an all expenses holiday and £100,000 if you helped me on this on Razor and that's exactly what you'll get. The flights are booked up for tomorrow night so all we need to do is pack. A couple of the boys have agreed to house-sit for the next two weeks until we get back just in case Dean does gets any funny ideas."

"Bring on the birds!" Razor replied as he opened a bottle of beer.

Chapter 46
Week 11 - Saturday

Urban was woken by the sound of his phone ringing. His mouth tasted of vodka as he opened his eyes. He was disturbed to note that he didn't recognise the room and was about to start piecing together how he got there when he remembered that he'd moved house. Daisy had managed to find a five bedroom house to rent in Putney and he'd moved in along with Rod, Tim and Mick the previous evening. After they'd carried all of the boxes and bags into the house one of them had come up with the bright idea of having a few drinks as a housewarming and the next thing Urban knew he was waking up fully clothed on the living room floor. He pulled his phone out of his pocket and saw that it was Dean calling. No-one had heard from him since the incident with Dougie the previous Friday night and Urban decided he was too hung-over to deal with him and let it to trip to voicemail. He then got up and went to find his bedroom. An hour later he was woken again, this time by Daisy.

"Have you had a message from Dean?" Daisy asked as he poked his head around Urban's bedroom door.

"What?" Urban replied groggily. "Yeah, he rang me earlier but I never took the call. Why?"

"Because he's left a message on everyone's mobile saying there's something that he needs to tell us all and asking us all to meet him at one o'clock at the Worlds End pub in Camden. Do you know it?" said Daisy.

"Yeah, it's a decent boozer. The birds are a bit bohemian for my liking but it's alright. What does he want to tell us?" Urban replied as he sat up.

"No one knows but get your arse out of bed as we want to have a chat about it downstairs before we decide whether to go or not."

"Fair enough" said Urban looking for his boxer shorts. Once he'd got dressed he headed down to the living room where everyone else was sitting.

"So what do you reckon this is all about?" Rod asked as Urban walked in.

"Well the way I see it he's either going to ask us if he can crash with us, ask if we can help him bury Glynn's body or try to blow us all away with that fucking gun" Urban said as he flopped onto the end of the couch nearest to the door.

"Fuck, I never thought of that" said Rod. "Maybe he deliberately picked the Worlds End pub as an omen of what to expect."

"You're both talking bollocks" said Tim "I'll bet he just wants to try to patch things up with us."

"If that's the case I'm walking straight back out of there" said Mick. "I don't drink with murderers."

"Right, so are we all agreed that we're going then?" Tim asked. They all nodded their agreement. "OK we need to set off in about an hour."

An hour and a half later they arrived at Camden tube station and made their way to the Worlds End pub. They headed to the bar and Urban went to look around the pub for Dean. He returned a minute later and gave a shake of his head to indicate he couldn't find him.

"If he is going to shoot us he'll wait until we've got a table first as it'll be easier to get us all if we are sitting down" said Rod looking around anxiously.

"Oh shut the fuck up" Tim replied as he picked up his pint and headed to a large table at the back of the pub. They all sat down and waited for Dean to appear.

They didn't have to wait long. Five minutes later Dean walked over to the table. Rod was relieved to see that he was carrying a pint of Guinness rather than a gun. As Dean sat down there was an uncomfortable silence.

"So what's so urgent that you needed to see us all today then Dean?" asked Urban once Dean had settled himself into his seat.

"I'm heading off for a while and I wanted to see you all before I go" Dean replied.

"Is that it? Well you've seen us now so you can fuck off" Mick replied aggressively.

"I understand you're still pissed off with me Mick, but there are a couple of things that I need you to know" said Dean as he lifted his rucksack onto the table.

"If you're going to say you're sorry for what's happened you can stick it up your arse" said Mick. "Whatever you say won't bring back Glynn will it?"

"It's funny you should say that" said Glynn as he walked out from behind an adjacent wall. The whole table fell silent and everybody froze as they watched him walk over and sit down at the last remaining free seat. He had a large bruise on the side of his face and a number of cuts and scratches but apart from that he was remarkably alive.

"What the fuck's going on?" Urban asked as he stared at Glynn.

"You fucking doctored that bullet didn't you?" Tim said shaking his head and smiling. "I thought it looked funny when I took it out of the gun but I was shitting myself so much that it didn't register."

"What are you talking about?" Rod asked.

"The bullet I used for the Russian Roulette was a blank" said Dean with a smile. "I decided that there was no way that we could play the game for real but if I'd have told any of you it was a blank I would have failed the challenge. My mate Moonie from back home knows a bit about guns and he doctored one of the bullets so that it would sound real but not actually kill anyone. I practiced spinning the barrel so that I could make it land on the bullet and I then set Glynn up."

"So were you in on this then Glynn?" Rod asked.

"No" Glynn replied shaking his head.

"I couldn't risk telling him in case Razor found out. Moonie had told me that the powder blast a blank gives off is the equivalent of being punched in the head and I just took the view that combined with the shock it would be strong enough to knock Glynn out. That gave me enough time to get his 'body' out of the house leaving you lot to think he was dead."

"So that's why there was no blood then?" Tim said nodding.

"Exactly" Dean replied. "The plan was for Glynn to stay at my mate's flat until I picked up the keys to the house."

"Except you never banked on Dougie reappearing and spoiling your game plan" Mick added.

"No I didn't bank on that, but I have got a bit of money that I want to split with you before I head off" said Dean.

"Is it going to be enough for a piss up?" Rod asked "as I'm in the mood for celebrating Glynn's resurrection."

"What do you want to do with Glynn's erection?" Urban asked laughing. Rod responded by pulling an un-amused face.

"Yeah, it should be enough for a decent piss up" said Dean as he handed a cheque to each of them.

Urban was the first to look at his. "Fucking hell, two hundred and fifty thousand pounds? Where the fuck did you get this from?"

"Well, as well as being a musician it turned out that Dougie was also a collector of instruments and memorabilia? He'd kitted out his whole basement as a state of the art recording studio and the place was an Aladdin's Cave with all sorts of guitars, keyboards, and other musical instruments as well as some rare memorabilia. Razor and I found it on the first day we moved in and I decided that sell it to make a bit of cash even if I didn't succeed with Dougie's challenge. So I called Sotheby's. They came round, took all of it away and put it for auction. It turned out that there was some really rare stuff in there - guitars used by the Beatles and Jimi Hendrix, original artwork from albums, that sort of thing - and the whole lot sold for just under two million quid. Most of the stuff had authenticity letters with it and had been registered as Dougie's address. As I could prove I lived at the house and none of the equipment was listed as stolen they released the money to me a couple of weeks ago. So gentlemen, the cheque I have just given each of you represents your share of Dougie's life's work" Dean said raising a glass. "I think a toast is in order. To Dougie" he said taking a long drink from his pint.

"To Dougie!" they all responded simultaneously.

"He's going to fucking freak when he finds out" said Urban laughing.

"I certainly hope so" said Dean with a chuckle. "Couldn't happen to a nicer guy though."

"So where are you off to then?" Rod asked.

"I'm off to see a bit of the world on Dougie's money" Dean replied. "I'm starting off in Brazil if anyone fancy joining me?"

They all looked at each other and a nod started rippling its way around the group.

"Why don't we all go? It'd be a right laugh" said Urban.

"It's just as well that I've bought you all a ticket then isn't it?" Dean said as he emptied seven tickets out of his rucksack and onto the table.

Chapter 47

A week later Dougie and Razor arrived back at the house after their two week trip to Ibiza. They threw their bags down in the hallway, grabbed a beer and headed for the sofas in the living room. After an hour Razor announced he was going to bed for a kip and Dougie decided to chill out by playing a few of his guitars. He headed through the kitchen and down to the basement. The door was locked and he took out his keys and unlocked it. As the door swung open and he entered the room he couldn't believe his eyes. The room had been stripped bare. All of his life's work, all of the new jingles he'd been working on and all of his precious instruments were gone. He felt a sick feeling hit him in the stomach and tears started flowing from his eyes.

He looked up at the blank wall in front of him, which previously had been covered with the original art work for albums by the Beatles, U2 and Queen. Now all that was there, spray-painted in Dean's handwriting, was simply the word **'THANKS.'**

THE END

About the Author

Joe Platt was born in 1968 and grew up in Birkenhead, England. He currently lives in London with his wife and daughter and began writing after a fifteen year career in finance. **The Inheritance Game** is his first novel.

Printed in the United Kingdom
by Lightning Source UK Ltd.
129425UK00001B/291/A